I0691618

The Wind and the Word

Book One: Tears of Stone

A Novel

By Stephen Kroh

ISBN 979-8-9862512-0-2

First Edition

For Lynne and Justin

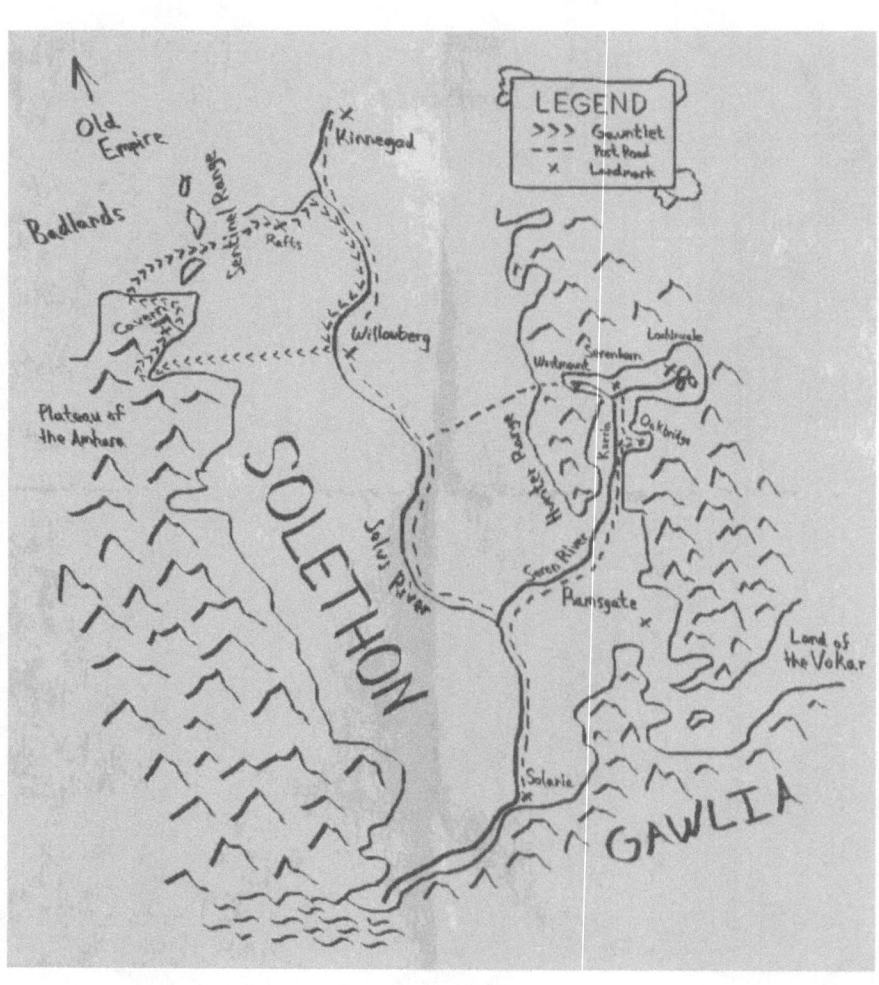

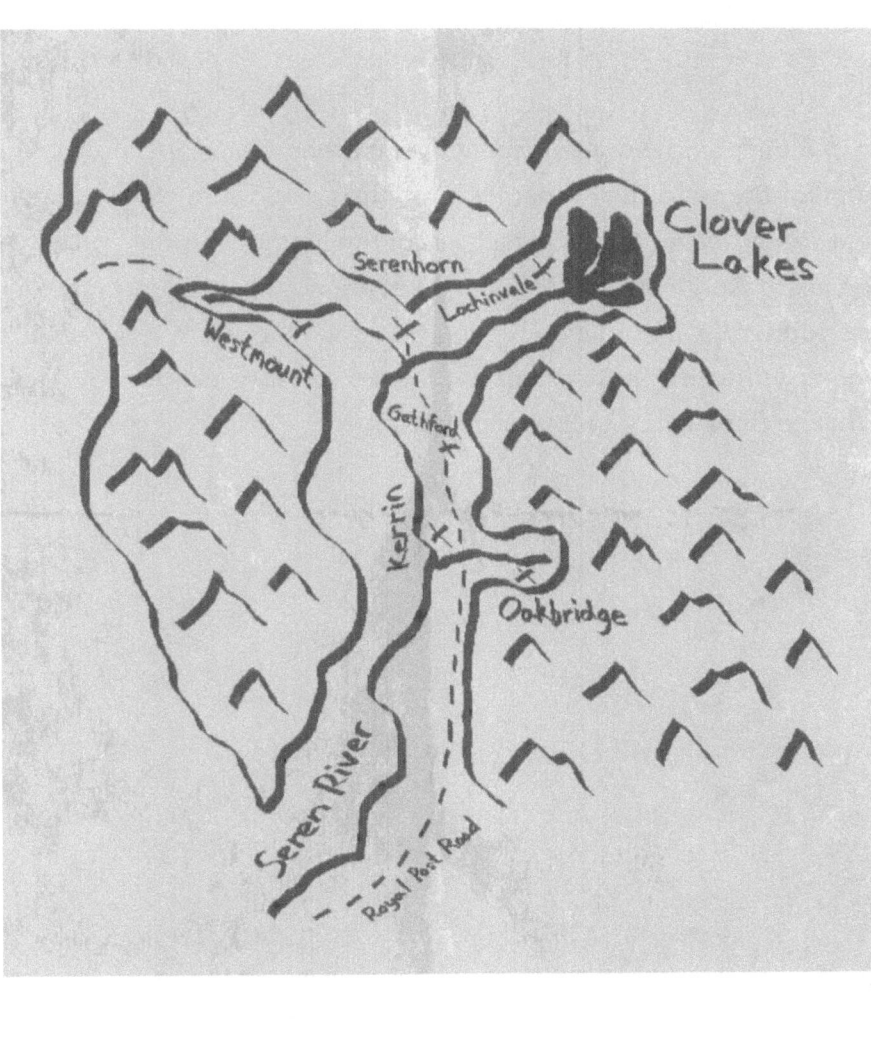

Clover Lakes

Serenhorn

Lochinvale

Westmount

Gathford

Kerrin

Oakbridge

Seren River

Royal Post Road

Introduction

In the deep winters, men hunger. Then they discover the brotherhood of the wolf, the desperate hunt, the pack. There come hungers that reach deeper than the belly—hollow longings in the bottom of the heart. And there come winters that are not made of snow; the ice lies hidden in the marrow of men. Many years from now, such a winter will come. In it a man will seek a fire to warm his soul, and what he finds will set his world ablaze.

Prologue

Those who sow in tears will reap with songs of joy.
—A saying from the Word

We know him only as the Scribe. He sat at his worktable on that terrible day, finishing a long and dangerous project. He etched the final mysterious phrases into the last clay tablet and placed it gently into the stone coffer with the others. Now the record of the forbidden document was complete. Even assembling a comprehensive collection of the unlawful texts had been difficult. Scraps of passages that were circulated carefully, large portions obtained from distant provinces, indirect references in other works—all these had to be brought together to recreate the whole. In the center of the city, that whole had existed in far greater form for centuries, but even now was being extinguished by a madman.

The Scribe stood after sliding the heavy lid of the coffer into place. He walked to the window and looked sadly at the darkening sky. This time the Mad Emperor would succeed—one could sense it in the air, the power of dark energies summoned for an evil purpose. The streets reeked of insanity and perversion. Death bided its time. Tonight the Word would be smitten and light would leave the world.

The wind carried a rising tide of wailing and screeching to the Scribe's ears. He turned with a sigh and clapped for his two remaining servants. They would carry the stone coffer to its resting place in the vaults below the house, and then he would release the men to flee as well as they might.

The sky was almost black when they finished, though it was only the middle of the afternoon. The Scribe lit a candle and sat by the window, waiting with patience for the final horror to overcome his people. He did not wait for long.

Chapter 1

Ask and it will be given to you; seek and you will find;
knock and the door will be opened to you.
—A saying from the Word.

Rand was most definitely not thinking about Lyssa. It was the only thing he was sure about. He sat with his back against the tree and carefully spread the parchment out across his knees. His fingertips refused to imagine that they were caressing her skin. His eyes insisted that they saw his school lesson, not the glitter of her hair. And his ears heard only the wind, not the mocking laughter of Karl. This carefully constructed state of affairs lasted for almost two minutes. Rand was not disappointed—it was the best he had managed in a long time.

After all, how could he help it? Lyssa was the one—the girl with the musical voice, the smiling eyes, the finely chiseled face. Rand watched different boys react to her in different ways, each according to his temperament—some with gallantry, some with humor, some with affected coolness—but each of them turned whenever she appeared, as surely as iron filings toward a lodestone. She was an elemental force in the life of the village, the Girl Every Boy Wanted. As for Karl—he was an elemental force of a different kind.

Rand leaned his head back against the tree in his uncle's apple orchard and soaked in the elements around him. The wind sighed through the boughs, hissed through the leaves, and tugged at his hair. Layers of cloud danced slowly across the overcast sky in various shades of gray. It was a cool day but not cold; a moist smell spoke of the possibility of rain without threatening it too loudly. The afternoon was full of energy and expectation. He closed his eyes and pictured himself racing down the road with the wind at his heels, running until he had discovered everything that lay beyond this valley—a valley he had never left in the sixteen years since his birth.

Rand shook his head in resignation and turned back to the folk song he was supposed to be studying. Daydreams and strange tastes in weather—no wonder Lyssa ignored him and Karl bullied him. Every time Rand opened his mouth, his conversation branded him as an outsider. He saw it in people's faces, the anger, contempt, and sometimes even hurt. He guessed he understood them no better than they understood him. He had to try harder somehow.

His school work was something at which he might do well, though. Not only was he to recite the song from memory, but he was also expected to produce some poetry of his own. Rand enjoyed playing with words. More than once he had made his young brother Denny laugh with rhymes that flowed naturally into his thoughts.

The song he needed to memorize was an old one that he had heard before, spilling out into the night from the doorway of the town inn. It was one of those simple country tunes that didn't make a lot of sense, but the silly doggerel verses were fun to sing and easy to remember.

> Remember ye the red-barked tree
> And the folk o' the sign of fish
> If quit ye will of the thrice-cursed hill
> Be careful what ye wish

Yo, hey, hey, ho, the fire is burning blue
Hi, yo, hee, yo, the fire can catch ye too

So strike the hammer as the demons yammer
And run with all yer might
For the raining stones will chase ye down
'Til yer backs are out of sight

Yo, hey, hey, ho, the fire is burning blue
Hi, yo, hee, yo, the fire can catch ye too

Rand went over the curious verses three times with his eyes closed so he would remember them perfectly when called upon. All that remained was to fashion some poetry of his own. He could think of only one suitable subject, of course—Lyssa. He took the blank slip of paper that had been provided for him and a stick of charcoal, and labored slowly over the rhymes and images that took shape in his thoughts.

What is this cloud of gold I see
Spun finer than a wire?
What are these gems that gleam at me
A pair of pale sapphires?

What is this lilting melody
That tinkles in my ears?
Is this hair, and are these eyes
Is this a voice I hear?

I cannot find the coin to buy
Such priceless hidden treasure
To meet its cost I can but try
To make my heart the measure

There, he thought. That should tell her a small part of how he felt. He would have used her name to drive home his intent, but he couldn't think of a rhyme for Lyssa. Well, it would have to do. He would catch her eye as much as possible while reciting it. With that done, he tucked the paper away and pulled out the rolled parchment with the folk song to practice it one more time.

At that moment a gust of wind whipped around him, yanking the roll loose from his fingers and sending it skittering away down the rows of trees. With a muffled oath Rand shoved himself up from the ground and dashed in pursuit. He didn't know what would happen if he lost one of the precious documents from the school's small library, but it would be unpleasant. His lean body, so inconvenient when dealing with the likes of Karl, served him well as he dashed and twisted between the trees.

After several nerve-wracking moments he drew close to the parchment, coming within a step or two as the fickle breeze plastered it against a tree trunk and held it there. He lunged after it, but the wind burst forth anew from a different angle and snatched it away again. Thus began a maddening chase through row after row of the orchard, the roll bouncing along the ground, tangling in the branches, or spiraling aloft in an open aisle between the rows. The wind acted like a living adversary, teasing him by letting him almost touch his quarry before pulling it away again. The gusts whipped at his hair, whistled in his ears, and roused chattering laughter from the leaves. His legs were aching and his lungs were pumping like the bellows in his father's smithy.

His strength was faltering; if he had to stop for breath, he would fall behind for good. A lull came in the wind. The roll paused briefly against the base of an old and gnarled apple tree. Rand leaped headlong with his arms spread to encircle the roll and trap it against the ground. He landed hard, knocking his head against the tree trunk and banging his knees and elbows into the earth. Shaking his head to clear it, he looked down. There, flattened under his chest, was the roll at last. He gripped it tightly as he rolled onto his side, and then tucked it firmly inside his tunic. Only when he was sure that it was secure did he spare a glance for his surroundings.

The chase had led him down into a shallow valley deep within the orchard. The trees here were older than he was used to seeing, the almost-ripe apples fewer on their branches than on the vigorous young trees closer to his uncle's manor house. As Rand looked about, there was nothing in sight but more trees—no fences or sheds or country lanes. He pushed himself up to a sitting position; as he did so his hand pressed against something hard and sharp-edged. Surprised, he leaned over and brushed at the soil to see what it was.

The object in the ground was oblong and dark, a chunk of stone about three inches long. Its edge looked almost as keen as a knife. Rand was grateful that it hadn't cut his hand. He slowly pried it loose from the earth. Once it was free he brushed away the dirt to get a better look; he was surprised at how easily the soil fell away from the glossy surface. So intent was he that he failed to notice when the gusts of wind which had tormented him on his chase faded back into the general breeziness of the day.

When he had cleaned the stone, he could see it was dark gray and smooth as glass. He first thought it was obsidian, but it wasn't heavy enough. It was thin and flat, with regular angles except on the side where it had broken off so sharply. The patterns that flowed across the flat surfaces were arranged in rows. He felt a strange excitement They must be some kind of characters, he thought. This was no mere slab of rock—it was a tablet formed by intelligent hands.

Rand rose slowly to his feet, turning the fragment over and continuing to remove as much dirt as he could. There was little doubt now that the object must be a portion of a tablet carved with words of some kind. The language was not his own, and though he had seen examples of the characters of outlanders, the marks on the stone bore no obvious resemblance to either the flowing script of the Gawlians or the rough runes of the Vokar. He knew where to go next, though: his uncle Bowin had been to the Academy of Serenhorn as a youth, making him the most educated man in the town of Oakbridge. He also had the only real library other than the one at the school. If anyone could tell Rand more about this odd stone, it was Bowin. Rand retrieved his school-bag and marched off through the orchard toward the manor house.

Chapter 2

*There is a time for everything--a time to scatter stones,
and a time to gather them.*

As Rand neared the center of his uncle's estate, he saw signs of the coming harvest all around him: barrels stockpiled near the door of the carpentry shed; carts being repaired and oiled for the many trips they would make through the orchard; hired men clearing rocks, ruts, and brush from the paths between the trees. He broke into a jog when he neared the house, smiling and waving at people he recognized as he went. He took the stairs to the front door of the manor two at a time, then skidded to a hasty stop as he reached the porch.

His aunt Cora was standing just outside the manor's tall oaken doors, watching the bustle of the estate at work. She looked on with amusement as he recovered his balance.

"Well, Rand, you appear to be on a mission of some importance! What are you chasing, or is something chasing you?" said Cora. She was a kind and quick-witted woman who had always been a friend to Rand; still, he sometimes struggled to find the right words when speaking to her. She was elegant and refined, the daughter of a wealthy family somewhere far away. Bowin had brought her back to Oakbridge with him after meeting her during his years abroad.

"I, er, found a strange stone while studying in the orchards, Aunt Cora. Is Uncle Bowin home? I would like to ask him about it."

"You two and your artifacts," she said with a smile. "Always mulling and muttering over them! Well, I'm sure Bowin will be glad to inspect your latest treasure for you. He is working in his study."

Rand made a little bow and slipped into the house. The soft light of the overcast day filtered in through the tall windows on each side of the doors, glowing on the polished hardwood floor. To his left a corridor led away from the high-ceilinged entrance hall. He turned into it, walking silently down the runner of carpet in the center of the floor as he passed doorways on each side. The hall ended at a large door that stood open, offering him a view of a room crowded with mismatched furniture, its walls lined with shelves of books. A large bay window that looked out over the orchards dominated the opposite wall. In front of it a heavy oak desk faced the door, and sitting behind the desk was Uncle Bowin.

"Uncle, may I speak with you?" said Rand. He paused just inside the doorway, giving Bowin time to acknowledge him. Bowin was leaning over the ledger books of the orchard, quill in hand, making notations doubtless related to the coming harvest. He was lean and lightly framed, not unlike Rand, with thinning silver hair and a ruddy face from much time spent outdoors. Even seated, he had an air of poise and confidence. He looked up sharply when Rand spoke.

"Welcome, lad! What brings you to my door? I see it brought you in haste," he added, noting the state of Rand's clothes.

"Uncle, I was studying in your orchard just now when I found something half-buried in the earth. I hope you can tell me what it is," Rand said, pulling the stone from his tunic as he crossed the room to stand in front of the desk.

"Rand, you know I'd love to inspect it for you, but just now I have other ..." Bowin's words faded on his lips as he got a closer look at the fragment that Rand held across the desk.

"So, that's no mere curious pebble, is it? Bring it around here where we can look at it in the light from the window," he said, gesturing with one hand while taking the stone in the other. Rand moved to his uncle's chair. He hoped the tablet would prove worthy of a thorough investigation. He enjoyed few things more than deciphering the past with Bowin.

"Hmmm, these are obviously characters of some kind—not a common local language though," said Bowin.

"I thought the same, Uncle," said Rand, feeling a tinge of pride.

"This material's queer, too," Bowin continued, turning it over in his hands and hefting it. "It's dark and smooth as polished granite, but almost as light as wood. Here now, wait a moment ..." He rose from his chair, crossing to a bookcase near the windows. After a short search he found the book he wanted and brought it back to the desk. He laid the stone aside and stood there leafing through the book.

"This was one of my history texts at the Academy when I was a young man," he explained. "My antiquities master used to tell a story about certain rather special stone tablets. Ah, here we are." He set the book on the desk and pointed to a series of woodcut illustrations.

"Here you see examples of tablet fragments that have been collected over the years. The artist didn't include a very detailed rendering of the characters, but if you look closely, there's certainly a resemblance between them and this piece that you found today." Rand looked from the pages to the stone and nodded agreement.

He had searched like this with his uncle since he was a small boy. One time they might try to identify a curious mineral. The next they might attempt to determine the uses of an ancient tool. There was a different feeling this time, though. Learned men like the creator of his uncle's book did not devote serious study to the castoffs of farming hamlets. The fragment was something older and grander than anything made by the people of Rand's valley.

"Does the book tell how to read the markings?" said Rand. Bowin shook his head.

"I believe there are a few historians who study these stones," he replied. "They can make out a little of what is written upon them. Of course, it is difficult to make much sense of them when each contains such a small portion of the whole."

"Where did they come from, and how did one of them end up here in our valley?" asked Rand.

Bowin slapped the book in excitement. "That's the nub of it boy—good question! These stones are old; I've no need to tell you that. What you don't yet realize is how truly old 'old' can be. They come from before the settling of Oakbridge, indeed before our kingdom of Solethon was even founded. Those who study them believe they are entwined with the history of the Trail of Sorrows itself."

"Trail of Sorrows?"

"You don't know of it then," said Bowin. "Not surprising, really. It may be only a legend. The short of it is that our people originally came to these lands as part of a mass migration, and that they suffered great hardship on the journey."

"Ah, that explains the name I guess," said Rand. "But why did they do it? Where did they come from?"

"They were the citizens of an empire far beyond the Badlands," said Bowin. "Do you know those?"

"Yes," said Rand after some thought. "North and west of our kingdom, is that right?"

"Correct. Some great calamity destroyed their empire so utterly that all who survived had no choice but to flee. They crossed the Badlands at great cost, and when they passed through the Sentinel Range and found the valley of the Solus River, they made a new life for themselves here. Much of the customs, the history, even the tongue of their lost empire did not survive the travails of their wandering. With the passing of many years their villages grew into towns, then cities, until at last they banded together and the realm of Solethon was born."

"What part would broken stones like this one play in such a story?" said Rand.

"They were part of some buildings or monuments—something important to the people of the empire," said Bowin. "The force that destroyed their homeland blasted these tablets to pieces and threw them high into the skies, so that they were scattered over many lands. Debris fell like a deadly rain after the fall of the empire. Every now and then the refugees would come upon one of these fragments as they traveled. Each time it was a bitter reminder of all they had lost."

Rand could contain himself no longer. He burst out laughing.

"What kind of blast could do such a thing, flinging stones into the air to hang for hours, scattering them across many leagues? Really, Uncle, you haven't told me this tall a tale since I sat on your knee!"

"I know," Bowin replied with a wry smile. "It is a legend, as I said, and a curious one. But it is the tragedy and the falling of the stones that gave them their name—the Stone Tears."

"Stone Tears," Rand repeated as he examined the jagged sliver again. "Have many been found?"

"No," said Bowin thoughtfully as he watched his nephew. "Never before in this valley, and only rarely across the length and breadth of Solethon. In fact, tradition holds that it is an omen to find a Stone Tear."

"Omen of what?" asked Rand. He hastily replaced the stone on the desktop, feigning a casual air. Bowin tried to hide a smile.

"It depends on the heart of the one who finds it, I think," he replied. "Perhaps victory, perhaps tragedy, but a sign of destiny nonetheless."

"What do we do with it now?"

Bowin picked up the fragment and carried it to the window. Rand saw a faraway look in the man's eyes that he had learned to recognize. His uncle was wrestling with the beginnings of an idea.

"I am unsure as yet, my boy. Why don't you leave this with me for a time and let me think on it? You'd best be getting along home before your father loses patience with both of us."

Chapter 3

Think on him who faced such opposition from wrongdoers,
that you not grow weary and lose heart.

Rand scarcely saw the road before his feet as he made his way back to the village. What had he gotten himself into? Stone Tears, a Trail of Sorrows, omens—everything his uncle had told him was too big to fit into his everyday thoughts. He was impatient with the small world of this valley and thought more often with each passing season of how he might find a way out of it. Now that the wider world had come rushing to meet him, he found that he much preferred approaching it on his own terms.

Lost in thought, Rand marched over the brow of a hill and down into the tree-shaded dell beyond. His uncle's house was out of sight and earshot now. In the sudden gloom, he failed to take notice of a presence beside the road until it moved in front of him, stopping him with a rough shove to the chest. He staggered back in shock.

"Watch where ye step, soot-face," the figure said in a cold tone that Rand knew well.

"Karl! I didn't see you—"

"Aye, a one-eyed fence post sees more'n you. Now me, I see plenty." Rand's eyes were adjusting to the dim light beneath the thick canopy of branches that overhung the road. It hadn't helped that Karl wore the usual clothing of the farmers around Oakbridge, rough woolens in brown and gray. Karl and Rand were about the same height, but Karl was broad in the shoulders and deep in the chest. Every part of him was hardened and thickened by the labors on his father's farm, which lay here along the road between Bowin Porter's orchards and the village.

"I'd best be along then," said Rand as casually as he could manage. "I'm late to my chores, and my father will have my head in a vise if I don't hurry." He made to pass by, but Karl again stopped him with a shove of his hand.

"I see plenty," he repeated, "watching you moon over her as you trip and trundle down the road, making eyes at her in the schoolyard. Ye best leave off that track, if ye mind yer health. Lyssa's a' going to be squired to the harvest fair by a true man, not by a wind-blown reed the likes of you."

Rand's wariness was overcome by a surge of anger, fueled not only by Karl's insults but by his own embarrassment at having his private longings so easily stripped bare. He shoved back at the other boy, who scarcely shifted his weight under the attack. Karl swatted at Rand with deceptive mildness, and his thick farmer's hand slapped the side of Rand's head like a hammer from his father's forge. Rand fell in a heap, his ear ringing and throbbing with pain. Karl knelt on his chest, pinning his shoulders to the ground and squeezing his ribs so that he could hardly breathe. He tried to heave Karl off, but he couldn't get any leverage. His fists bounced harmlessly off Karl's leg.

"None of that, you village rat, or I'll take time and trouble to teach you a lesson proper." Karl slowly lowered his other knee onto Rand's neck until his breathing was cut off altogether. His eyes started to bulge with the strain. "I've got work of my own to tend to now, but just you mind what I told you." With a chuckle, Karl rose and left Rand lying in the road.

After a few seconds of gasping, Rand was able to sit up. Karl had moved off the road and was vaulting a fence that marked the edge of his family's farm. Rand rose slowly to his feet and dusted himself off. As he collected his satchel and made his way up the next hill, he tried to keep his thoughts on the poem for Lyssa. Karl's strength was more than enough to win fights, but that didn't mean it was enough to win a girl's heart. Perhaps in such a battle as that, Rand's weapons would prove the stronger.

Chapter 4

My boundaries have fallen in pleasant places;
truly I have a delightful inheritance.

When he finally reached his father's smithy, Rand was an hour late. In spite of his throbbing head, aching ribs, and injured dignity, he had to work doubly fast to finish his chores before supper time. Throughout the labors of stocking the wood, feeding the fire, and manning the bellows, his normally taciturn and ill-tempered father glowered at him with an extra measure of disapproval and suspicion. Mercifully, he asked no questions, and Rand volunteered nothing.

Supper time came at last. Rand shut and latched the large outer doors of the smithy. He and his father took turns ladling water from a barrel in the corner over each other's hands as they washed away the soot and sweat of their labors. Then they left the smithy by a side door that led through the pantry into the house proper.

Rand found it difficult to concentrate on eating. His mother could tell he wasn't himself. She made a point of passing bowls and platters to him and insisting that he take more helpings. Once as she made her way to the kitchen hearth to fetch more stew, she paused at his chair and rested her hand on his shoulder—a brief, simple gesture that communicated a wealth of tenderness and concern.

Rand escaped from the table as soon as he could without further arousing his mother's concern or his father's ire. In the smithy, all was now quiet. He swept soot and metal scraps up from the floor and hung his father's tools on their assigned pegs along the walls. Next he scooped up bucketsful of ash from the forge and used them to bank the glowing embers there so that the fire could be built back up quickly in the morning. With all set in order for the night, he washed once more at the water barrel and went back into the house.

Rand passed his younger brother in the pantry; Denny was cleaning out the dishes from the evening meal. That meant the rest of the family had finished their supper, just as he had hoped. When he entered the kitchen his mother was gathering up scraps to feed the dog. Through the archway on the far side of the kitchen table he could see the silhouette of his father seated by the smaller hearth in the parlor, resting his feet on a stool and puffing slowly on a pipe.

"So, Rand," said his mother over her shoulder as she continued working. "What were ye up to this afternoon? Yer father's none too happy, though it's quieted him some that ye caught up on yer work. And what's become o' yer face? Don't tell me 'nothing,' neither."

Rand winced; he should have known there was no escape from his mother's watchfulness. He glanced around quickly to make sure he would not be overheard. His father was out of earshot in the next room, and the door between kitchen and pantry was more than half shut.

"It was an afternoon full of surprises, Ma," he replied quietly. "After school I went to Uncle Bowin's place to do my study work. I found an ancient stone in the orchard, and he thought it was something important. We looked it over for a while, and by then I knew I was late so I hurried back. I didn't mind where I was going, and Karl caught me unawares down by his farm."

"Karl Morgan! Has he been at ye again? What is it makes him so hateful to ye?" said his mother. She set aside the pot she was scraping and turned with her hands on her hips to look at him. He knew that she would stand there until she had an answer from him, and no half-truths would escape her notice.

"There's this girl at the school—Lyssa—and Karl thinks he has a right to her. He told me off about her, and I didn't take well to him givin' me orders, so there was some scuffling."

"Aye, ye've got a proud streak in ye, same as yer father. But ye'd as soon knock over an oak tree as gain ground in a tussle with that ox of a boy. Now this Lyssa—is she that little missy goldilocks, the storekeeper's daughter?" Rand nodded and looked down at the floor without speaking.

"I might've known. I saw her at the May fair this year, flouncing about in her party dress to catch the eye of every boy she crossed paths with. I marked her for a maker of trouble then, and now we see it come to pass."

"But Ma, she's—"

"I know, Rand, I know. She shines and glitters and sets you all aflutter. But not all that shines has true gold at heart. Mark it well."

"Yes'm," said Rand. When his mother had her mind made up, that was the best and only answer. She reached out and lifted his chin, forcing him to look her in the eye. She searched his face for a few moments and then the most amazing thing happened—her ruddy, careworn face broke into a smile.

"Other mothers're warning their daughters about you this very night, I shouldn't wonder. Ye've too much o' that smooth-talkin' uncle o' yours about you." She chuckled as she turned his face from side to side. He blushed profusely but smiled in spite of his embarrassment. Not for the first time he looked at this simple, sweet-faced woman with her thick country brogue and wondered at the differences between his family and Uncle Bowin's. Maybe this was a time to ask some questions that had vexed him for long enough. He glanced back toward the parlor; his father appeared fully occupied with carving a bit of wood.

"Ma, since you mention it, why isn't Da himself more like Uncle Bowin?" he asked. "They are brothers after all."

"Hmm, aye, ye'd scarce think 'em kin, would ye?" she said. "One fine-spoken and blessed with all manner o' worldly goods, and t'other dark and quiet as a stone. Weeell, 'tis not uncommon for brothers to have different natures. You and little Denny are not so much alike as all that."

"Yes'm, I can see that. But why do they live so differently too?"

"Fer that ye'd have to look to their father. You never knew your gran'da Porter."

"No, and neither Da nor Uncle Bowin ever speak of him."

"Old Porter, as we used to call him when I was but a girl meself, was a hard man, Rand. He had more pride than you and yer da put together. He was a stickler for tradition, too. There was never any question that the customs common to highbred folk would be followed without swervin' to left or right. That meant that the house and lands and family business must go to the eldest child—yer uncle, o' course."

"So Da was left with nothing? No wonder he's so grim."

"Oh, 'twas not so hard as that, Rand, nor so simple," his mother said. "The traditions allowed for a portion o' the family's wealth to be set aside for the younger heirs, an' the eldest could share as he or she pleased from the birthright once it had passed down. No, 'twas more my meaning that Bowin was the favored one from the day o' his birth, and Eli, yer father that is, was always in the shadows so to speak—and not always for bein' the second son, neither.

"Bowin and Eli were light and shade, folk used to say. The older was fair and friendly, full o' charm and wit. The younger was quiet an' somber-like, given more to ponderin' than talkin'. Bowin loved books and music; Eli liked to work more with his hands than his head."

"Did they hate each other, then?"

"Nay! Oh aye, they fought as brothers do. Still do, ye know," his mother replied with a smile. "But they stood by each other when it came to it. In truth they probably had less cause than most for strife, being too different to want or care about the same things. The real trouble was their father."

"How, Ma?"

"As I told ye, yer gran'da Porter was fearsome proud. The family o' the Porters was not o' noble stature, but it was old and respected. Old Porter expected his sons to be learned and courtly-like, to go off to the fine schools in the cities and learn manners. That was a path that suited Bowin's nature well, but it held no charm for Eli. They both attended the village school as children, o' course, same as you. But as the time approached for them to move on, Eli's attention was caught elsewhere.

"See, when yer da was scarcely older'n Denny, he used to stop on his way home from school to watch the village blacksmith at work. The ringin' o' the hammer was like music to his heart. Afore long the smith took a likin' to him, for he could see that Eli had a natural bent toward work o' that kind. Soon the smith was lettin' him help around the workshop, teaching him a little of the trade."

"The smith was your own da, wasn't he?"

"Aye, Rand, he was—the only gran'da you ever knew, though you were young yet when he died. Well, Oakbridge is a small place for news, and Old Porter heard soon enough what Eli was about. He didn't like a son of his bein' seen around the town workin' as a common tradesman. He and Eli fought no end over it, but some of Eli's true mettle showed then. He had never been one to give his father any chaff before, but once he had his heart set on somethin', he wouldn't be moved. The more Old Porter raged, the more he dug in his heels.

"Back and forth it went, and a few stormy years passed. Bowin finished at the village school and went off to the city. Then the time came for Eli to do the same. But he had already made up his mind to do otherwise. He announced that he was going to apprentice to my da and become a blacksmith himself."

"There must have been a mighty row over that."

"True enough, son. Old Porter threatened, but Eli didn't flinch. The old man even tried to buy off my da, but he should've known better. In the end, he cut Eli off from the family fortunes and banned him from the house. That hurt Eli some—he loved his father in his way—but he knew that the Porter life was not for him. He took up his 'prenticeship and slept on a straw pallet out there in the smithy. Was no more'n a season older than you, he was."

"What did his father do then?"

"Why, 'twas nothin' he could do. The law o' the land says that none may gainsay a lad's right to enter into a trade once it all be done right an' proper, and the master willin' to take him on." Rand's mother stopped for a moment and smiled quietly to herself before going on. "Along that time, I was becomin' a young woman, and what with us bein' under the same roof every day, yer da and I soon took notice of each other. By the time Eli made journeyman, we were fast in love. When he finished his service we were married, and would have moved on to start a shop of our own somewheres.

"My da couldn't bear to let Eli go, though. He had no sons of his own, and Eli was dear to him. He asked us to stay on and for Eli to be his partner, share an' share alike. When my da could work no more, the smithy would pass to yer father, and so it did.

"Now, here we all are. Yer uncle went to the city, saw the world, and brought his Cora back with him. Me'n yer father had you an' Denny, the shop keeps us fed, and the work keeps him happy."

"Happy?" Rand looked at his father in the other room. "Are you sure?"

"Yes, dearie," his mother said with a chuckle. "I know he doesn't look it most times, but he followed the path that suited him. At the end o' the day he knows what he's done, and that it's done well. He sleeps easy and wakes with a clear conscience, though his troubles left a mark on him all the same. He sees it his duty to be hard with you and hammer you into shape like he does his iron. He don't know another way. And it worries him when he sees you spend so much time with his brother."

"Why, Ma? I thought you said they were at peace with each other."

"Bowin never had any ill will toward yer father, and when Old Porter died he used his right as the firstborn to set aside a sum for us. Yer father wouldn't take it though—too proud, wanted to make his own way and knew he could do it, too. Now he sees you up at the big house all the time and wonders what's to come of it. He doesn't want to see you drawn into the life o' the Porters after all he did to leave it."

As his mother paused, Rand's father shifted in his chair and called into the kitchen to ask if there were any barley cakes left from supper. His mother went to fetch one from the cupboard, and Rand decided that he had trusted his luck far enough for one evening—it was time to turn in. He had to be up before the sun next morning to help his father get the smithy going, and then off to school. He was in bed quickly but lay long in the dark thinking on all his mother had told him.

Chapter 5

There are three things that are too amazing for me,
four that I do not understand: the way of an eagle in the sky,
the way of a snake on a rock, the way of a ship on the high seas,
and the way of a man with a maiden.

The first rays of sunlight broke over the mountains to the east of Oakbridge. A falcon launched from the crags into the crisp air and followed Oak Creek in search of its breakfast. As the bird passed over Rand's village, its sharp eyes noted people stirring abroad to begin their day. It saw Rand as he shuffled along to the schoolhouse, weary from his morning chores. The predator's mind classified him as a straggler, possible food, then discounted him as too large to carry and promptly forgot him.

The falcon soared westward above Oak Creek, seeking a juicy rodent as the stream left the smaller valley and flowed down into Serenvale. The bird came to the Seren River and turned to follow it as it meandered south by southwest. Good hunting could be found in the marshy meadows where the Seren joined the Solus, the main artery of Solethon.

Having reached the confluence of the two rivers, the falcon turned to circle over its favored hunting grounds. Sunlight streamed through the pass called the Ram's Gate, illuminating verdant grasslands. Just before it dove upon an unwary water rat, the hunter's eye caught a flash at the very limit of its keen vision—the glint of metal above stone battlements. There, far to the south, the Solus turned westward and flowed past the foot of cliffs that marked the southern border of the realm. Between the river and the cliffs lay the city of Solaria, capital of Solethon, crowned by the citadel of the king.

On the battlements of the citadel, the royal honor guard tramped and jingled through the daily ritual of the morning flag-raising. The polished silver ball at the top of the flagpole reflected the morning light as it broke through the Ram's Gate, but on the granite pavestones below, the light was still dim and the soldiers' breath steamed in the autumn chill.

Deep within the fortress, a candle burned low on a broad stone table. The table rested in a private study, part of a suite of rooms never touched by the light of day. A black-robed man sat with his head bent over the table, fatigued from working through the night. He found it easier to concentrate on his auguries and alchemies when common folk slept, his labors best suited to darkness. He was the Royal Vizier.

All the court—even the king—knew him by his title alone. Holders of his office had long practiced this tradition, along with his shaved head and the arcane symbols tattooed across his face. He thrived on the cultivation of mystery. His naked head and unveiled face, seemingly so open, formed a mask hidden in plain sight. People struggled to distinguish the present Vizier from the last one, or the one before that. Some whispered that his unnatural powers had rendered him immortal—that in reality there had been but one Vizier from the beginning. These rumors were false, of course, but holders of the title secretly encouraged them. The order held this as one of their guiding principles—they could easily awe people who had already overawed themselves.

Normally the Vizier relished his work. Not this morning, though—recent developments troubled his mind. King Anthon, the public face of the governance of Solethon, had contracted a deep and chronic cough with the onset of cool weather. The court physician had done nothing to improve it with his brews and poultices. This winter might be the death of the king.

It would be no great loss, thought the Vizier. Anthon played the part of a cooperative tool, but not a particularly energetic one. Still, mounting a Royal Gauntlet to determine the king's successor would be a formidable undertaking, not to mention orchestrating the gauntlet to secure the sort of successor that the Vizier required.

He had begun the night by casting horoscopes to glean insight for the many plans he needed to make, but what he saw in them alarmed him in an unexpected way. He sought confirmation, and one omen after another—tossing the bones, drawing lots, the divining rod—confirmed it. Something stirred regarding the Enslaver. The ancient nemesis of his order rested uneasy in its grave. He did not yet know what form this stirring would take, but he found it disturbing in conjunction with the approaching change upon the throne.

The Vizier lifted his head from the stone table. He stared into the darkness beyond the guttering light of the candle as though he might pierce the stone walls of the citadel with his gaze, and allowed himself a grim smile. He would be very watchful. He excelled at that.

Rand reached the schoolhouse before most of the other students. He took a seat close to a window so he could practice his recitations in good light. There were three other students in his age group at the school; they were taking their final year before leaving and embarking on more practical pursuits. The Widow Liston taught all the ages together in one room, giving each their work in turn and maintaining order among the twenty-three children in her care.

The other boy in Rand's group, a farmer's son named Bart, came in and sat near the back of the room. Rand guessed by the forlorn look on his face that his attempt at composition had not turned out very well. Younger children came in by twos and threes to join those who were there already. Last of all came Lyssa and her friend Cami. Rand did his best to appear disinterested, but she caught him sneaking a glance and made a face before whispering something to Cami that made both of them laugh. Rand sighed and turned toward the window—a poor beginning to the day when he planned to declare his heart in rhyme.

Widow Liston called everyone to order and started her lessons. She saved the recitations of the eldest students until the end of the day as a special treat. Time dragged on as they worked their way through other subjects, ate lunch, and the younger students competed in a spelling contest. At last Rand and his peers took their turn.

Widow Liston called upon Bart first. He made it haltingly through the song he had memorized, with occasional prompting from the teacher. Then he brought out the battered paper that held his own poem. He flushed, cleared his throat twice, and read through it doggedly with a woebegone expression.

> I planted a tree.
> It grew for me.
> I wanted a pear
> But none was there.
> It'll bloom in the spring
> Or I'll chop down the thing!

Lyssa and Cami burst out laughing. Rand quickly covered his mouth to hide his own smile. The younger children dissolved into giggles and squeals. The seriousness with which Bart delivered his verdict on the tree only made it funnier. His flush of embarrassment quickly transformed into the brick red of anger. He tried to storm out of the schoolhouse, but Widow Liston intercepted him at the door and steered him toward a seat, quieting the rest of the students with stern reprimands. When she had restored order, she addressed Bart in a manner clearly intended to be heard by them all.

"Thank you, Bart. You performed your assignment just as you were instructed. I couldn't ask any better of you. Lest you fret over much about the reaction of your fellow students, remember that laughter is a gift to one's audience that not all are able to give." Bart, still visibly unhappy, nodded and relaxed a bit.

Widow Liston called on Cami next, who followed her folk-song recitation with an ode to a robin on a branch outside her window. Then it was Lyssa's turn. Rand couldn't focus on the content of her poem—he was too busy basking in the cadence of her voice, the movement of her lips, and the delicate tilt of her chin.

"Rand!" Widow Liston rapped the top of her table with her pointing stick. "Stop chasing moonbeams and get up here. I said it's your turn."

Rand glanced around and saw that the other children were looking at him expectantly. Lyssa had already returned to her seat; he had been so carried away in his thoughts that he hadn't even noticed she had stopped speaking. He wound through the benches to the front, feverishly reviewing the folk-song and his poem under his breath as he went.

Widow Liston nodded for him to begin. He turned to face the room. All eyes were on him, including Lyssa's; she wasn't smiling, but at least she was paying attention. He launched into the folk-song with more gusto than he had intended, being full of nervous energy. It was his good fortune to have a decent singing voice, though. The class was soon tapping and clapping along with him, even Cami and Lyssa. He felt his oats enough to finish off the song with an extra repeat of the chorus.

When he stopped, the younger students gave a cheer. Cami laughed and Lyssa smiled. Rand felt a swelling sense of confidence and opportunity. Without waiting for any prompting from the teacher, he raised his hands for quiet and launched into the poem he had written himself.

Rand kept his focus resolutely on Lyssa as he spoke. She looked puzzled at first and glanced from side to side, clearly wondering why he didn't address the entire class. The words poured out of him; she realized that he was speaking about her. She looked down and blushed. Then she looked back up at him, lips parted, eyes half-closed, inhaling each word. He finished and stood silently, unsure what to do next.

Widow Liston cleared her throat. The sound broke the spell. Children giggled and pointed, and Cami snorted derisively. Lyssa turned away and refused to look in his direction. Now it was Rand's turn to blush. He nodded to the teacher and retreated quickly to his seat.

"My, my, that was certainly ... heartfelt, Rand. Thank you. That will do for our studies today, children. My thanks to all of you who shared your compositions with us. I will see you tomorrow."

Rand went back to his seat to get his bag. Sitting by the windows had put him across the room from the door; he had to wait while most of the students filed out ahead of him. Cami continued to gesture in his direction while whispering to Lyssa and laughing.

Rand struggled between anger and self-loathing; he contemplated climbing out a window to escape the torture. The girls reached the doorway and Cami stepped outside; Lyssa paused and turned. Rand expected a mocking smile or a hateful grimace, but she just stared at him with a sort of doubtful wonder. Then she vanished through the door.

Rand didn't know what to make of that, but it seemed preferable to outright rejection. Soon he reached the door and slipped outside. He paused and adjusted the strap of his satchel while his eyes grew accustomed to the afternoon sun. The flour mill stood across the dusty road that split the village, and Bart leaned in the doorway next to a wagon filled with sacks of grain. The driver of the wagon turned to look at Rand—Karl. From the dark look on his face, Rand guessed that Bart had given him an account of what happened in school that day. Since Karl had finished his schooling the year before, Rand thought he might not hear about the poem, but no such luck.

Rand decided not to wait to hear Karl's thoughts on the subject. He turned and strode quickly up the street toward the smithy as though he hadn't noticed the other boys. He passed the town's general store, which was owned by Lyssa's family. When he reached the far end of the storefront, a call whispered from the narrow alley between the store and the house beyond.

"Rand! Over here!" He peered into the shadowy space. Lyssa stood there, beckoning impatiently. He hesitated only a moment, deciding not to stand gaping in the street with Karl so close at hand. He moved into the alley; Lyssa retreated farther, drawing him away from the sunlight and passersby. Satisfied that they were far enough removed from prying eyes, she stopped and leaned closer to him, gesturing for him to do the same.

"Well, Mr. Rand Porter. What were ye about in that school to-day? Did ye mean all those fancy words of yours?" Her expression was serious, but not angry. He felt acutely aware of how close she stood to him in the narrow space of the alley. He cleared his throat and did his best to answer with a steady voice.

"Yes, Lyssa, I meant every word. I feel so much—my heart just—when I see you, I—" She stopped him by touching his arm and smiled warmly. Rand felt his knees weaken at the sight of that smile, and for a moment he didn't know if he would stand or fall.

"You're certainly full of surprises, boyo. I'd never have thought you had it in you. By way o' thanks, you can kiss me if you like." Rand's mind reeled in shock; he hadn't dared to hope for this. She waited with an expectant smile; he knew he had to act before she changed her mind. He leaned closer, uncertain how to place his lips on hers, but she resolved any difficulties by meeting him halfway and planting her mouth firmly on his. Her hands caressed his cheeks, and he found it the most natural thing in the world to wrap his arms around her slender waist. Moments passed and still she lingered; he supposed it must count as a single kiss, for their lips never fully parted, but many kisses danced between them, each melting into the next.

Lyssa pulled back at last, flushed and out of breath. Rand stared at her wordlessly, feeling feverish or trapped in a dream.

"Mercy, Rand, aren't you the passionate one indeed? Perhaps we ought to know each other better after all. Why don't you meet me after supper tonight, down the west road by the big willow tree—d'ye know it?" Rand nodded; it grew along the way to Uncle Bowin's place.

"Good. Perhaps you can sing me a song or two, and I can thank you again." Lyssa stepped away from him, flashed a mischievous smile, and turned with a light laugh to dash into the rear yard of her father's store. Her steps tapped swiftly up the stairs to the back door, and she was gone.

Rand shook himself to clear his head and followed the alley back to the street. He craned his neck around the corner toward the mill; the wagon was there but Karl and Bart were out of sight. No one looked his way; he hastened up the road to his father's workshop.

Chapter 6

Teach a child to choose the right path,
and when he is older, he will remain upon it.

The Porters did plenty of work in the smithy with harvest time coming. Rand labored over the grinding wheel to sharpen the edges of scythes while his father hammered the dents out of plow blades that had run against rocks buried in the earth. Just before supper, Rand went to the door to catch his breath between one scythe and the next. He heard voices in the street and stepped out to see what was happening.

One of the women of the village called to two of her friends and pointed up the road leading into town. They stood together, leaning this way and that, peering into the distance. Rand couldn't tell what they were pointing to from his side of the street. He moved a little farther to look around the corner of his house.

A rider approached on horseback. The mount was no common plow-horse; it had a light frame and stepped up the road with a crisp gait. As it trotted closer, Rand realized that he knew it—Challenger, his uncle's favorite horse, ridden by Bowin himself.

Rand jogged up the road to meet him. Bowin rarely came into town; one of his hired men usually took care of any ordinary errands that would have brought him this way. Today's business must not be ordinary, then. As Rand came near, Bowin reined his horse to a halt and smiled in greeting.

"Ah, Rand, I hoped to find you! Doing well this fine day?"

"Very well, Uncle, thank you! What brings you into town? Has Challenger thrown a shoe?"

"Nay, lad! I thought I might see if your mother was serving her incomparable meat pies for supper tonight." Bowin leaned low in the saddle and spoke quietly. "And I've been giving some thought to that stone you found. I'm glad you met me in the road. We can talk a while before we get to your house." He started his horse forward at a leisurely walk and Rand fell in alongside.

"As I told you yesterday, I think it is no small matter for you to find a Stone Tear. It's of great interest to scholars, and I believe it represents a turn in the path of your own life as well. It should be taken to the Academy in Serenhorn without delay. What's more, I think you should take it."

Rand stared up at his uncle in disbelief. Could Bowin be serious? He certainly didn't look like he was teasing. Rand didn't know whether to be overjoyed or terrified at the prospect of going to the city alone. Larger than that, however, loomed the problem of what his father would say.

"Uncle, that's—that's amazing, but my father would never allow it."

"He would think this business about the stones was complete foolishness. I don't plan to put it to him that way, though. I have some contracts for this year's cider production that need to go to the merchant house in the city. I have no unoccupied hired hands that I would trust with them, and they must get there soon. I'll pay Eli for your time to be my messenger, and I'll take the line that a boy your age needs to see a little of the world if he's to have a good head on his shoulders. Follow my lead, and don't speak more than you have to; we'll bring him around, just wait and see."

They arrived at Rand's house as he finished speaking. Bowin dismounted and tied Challenger's reins to the hitching post by the smithy door. Rand's mother must have seen them through a window; she burst out through the front door before they could reach it.

"Bowin! Mercy, but ye're a rare sight! What brings ye to our home?"

"Good afternoon, Lydia. I wondered if there might be a spare plate at your table tonight. I've been pining after those meat pies of yours."

"Ah, pish and twaddle, man! I know well that you've an army to cook and clean fer ye and all manner o' things." Rand followed them into the house as they continued to banter with each other. His mother sent Denny out to the shop to let their father know they had company.

Eli appeared shortly and extended a hand to his brother in greeting. Rand watched carefully—his father was reserved, perhaps even wary, but he didn't look angry at the unexpected visit. Before long they were seated around the dinner table, enjoying the meal while the elders exchanged news and stories. Rand observed Bowin as he discreetly turned the conversation toward talk of his contracts and the need for a trusted messenger. Eli snorted and observed that few of Bowin's hirelings had the wit or the character to be given such responsibility—they'd get lost in the city or spend all their travel money on drink at the first inn along the way. Bowin agreed with a rueful chuckle; then he broached the subject of Rand with the air of having just thought of him.

Rand's father immediately dismissed the suggestion—he needed Rand's help this time of year, and the boy was too young for the city. Bowin took up this theme, pressing the idea that a trip beyond

Oakbridge would help to season and mature Rand now that he was becoming a young man. He also appealed to Eli's family pride, emphasizing the advantages of keeping important matters in the hands of a trusted relative. When money was mentioned, Eli brushed it aside; he had never made a family decision for the sake of coin, and he wouldn't start now. Still, Rand was surprised that his father seemed to waver on the question as a whole. Then Bowin played his final card.

"You know well the treasures of my house, Eli, for once it was your house too, and you are always welcome there." Rand scarcely dared to breathe—what was his uncle up to by turning the talk to matters such as these?

"Yet with all the wealth that is stored under my roof," continued Bowin, "there are riches in your keeping that I will never know. You have two fine boys—healthy, strong, and helpful to you in your labors. In my hour of need, will you not lend me a little of your bounty?"

Rand was surprised. He had never thought much about the fact that Bowin and Cora had no children, or about what hardships that lack might impose. He looked to his father to see what the response to such an unexpected sentiment would be.

Eli rose slowly and leaned on the table with both hands. He returned Rand's gaze with a searching stare of his own that Rand dared not look away from. Then he nodded and turned to his brother.

"You have me there, Bowin. You may have Rand's help for a week. It's time Denny learned more about the work in the shop anyway."

Bowin stood also and shook his brother's hand warmly. "Then it's agreed. I'll see that he returns by then." He turned to Rand.

"Why don't you gather up some clothes for the trip and come to my house tonight? We can finish provisioning you for the journey, and you can get an early start in the morning."

Rand looked to his father, who nodded and waved for him to get moving. Rand was clumsy with excitement as he left the table and climbed the stairs to the small room he shared with Denny in the attic of the house. Bowin excused himself with kind words for the meal and called after Rand that he would see him at the estate. Rand couldn't believe that things were moving so quickly. He would be gone to the city in the morning! What should he take? In the end, he bundled up all the clothes he had, for they amounted to little.

When Rand came back down into the kitchen, his father and Denny were gone. His mother was picking up the mugs and plates from the table to take to Denny in the pantry. As Rand reached the ground floor, she turned and took his face in her hands.

"Oh, Rand, me boy—ah, me boy. ... 'Tis good for you to go abroad, my heart tells me 'tis true, but I know it will change you. Mind what shape that change will take. Mind who you let yourself become, and come back safe, ye hear?"

"Yes'm." Rand fought back the tears that welled in response to hers. She embraced him so tight as to never let go. Finally she stepped back and composed herself.

"Go out through the shop as ye leave. Yer da wants to have a word with ye afore ye go."

Rand looked toward the pantry door with reluctance. It wouldn't do to upset his father by dragging his heels, though, when Bowin had so narrowly won permission. He lifted his bundle and went.

He had to pass Denny in the pantry. His little brother followed him into the smithy, eager to join in the excitement of Rand's departure. Their father sent Denny back to the cooking pots with a shake of his head and a pointed finger. Denny turned back with his head hung low in disappointment. Rand managed to tip him a wink that earned a smile in return.

"Close the door, lad," said Eli once Denny was gone. "We have matters to discuss." Rand complied and turned slowly to face his father.

"So, young man—going off on your own, eh?" Eli leaned across the anvil and regarded Rand with a searching stare. "There's a lot my brother says that I put little stock in, but I can't deny he's right in one thing—you're growing up fast. It's time you learned to stand on your own two feet; this jaunt to the city is as good a way as any. You must leave off your songs and larks and be serious about your life. I don't need his silver, and I don't think his business dealings are ours to worry about, but him asking me for help—that was something new."

"Yes, sir." Eli turned and went to a cupboard on the wall behind him. He retrieved a small bundle wrapped in oiled cloth and tied with leather thongs. Rand had seen it before while tidying the shop but paid it no mind, thinking it to be a set of tools.

"Bowin will give you most of what you need for the journey— food that will keep while traveling, some coin for expenses, and the like. But there's one thing I can give you that no man should be without on the road. If you need to hunt, cut a path, or—luck forbid—face an enemy, you shouldn't be empty-handed." Eli unfolded the cloth and lifted the object within toward the overhead lamp for inspection—a knife in a well-crafted leather sheath. The straight blade was twelve inches long. The hilt was leather-bound and wound with a fine wire that appeared to be silver; it had a guard as well, and that, together with the length, signified that the knife could serve as a weapon if need be. Rand's father had taught him that a guard stopped an opponent's blade from sliding down your own and cutting your hand.

Eli handed the knife to Rand and he drew it slowly from the well-oiled sheath. It was double-edged and finely balanced, free of rust, nicks, or dents. The metal had a bright sheen that was unfamiliar to Rand.

"It's not made of silver is it, Da?"

"Nay, not silver—silver's too soft; that's a special kind of iron, lad. It's called steel. Very few know the secret of its making and they guard that knowledge closely. I don't know that there are any smiths in all of Solethon who possess such craft." Rand's estimate of the knife's value—already a lordly sum—rose even higher. It must be worth more than the shop earned during an entire year.

"Da, where did you get this?"

"I've had it a long time, boy—since I was younger than you. My father cared only for business, first, last, and always. My grandfather, though, was more adventuresome. He traveled far when he had the chance and brought back many trophies that he collected along the way. I spent a fair amount of time with him during his later years; he loved to tell stories, and I loved to hear them. What with Bowin in line to inherit the estate and the business, I guess my gran'da thought I might strike out on my own some day and be a traveler too. He gave me the knife, something he picked up in the lands away south, to take with me and remember him by."

"Did you ever go?" After talking with his mother the night before, Rand thought he knew the answer.

"No, lad. I did strike out on my own, but not on the road. I found that life here at the forge was adventure enough for me. As you are about to make one journey at least, the blade ought to pass on to you now. It wasn't made to sit on a shelf waiting for time and rust to ruin it."

"Thank you, Da. It's the finest gift I've ever had." Rand worked at threading the sheath onto his belt.

"As I said, boy, it's time for you to stand on your own feet; that's why I'm letting you go. It's only the beginning, though. I want you to keep your head clear out there. You're not on holiday; remember the charge entrusted to you by your uncle. Remember also that the end of your path lies right back here, not off in the city or elsewhere in the wide world. Since you're to start learning how to be a man, I judge it'll be time for you to begin your apprenticeship when you return."

Rand's heart sank. He had known his father would soon expect him to train in earnest, but the thought brought him no joy. Now Eli would work him twice as hard, watching every step and demanding perfection. Rand would be sore, seared, and exhausted from after school until nightfall. When he finished school early next summer, his world would shrink to the space within the walls of the shop.

"Yes, Da." He did his best not to look unhappy; he knew his father counted it a privilege to learn the secrets of smithcraft.

"All right, then, off with you—it's getting dark already, and you've a long walk ahead of you." Eli thrust out his hand. Rand stared at it in surprise, then took it in his own. They shook hands solemnly; Eli cleared his throat and turned to put some tools on their pegs along the wall. Rand thought his father's cheek looked wet in the lamplight. He shouldered his bundle and slipped quietly out of the shop by the main street door.

Rand took a deep breath and headed northward over the bridge that gave the town its name. On the far side of the bridge the road turned west to follow Oak Creek downstream. As he made the turn, a sudden thought made him cry out in alarm and sent him dashing down the road as fast as his burden would allow—he had forgotten about his rendezvous with Lyssa.

Chapter 7

What causes conflicts among you? Don't they come from your desires that battle within you? You desire but do not have, so you kill. You covet but you cannot get what you want, so you quarrel and fight.

The sun had already set and dusk faded into twilight in the sky ahead of him. The willow tree where he had agreed to meet Lyssa stood along the bank of the stream, past the first bend in the road as it left town. Rand sprinted as fast as he dared, stumbling over wagon ruts in the shadowed roadway. Finally, he rounded the bend and saw the willow. No sign of Lyssa, but that counted for little in the gathering dark. Rand slowed to catch his breath; it would hardly impress the girl if he arrived gasping for air like a fish.

He came to the willow, but still saw no one. *Curse you, Rand, if you kept her waiting too long, she'll never give you another chance.* He tried not to lose heart; perhaps Lyssa was waiting by the stream to avoid travelers. He circled the low-hanging branches of the tree until he reached the water's edge. His hopes faded—no one was there.

"Lyssa?" There was no answer. With a groan he turned to continue on to Bowin's house.

"Hsst! Rand! Under here!" He remembered that urgent whisper from earlier in the day. His hopes leaped upward even faster than they had fallen—Lyssa was hiding under the shadow of the boughs. He pushed through the branches and found her.

"I nearly fell asleep in here waiting on you. If you hadn't made such a clatter coming up the road, I might have missed you altogether." Rand's eyes adjusted to the gloom beneath the tree until he could see the disapproval on her face.

"Don't make me wait again. I'm not in the habit of needing to wait on any boy. Hullo, what's this?" she said as she spied the bundle slung over his shoulder. "A change of clothes? Really, Rand, what sort of girl do you take me for?"

Rand flushed in acute embarrassment at the misunderstanding. But wait—the coquettish smile on Lyssa's face hinted that she could be taken for a lot more than he had imagined. As if to confirm the idea, she leaned forward so that the soft warmth of her bosom pressed against his chest. His romantic notions about her were pushed aside by a rush of physical desire. He dropped the bundle and grabbed for her. She laughed and returned his embrace, meeting his eager kisses with her own.

Time stopped. A voice deep inside warned him. This was strange territory—did he know where he was going or what it might cost? There was a louder voice shouting from a much shallower place that drowned it out—onward! More, more! She was so soft and alive in his hands. He ran his fingers through her long, curly hair. She pulled his head down to her neck, then lower still, pulling her neckline lower to bare more of herself to him. As he moved his mouth over her bosom, his hands slid under her skirt and began to explore below her waist.

Her giggles turned to moans. He felt her hand grasping at the front of his trousers, and it was his turn to moan. She toppled back onto the ground, pulling him down on top of her. He knelt there, gasping and shaking his head. What was happening?

"Don't worry, Rand. I'll show you what to do."

At that moment the boughs of the willow were shoved aside. A deep voice growled a harsh oath, and rough hands took hold of Rand's tunic and threw him to the ground beyond the circle of the tree. Lyssa squealed. Rand rolled over to face his assailant. Karl stood over him with murder in his eye.

"Karl! What are you doing?" cried Lyssa as she rushed to join them in the open air.

"I might ask you the same, wench! I thought we had an understanding between us. What're ye doin' in the arms o' this whelp?"

"An understanding, is it? I belong to no one, Karl Morgan, least of all a bullying brute like you. What have you shown me to prove you've any claim on me?" While Karl was distracted, Rand got quietly to his feet. He braced himself as well as he could and prepared to strike with both fists. Karl's next words brought him up short.

"Ye spoke better of me that night in the barn, ye she-witch. Did I not show ye enough then?"

"Hush that talk!" cried Lyssa. She turned to Rand. "Pay him no mind! He lies!"

"If I'd happened along much later, I expect he would know for himself if I lied or not." Karl turned to Rand. "But then I doubt ye'd know the difference at that, stripling. Believe it or no, she's no maiden any more, this one."

"Have it your own way, then," sniffed Lyssa with an injured air. "You press your will on me all hot and masterful, then pretend it makes me a strumpet. This one sings me his pretty love songs, but his blood runs as hot as yours when he sees his chance. How about it then? Is either of you man enough to promise me more than a night o' misbehavin'?"

"Wait a moment," said Rand. "Karl, how did you end up here tonight?"

"Not that I answer to you, skinny-britches, but I was here by right. She's my lass, and she asked me here."

Rand turned and stared at Lyssa in disbelief. She raised her chin and glared back at him defiantly. He saw a glimmer of what was happening. "You tricked us! You brought us out here to fight over you like roosters in a barnyard."

"What if I did? I have a right to a man who'll fight for me. I'm not some common kitchen drudge, and my heart will not be bought cheaply."

"If this is the price I have to pay, I'm afraid I can't afford it," Rand replied. "Karl, I'm sorry—I didn't know ... that is, I guess there was a lot I didn't know. I have many things to do tonight; I think I'd best be off now." Karl scowled at him but made no move. Rand went to retrieve his bundle from under the tree. Lyssa stared in disbelief, then spat on the ground.

"Go then! I don't know why I wasted a thought on a coward like you anyway." Rand grimaced but started down the road just the same.

As he passed over the next hill and left the pair behind, he could still hear them quarrelling.

Once the bickering was out of earshot, he slowed, his feet heavier in tandem with his heart. After the daydreams of the afternoon, the cold shocks of the evening were bitter beyond measure. One moment he hated Lyssa for her faithlessness; the next, he vowed he would prove himself worthy of her undivided attention.

He was about halfway to his uncle's house when he heard a loud rustling among the bushes beside the road. His hand happened to brush against the hilt of his new knife. He had forgotten all about it. He stopped in the road and drew it from its sheath, but the noise in the undergrowth did not continue. He tested the weight and balance of the weapon by swinging it in a figure eight. It felt secure in his hand and responded to his will with a smoothness that inspired confidence.

As Rand held the blade before him in the twilight, thoughts came unbidden—thoughts of how differently the confrontation with Karl and Lyssa might have gone if he had remembered the knife. What if Karl had carried out his jealous attack? Rand imagined the look of surprise spread over Karl's face as he moved to strike and instead felt cold metal slide into his belly.

And what of Lyssa? Once Karl was lying on the ground, feeling his lifeblood seep through fingers clutched over a mortal wound, might not Rand deal with her as he saw fit? Maybe he should do the village a service by killing her as well and putting an end to her devious ways. In fact, maybe it would be best to simply slay her instead of Karl. He and Karl would both be free of her then; they might make peace with each other.

Then again, Karl had more than just Lyssa to answer for as far as Rand was concerned. Rand should kill him after all. After that, Lyssa would spend the night with him under the willow tree as he explored the forbidden secrets and uses of her body.

A cool breeze blew Rand's hair into his eyes, causing him to stop and brush it away. Stop? He suddenly became aware that he had been retracing his steps, faster and faster back toward the willow with his knife clenched beside him in a white-knuckled grip.

He shook his head in disbelief; would he really have done such things? He carefully put the knife back in its sheath and turned toward Bowin's house again. Dread of his own anger and jealousy made his knees unsteady. As he trudged back past the place where he had remembered the knife, slitted yellow eyes regarded him from the shadow of a gnarled oak, then turned and disappeared into the night.

Chapter 8

Small is the gate and narrow the road that leads to life,
and only a few find it.

Stars were appearing above when Rand arrived at the lane leading to the Porter estate. His heart felt lighter at the sight of the warm lights of the manor house gleaming from the top of the hill, and he quickened his pace until he was almost running. The housekeeper let him in and took his bundle of clothes before leading him to the dining hall.

Rand found his aunt and uncle seated at the far end of the long table. Bowin had eaten earlier at Rand's house, of course, but he was chatting with Cora to keep her company while she ate her own supper. They both smiled as he approached.

"Come and sit, my lad," said Bowin. "I've just been telling your aunt about my talk with your father today. Now, tell us what happened after I left." Rand gave an account of his father's farewell and held out the knife for them to see.

"Grandfather's old Hamedan blade," said Bowin with a low whistle of appreciation. "I'd forgotten about this. It's quite a piece of workmanship, isn't it?"

"Yes, Uncle—like nothing I've ever seen." Rand tried to maintain a cheerful tone for their sakes, pushing aside the memory of his blind, murderous anger. He had no intention of telling anyone about Lyssa or Karl. Bowin stood and led Rand to his study.

As Rand took a seat he noticed a leather backpack leaning against a bookcase nearby. Bowin sat at the desk and took a small key from his waistcoat. He unlocked a deep lower drawer, from which he removed a drawstring bag and a fat packet of papers. He handed the bag to Rand.

"There's your Stone Tear. Thank you for entrusting it to me, but it belongs to you and no other. Don't forget that, whatever befalls you in the city or on the road. When something like that comes to you, you have to hold fast to it or it might slip away."

"Would someone try to steal it?"

"Perhaps not. Most would think it nothing but a curiosity. If someone recognized it for what it was, though, they might be keen to have it for themselves. At the very least it could attract attention. I learned in my own youthful travels that it's best to draw no notice to yourself if you can help it. The folk who first take an interest in you are always the kind that you least want to meet."

"I think I see your meaning."

"Good." Bowin clapped him on the shoulder and turned to the packet of papers. "These are the contracts for our cider. There are two sets, one for the merchant house and one for me. I've signed and sealed them as you see. When you return these to the merchant house, they will sign both copies as a final agreement, and you will bring my copy back to me when you return."

Bowin strapped the leather folio closed again and turned toward the pack by the wall. "This was my traveling pack when I was abroad. There's a tinder box and a bandaging kit inside. We'll give you a good store of hardtack and dried meat, and a thick woolen blanket for a bedroll. Tuck the Stone Tear deep within and leave it there, and the contracts too."

Bowin spent the next hour sketching out a rough map of the route from Oakbridge to the Seren River, then upriver to Serenhorn, and finally from the riverfront docks to the merchant house and the Academy. He rolled it up and placed it in the pack, then helped Rand to put it on and showed him how to adjust the straps. Finally he led Rand to a bedroom and bade him good night. Rand took a quick look at the Stone Tear, but weariness soon overcame him. He extinguished the lamp and climbed into bed.

When the first rooster crowed to greet the dawn, Rand dressed quickly, shouldered his pack and stopped by the kitchen for a quick breakfast. Miss Curdy, the cook, had laid out bread, cheese, and fresh Porter apples for him. His uncle took the opportunity to share a few last thoughts with him while he ate.

"Remember to take this letter of introduction straight to the headmaster of the Academy when you arrive there. They do not welcome interruptions at the school, so you don't want them to take you for a casual visitor. I think Master Parma holds the office now. When you've paid him your courtesies, seek out Master Zekiel. He is the Master of Antiquities, including the Stone Tears. You can let Parma know you are interested in the Tears if he presses you, but I wouldn't let anyone other than Zekiel see your fragment or even know you have it."

"Right," said Rand around a mouthful of bread. "Always lay low."

"That's the spirit, lad. Now, before I forget and let you run off without it, here's your traveling money." Bowin handed Rand a small leather bag on a long string. "Keep it around your neck, inside your shirt; when you need to get into it, do so quickly and put it out of sight again. If you hang it from your belt the way some folk here in Oakbridge do, you'll soon find out why petty thieves in the city are called cutpurses."

The bag felt heavy in spite of its small size and Rand wondered how much it contained. He put it around his neck and tucked it inside his tunic. It would be more polite to count it later. He took a last bite of apple and reached for his pack.

"I suppose it's time to stop plying you with advice and let you go," said Bowin. "Your aunt will be waiting on the front terrace to say farewell." When they stepped out, Cora kissed Rand's cheek and wished him luck on his journey. Bowin shook his hand heartily.

"I was just thinking. Six generations of Porters have held this land since we settled here. Today the story of the seventh generation starts with you, Rand. That's a number with good portents. May they follow you from this day on."

Rand smiled, waved, and marched down the hill. Bright morning sunshine filled the air. Soon he reached the gate and turned onto the main road.

He stopped to adjust the straps of his pack as he faced west. His shadow stretched out tall before him. Looking down the road, he realized that he had never followed it more than a few dozen yards past his uncle's gate. A twinge of anxiety passed over him now that he was about to enter the unknown. It faded when he realized that he was about to taste true freedom for the first time. He had food, a map, a full purse, and a secret; what more could a boy wish for? He grinned and started walking.

Oak Creek ran on the left and his uncle's orchards were on the right. The beginning of the story of the seventh generation, Bowin had said. Thinking about it that way changed things. Rand was no longer just a blacksmith's son running an errand for his uncle—he was an agent of the Porters, carrying the seventh generation's torch into the world. The orchards he was passing were not just his uncle's land; they were the ancestral domain of Rand's people—a foundation with deeper roots than he had realized.

Rand stopped at noon to eat lunch along the water's edge, letting his tired feet dangle in the icy flow. He had met few people on the road. Since no one was in sight at the moment, he took the opportunity to examine the contents of his purse. He counted twenty-five coppers and ten silver crowns. More than he had expected, but his uncle must want him to have a margin of safety. In the bottom of the purse Rand found a small packet of folded paper. The words "For Luck" were printed on it in his aunt's elegant hand. It contained a coin he had heard of but never seen before—a gold royal. He quickly put the money back in the bag and hid it away. He would be doubly careful now that he knew he carried an unimaginable fortune.

Midway through the afternoon, Rand's progress took him beyond the narrow walls of his own valley and onto the eastern slope of Serenvale itself. The trees thinned out on the grassy hillside as the road switch-backed down to the valley floor.

The sun hung low over the Hunter Range in the west as he reached the brow of the last hill. The road ran straight now on its final descent. Rand could see stretches of the Seren River sparkling in the golden autumn light. The smell and haze of wood fires hung in the air. He estimated that there was about an hour of good light left; that should be enough for him to reach Kerrin, the town where the road from Oakbridge met the river.

Rand resettled his pack on his shoulders. As he started down the hill, he whistled the folk tune he had sung in school. Evening breezes rustled in the browning grass on the hillside, whispering their own song of roads to follow and deeds to be done. It was a moment balanced between haste and reflection, desire and fulfillment, boyhood and manhood. Simple and perfect, unnoticed by the world, it soon passed—but in Rand's heart it would never be forgotten.

At the Porter estate, work in the orchards drew to a close for the day. Bowin stood in the garden outside his study windows, watching the velvety autumn dusk steal over the tree rows. He heard the glass door open behind him. A rustle of silk told him who was there. He reached back a hand without turning to look, felt it joined by the hand of his wife, and drew her to his side.

"Beloved, you have been troubled of late," he said.

"You know me too well, husband. Can you also guess the reason?"

"Perhaps. And yet I depend greatly on your counsel." She squeezed his hand and released it, stepping away to gather her thoughts.

"I do not know how much of this expedition of Rand's came to you as impulse and how much as plan. I suspect you do not know either, but I know this much with all my heart: you have done something that cannot be undone. No matter how quickly he returns, Rand will never truly come home."

"It is true that there will be changes in him and in his life. I have been impatient sometimes with Eli's plans for him, but then Eli is his father and I am not. I am not playing a game to mold his future into something more to my taste; there would be no honor in that. If anything, I feel it is more likely that something is playing a game with us all."

"How so?"

"It was no small thing, don't you think, for Rand to find a piece of history beneath a tree in our orchard? From the moment I saw it in his hands, I felt we were being carried along by an unseen tide."

"You have indeed had a strange look in your eye." Cora stepped close to him once more.

"Stone Tear or no Stone Tear," he said as he put an arm around her to shield her from the evening chill, "Rand would have faced considerable changes in his life someday."

"Must you say it, Bowin?" He looked down at her and saw the pain of long childless years in her face, the pain that she usually hid so well with her grace and humor.

"Yes, beloved, the time has come that I must. We both have known it long enough. So has Eli." He gestured across the tree-covered hills with his free arm. "One day all this will be given over to someone, and we know who that someone must be. All that remains to be seen is when and how."

Chapter 9

Stand at the crossroads and look; ask for the ancient paths, ask where the good way is, and walk in it, and you will find rest for your souls.

Rand reached the outlying houses of Kerrin about a quarter of an hour after the sun sank behind the mountains. The moist smell of the river thickened the evening air and drew him toward the docks. He resisted, though; Bowin had advised him that the safest lodgings were found well away from the waterfront.

A man in ragged clothes leaned against the corner of a building several yards ahead. He scowled at Rand and spit a stream of tobacco juice into the dirt. He looked like he was about to move closer. His attention shifted toward angry voices down the street. A group of men spilled out the doors of a tavern, shoving and punching at one another. The man jogged in that direction, eager to see what was happening. Rand let out his breath in a sigh of relief and stepped under the shadow of an awning to his left so he could get his bearings without making an easy target for any other members of the local welcoming committee.

The town lay clustered along the riverbank and the first hundred yards or so of the road to Oakbridge, and that was the sum of the place as far as he could see. Still, it was about twice the size of his own town. His uncle had recommended the Lantern House as a decent inn for the night; Rand soon found the sign for it on the right side of the street. He slipped quietly across the road and stepped inside.

The interior was much the same as that of the small inn back in Oakbridge—a dining room with a raised counter at the back. The man behind the counter looked him over cautiously and asked what he wanted. Rand tried to sound casual and worldly-wise as he inquired about a meal and a room for the night. The innkeeper nodded curtly and appeared to relax his guarded posture.

"Five coppers fer supper and a crown fer the room. Follow me and we'll get yer pack stowed away first."

Rand followed him up the stairs at the right side of the bar. The room was barely big enough for the narrow bed and washstand that it contained, but it was clean and the linens were fresh. After he shed his pack and washed some of the dust of travel from his face, Rand went back downstairs and enjoyed a hot bowl of beef stew with a hunk of bread. When he returned to his room he had no trouble dropping quickly off to sleep in spite of the relatively early hour.

In the citadel of Solaria, the Vizier was just finishing his evening meal—supper to others, breakfast to him. He turned sharply at the sound of tapping on a small metal grate set into the wall at floor level. Checking that none of his servants were presently in his private chambers, he went to the grate and worked an intricate latch to open it. Then he returned to his seat at the table and waited.

An enormous black beak extended tentatively into the room, followed slowly by the head and body of a large raven. The bird turned its head rapidly from side to side until satisfied that the room was empty of threats, then hopped across the floor and flapped heavily upward to alight on the table.

"Welcome, Garrak," said the Vizier, inclining his head solemnly. "Eye of my mind, wing of my spirit, what tidings do you bring?"

The bird turned its head to one side and regarded him for a moment, then responded with a rasping cry that was piercing in the enclosed space. In sibilant, croaking tones, it spoke.

"Hail, master. Mind of my eye, spirit of my wing, I bring tidings from our spies among the beasts," it completed the ritual greeting.

"Tell me then."

"Prince Uthor of Ramsgate killed his younger brother in order to take his fiancée from him. It was made to look like a hunting accident, but one of my ravens witnessed the deed."

"A man who possesses strong desire and the will to fulfill it—excellent. Continue."

"Princess Jylla of Kinnegad has been reading some of the tales of our old friend Curhoven. She has developed a taste for the mysteries of the spirit world and fancies herself a budding seeress."

"Interesting. I really must see about finding a new storyteller to make more tales like Curhoven's. They have often proved fruitful. In any event, we should encourage the princess's pursuits, Garrak."

"Indeed, master."

"Might we introduce her to a familiar?"

"Yes, master. There is a cat in the area who should find it easy to gain entrance to her home."

"Let it be done. These are promising tidings so soon in our preparations for the Gauntlet. Tell all of our friends to continue their efforts to discover the most worthy candidates."

"Yes, master." The bird remained, regarding the Vizier first with one eye, then the other.

"Well, Garrak? Have you more to say?" The bird shifted from foot to foot and resettled its wings before answering.

"There is one other matter, master. On my way here, I was stopped by one of the Others. He wished me to tell you of something." The Vizier was immediately on his guard. The Others were powerful allies in the cause of man's knowledge and freedom, but they were capricious and dangerous to treat with. They served the Banished One the same as he did, but they were not under the Vizier's authority.

"What is it?"

"This Other walks in the form of a panther, prowling the vale of the Seren River to the north. In his search for willing pupils, he came upon a boy who had been jilted by a faithless girl. He was speaking to the boy's thoughts, encouraging him to take action. Things were progressing well when something intervened."

"Something? How?"

"A breeze distracted the boy at a critical moment and he came to himself. After that, the Other could no longer reach his mind."

"Why did you not include this boy in your report?"

"He is not of noble family, master."

"Hmmph. Why waste our time then? Why does this Other think a commoner and a puff of air are so important?"

The raven became agitated. It cawed several times and fluttered its wings. When it spoke again, its voice was not as birdlike as before.

"Beware! Beware! The Others are not to be gainsaid lightly. They are of a higher order. Though I and my fellow familiars are of lesser kind, we answer to the same lord as they—as do you... master." The Vizier felt a chill pass over him. It was too easy to become complacent in dealing with dark powers when they were eager to do one's bidding. He must not allow himself to speak so carelessly again. On the other hand, he must not show weakness. The servants of the Banished One looked ever for advantage in their struggle for supremacy, as was proper.

"I know my duty, raven," he said with as commanding an air as he could summon. "You will not remind me of it again if you value your place as my servant. It is my duty that compels me to question anything that might distract me from my mission. Answer me now—what does this matter have to do with me?"

"Very well, master. The Other bade me tell you of this for two causes. First, the Others know from experience that only the influence of the Enemy may shut them out so completely as happened with this human. Second, the Other caught the scent of the Enslaver about the boy."

"The Enslaver! Omens have pointed to it of late. Did the boy have a fragment, then?"

"No, master. The Other did not sense it strongly enough for that. He was certain, though, that the human had come into contact with it or had been influenced by it in some way."

"Right, then. Though we may not yet understand these tidings, I agree that anything attracting the interest of the Enemy warrants our attention. Arrange for a watch to be kept on this boy, Garrak."

"Of course, master." The bird hopped to the edge of the table and fluttered down to the floor. In moments it had disappeared into the small opening from whence it had come—the inner end of a ventilation shaft that led to the outside wall of the keep. The Vizier rose and latched the grate over the hole once more.

He knew that fragments of the Enslaver came to light at rare intervals. His order and its allies had decided long ago that it was better to feign indifference to them than to arouse curiosity by taking an active interest. Now that the omens were raising an alarm, he must take seriously any hint of renewed activity, even if it took the form of a clod-footed farm boy from the provinces. Still, the best approach was subtlety. The Vizier was confident that Garrak and his friends could manage that.

Chapter 10

Whoever believes in me,
rivers of living water will flow from within them.

Rand woke refreshed the next morning, although his legs were stiff from the long march of the day before. He pulled aside a curtain and saw that the sun had not yet risen. The sky was brightening, though, and townspeople were abroad in the street below. He cleaned up at the wash stand and went downstairs to see about breakfast.

He found a table among the guests who had risen before him. The innkeeper's wife brought him a plate piled with hot and hearty food. When he was finished he settled up his bill with her—a silver crown for the room and ten coppers for the two meals. If rooms in the city could be had for about the same, he would be well provided for on the rest of his journey.

Rand went back to his room, retrieved his pack, and dropped off the key at the counter downstairs. Then he set off for the docks. As he walked along the planks that ran in front of the shops and houses along the Oakbridge road, he passed a cat sitting on top of a barrel. It watched until he was several yards down the street, then hopped down from its perch and followed.

Rand soon came to the intersection of the Oakbridge road and the street beside the river's edge. It was busy—there were more people gathered here on this normal workday than he would ever find in one place back in Oakbridge unless there was a festival. Tradesmen bustled to and fro with loads of goods. Wagons arrived from the countryside full of barrels and crates, along with empty ones that lined up to receive river shipments. The west side of the intersection was formed by the river docks themselves; stevedores labored over piles of sacks and crates under the watchful eye of cargo masters and river captains. Three long, low river barges were tied up along the bank.

Rand stood at a corner of the intersection, taking it all in as he sought for an inkling of what he ought to do next. He became conscious of the hurrying people that were flowing around him, some of whom were impatient with the obstacle he represented. This was a case where standing still made him stand out in the crowd; remembering his uncle's advice about not attracting attention, he stepped cautiously into the street and crossed over to the docks.

As he went he recalled that Bowin had told him there would be a schedule posted for the arrivals and departures of the day. When he reached the dock side of the street he looked up and down the waterfront. There was a large board standing on poles by the water's edge with a slate mounted on it. Words and numbers were written on the slate with chalk in neat rows and columns. Rand thought this must be the shipping schedule, and as he drew closer to it he saw that he was right.

The first listing was for a barge named the *Dolphin*, showing that it was headed downstream. The next was for the *Kelpie*, due to depart for Serenhorn within the hour. The *Elsbeth* was also headed to Serenhorn but wasn't expected to leave until the afternoon. Rand went in search of the *Kelpie*.

The barge nearest the schedule board was the *Elsbeth*; Rand decided a boat bound for Serenhorn would probably be docked upstream and headed that way. Sure enough, the barge at the northern edge of the docks proved to be the *Kelpie*. Like the other two barges it had a blunt stern and a rounded prow. Most of the deck was occupied by a slant-sided, flat-topped housing that protected cargo from the elements. The gunwales were only a yard or so high; in fact the entire craft stood less than a man's height above the water.

Rand turned his attention back to the activity on the dock. Workmen rolled crates and bundles on handcarts up the two gangplanks at each end of the barge and down through open hatchways into the cargo hold. One man stood still amidst the frenetic activity, noting each item on a sheaf of paper clipped to a board. Rand sidestepped carefully between the racing carts to stand beside him.

"Excuse me, sir," he said, "who do I talk to about buying passage to Serenhorn?" The man glanced briefly at him in between checking cargo, waiting for a pause between loads before answering.

"Why, that would be me, young man," he answered. "Captain Beck, I am; also first mate, cargo master, chief purser, and galley cook. To cut straight to it, this here's me boat and I make 'er run. Who's askin' and how many?"

"Just me and my pack here. My name's Rand, Rand Porter."

"Ye look a bit young to be travelin' alone. Not a runaway, are ya now? I don't like trouble on my boat, and runaways are nothin' if not trouble."

"No, sir! It's nothing like that. I'm just running an errand for my uncle's business."

"I suppose ye look none too ruffian-like at that, boy. Head on board, then, and ask for Kennit to show you a berth. Passage to Serenhorn is a crown, which I'll expect before we shove off."

Rand nodded and turned toward the gangplank at the stern of the barge. He saw that the transfer of cargo onto the boat appeared to be complete. The crew was now busy securing everything in place for the journey upriver. He stepped aboard and asked the nearest man where he might find Kennit; the man gestured wordlessly into the interior of the deckhouse. Rand slipped his pack from his shoulders and maneuvered his way into the dim and crowded interior, where he found a team of men packing cargo into every available space under the watchful eye and sharp tongue of an older crewman.

"Kennit?" asked Rand. The man nodded; once Rand had explained that he was a passenger, Kennit led him forward. They ducked through a narrow passage between two rooms that were located midway up the deckhouse. The one on the right was the galley; the door on the left was closed and bore the captain's name in neat capital letters—evidently it was his private quarters. As they proceeded forward, they came into another space packed with cargo, but the rafters were also strung with hammocks for the crew. Kennit showed Rand where he could stow his pack, then retrieved a spare hammock from a storage locker and began to tie it in place. He suggested that Rand go on up to the bow while the crew readied the barge for departure.

Rand moved forward and found a stairway leading up onto the deck that was identical to the one at the stern. As he emerged, he saw that the sun had risen over the eastern mountains while he was below. Captain Beck was aboard now, bellowing orders from the upper deck formed by the roof of the cargo hold. Crewmen stowed the gangplanks and began casting off the lines that tied the *Kelpie* to the pilings of the dock. Others stood on the upper deck with the captain, holding long poles at the ready to push off from the dock and then upriver.

Rand moved to the snub-nosed prow of the barge; from here he had a good view of everything that played a part in getting the ship underway. The crewmen who had been untying the lines on the dock now leaped aboard. The polemen on the starboard side set their poles against the pilings and pushed the *Kelpie* away from the dock. Those on the port side dug in with their poles to keep the ship from drifting downstream with the current. At the aft end of the upper deck, two men worked the long handle of the sweep back and forth between them. It was a long angled paddle, part rudder and part oar, that provided much of the power to push the barge upstream against the current.

Once they were completely clear of the dock, the polemen fell into rhythm, two on each side of the upper deck. They alternated — first the port forward and starboard aft poles pushed, then the starboard forward and port aft. This pattern helped to keep the course steady and gave each pair of polemen a breather between strokes. The overlapping timing also allowed them to keep one set of poles pushing at all times, smoothing out the forward motion and making the load lighter for the men on the sweep. The boat kept close to the bank where the going was much easier upstream than it would have been against the current that flowed in the center of the river.

Captain Beck paced along the upper deck, calling out the strokes and ordering course adjustments. There were another two men who stood by for the time being. After a quarter hour had passed, the captain signaled and these took over for two of the polemen, who then moved to the sweep. The men on the sweep sat with their legs hanging over the edge of the upper deck, waiting for the next rotation to take a turn with the poles. As the pattern continued in its round, the men struck up a chantey to the rhythm of their labors. Thus the morning and the miles slid by against the slow, heavy hand of the river.

At noon the crew tied the *Kelpie* to a pair of sturdy trees along the bank and took a break for lunch. Captain Beck served up generous portions of cold meats, bread, and dried fruit for everyone. As they ate, he moved among his crew, checking their hands and rubbing their shoulders. His genuine concern for them was obvious, as was their loyalty to him. Rand found himself wondering if the life of a boatman—always on the move, singing while you worked, looked after by a good master—might not be better than the life of a blacksmith.

Lunch soon ended and the men fell back into their routine. Two boats out from Serenhorn passed by in the course of the afternoon, gliding swiftly in the heart of the current. As the sun touched the peaks of the Hunter Range in the west, Captain Beck had the men take the barge in close to the bank again and tie up for the night. The day of the rivermen had come to a close. No one, Rand least of all, paid any attention to the raven that sat high in an oak tree nearby and watched over them as they ate a supper of beef stew on deck and sang a few songs before settling in for a night's rest.

Chapter 11

But let justice roll on like a river,
doing the right like a never-failing stream!

The next morning, Rand woke to the sound of polemen's feet pounding on the roof of the deckhouse just over his head. The *Kelpie* was already under way. He tumbled out of his hammock and dressed quickly in the semi-darkness of the hold. When he emerged on deck, autumn mist was rising in streamers from the surface of the river in the pre-dawn light.

He asked one of the polemen who was waiting his turn in the rotation how soon they would arrive in Serenhorn. The man paused and pointed upriver.

"See that wooded hill a few miles ahead on the starboard side? The river bends around the hill and then it's straight into Serenhorn. We should be at the docks in two hours' time, maybe three."

Rand thanked him and went to sit in the bow of the barge. The hill crept slowly closer as the mist melted away in the morning sun, but the pace was agonizing. He gave it up after a while and went below to see what he might find in the galley. He gathered bread and cheese, then filled a pewter mug from the water barrel and returned topside. He had learned by watching the movements of the crew that there were places on the upper deck where he might sit without interfering with their work. He watched for his chance and maneuvered into one of these places now, hanging his legs over the edge of the deckhouse and eating his breakfast while watching the green countryside slide by in the morning sun.

Rand looked at the distant farmhouses that appeared from time to time and wondered about the lives of the people within. Was there a town nearby to which they drove a wagon on market day? What was it called? He had grown up knowing the name of everyone in Oakbridge and the surrounding farms. Here, a mere two days' journey from his home, were people just like himself whom he had never met and probably never would. It made the world strangely immense and tiny at the same time.

Rand finished his breakfast and rose to take the mug back to the galley. When he turned to face upriver he discovered that the *Kelpie* had covered half the distance to the hill where the river turned. He could already make out the mouth of the bend that would take them past it and into the city. The apparently languid pace of the barge against the current had concealed the effectiveness of the men on the poles and the sweep as they pushed steadily along.

As soon as he returned from the galley, Rand took up his watch at the bow of the barge. There were more farmhouses scattered along the banks of the river now. Boats passed them headed downstream, or drifted in shady spots where the fishing was probably good. Once in a while he could see the distant figure of a farmer working in his fields. All the while the *Kelpie* drew closer to the hill and Rand could see farther into the river bend ahead.

At last they pulled even with the hill and started around the curve in the river. The main current swung wide here, pushed against the western bank by its own momentum. In contrast, the water where the barge ran along the eastern bank was virtually still. At times eddies spun away from the main flow in counter-currents that actually helped to push the boat upstream. As the morning passed, Rand had doubted the crewman's estimate; now he could see why the last leg of the trip would be the fastest.

The Kelpie was now coming out of the bend on the upstream side. The river stretched broad and straight before Rand in the morning sun., taking them northeast. Just at the edge of visibility he could see a cluster of shapes that were distinct from the natural terrain. His pulse quickened—that must be Serenhorn.

The crew launched into a chantey more cheerful and up-tempo than they had sung thus far on the journey. The pace of the barge quickened in time with the song. Evidently the sight of their destination was an inspiration to the crew as well, though perhaps not in the same way as it was for Rand as he looked on it for the first time.

Traffic increased as they got closer to the city. The wind was favorable and the boats that bore sails were able to use them to good effect. Small docks appeared here and there on each side of the river. Some were connected to roads that led away into the countryside. Others were for the private use of houses, some of which were larger and more opulent than any Rand had ever seen. The further up the river they went, the more numerous and extravagant these waterfront mansions became.

As the banks slid past to the rhythm of the poles and the sweep, more and more of the city came into view. It looked to Rand as though Serenhorn was reaching out its arms to greet him. Country estates gave way to scattered hamlets and occasional commercial buildings. Before long the buildings closed ranks on either side in rows that were punctuated only by city streets. The *Kelpie* was now within Serenhorn itself.

The river curved gently back to the north now. Up ahead, it appeared to separate into two diverging paths. Rand asked a crewman who was taking his rest break in the rotation about this.

"Aye, lad," the man replied, "those be the branches of the Seren River—the East Horn and the West Horn. The center of the city lies yonder where they meet, for there is where 'twas founded at the first. And 'tis from the horns o' the river that the city takes its name." The man rose and rubbed his hands on his breeches. "Yer pardon, but I'd best get busy. Where the horns meet is also where the main docks lie. We'll be tyin' up there soon."

Chapter 12

Wisdom makes one wise person more powerful
than ten rulers in a city.

The sun had climbed more than halfway to its zenith by the time they reached the center of the city. As the day grew warmer, one of the less savory aspects of city life intruded on Rand's awareness— the smell. The water stank of sewage, garbage lay piled in alleyways, and tanneries and slaughterhouses added their own unique tang to the mix. Although it never completely lost its unpleasantness, he was thankful that he grew accustomed to it as they drew near to the docks.

Rand was impressed by the activity all around him as the *Kelpie* picked its way through the river traffic toward an open berth. He counted eight other barges and dozens of smaller boats—light haulers, fishing boats, water taxis, and even a couple of floating kitchens that were selling hot food as they went from one vessel to the next.

The docks themselves were almost overwhelming. Rand had thought the waterfront at Kerrin was a bustling place. Here in Serenhorn it was as though a giant had kicked over a human anthill. Throngs of people were moving in every direction at once, and they all seemed to be shouting at someone or something. Unconsciously he backed away from the rail as he tried to take it all in.

The *Kelpie* reached its berth and the polemen strained to push it into place. The sweep was of little use in such tight quarters. When they were close enough, two of the crewmen leaped to the dock with rope lines and helped pull the barge in. Once it bumped against the pilings, the ropes were tied off and those aboard set aside their poles to put the gangplanks in place.

Rand flinched as a heavy hand fell on his shoulder. He turned to find Captain Beck standing there.

"Ye've made it to the city, lad. What d'ye think of 'er?" he said.

"So many people," said Rand quietly. "How does anyone find their way?"

The captain's expression took on a fatherly concern. "Ah, that's how it is, is it?" he said kindly. "Where are ye bound for, now that you're here?"

"First I'm supposed to go to the Merchant Hall," Rand replied.

"You're in luck then, me boy," said the captain. "I'm bound that way myself to find another load of cargo. I'll take you there personally. Kennit and the boys will see to unloading the ship well enough without me. Now then, let's settle up the fare for your passage. Hold on now," he warned, holding up a hand as Rand started to reach into his tunic. "Turn away from the dockside afore ye reach for your purse. That'll be one silver, if you please."

Rand heeded the captain's warning and used his body to shield the transaction from prying eyes. Kennit came up to them and handed Rand his pack before turning his attention back to the cargo hold. Captain Beck clapped Rand on the back and led the way onto the dock.

As the crowd on the dock swirled around them, the smell of the river was immediately replaced by the pungent odor of many unwashed bodies in close proximity. People with grotesque deformities sat in heaps of dirty rags, begging for the smallest kindness with outstretched bowls. It was impossible for Rand to discern the age or gender of most of them beneath the dirt and tattered garments. More than once Captain Beck was approached by women in bright colors whose strong perfume temporarily overpowered the ripe smells of the crowd. Each time he rebuffed them with a raised hand and a shake of the head. On at least one of these occasions, though, Rand thought that the woman and the captain knew each other. Rand guessed that such encounters may have gone differently if he hadn't been there.

As they approached the row of buildings that stood along the dock, Rand saw that every available space against the building walls was occupied by small stalls where merchants loudly declared the merits of their wares to passersby. One of the hawkers even darted from his stall to tug on Rand's sleeve and implore him to buy a trinket for "the girl back home." Captain Beck shoved the man away roughly and pushed Rand forward through the crowd.

They reached a gap where a street opened onto the docks; the captain guided Rand into it. Much of the noise and smell of the docks died away almost at once. Rand breathed a sigh of relief and started up the stone-paved walk at the side of the road. Captain Beck tapped his arm and motioned for him to move into the center of the street.

"Ye don't want to walk too close to the walls here, young master," he said with a wink and a grin. He pointed further up the hill. Rand looked and saw a woman lean out of an upper window to dump a bucket of slops onto the road below. He stood there for a moment, stunned by his narrow escape. Then he laughed at the vision of himself caught in that unexpected shower. The captain chuckled along with him and they continued on.

Most of the buildings that lined the street housed storefronts of one kind or another in their ground floors. There were bakeries, clothiers, and ironmongers, but the ale houses outnumbered them all. As it was still morning, the latter had not opened yet. Once in a while Rand and the captain had to step aside for wagons or carriages running to and from the docks. On these occasions Rand was careful to move back into the street as quickly as possible. A few hundred feet up the hill they came to an intersection with a broad avenue that bore a steady stream of traffic. Captain Beck stopped and pointed out a nearby post with crossed signs nailed to the top.

"See there, lad, this street we've been followin' is called Dock Street, as ye might've guessed. The big one here is Hornside Way. We turn right on Hornside and follow it along, and it takes us to the Merchant Hall."

Rand recognized the route from the maps drawn by his uncle, but he was glad to have a guide familiar with the city all the same. If nothing else, it allowed him to avoid standing along the road while gawking at a map and trying to decide his next move. That would mark him as an ignorant newcomer and draw unwelcome attention. When it came to it, Rand doubted he could have crossed the docks to the street by himself without getting into some kind of trouble, judging by what he had seen today.

Hornside was apparently one of the more important streets in the city. Most of the buildings they passed were made of stone or brick rather than wood. Across the street on the east side, some of the buildings were surrounded by open space that was protected by walls or iron fences. Captain Beck told Rand that most of these were the city homes of noble families; others were government offices or guild halls.

After they had walked a quarter of a mile or so, a massive square building with a high domed roof came into view. The front was lined with thick stone columns and featured an ornately carved double door set in a tall stone arch.

"There it is, lad," said Captain Beck as he pointed at the forbidding structure. "Merchant Hall. Now, watch me and follow lively. We've got to cross the road without losing our skins." The captain watched for his chance and darted into a gap between passing wagons. Rand followed, trying to match him step for step and not be distracted by the noise and motion all around them. They paused in a narrow space between two rows of southbound traffic, then lunged forward again. Now they had to reverse their orientation and pick a path through the northbound flow. By copying Captain Beck's every move, Rand made it at last to the far side, although a passing carriage wheel did strike a glancing blow to his backpack at the end of his final dash.

They took a moment to catch their breath; then the captain led the way up the broad stone steps to the great doorway of the hall. The doors stood open and a steady stream of people flowed in and out. Rand wondered if he should wait a moment and consult his uncle's instructions, but the captain entered without hesitation and he decided it was best to follow.

Daylight spilled through the archway onto granite floors inlaid with marble mosaics. As Rand's eyes adjusted to the dimmer light from the lamps scattered across the vast hall, he saw that the distant walls were paneled in oak and decorated with tapestries and paintings. A long desk faced the entrance; several clerks were seated behind it and spoke with visitors as they approached. Behind this reception desk and separated from it by a wooden railing was an area where row after row of smaller desks stood, each manned by a clerk. Some of the clerks were speaking with visitors, but most were absorbed in writing notations with quill pens into massive books.

Captain Beck spied an opening at the front desk and stepped forward. The reception clerk regarded him disinterestedly.

"State your name and business," he said in a rote monotone.

"Cyrus Beck, captain of the river barge *Kelpie,* looking for fresh cargo to haul downriver." The clerk made an entry in the ledger before him and then pointed to a distant corner of the hall.

"Shipping, desk three. Jurgen Mercantile has some timber, I believe." The clerk immediately went back to his notations. Captain Beck nodded and turned to Rand.

"I have to look after my own matters now, boy. Best of luck to ye, and mind those upper windows," he added with a smile.

"I'll do that," said Rand and smiled in return. Then the captain was gone and it was his turn at the desk.

"State your name and business," said the clerk with exactly the same tone and expression as before.

"Rand Porter, bringing cider contracts to be finalized on behalf of Bowin Porter of Oakbridge." The clerk grunted and reached for another ledger. Rand watched others come and go while the clerk searched for an entry regarding Porter, cider, and Oakbridge. Bowin had done his best to explain how this place worked. It served as a sort of exchange or matching service. The clerks at the desks in the hall each represented a group of merchants that fell into a particular category. Buyers, sellers, and those who offered services like Captain Beck came with offers or requests; the clerks passed the information along to their clients or made deals on the spot if they had standing orders. They usually did more business with one another than they did with people walking in off the street, but they were prepared to accept any transactions that came their way. The clerk cleared his throat impatiently and Rand turned his attention back to his own mission.

"Yes, the Porter cider contracts," said the clerk. "Foodstuffs, desk five." He pointed toward the opposite side of the room from the one where Captain Beck had gone, then turned his attention back to his ledgers. Rand was uncertain how to find "foodstuffs, desk five," but he didn't want to try the man's patience or appear ignorant. He made his way past the other visitors at the reception desk and approached the railing in the general direction indicated by the clerk.

Swinging gates offered passage through the railing to each aisle between the rows of desks. As Rand moved toward one of these he noticed that neatly lettered signs stood on brass poles here and there among the desks. They bore legends such as "Commodities," "Raw Materials," and "Exports." Each desk had a small placard on the front that indicated its number within a particular section. "Foodstuffs" wasn't visible from his vantage point. He pushed through the nearest gate and moved deeper into the room, careful to keep his pack from knocking into desks as he passed by.

"Foodstuffs" appeared at last, close to the back right corner of the room. Rand was in the wrong aisle, but fortunately there were cross-aisles at intervals down the rows of desks. He didn't think he could have slid between desks otherwise without running the risk of bumping a clerk on the back of the head with his pack, and he felt conspicuous enough as it was. The clerks wore fine linen shirts in a variety of colors, topped by well-tailored coats or vests. Rand's woolen tunic and homespun shirt were drab and crude by comparison. He winced at the thumping sound made by his heavy boots in contrast with the whispering footfalls of the soft leather shoes worn by the city folk. Most of the clerks ignored him as he passed, but the few who looked up made no effort to hide their amusement at his appearance.

Rand arrived at the foodstuffs section and walked along until he found the fifth desk. The clerk stationed there was a short, heavy man with a round bald head that reminded Rand of a melon. He was absorbed in his bookkeeping, mumbling to himself in a sing-song way while he worked. Rand slipped his pack from his shoulders and set it on the floor so he could retrieve the folio of contracts from within. The sound of the pack striking the floor brought the clerk abruptly back to awareness of his surroundings.

"Goodness me! Whatever is this?" he cried.

"Beg your pardon, sir; I didn't mean to startle you. They told me at the front that you were the one I needed to speak to," said Rand. The man leaned forward and examined Rand's pack.

"That's all well and good, young fellow, but I'm afraid I don't barter for goods from the hinterlands," he said. He jabbed a finger at the pack. "Whatever pelts or berries or hand-carved whatnots you have stored away in there would best be disposed of in one of the market squares—I believe there's one not far down the street from here."

"But sir, it's nothing like that," said Rand. He quickly undid the strap on the top of the backpack and plunged his arm within until his fingers found the folio. He pulled it out and handed it to the clerk. "See? I've been sent by my uncle with contracts for his cider." The man hesitated a moment before taking the bundle. When he opened it and saw the contents, his demeanor visibly improved.

"Ah, I see," he said. "This is quite another matter! Pardon the misunderstanding, young man. Please, be seated! Let's see what we have here." He indicated the small chair in front of his desk; each clerk had one for visitors like himself. Rand sat, grateful for a chance to rest after his hike from the docks. The clerk resumed his curious humming as he sorted and examined the sheets of parchment. He pulled a ledger from one of his desk drawers and thumbed through the pages until he found the reference he sought, then compared it to the contracts.

"Yes, here we are," he said. "Bowin Porter solicited offers for this year's cider production on August 11th, and three of my clients expressed interest. Porter cider is considered to be of particularly good quality here in the city, so the offers were generous. Bills of purchase were drawn up and sent to Oakbridge on the 19th of that month. Evidently Mr. Porter has accepted the offers, signing and sealing in the appropriate places on—let's see—yes, the date is noted as September 3rd." He paused and made several entries in his ledger. "Now then, I will confirm receipt of the completed bills of purchase on behalf of my clients."

The clerk reached into another drawer and retrieved a small tray that he placed on his desk. The tray contained a seal for stamping documents and a small bowl of red wax. The bowl's base consisted of a curious stand or frame. When the clerk lifted the bowl and fitted it onto the top of the oil lamp on his desk, Rand saw that the frame was designed to hold the bowl securely so the heat of the lamp could melt the sealing wax.

"There we are," said the clerk. "That will take a few moments. While we wait, permit me to introduce myself. I am Sima, of Feydle and Sima Fine Foods Distributors. You said you are Bowin's nephew, I believe?"

"Yes, Mr. Sima. I'm Rand Porter, his brother's son."

"Well met, Rand. Give your uncle my greetings if you would. We studied together at the Academy in our youth. Ah, the wax is ready," said Sima, taking a cloth from the sealing tray and using it to remove the hot bowl from the lamp. Rand sat upright at the mention of the Academy and leaned forward.

"You know the Academy then?" he asked. "That is where I am bound next. When you are finished, could you confirm the directions my uncle gave me?"

'But of course, Rand," said Sima as he continued his work. He took a spoon from the sealing tray and used it to carefully pour wax on each of the documents. While he waited for the wax to gel enough to take the seal, he initialed each document on the appropriate line with his quill pen. Then he took up the seal itself and pressed it into the wax on each contract.

"There," he said with satisfaction. "A deal well completed, and good for all concerned. When accounts are settled at the end of the day, the agreed deposits will be transferred to your uncle's account at the Bank of Serenhorn. While we wait for the seals to finish hardening, let's look at those directions of yours." Rand reached for his pack and dug within it until he found the scrap of paper that held Bowin's map from the docks to Merchant Hall and on to the Academy. Sima took it and studied it carefully.

"Yes, this looks right enough," he said. "When you leave the Hall, turn left and continue south down Hornside until you reach Ridge Road. Bowin's map doesn't show it but you'll have to cross several busy side streets as you go, so be careful. Go left on Ridge, which takes you east up a fairly steep grade. When you get to the top you'll find the Academy. It was built there two centuries ago— chiefly for the view I suppose—when all that area was still open countryside. You can't miss it; it looms over the whole district.

Now, these papers are ready at last." Sima stacked the copies that were to be returned to Bowin neatly in the folio and strapped it shut before returning it to Rand. It was easy to see why he had entered into the life of a clerk. He did everything with patience and strict attention to detail.

"Thank you for all your help, sir," said Rand. He tucked the folio back into his pack, strapped it shut, and hoisted it up from the floor.

"Not at all, Rand; it's a pleasure to meet family of an old friend. As I said, remember me to your uncle, and luck to you on the rest of your journey." Rand nodded and turned to retrace his path to the front of the hall.

Chapter 13

Choose my instruction instead of silver,
knowledge rather than choice gold.

It was noon by this time and the reception area was full. Rand had to pick his way around the outside of the chamber to reach the doors. When he slipped out onto the front steps, he was blinded for several seconds by the bright sunshine. He moved to his left along the row of columns that topped the stairs. From this vantage point he could see more than a mile down Hornside. The avenue was a veritable river of humanity. He looked around carefully; as far as he could tell, no one was paying him that unwanted attention his uncle had warned him about, but this time he wouldn't have Captain Beck to watch over him. He headed down the steps, trying to strike a balance between hurrying and not appearing to hurry.

Street vendors filled the air with delicious smells and promoted their offerings to the lunchtime crowds. Rand became keenly aware of how long it had been since his breakfast aboard the *Kelpie*, but he didn't want to risk digging into his purse on the crowded street. Before long he came to the first busy intersection that Sima had warned him about. He again regretted the loss of the river captain's help, but after a few false starts he hit upon the method of waiting for a city-dweller to cross the street and mimicking them. In this way any knowledgeable pedestrian could be his guide without him even asking for assistance. In no time he was safely across, and at each subsequent intersection the method worked equally well.

He had come about a mile when he reached the intersection with Ridge Road. Traffic had been falling off on both the main avenue and the side streets as he moved away from the heart of the city; on Ridge Road it was sparse by comparison. As he turned and walked up it, the street climbed rapidly, just as Sima had said.

There was one last food cart in sight on the sidewalk ahead. Rand decided to risk fishing a few coppers out of his purse now that he was no longer surrounded by pressing crowds. The coins were enough to buy him four hot sausages on a skewer and a cup of sweet tea to wash them down with. He couldn't remember the last time a meal tasted so good.

Thus fortified, Rand hooked his thumbs into the straps of his pack and resumed his march up the hill. The buildings on either side quickly transitioned from shops and hotels to private residences. Sometimes there would be a bakery or butcher shop, but these became less common the farther he climbed. The houses grew in both size and quality—evidently the higher parcels of land were more prestigious and desirable. By the time he neared the Academy at the crest of the hill, the homes rivaled the noble mansions Rand had seen near the Merchant Hall. He supposed that many of the hilltop residences must be owned by nobles as well.

The Academy itself dominated the skyline in keeping with Sima's description. It was a complex of halls, towers, porticos, terraces, arches, and columns. The jumbled appearance and the varied colors of the stonework showed that it must have grown slowly with the passing years; it was not unlike an ancient gnarled oak, Rand thought. Ridge Road ran right up to a gate in the wall that enclosed the complex. The gate was open and no one was guarding it, so Rand continued into the stone courtyard beyond.

He could see young people in gray robes scattered here and there throughout the grounds. None of them were nearby, nor did they notice his arrival. He paused to retrieve Bowin's letter of introduction from his pack, then proceeded to the large door that stood directly opposite the main gate. When he tried the handle it was unlocked, so he opened it quietly and stepped inside.

He was in a tall, narrow hallway with a polished stone floor. Shafts of light fell from narrow windows set high in the walls. Many doors opened on either side. Youths in their gray robes moved to and fro; Rand supposed they must be students. He could also see older men and women who wore robes of dark blue—these must be the masters. Someone cleared his throat for attention nearby. Rand turned and saw two blue-robed men standing to one side of the door; they didn't appear pleased by his presence.

"What is your business here, young man?" said one of them, approaching to get a better look at him. Rand held up the letter.

"I'm to speak with Master Parma," he said. "My uncle was a student here once. He gave me this letter of introduction." The man took the sealed envelope and scrutinized it for a moment before sighing in resignation.

"Very well," he said. "Master Parma is quite busy administering the Academy, you know, but I suppose I must take this to him. You may sit over there; do not move until I return." He pointed to a stone bench to the left of the door.

"Yes, sir, thank you," said Rand, moving quickly to comply. The man rolled his eyes toward the roof and turned away, striding briskly down the hall and through a set of doors on the right. Some of the passing students took note of Rand's presence. They seemed to find his appearance at least as entertaining as had the clerks at the Merchant Hall. He gritted his teeth and strove to ignore them. After interminable minutes had passed, the master reappeared in the hall and marched toward him.

"Master Parma has a meeting with some of the faculty just now, but his secretary believes you might be able to see him later this afternoon. Apparently he does make it a point to accommodate alumni and their families, though I scarcely know why. You may wait in the central library until his secretary comes to get you. This way, please." The man turned and left without waiting to see if Rand would follow. Rand jumped up, grabbed his pack, and sped after him.

The master led him all the way down the corridor and through the double doors at the end. They passed from the sharp echoes of the stone hallway into carpeted quiet. Dust motes danced in shafts of light from many windows. Rows of long narrow tables lined each side of a wide central aisle. Beyond the tables stood a line of bookcases with their ends toward the entrance. The walls of the room, where they were not punctuated by windows, consisted of shelves filled with books as well. In a space between the study tables and the bookshelves an ornate desk was set on a raised dais. A thin, white-haired man sat there watching them. Rand's guide approached the desk and signaled for him to follow.

"Master Atticus, this boy is waiting to see Master Parma," he said to the older man. "I thought it best to keep him here under your watchful eye rather than leave him footloose in the halls."

"Very well, Master Roland. I'll see to it that he remains out of trouble," said Master Atticus, examining Rand with an unreadable expression. Roland wheeled about and marched crisply back to his duties. Rand turned to find Atticus regarding him as enigmatically as ever. Finally the man spoke.

"As you heard, I am Master Atticus, and as you undoubtedly may surmise if you have some wit about you, I am the librarian of the Academy. Tell me your name, if you please."

"I'm Rand Porter, sir."

"I see. Can you read, Rand Porter?"

"Oh, yes sir. I'm in the final year of school, that is, in our little village school at home."

"That is well," said Atticus. "What sort of books do you enjoy the most?"

"History mostly, sir. Sometimes natural studies, too, or poetry," said Rand.

"Indeed; then I propose that you make some use of your time while you wait. The history section is along that wall. Find a book that interests you and read it at one of the tables."

"Thank you, sir," said Rand with a smile. He looked over at the indicated shelves, his eye caught by first one volume and then another. They were of many sizes, colors, and thicknesses. He approached the wall and took his time before selecting a book about the founding of the kingdom of Solethon.

Time passed slowly as he read; the only sounds were the turning of pages as he and Master Atticus pursued their separate inquiries. Rand had just finished an account of the cities that joined in the First Alliance—the forerunner of the present kingdom—when a young man entered and introduced himself as Matthew, Master Parma's secretary.

"If you'll follow me, Master Parma will receive you now," he said. Rand stood and thanked him, then turned to take his book back to its place.

"Never mind that, Mr. Porter," called Atticus. "I prefer to be the one who shelves the books. Run along to your appointment." Rand nodded and followed Matthew back into the main hall. Most of the doors stood open now—it appeared that classes had ended for the day. Matthew turned at the doors where Master Roland had gone with Rand's letter of introduction earlier in the day, leading him within.

They walked down a short hallway lined with small offices and through a door at the far end. They were now in an anteroom with a desk at one side. Matthew knocked on a door opposite the one by which they had entered.

"Rand Porter to see you, sir," he announced. A muffled voice spoke from within. Matthew opened the door and waved Rand in.

Master Parma awaited Rand in the center of a large office, the size of which was surprising compared to those that preceded it. He was a tall, heavily built man with a round ruddy face and a quick smile. His grip was almost overpowering when he shook Rand's hand, but somehow his smile didn't reach his eyes. Rand decided to be cautious with him.

"So, you're Bowin Porter's nephew, eh? He was a fine student here in his day. I understand he's done well with the family business since he left us. Come, sit!" Parma indicated a pair of high-backed chairs on either side of a fireplace to the left of the door.

"Now, then," he continued once they were seated. "Your uncle's letter spoke very highly of you. He says you are interested in history, is that right?"

"Yes, sir. I'm afraid I've often tried his patience with questions," said Rand, doing his best to play the part of a wide-eyed schoolboy who had no secret artifacts, only curiosity. "He told me I should ask after Master Zekiel—I guess he hopes I might use up some of my questions while I'm here."

"Really?" said Parma with a note of skepticism. "Zekiel is our master of antiquities. History is his field, granted, but he's something of a specialist and not a little eccentric. Odd that your uncle didn't direct you to the chairman of the history department." He maintained his jovial air, but the unsmiling eyes were watchful. Rand shrugged his shoulders, spread his hands in a gesture of helplessness, and smiled as agreeably as he could.

"Perhaps Master Zekiel and your uncle were close," Parma continued. "I can't say I remember. In any event, I suppose it makes little difference. I will have Matthew take you to Zekiel. Enjoy your visit and take in all you can. It will be of benefit to you if you become a student here yourself."

"Oh, there's little chance of that, sir," said Rand with unfeigned surprise and awkwardness. "My father, Bowin's brother, is a blacksmith and intends for me to follow in his trade," said Rand.

"Is that so?" Parma's sunny demeanor dimmed like the closing of drapes over a window. "Pity. Ahem, let's get you on your way then." Parma stood and ushered Rand to the door of the office. He called Matthew over.

"Show Rand here to the Hall of Antiquities, would you? He wants to chat with Master Zekiel." Parma gave Rand a pat on the back and turned away, closing the door behind him. Rand was concerned that he might have offended the man, but relieved that he had gotten through the interview without having to discuss the Stone Tears. He felt certain that Parma would have pounced on that and questioned him until he told the entire story. It was likely that the headmaster would deem him an unworthy custodian of ancient mysteries—that somehow Parma would compel him to surrender the fragment and send him back to his ordinary life with scarcely a fare-thee-well. Rand was not prepared to return to the ordinary just yet.

Chapter 14

And afterward, my Wind shall blow on all people.
Your sons and daughters will speak of unseen things,
your old men will dream dreams, your young men will see visions.

Matthew led him back into the main hall and then through a veritable maze of rooms and secondary hallways to a door that exited the building at the back. They passed from there along white gravel paths through the well-tended grounds of the academy, under arches and down long colonnades until they reached a low rectangle of a building that stood against the wall in the far left corner of the complex.

"The Hall of Antiquities," said Matthew, opening the door and bidding Rand to follow him into the dim interior. Rand's eyes adjusted slowly until he could see that they moved through a large open room filled with display cases, waist-high with slanted glass tops. Dozens of objects rested within them, each labeled with a neatly-printed white card. Rand wanted to browse among them for anything related to Stone Tears, but Matthew walked swiftly without pausing. Most of the displays throughout the room were the same kind as those Rand now passed, but tall ones stood here and there holding larger relics such as stuffed animals or suits of armor.

Matthew turned right at an intersection of aisles and led Rand toward the south wall of the exhibit hall. A wide doorway stood open there that proved to be the entrance to a hallway like those in the building where he had met Parma. The first door on the right was an empty lecture hall. Several on the left were offices that appeared to be unoccupied. The last was closed, and it was there that Matthew stopped and knocked.

"Master Zekiel?" he called. "It's Matthew, Master Parma's secretary. I've brought you a visitor." They waited in the silence of the empty building. Rand heard the muted sounds of papers shuffling, then a chair creaking, and finally slow, heavy footsteps. The door handle moved and the door opened inward a few inches. The occupant of the office stuck his head partway out to speak to Matthew. From Rand's vantage point the face was in profile—a long, iron-gray beard, a great hooked beak of a nose, and a bushy eyebrow over an eye so deep brown that it looked black in the dim light of the hallway.

"Visitor?" he barked. "Not expecting any visitors! Why is Parma bothering me with this foolishness?" Matthew pursed his lips in disapproval of the man's hostility, but looked unsurprised by the reaction. He gestured toward Rand.

"This young man asked for you by name, Master Zekiel," he said. "His arrival was as unexpected to us as it is to you. He is the nephew of a former student of yours who sent him with instructions to seek you out." The master opened the door wider and craned his neck through to get a look at Rand, who took a step closer and dipped his head in a little bow.

"Hmmph," said the man as he looked Rand over. "Nephew? What is that to me? You don't look like anyone I know."

"My name is Rand Porter, sir," said Rand as respectfully as he could. "My uncle is Bowin Porter. He would have been a student here some twenty years ago." The man blinked slowly as he stared at Rand; it reminded Rand of a barn owl.

"Hmmm," mused Zekiel. "Lad from the country, was he? Of a merchant family?" Rand nodded and chanced a smile.

"I think I remember him," the master murmured. "Took history seriously, that one. Showed some respect, not like these upstarts today." The old man jerked a thumb at Matthew, who raised an eyebrow in amusement.

"All right, then," said Zekiel with a sigh. "I suppose I must give you a fair hearing, boy. Matthew, you can run along to trot at the heels of your master." The secretary reddened at the jibe, then made a curt little bow and left the way he had come. Zekiel opened the door wide and motioned impatiently for Rand to enter.

"Come in and sit, boy. This nonsense has wasted enough of my time already." The master shuffled around his desk and sat behind it. Rand removed his pack and took the only other seat available, a smaller chair that faced the desk.

"Well?" said Zekiel. He propped his elbows on the desktop and laced long, great-knuckled fingers together, resting his chin on them while he glared at Rand expectantly.

"My uncle sent me to see if you could help us," said Rand. "He told me that you are the only man in Serenhorn or elsewhere in the Vale who knows something about the—that is, the history of such things as we wish to understand." He trailed off, struggling for words in the face of the man's unyielding stare.

"What things?" snapped Zekiel with growing impatience.

"The Stone Tears, sir! The-the fragments of the ancient tablets," stammered Rand.

Zekiel unlaced his fingers and pressed his palms on the surface of the desk, rearing back in his chair and regarding Rand through eyes narrowed in suspicion. "The Stone Tears!" he cried. "They are not a matter fit for the ignorant to speak of."

"I'm sure you're right, sir," said Rand, struggling to keep his voice steady. "From the little my uncle could tell me, they are something far beyond me. But you see, I had no choice—the matter came upon me unawares."

"What do you mean?" said Zekiel in a deep, gravelly voice that reminded Rand of the growl of a wild beast. He leaned over the desktop as though he might pounce at any moment. Rand held up his hands in a silent plea for patience and bent to open his backpack. After the shifting of contents in the progress of his travels, it took him several agonizing moments to find the drawstring bag that held the fragment. He pulled it out of the pack and set it on his lap to undo the strings, struggling with shaky fingers. At last the bag opened; Rand pulled the fragment out, setting it carefully on the desk in front of Zekiel.

"I was doing my lessons in my uncle's orchard, not yet a week ago, when I found this buried in the earth," he said. Zekiel's eyes widened in shock as he saw the piece of tablet. He reached a hand to touch it; Rand was surprised to see the hand tremble as it moved.

"Another," Zekiel whispered, "you have found another." He lifted the piece carefully and scrutinized it closely. "Yes, it's real—it must be. No other stone like that." He turned his attention back to Rand. His expression softened for the first time since Rand had met him. "Your uncle did right in sending you to me—I'm sorry, what was your name? I'm afraid I wasn't really listening before."

"Rand Porter, sir."

"Rand, yes. Please excuse my impatience earlier; I had no idea," said Zekiel. His face stiffened at a sudden thought. "Did you say aught of this to Parma?" Rand shook his head.

"Not to that smirking sycophant Matthew, or any other soul?" pressed Zekiel.

"No one but you, sir, and my uncle," said Rand.

"That is well," said Zekiel with a sigh of relief. His countenance relaxed again. "You showed discretion, lad. I can't say for certain what Parma would have done, but he would no doubt have tried to turn the affair to his own advantage somehow. Ever an opportunist, that one, and his secretary is his true disciple." The master found a match somewhere and struck it, lighting an oil lamp on his desk. "You've no idea what this means to me, boy."

"No, sir," said Rand, waiting quietly with the hope of being enlightened.

"For over thirty years now I have held custody of what little the Academy possesses concerning the Stone Tears," said Zekiel. "My predecessor fulfilled that duty for almost forty years before me. It is a post that has fallen into disfavor in these progressive times, but the tradition still endures that the master who is entrusted with it holds it for the remainder of his or her life. When she took up the mantle in her youth, the master before me took charge of a collection that included two Stone Tears. Can you guess how many there were when she at last bequeathed them to me?" Rand shook his head and remained silent.

"Three," said Zekiel grimly. "And during all my years as the master of these archives, how many new ones have I myself seen? Until today—until this very hour—none." His voice fell close to a whisper again as he finished. He cradled the Stone Tear in his hands, clutching it as though it was a morsel of bread and he was dying of starvation. He leaned closer to the lamp to get a better look at the symbols on the stone; Rand was amazed to see the tracks of tears down his weathered cheeks.

"Have I upset you, sir?" he said.

Zekiel hastily wiped at his face with the sleeve of his robe. "Yes, of course you have!" he cried. At the sight of Rand's pained expression, he burst out laughing. "You misunderstand me. Yes, you have upset me—upset me from dusty days of boredom and hopelessness. Thank the heavens that you upset me!"

Rand smiled in relief. "Sir, do you know what it says?" he asked, unable to contain his frustrated curiosity any longer.

"That's the hard part, you see," said Zekiel. "Given time, I can compare these pictograms to others and make guesses as to the basic ideas they express. Then we can string them together and see if they convey a coherent story or thought, but there is so much ambiguity. We are not certain of the meaning of any of them, and even if we were, the meaning might change in different combinations. Context is everything when interpreting language, lad."

Rand nodded, feeling no little disappointment. "I was afraid of that," he said. "Uncle Bowin told me that it was difficult to learn anything from them—that the original language had been lost."

"Yes, along with a great deal more," said Zekiel thoughtfully. "Did he tell you the story?"

"He told me what he knew, though it wasn't much," said Rand. "About an ancient empire that was destroyed, and our ancestors fleeing here. That these stones were part of the ruin and were scattered over the earth."

"No more than that?" asked Zekiel. Rand shook his head. "Well, I've learned a few things in the years since—it's possible I told him little more than that at the time. It's also possible that he paid a little less attention than he pretended." The old scholar winked conspiratorially, and Rand laughed in spite of himself.

"I'm not alone in my studies, of course," Zekiel continued. "There are academies in the other provincial capitals, in the royal seat at Solaria, and a few other places. Most have a handful of Stone Tears and someone who looks after them, like me. We share copied sketches and charcoal etchings of the symbols on our fragments. Some of the collectors are not interested in cooperation, though. They prefer to work alone; mayhap they even dream of being the ones to unlock all the secrets of the fragments and claim glory for themselves. But those of us who work together have managed to compile a sort of history of the fragments and the tablets from which they came."

"Sort of?" said Rand.

"Yes, lad, I'm afraid that's the best we can offer. You see, all that we know is gathered from oral tradition—remembrances that were handed down as stories over the generations. No written records were made in the chaos of the empire's fall or the hardships of the Trail of Sorrows. We have taken these stories and gathered them together, combining pieces from one to fill gaps in another, trying to resolve contradictions, and so on. I can tell you the story as best we know it now, but remember that it is uncertain."

"I understand," said Rand. "Please, tell me."

"Before I begin, there is one more thing you must understand," said Zekiel. "I am not one to love ancient bits and pieces for their own sake, as some collectors and curators are. Neither are the best and closest of my colleagues elsewhere. The sight of a rusty sword or a long-dead princess' secret diary does not move me to weep. What drives me is the certainty that the value of the Stone Tears lies neither in their antiquity nor even so much in the history surrounding them, but in the message they contain. If the story we have reconstructed is true, that message is now and has always been of vital importance to our people. That is why the discovery of even one new fragment is so precious—it gives us hope that the message may be known again."

"How many Stone Tears do you and the others have so far?" asked Rand.

"An excellent question," said Zekiel with a wry smile. "The answer will help you understand why we know so little. We suspect there may be many that are hidden from us in private collections and the like, of course, but there are twenty-nine that we know of— thirty, counting yours. Of those, only twenty-two have been shared openly. Now, I will try to tell you their story."

Chapter 15

How great are his signs, how mighty his wonders! His kingdom is an eternal kingdom; his dominion endures from generation to generation.

"A thousand years ago," Zekiel began, "a powerful empire lay far to the northwest of our land. How long it had stood before that time we do not know, but it was certainly not young. In fact, its people were a tired and unhappy race. Commerce flowed, political intrigues unfolded, artisans presented their achievements to the public eye, but underneath the surface of life the people felt hollow. There was a restlessness in their hearts that they could not explain. The hardships of life and the mysteries of nature they accepted, but something else disquieted them—themselves.

"They came to see that they had certain ideas about what was hurtful or helpful, right or wrong, but they couldn't do as they felt they should. The empire had defeated all external enemies, but its people could not master themselves. Some gave up trying, and abandoned themselves to cruelty that brought much suffering into the lives of others.

"But there lived people in the empire who questioned why this must be so—why they saw laws within themselves that they could not obey. They saw the birds and animals, how each lived according to the laws of its nature and never did anything without cause; why was man not the same?

"These few men and women searched all the recorded wisdom that they could find. Therein they discovered mention of a book about the law of man's nature, a book rumored to explain the source of the law and of man himself, and how he had become cut off from that source. It told the history of the power of the source seeking and finding a way to rejoin with men."

"The source of man?" said Rand. "But we are born from our mothers and fathers and always have been. What do you mean by the source of man?"

"Yes, Rand, we are born of our fathers and mothers—but where did the first mother and father come from? Or the first cow and bull, or the first mare and stallion? What was their paternity, or indeed that of the earth beneath our feet and the stars in the heavens?"

"I—I don't know," said Rand. "It never occurred to me to question such things."

"Isn't that curious?" said Zekiel. "Once, long before even the story I tell you now, men questioned such things without end. They supposed many kinds of makers or forebears as the source of all things, and some even proposed that the world made itself out of nothing at all, by mere happenstance. Questions such as these even provided the pretext for wars, but then men always find a pretext for war. In the great breakings, remakings, and struggles that wiped away the remnants and even the memory of the early times, we have chosen to forget such questions altogether. But those questions have not forgotten us. Ahem—other tales for other times. Let us return to our people of the empire.

"In the depth of their weariness a small tremor of hope was born. What was this book? How had it become lost? Could it be found again? The records they pored over held no answer—brief allusions to the book and nothing more. So they embarked on an ever-widening hunt for traces of the book and its contents. Months turned into years as they continued looking throughout their land; many scoffed at them, and those who had embraced cruelty sometimes attacked them. Finally they were forced to accept that the answers they sought could not be found within the empire's borders. However, among some of the conquered peoples who lived in the easternmost provinces, they found handed-down stories of a place far away that was touched by the power and mystery of the maker of the world, called by them the Speaker. It was known as the Temple of the Wind.

"Here at last was a frayed thread that tied to something tangible. Now that they had a place with a name, they might be able to follow the name until it led them to the place itself. During the years of their pursuit, things in the empire had only gotten worse. Lack of confidence in the foundations of their culture strained the threadbare fabric of their society to the tearing point. People in search of hope joined with the few dozen scholars and noblemen who had initiated the effort, swelling their ranks to hundreds. They pooled their resources to outfit an expedition to find the temple. It included the hardiest and most well-traveled among them, along with bearers, guides, and hired guards.

"They skirted the northern edge of the Badlands and came south through the land of the Vokar. Then they came to the southeastern borders of Vokar territory and the lands beyond, of which we know nothing. In the trading posts along the Vokar frontier they made contact with merchants from these distant places. Some of them had heard tales of the Temple of the Wind. The flagging spirits of the seekers were revived. Thus emboldened, they pressed on into the nations south of the Vokar and east of the Gawlians.

"As they went, word of the temple grew stronger and they pursued it like hounds on a freshening scent. Rumors grew into legends and legends into history. The day finally came when they stood at the foot of a mountain and looked up at the temple, perched on the very peak.

"They had supposed that such a temple would have its retinue of priests or monks, but the people living at the foot of the mountain told them that it was uninhabited. It was a long climb to reach the place and few of the locals ever bothered to make the trip. There was nothing to see. The only sign of life was the ceaseless interplay of winds through the many stone portals in the main hall; some who had been there swore they heard voices in the winds, which led to the belief that the temple might be haunted and served to further discourage visitors. Even if someone had wanted to live there, the height at which it stood was inhospitable to life; a permanent resident would have needed a continual supply of food and other goods from the valley below.

"Discouraged but undaunted, the searchers replenished their supplies and climbed the mountain path. At the summit they came to the temple at last and found it just as the valley folk had described it. Steps cut directly into the rock of the mountain led to a pillared entrance hall. Beyond that was a tall, circular room capped by a great dome. Narrow windows pierced the stone walls of the circle every few feet; winds whistled and moaned back and forth through these openings, and the company could well appreciate how a visitor might believe he heard voices in them. There was a circular slab of stone in the center of the room, a sort of pedestal or plinth. Other than that, it was devoid of features or markings of any kind.

"The party was at a loss for what to do next. Their hopes had rested on finding a person or an inscription, something that would tell them how to find the lost book. They camped in the room for a day but nothing happened. It was disappointing, yet they knew in their hearts that this was the right place. The longer they listened to the winds, the more convinced they became that voices were trying to speak to them somehow. On the morning of the second day, the elder scholars of the group took counsel together and formed a plan. The party would withdraw from the temple and make camp outside. A select few would re-enter the great room and speak to the winds as reverently and persuasively as they could. Perhaps an answer would come.

"The plan was set into motion. By the time the searchers had removed their gear from the temple and set up camp outside, it was almost dark. The chosen emissaries entered the temple and stood near the stone at the center of the room.

" 'We have heard of the law of man,' they called, 'and that the power which made the law once sought after man and found him. We have heard also of the book which taught the law and told the story. Finally, we have heard that the power of which the stories speak has touched this place. We have traveled far to reach it, hoping to learn wisdom and hope for our people. If one dwells in this place who can hear and will answer, look favorably upon us and grant that we may know the book again.'

"The representatives waited for a few tense moments, but nothing seemed to happen. They were soon to realize, however, that something had started to happen at once—it simply was not noticeable at first. One by one, the winds that flowed through the various portals were dying away. By the time the scholars noticed this and made it known to one another, the last whistling breezes were fading. Eddies of swirling ice crystals were falling silently to the floor. Soon there was no sound other than the labored breathing of the visitors in the thin mountain air.

"Time stretched to a breaking point. The seekers wondered if the silence was a sign or merely a natural shift in the weather. Then they heard a muted rumbling in the distance, as if they were hearing waves crashing on the shore from the other side of a hill. The sound grew in intensity until it vibrated through the rock on which they stood. The group huddled together by the stone pedestal, trying to look in every direction at once. Suddenly, powerful blasts of wind came through every portal simultaneously and converged at the center of the room. The party threw themselves to the floor and covered their heads with their arms. The noise was deafening and the strength of the wind tore at their garments.

"The sound abated only slightly as moments passed, but the violence of the buffeting faded. The scholars regained a little of their courage, lifted their heads, and looked about the temple. A whirlwind rested on the stone platform, spinning and twisting like a great snake but remaining in one place. A blue-white glow emanated from its interior and grew in intensity until it was painful to look at directly. The eldest of the scholars, a woman frail in body but great in will and determination, rose slowly to her knees and spoke.

" 'Are you the power we have sought?' she asked, almost shouting over the shrieking winds.

" 'I AM,' came the answer in a voice like thunder crackling across the sky. As the voice spoke, all winds but the whirlwind fell away and the noise became bearable.

" 'What shall we call you?' she asked cautiously in the relative quiet.

" 'I AM,' the voice repeated. 'I AM the beginning and the end. I AM the maker of all things. I AM the Speaker who sends forth the Word.'

" 'Speaker, it is your Word we have sought. Long has it been lost to us. What must we do to receive it again?'

" 'I shall give you the book of my Word again, not over centuries as first I did, but complete and enduring. Should this book I give be lost by those who dwell in this age, it would be better for them that they had not been born!'

" 'Mighty Speaker, we shall treasure it and teach it all of our days.'

"Then the voice withdrew, and the light and the whirlwind departed with it. The earthly winds common to the many-portaled chamber resumed their ceaseless interplay. The searchers climbed slowly to their feet. One of their number gasped and pointed to the stone pedestal—it now held a neat stack of tablets. The scholars approached them carefully and examined them. Each was three feet square and engraved with text on both sides. The substance was the same as the Stone Tear you hold now, of course—hard and dark like polished granite, but much lighter in weight.

"As the emissaries read the tablets, they made an even greater discovery. Several of the scholars had come from diverse peoples within the empire, descendants of the nations from which it was formed. They were accustomed to speaking, reading, and writing in the empire's common tongue, but as children they had first learned the languages of their own distant forebears. When they looked at the tablets, they realized with a shock that they were seeing the text in their own tongues. Moving from one tablet to another and comparing with their friends, they confirmed their suspicions—the tablets appeared to each reader in his or her native language.

"In the meantime, all that they had experienced had caused them to forget about their companions camped outside the temple. A scout sent from the camp crept fearfully into the room and found them there, poring over the tablets with wonder and delight. When he called to them, they surrounded him, shouting all at once about what had happened. Then they rushed out of the temple door to tell the entire company.

"It took time for the others to lose their fear of those who had spoken to I AM, for their faces glowed with a remnant of the light that had come from the whirlwind. For the next three days the expedition huddled around the tablets, reading with amazement the story of the Speaker, the Word, and mankind. At last their supplies ran low; they knew they must leave the mountaintop and take the Word back to their people.

"When they reached the village at the base of the mountain, it appeared deserted. The company soon discovered that the inhabitants had shut themselves up in their homes and would have nothing to do with the travelers who had called forth light and thunder on the mountain. When the villagers peeked through cracks in their doors and saw the faces of those who were touched by the blue light, they cried in renewed terror and demanded that the company leave at once.

"Saddened, the seekers took what supplies they might from the untended stores of the village and left payment for the owners to find once they emerged. Those who had beheld the whirlwind contrived veils to hide their faces. The expedition set out for home.

"The light on the faces of those who had received the Word faded with time, but the light burning in their hearts marked them almost as strongly. Many times on their journey back to the empire they tried to share some of what they were learning with the people they met, but their efforts were always received with fear and suspicion. In the end they had to content themselves with trying to reach home and gain a hearing from their own people.

"They returned to the empire at last and brought the Word to the court of the emperor. His name was Straban. The seekers succeeded in convincing him of the Word's importance. He became a disciple of the Word himself and commanded that the tablets be mounted on display for all to see. Scribes were assembled to copy the message of the tablets so that it might be spread throughout the empire. Many people ignored or attacked the teachings of the Word, but many more rejoiced to hear the truths they had hungered after for so long.

"The empire prospered once more during this time. When the emperor's son took the throne, he continued to support the teaching of the Word. He was called Shamal the Priest-King, brought up in the Word by his father, wise and generous.

"It was in the third generation that troubles began. As often happens, the son of Shamal could not accept his father's imperfections when measured against his public policies, and so he plotted rebellion against both. Shamal's strict adherence to the Word was unpopular with many powerful people in his empire. They found a useful tool in his restless and scornful son. Shamal died under suspicious circumstances and his son was crowned emperor, taking the name Vancour. He did not openly attack the Word but he pointedly ignored it. This set a tone of ambivalence that was to muddy the clarity of events for generations to come. Supporters, detractors, and desecrators of the Word took their turns on the throne. The more definite their stand, the shorter their reigns lasted. We know nothing specific about most of them except for the last.

"The empire was once again approaching dissolution. It had already endured an unusually long time; now pressures from without and within were tearing it apart. The last emperor took the name of Vincitor. He became known as Vincitor the Mad. He was weak and unstable, the product of imprudent intermarrying among the nobility. In his obsessive search for a single, all-encompassing source of the empire's ills, he focused his hatred on the Word. Others before him, notably Caramanth the Pitiless, seventh emperor from Straban, had suppressed the Word with forceful measures. Vincitor made possession of any copied portion of the Word treason; he even removed the original tablets from the great plaza where they stood on public display.

"His decisions added fuel to the fires of rebellion that were already spreading under his incompetent leadership. Hostile nations had arisen to the south and east. They continually harried borders that were guarded by corrupt and poorly trained troops. The situation worsened for more than a year, during which Vincitor's obsession deepened. At last he conceived what to him was the final necessity—he resolved to destroy the seemingly indestructible tablets of the Word.

"Months of concerted effort failed. No solvent, no weapon, no fire could be found that would mar the tablets. But Vincitor had a terrible cunning sometimes seen in the insane, and he saw an answer to his problem in the Word itself. The Word told about the enemy of the Speaker—a rebelled servant named the Shadow. It taught that all philosophies contrary to the Word were ultimately devices of the Shadow, evil toys invented to seduce and destroy the children of the Speaker. As he sought more knowledge about the Shadow, Vincitor found that there were some who even worshipped the dark spirit. He realized that this enemy of the Word was his best possible ally. He turned from brute force to sorcery, and the empire's decay took on the stench of death.

"Some time later he emerged from his terrible researches with an answer. It would bankrupt the treasury and require the death of hundreds of innocents, but it would work. For thirteen days he labored over the tablets, muttering incantations and slaughtering children by his own hand. The skies over the central empire darkened with storms that would not dissipate; violent earthquakes were reported in many districts. The hordes in the south and east chose this chaotic time as the signal to attack and overran the borders, pillaging as they went.

"On the fourteenth day Vincitor took up a massive hammer crusted with diamonds. It was almost more than his weak limbs could manage. He ordered his personal guards to stack the tablets in the courtyard of the palace. Dark priests who had assisted him in his sorceries brought forth a cauldron of blood from his victims and poured it over the pile. He lifted the hammer and brought it down with a final terrible curse. The tablets were not destroyed utterly, for no work of the Speaker could come to nothing, but they were shattered into the myriad pieces we now call the Stone Tears. Only a handful of those who fled in despair at the sight survived to pass on the portion of the tale I tell you now. For the rest, we will never truly know more than was seen from afar.

"A howling wind broke over the city from the storm clouds overhead. The earthquakes blended together into a terrible wrenching roar. Those faithful to the Word were already evacuating the city; as they looked back from the distant hills they saw a great blue fire spreading out from the palace.

"That fire swept slowly across the lands of the empire, and where it passed nothing but barren rock and scorched earth remained. The citizens that had not died in earthquakes or at the hands of the invaders now fled before the fire as refugees. Any who could not keep ahead of it were consumed. The invaders retreated to their own lands in terror, leaving an open avenue of escape to the southeast. The refugees thus came into the Badlands. Fierce nomads inhabited that region then as they do now, but they were a skittish people; when they saw what pursued the fleeing imperials, they hid in their desert caves and let them pass unmolested.

"The Blue Fire faded away once it came to the borders of the empire, but the refugees were not safe yet. Once the immediate terror of the empire's fall had faded, the nomads began to steal forth from their hiding places and raid the camps of the imperials, who had no choice but to gather themselves as best they could and seek a better haven elsewhere. For weeks they marched through the pathless and inhospitable wilderness. Many fell to starvation or lack of water, others to the continued harrying of the nomads.

"On the far side of the Badlands the refugees found a wide, fertile valley. They settled there and built a new life. Eventually their settlements grew into the kingdom of Solethon as it is today. No one has ever ventured back across the Badlands to see what became of the ancient empire's waste."

Chapter 16

We all, like sheep, have wandered off, each of us has gone our own way and the Speaker has laid on him the wrongdoing of us all.

Zekiel fell silent and sat contemplating the Stone Tear on the desk before him. Rand's thoughts were consumed by all he had heard. The story of the blue fire in particular had taken him aback. He had never heard of blue fire before except one other time—the old folk song he had memorized for school.

"Sir, there's something odd that I wonder if you can explain," he said. Zekiel looked up and nodded for him to go on. He recited the song and noted the mention of blue fire.

"Yes, Rand, such a thing is not uncommon," said Zekiel. "Many a saga and folk song preserves echoes of events from long ago. It was from such sources that we collected most of the tale I just told you."

"I understand the part about the hammer now, and the rain of stones, but what are demons?" said Rand.

"Have you never heard tales of evil spirits?" said Zekiel. Rand shook his head.

"The world certainly has changed since the times long lost," the master continued. "Sometimes I forget how much. Our distant forebears, those who lived before the reshaping of the world, tended to believe that unseen powers were all around them. Some believed that one great powerful mover and maker of all things was behind it all, like the Speaker of my story. Others subscribed to the idea of many such powers, each ruling over one part of the whole. Whatever the case, these powers that moved unseen in the mysteries of the world were called gods. And whether there was one great god or many, most beliefs agreed that they would have lesser servants. The servants of evil powers, or evil gods themselves, were known as demons. In the saga of the Stone Tears, the Shadow that Vincitor chose to serve was not a god—rather he was an outlaw servant of the Speaker. But he had been one of the mightiest of the Speaker's servants; he took many other servants into exile with him, and they are all what we would call demons."

"Why don't people talk of gods and demons now?" said Rand.

"I hear that some still do in other lands—the Vokar and the Hamedans in particular keep such beliefs alive," said Zekiel. "But as I understand it, many people rejected the idea of unseen powers in the last age of the early days. When the world was shaken, even the people who still believed abandoned their faith in those things, feeling that any gods who might exist must have turned their backs on us. The loss of the Speaker's book, the Word, meant there was no record or testimony to teach them otherwise. People wonder about unseen powers now and then, and they sometimes crop up in stories. Otherwise they receive little mention."

"What about the red-barked tree, or the thrice-cursed hill, or the sign of fish?" asked Rand.

"I don't know, lad," said Zekiel. "I have no doubt they mean something, but that part of the tale is unknown to us as yet."

Rand reached out and touched the Stone Tear as a thought grew stronger in him. "I wonder," he said to himself.

"What do you wonder?" said Zekiel, regarding him with a penetrating gaze.

"This ancient tale or legend of yours—I don't know what to think of it, but here is this one solid thing," said Rand as he tapped the Stone Tear with his finger. "This fragment is made of no natural stone. It's too light and strong. Time has made no mark on it. I have heard of no explanation for it other than the tale you've told me."

"Aye?" The master leaned forward in his chair, patient but very aware.

"What I mean is, if this one part of the story is true, it's almost—I don't know—necessary that the rest is true," said Rand.

"Indeed," said Zekiel, giving no sign of his thoughts as yet.

"What about you?" Rand blurted out as the turmoil in his mind grew unbearable. "Do you believe it?"

Zekiel sat back in his chair and sighed. He stared at Rand for a long moment, waiting until the boy's agitation had subsided.

"Yes," he replied quietly. "I believe it."

"Why?" said Rand, his question not a challenge but a plea for help.

"First, as you said, there is the fact of the Stone Tears themselves," said Zekiel. "They present profound implications by virtue of their very existence. Then I look at humanity around me—indeed I look within my own humanity—and I see a story written there that agrees with the story of that lost empire."

"It does?" said Rand.

"Yes, lad. Think on it—open your eyes and set aside your assumptions of what is normal," said Zekiel with growing intensity. "Remember what you saw as you came here through the streets of our 'fair city.' I was not with you, but I know Serenhorn well enough to guess what was there: poverty, squalor, and disease; thievery and dishonesty; violence and murder; listlessness and empty-eyed despair. Did you see them?"

Rand recalled the beggars and hawkers on the waterfront. Human corruption and misery were certainly on display in that place. And what of himself? He thought back to his vengeful anger at Karl and Lyssa. Furthermore, what of their faults—Karl's bullying and Lyssa's selfish manipulation?

"I guess I did," he said.

"We're adrift, Rand, all of us—just as they were all those centuries ago. We know in our hearts that life should not be like this and need not be like this. But we go on living this way just the same. If we cannot find an answer, we will destroy ourselves. I believe the answer lies in the Word of the Speaker, just as it did for the men and women who found these tablets."

"What have you and the others been able to learn from the Stone Tears?" said Rand.

"Come, let me show you," said Zekiel, rising from his chair. "One of the more interesting fragments is here in our collection." He took his lamp from the desk and led Rand back down the corridor to the exhibit hall. It wasn't until Rand noticed how bright the lamp burned in comparison to the hall's shadows that he realized how late it must be getting outside.

"Are you always the only one here?" he asked as Zekiel led him through the displays.

"Yes," said Zekiel. "Once there was a team of instructors assigned here; I was a member of it myself before taking my place as master. We trained the students in the finding and identification of artifacts, and conducted research of our own. This hall was lit with lamp stands and students mingled with visitors from distant cities. Our allotment for research and acquisitions was reduced time and again by a succession of headmasters, though, Parma being the worst of them. The Academy ceased encouraging students to study antiquities as a vocation. With research curtailed and classes dwindling, the staff of the department shrank. Now I am a department of one! That lecture hall you saw across from my office sits empty but for two classes a week. I think Parma would shut the whole thing down and turn me out into the streets if he wasn't afraid that it might cost the Academy some prestige."

Zekiel stopped at one of the waist-high display cases. It looked no different from any of the others. Inside were three irregular pieces of the strange stone, neatly labeled and held in place by small metal clips. As Rand leaned closer he could see a placard next to each fragment.

"There you see the translation of each piece, as best as we can manage," said Zekiel as he indicated the placards. He handed the lamp to Rand. "Have a look."

The first of the Stone Tears was small, about the size of a large coin. The card beside it read, "Front: [Name1] has [killed or destroyed?] his [many?] and [Name2] has [killed or destroyed?] his tens of [many?]. Reverse: [Spirit?] who was [harming?] the people, '[Completed or enough?]—pull back your hand."

The next fragment was a rectangle, somewhat smaller than Rand's but larger than the first. Its placard said, "Front: This is a list of names in the form: [Name1] [produced or fathered?] [Name2], [Name2] [produced or fathered?] [Name3], etc., apparently a genealogy. Reverse: [Name1] lived in [place1] and [made or built?] towns for [protection?] in [place2], [place3], [place4], ... [place16]."

The last Stone Tear was the only one in the collection that had a straight edge like Rand's. In fact it had two at right angles; it must have been a corner of one of the original tablets.

"This is the fragment I especially wanted you to see," said Zekiel. "The other two tell us little, but this one speaks of the Word itself."

Rand held the lamp over the final placard, which read, "Front: From [start?] was the Word, and the Word [beside?] the Speaker, and the Word [mirror?] the Speaker. Reverse: "… at the [entrance or door?]. Suddenly a [spirit?] from the Speaker appeared and a [light?] shone in the [cage?]."

"You see," said Zekiel, "the Word and the Speaker are linked somehow at a fundamental level. Of course any message from a being with the Speaker's power is important, but the Word was more than just a message; it was somehow one with the Speaker, an expression of the Speaker's very being."

Rand pondered that for a few moments. "Do the fragments held by others reveal any more of what the message actually was?" he asked.

"There are some tantalizing glimpses," said Zekiel. "Many of the passages are historical records of times and people that mean nothing to us without a proper context, like the first two here. But some appear to be principles of wisdom or proper behavior. It appears that there was a teacher of these truths who moved among the people of that distant time, followed by students who spread his teachings to others."

"What must you do to translate the symbols on my fragment? How long does it take?" said Rand.

"I will require several hours to compare—" started Zekiel when the main doors of the exhibit hall creaked open. A figure in the gray robes of a student entered and came toward them, holding aloft a lamp that was enclosed for carrying out of doors. Zekiel tugged at Rand's sleeve and went to meet the visitor partway. Rand realized that Zekiel intended to obscure the fact that they had been examining the exhibit of the Stone Tears; he followed closely after the old scholar.

"The headmaster's office sent me," announced the student when he met them. "The hour is growing late and they wish me to escort the, er, visitor to the gate."

"This young man has traveled far," said Zekiel. "May he not remain as my guest?"

The student shook his head. "The headmaster's secretary thought you might say as much," he said. "He asked me to tell you that there are no unoccupied lodgings on the Academy grounds at this time, and to remind you that even if there were, Master Parma prefers not to have visitors at the Academy overnight."

"Wait here while we collect his things from my office," grumbled Zekiel. The student flinched a little at the man's displeasure. Zekiel motioned for Rand to precede him, raising an eyebrow in a way that Rand interpreted as an admonition for silence.

"Best not to push Parma and his errand boys too far, lad," Zekiel said in hushed tones when they had reached his desk. "There are decent enough lodgings along Ridge Road to keep you for the night. The Academy's gate opens at dawn to admit tradesmen and the like. I will meet you there and escort you. To most of the students and no few of the masters, I'm a fearsome old crank that they'd just as soon avoid," he said with a crooked smile. "If we're quick about it and take the less-traveled paths, I doubt anyone will trouble us."

"If you say so, sir," said Rand.

"With your permission," said Zekiel, and to Rand's surprise he made a slight bow, "I would be honored if you would allow me to keep your Stone Tear until morning. In that way I could begin working on it immediately."

"Of course, sir," said Rand. "I really don't think it's my place to say what's done with it now."

"On the contrary, lad, it's your place and yours alone. The Stone Tears are not common relics that come to light by chance, revealing themselves to anyone who passes by. This one came to you for a reason, and though I did not know you before, I would venture to say that your life is already changing because of it. It is not for me or anyone else to decide for you what to do with it. You must follow the counsel of your own heart."

"Uncle Bowin said something like that before I left. I guess I assumed you had more right than I, being a scholar of such things," said Rand. "All right, then: if I must decide, then I am happy to leave it with you tonight."

"Very good," said Zekiel. "I will meet you in the morning. Do not make me linger long at the gate. That would attract a great deal of attention indeed. Now get your pack and run along. That student is no doubt wondering what's keeping you."

Rand retrieved his pack and returned to the hall. The student looked relieved to depart from the darkening, empty building. He displayed no interest in speaking and Rand decided not to try and draw him out. Within minutes they had reached the front gate and Rand was left standing in Ridge Road in the deepening dusk.

Chapter 17

The violence of the wicked will drag them away,
for they refuse to do what is right.

As he looked down the hill, Rand saw lights here and there along the road. Some came from the windows of the large nearby homes, others from lamps that were mounted by gates or doorways. Tendrils of smoke rose from chimneys and collected into layers that glowed faintly in the light of the rising moon. Rand could smell the burning wood in the breeze. He started down the hill slowly, weary from a full day. He was having a lot of those lately, he thought as he trudged along. It was as if he was living faster to make up for all the dull, unchanging days he had known until now.

He arrived soon at the sign of one of the inns he had passed on his way up Ridge Road earlier in the day—the Rider's Rest. It was about halfway down the hill from the Academy. When he entered the common room his senses were almost overwhelmed—bright lamplight after the near-darkness outside; the smell of cooking, tobacco, and beer; and the noise of thumping mugs, clattering plates, and more than a dozen voices talking at once. Rand pushed through the crowded room until he found a small empty table along the wall to his right.

A large woman came by with four mugs of beer in each hand. She nodded to Rand and shouted that she would see him as soon as she had a spare moment. Rand smiled and nodded, turning his attention to the people around him. An elderly man with a craggy, deeply-lined face sat alone at the nearest table, staring morosely into his drink. His table held an impressive collection of empty mugs and nothing else.

The next table was occupied by three men engaged in some kind of complicated game with dice. They shouted with each successive roll, in joy or frustration depending on their luck. Suddenly one of them cried in outrage and grabbed the wrist of the man who was about to make his throw.

"Hold, ye snake!" he shouted. The room fell silent as the other patrons turned to see what the matter was. "I saw ye swap the dice in yer lap, Jarvis! What d'ye take us for?" Jarvis uttered an oath and tried to shake loose of the other's grip, but the third man came around the table and grabbed him from the other side. Together the two captors hauled Jarvis halfway up out of his seat; the movement dislodged a hidden set of dice that clattered across the wooden planking of the floor. Jarvis looked at them in horror as the other two growled anew and drew back their free hands to strike him.

"Easy, lads, easy," pleaded Jarvis, "that's just a spare set I carry in case no one else has 'em." He kicked at the dice with his boot for emphasis. When his adversaries looked down, he capitalized on the distraction by shifting his weight and knocking one man into the other. In the blink of an eye he had freed his arms and drawn a knife.

The serving woman cried out in alarm. From a table in the back corner of the room two hulking figures in heavy cloaks rose and pressed forward. They wore metal caps and as Rand watched, the cloak of one of them fell aside to reveal an iron breastplate emblazoned with a green coat of arms. A path quickly cleared through the crowded room as the soldiers passed. The two gamblers who had been cheated stepped back and lowered their eyes, their drunken fury gone as if it had never existed. Jarvis turned to see what had spooked his adversaries. When he saw the approaching men he dropped his knife and fell to his knees, holding his hands above his head.

"Please, sirs," he croaked. "I meant no harm—I had to defend myself!" The two men reached Jarvis and stood over him. They were clearly soldiers—whether they were city guards or members of the royal army, Rand did not have the experience to tell. One moved behind Jarvis and gripped the collar of his jerkin. The other swung a gauntleted fist and struck him across the mouth. Rand looked on in shock as blood and bits of broken tooth dribbled from Jarvis' mouth.

"Silence, thief! Aye, and ready to be a killer, too, by the looks of it." His comrade hauled Jarvis up onto his feet as though he were no more than a half-empty sack of grain. The first soldier punched the gambler in the gut and he collapsed in agony to the floor, retching. The two soldiers then kicked him two or three times each with their iron-toed boots as he cried out in pain and tried to huddle into a ball for protection. Then each one gripped him under an arm and hauled him up once more.

"No more testimony to give?" mocked the second soldier. "That's better. We likes it nice and quiet in the jailhouse at night." The two of them dragged Jarvis toward the door, his legs trailing behind him and his head lolling to one side. Everyone in the common room remained quiet and motionless until they were gone. The first to move were the two remaining gamblers, who quietly gathered up the spilled dice and scattered coins and slipped out into the night. Muted conversation rose slowly among the remaining patrons. The solitary old man at the nearby table smiled weakly at

Rand and shrugged his shoulders, as if to say that he expected no better from life. Then he took a long pull from his mug and resumed staring at the table as before.

The serving woman produced cleaning supplies from behind the bar and worked swiftly on the mess left behind by the altercation. Rand was surprised by how quickly and efficiently all traces of the incident were removed—evidently the woman had plenty of experience with situations of the same kind. When she was done she came to wait on Rand.

"Hope all that to-do didn't spoil your appetite, young sir. What can we get fer ye?"

"Ma'am, I hope you don't mind my asking, but I'm not from the city, you see—what was that all about? Who were those soldiers? Why did they beat that man when he had already surrendered?" The woman eyed him sidelong for a moment before answering.

"Ah, so you're in from the country I suppose," she said. "All right then, here's the way it is. Those were constables of the City Guard. They're a rough lot, I grant ye—hard men without patience or mercy. Some say they're little better than the criminals they battle with; others say they can't afford to be if they want to do their job. They themselves say that they have to act fast and hit hard to make an example—they're outnumbered, after all, and if they don't put the fear into people, they'll spend every moment arrestin' and fightin' and end up with a knife through their neck some dark night. I guess there's truth in that, but I say," and here she lowered her voice and leaned closer to Rand, "I say they enjoy it too much and take it too far. That Jarvis may be a crooked gamester and a dirty fighter, but he may never be whole again after the beatin' he took. May not live out the night, either, and there's more folk end up that way at the hands of the Guard than should."

"I better not break any laws," said Rand, his voice a little shaken. The woman patted his arm kindly.

"Don't let it make ye frightened, lad. Do what's right and you'll be fine wherever ye go. Now, are ye hungry?"

"I'll have the chicken and dumplings, I guess," said Rand. "I'll need a room, too, if it's not too expensive."

"Tell you what," she said with a smile, "since the commotion will put a damper on business tonight, I'll let you have supper and a room for two silver." Rand nodded gratefully. It was still more than he had hoped to pay, but Bowin had warned him to expect higher prices in the city.

Rand ate his dinner quickly when it arrived and went to the bar to ask about his room. The serving woman called a boy who was working in the kitchen to show Rand the way. His room was up three flights of stairs, and though it was larger than the one he had slept in at Kerrin, it was not nearly as clean, nor did it have a window.

While he waited for sleep, Rand thought back to his conversation with Zekiel about his belief in the story of the Stone Tears. Just as at the docks, symptoms were all around him of a wrongness or brokenness in the hearts of people, if he chose to see. The petty treachery of Jarvis and the brutality of the soldiers were obvious, but what of the loneliness and hopeless apathy of the old man? For that matter, what about the serving woman's indifference as she cleaned the stains of Jarvis' blood from the floor? Rand wrestled with these thoughts as he tossed and turned on the old and lumpy mattress of his bed; finally he fell into a fitful sleep.

Chapter 18

For the word of the Speaker is alive and active. Keener than any double-edged sword, it slices even to dividing soul and spirit, joints and marrow; it judges the thoughts and attitudes of the heart.

The kitchen boy tapped on Rand's door early the next morning as Rand had requested. He had time for a quick breakfast before settling his bill and striking out for the Academy gate. Marching up the hill in the pre-dawn light, he glanced behind him toward Hornside Way and wondered where the guardsmen had taken Jarvis. Would the gambler be set free this morning? Would he even be alive to witness the sunrise?

The gate to the Academy had not yet opened when Rand topped the hill. He hung back and loitered by a garden wall, looking out over the city and trying to appear as innocuous as possible. A small group of tradesmen gathered by the entrance as dawn approached. When Rand heard the clang of the gate being opened, he turned and sidled up to the rear of the group, blending in with them as they entered the grounds. There was a loud cough to his right; he looked to find Zekiel standing in a narrow path between the inner wall and a tall hedgerow. The master pressed a finger to his lips for silence and waved for Rand to join him.

Rand found it easy to slip sideways into the path without attracting attention. Zekiel turned and led the way without speaking. The path turned left sharply after a few dozen yards, following the wall around the perimeter of the Academy complex. The hedgerow was broken at intervals by paths that intersected their own, but the pair slipped by these openings quickly without seeing or being seen by others.

In time the path and the wall reached the far side of the Academy property and turned left again. The scholar covered what Rand estimated to be about half the distance along the back wall, then stopped at a break in the hedge and stepped through it. Rand followed and found that they had come out at one side of the Antiquities Building. Zekiel produced an ornate iron key from the recesses of his robe and unlocked the small door nearby. They entered the building and Rand saw that they were in the hallway outside of Zekiel's office.

Zekiel locked the outside door behind them and led Rand into his office. Only when he had closed that door as well and sat behind his desk did he speak.

"Our little bit of slinkery appears to have succeeded," he said with gruff satisfaction. "We should be safe from the headmaster and his pestilential underlings for as long as we like. Good thing, too—I am eager to tell you what I've found in the symbols on your Stone Tear."

"You were able to read it then?" said Rand eagerly, leaning forward in his chair. "What does it say?"

"Several of the symbols are ones for which we have no meanings, however uncertain," said Zekiel. "But here is my rough translation of the more familiar characters." He handed Rand a piece of parchment with the following notes: "The Word [changed? passed through?] [body? meat?] and [?] [with? next to?] us." Rand read it twice, trying to identify what made it so significant to Zekiel, but nothing suggested itself. He handed the sheet back and shook his head.

"Doesn't look like much, does it?" said the scholar. "This passage is full of possibilities, though. The Word with us, that is the gist of it, whatever the other symbols may refer to. Like that other fragment in the exhibit hall, it features the Word telling about itself; none of the other known fragments do so. What is it saying about the Word and us together, about our relationship to it? These are the kinds of things we need to know if we are to unlock the secrets of the Word's power to help us."

"Do you think one of your friends might be able to shed some light on it?" asked Rand. Something Zekiel had said about the Academy's collection was nagging at him, but he couldn't quite remember it.

"Yes, that is how we make progress in our studies, by collaborating," said Zekiel. "I will make copies of my transcription and send them to my colleagues, along with tracings of the original symbols. We never know how our different fragments may shed light on one another. We started out knowing the meaning of only a handful of symbols—and even that was by the strangest chance— and we have expanded our vocabulary by carefully placing unknown symbols into context with the known until their probable meaning becomes clear."

"What was the strange chance?" asked Rand.

"Now that was a curious story," said Zekiel. "One of the collections of Stone Tears is kept by the Academy of Ramsgate, the city that stands at the border with the land of the Vokar. Some two hundred years ago, the Master of Antiquities there went shopping in a bazaar where Solethonian and Vokar merchants exchanged their goods. A few of the traders did business in artifacts of various kinds and the master was always on the lookout for something new.

"He came upon a stall operated by a Vokar merchant that he had never seen at the bazaar before. He spoke with the man as best he could with his limited command of the Vokar tongue, for the trader was from the deep interior of Vokar country and spoke no Solethonian. On impulse the master pulled a copy of some of the symbols from his Stone Tear collection out of his pocket—he had it with him to study while he ate his lunch later in the day—and showed it to the man. The trader puzzled over the runes carefully and then grew quite excited. He rummaged through his wares until he found a particular book, which he opened to reveal an ancient and brittle parchment that he had preserved by keeping it pressed between the pages.

"The sheet had lines of characters arranged in two columns. On the left the text was in the runes of the Vokar. On the right, each line aligned with those in the left column, were characters like the ones found on the Stone Tears."

"A key!" exclaimed Rand with excitement.

"Yes, lad," said Zekiel with a smile. "I'm afraid the master from Ramsgate disguised his elation no better than you, for the Vokar saw that he had an eager buyer and he drove a hard bargain. When the haggling was over and the master's purse was significantly lightened, the old Vokar rogue burst out laughing as he handed over the prize."

"What did he find so funny?" said Rand.

"The master was at a loss for that until later, when he had the master of languages at his academy work out a translation of the Vokar runes," said Zekiel. "The document turned out to be a bill from an inn for food and lodging. The trader had obviously thought it hilarious that someone would pay so much for an old invoice. The scholar was not disappointed in the least by the contents of the parchment, though."

"Why not?" said Rand. He himself was a little disappointed by the nature of the find.

"For two reasons," said Zekiel. "First, the content of the document mattered little for the purposes of the scholar. It was enough that it provided a translation of the symbols into a known tongue. Second, the nature of the document was not so insignificant as it might have looked at first. Can you guess who might have left such a bill behind on their journey?"

Rand felt his excitement grow anew as he realized what the answer must be. "The travelers who sought the Temple of the Wind?" he said.

"Good lad, that's it," said Zekiel. "Who else from the ancient empire made a journey through the length of the land of the Vokar and back again? What most likely happened was that the owner of the inn made out the bill in his native Vokar runes; then a guide or escort of the seekers who knew both languages wrote it out again in their symbols so they could know what they were being charged for. Thus this commonplace remnant of commerce was compelling evidence that the story of the seekers was not fanciful legend but historical fact, and the trader's prank became the basis for all we know about the meaning of the Stone Tears."

"What a remarkable chain of events," said Rand. The thought that had been nagging him about the fragments was still there, hovering just beyond his reach. "Can I see the Stone Tear I gave you?"

"Of course," said Zekiel. He pulled the fragment from a cabinet behind his desk and handed it to Rand, who examined it carefully to see if anything about it would jog his thoughts. Something about the two Stone Tears that spoke of the Word directly, and the straight edge on the side of his fragment—what was it?

"I'd like to compare this piece to the one in your collection, the one that also spoke of the Word," he said at last. Maybe then the connection would suggest itself.

"Certainly," said Zekiel. He took a folio from the tall bookshelf nearby and pulled a sheet from it, laying it on the table before Rand next to the sheet he had shown the boy earlier. It was a transcription just like the other. Rand shook his head.

"Beg your pardon, sir," he said, "but I meant that I would like to compare the fragments themselves."

"Ah, well then," said Zekiel with a look of surprise and some discomfiture. "I suppose we could, but be careful—I do not like the pieces in our exhibits to be handled more than necessary. We must be discrete as well; others do not enter this building often except for the scheduled lectures, but unexpected visits do happen at times."

Rand nodded and stood, taking his Stone Tear from the desk. Zekiel rose also and led the way back to the display case in the exhibit hall. He produced a small key and unlocked the glass lid of the case, lifting it up and holding it to provide Rand access to the contents.

"If you rotate the retaining clips, you will be able to remove the fragment that interests you," he said. Rand did so and removed the Stone Tear with the square corner. Zekiel gently lowered the case lid and stood beside him watchfully.

"I was wondering," said Rand. "You said these two pieces were similar in their topic. Perhaps they came from the same tablet originally. The grain of the stone might look the same." He held the two pieces up side by side, but whatever flecks or whorls there were in the stone were so dark that it was difficult to tell if they bore any resemblance. As he tried to find some pattern or correspondence, Rand changed their orientation and held the Academy's piece above his own. Suddenly the relationship that had eluded him became plain—how had he missed it before? He held the pieces up for Zekiel to see, too excited to speak. The scholar's eyes grew wide.

"The edges—they match! Great thunder, boy—these two pieces were once connected! Try them and see." Rand carefully aligned the straight edges of the pieces on the left, then slowly fitted the matching curves and jags of the broken edges together. There could be no doubt now that they had once been joined. He shifted the alignment slightly and the pieces slid perfectly into place.

Three things happened at once then; any of them would have been stunning by itself, but together they knocked Rand to the floor in a daze. A brilliant flare of blue-white light burst from the crack where the two pieces touched, temporarily blinding him. It was accompanied by an explosive sound like a thunderclap that battered his ears. At the same time a biting, tingling sensation shot through his fingertips, causing him to drop the fragments as he fell. Zekiel was by his side in an instant.

"Rand! Rand, are you hurt?" he cried. Rand rolled over and sat up slowly, blinking as the afterimage of the flash faded. He shook his head—as far as he could tell, no permanent damage had been done.

"The stones—did I destroy them?" he croaked in desperation. Zekiel turned and groped on the floor until he found something.

"Here's one," he said. Then he looked more closely. "Wait, not one! Or rather, the two made one—look!" He handed the stone to Rand. It was indeed composed of the two fragments, but there was no sign of a crack or seam between them. They were fused together as if never broken.

Rand had been so intent upon the pieces themselves that he had spared no attention for the symbols engraved upon them—upon it, he corrected himself. Now as he looked at the text, he received the greatest surprise yet. He could read the words as plainly as if they were a lesson on the chalkboard of his schoolroom back home. With a trembling voice he read aloud.

"In the beginning was the Word, and the Word was with the Speaker, and the Word was the Speaker. The Word became flesh, and made his dwelling place among us." He looked at Zekiel. The old man stared at him in shock.

"How did you read that?" he said. Rand held out the tablet. Zekiel took it with unsteady hands. He breathed in sharply as he saw the text. "It lives! The Word lives again!"

Deep in the lightless, windowless recesses of the Vizier's quarters in the citadel of Solaria, the heavy tomblike silence was violated by the sound of something shattering. The Vizier was yanked from his deep midmorning slumber by the sound and reached quickly to uncover the shuttered lamp by his bedside. He rose and hunted through his apartments until he discovered the source of the noise. He kept a scrying glass on the wall of his library, a special mirror that—under the right conditions and with the proper rituals—could allow him to see afar through the eyes of a familiar. It now lay in jagged shards upon the floor.

As he searched in vain for the cause of this costly ruin, he heard a well-remembered tapping in the dining room. It was highly unusual for Garrak to seek audience with him in the middle of the day. As he went to open the ventilation grate, the Vizier was disquieted by the suspicion that his familiar's arrival so soon after the destruction of the glass was no coincidence.

The Vizier turned from the grate to place his lamp on the stone table and sat in his accustomed chair, but Garrak startled him by bursting into the room and fluttering against the low ceiling, uttering a storm of ear-piercing cries. The raven alighted at last on the table, but it still quivered with agitation.

"Alarm! Alarm!" it cried. "Our foe awakens—beware! Beware!"

"What has happened, Garrak?" said the Vizier sternly. "Calm yourself! Now answer me."

The bird shivered and fluttered on the table, then shook its head rapidly and collected itself enough to speak more intelligibly. "There has been a mighty tremor in the spirit realm, master. The Enslaver has awakened somehow."

"How can this have happened?" said the Vizier. "The Enslaver is hidden, broken, scattered across a thousand miles!"

"It is not yet whole, master," Garrak replied. "May it never be so! But some small part of it has been made whole, and the pain was felt by all spirit-servants of the Banished One. That fragment is now awake. We do not know how this was made to happen, but we know where."

"Where?" said the Vizier, leaning over the table as if to pounce on the bird and devour it.

"Serenhorn," said Garrak. "Even now the Others gather in shadowed places and wait for nightfall to investigate."

"What of your own spies?" demanded the Vizier. "Was there no warning of this, no sign?"

"They have been much occupied of late, master. They are spread abroad to keep watch over the candidates for the Royal Gauntlet."

"Yes, the candidates," the Vizier mused. "What was there about the candidates and the Enslaver? Ah!" he cried and snapped his fingers. "The boy, that commoner that the Other wanted us to take note of—what of him?"

"My spies have only just given me a new report of him, master. I was on my way here to relate it to you when the—the calamity happened." The raven became agitated again and struggled to settle itself before continuing. "The boy left his village the day after the Other found him; he traveled to the Seren River and embarked on a barge bound for Serenhorn. We were able to track him to the edge of the city, but we lost him there among the crowds."

"Again we see that the farm boy is connected to this somehow," said the Vizier, pacing back and forth as his mind picked at the puzzle. "But how? The Other said that the youth did not possess a fragment of the Enslaver; could he have been mistaken?" The raven became very still; it waited in silence until the Vizier halted his pacing and focused his full attention on it.

"With regard to the Enslaver, the Others make no mistakes," Garrak replied. "They fear it second only to the Enemy himself."

"Very well," said the Vizier. "We must work to discover the answer to this riddle before any more harm is done. I will need more frequent reports from you, Garrak. I can no longer watch through the eyes of you and your fellows." He told Garrak about the loss of his scrying glass.

"Suggestive," hissed the raven. "Some small part of the vision granted, in a sense, by the Enemy through the Enslaver is restored, and in turn an instrument of vision granted by our own lord is lost."

"You are indeed a wise creature, Garrak. We both had best get to work now to find out what happened, and how to prevent it from going further." The Vizier turned and began lighting more lamps around the room; there was no time for him to return to his day's sleep. The raven left by the grate without saying another word.

Chapter 19

Every word of the Speaker is flawless;
he is a shield to those who take refuge in him.

"What fools we've been," exclaimed Zekiel as he sat heavily behind his desk. He had urged Rand to return with him to the seclusion of his office once the initial shock of their discovery had abated. "Long years spent scrabbling in the dust for clues, puzzling over the symbols, each of us jealously guarding our own little store of relics and trying to build a private edifice of vanity for ourselves. And all this time, how many more of the Stone Tears might there be that could join together as these two did?"

"Do you think there really could be?" asked Rand.

"Perhaps not," said Zekiel. "After all, we have so few. It's impossible to know how many Stone Tears there are in all, but it would hardly be surprising if none of the others we have found come from adjacent portions of the original tablets. But now that we know it is possible for them to join, I must convince my colleagues to bring them together and try. I must also tell them of the message that our living fragment reveals."

"I am not sure I understand the meaning of it, even now that I can read it plainly," said Rand ruefully.

"Indeed, lad—it contains much mystery," Zekiel agreed. "But I am in awe of what it does tell us. Don't you see? The Word is not just a message from the Speaker; in some way it was once a messenger as well, coming in the form of a man to walk among men. Who was this man? What did he say and do? Why did the Speaker send him and not just the message itself? This is a key—much more of a key than that old Vokar parchment ever was. That helped us to decipher the symbols, but the words we saw today could help us to understand at last the message they contain."

"I hope you succeed, sir," said Rand.

"Me, Rand?" said Zekiel. "Nay, let us say 'we.' Much credit is due you for the victories we have now won. I wouldn't think of continuing without you."

Rand sat with his mouth open. What was Zekiel saying? "I'm sorry, sir—I'm afraid I don't understand," he said.

"Oh, come now, lad," said Zekiel. "You're just about of age to enroll in the Academy. Why wait? Don't you want to continue what you've started?"

"With all my heart, sir," said Rand. "I've loved studying history and artifacts since I was a small boy. But you see, I can't." He hung his head miserably.

"Why, what's the matter?" said Zekiel. "If it's a question of money, something could be arranged."

"No, sir, it's not that—not exactly," said Rand. As well as he could, he proceeded to explain about his father, his uncle, and the expectations his father had for him. When he finished, Zekiel sat looking at him with an unreadable expression. Suddenly the old man slapped the top of his desk in frustration.

"By thunder, but isn't this a fine mess? I've never heard the like," he growled. "You're a natural scholar—any fool could see it! I assumed that since your uncle came here, your family would send you too." Zekiel took a deep breath and sighed heavily. "Forgive me, lad. Of course you must respect your father's wishes. I simply assumed too much. Don't be surprised if your path changes, though. You've been caught up in the tale of the Stone Tears; I don't think they will let you go so easily."

"Perhaps you're right, sir," said Rand, although in his heart he doubted it. "I must return home now all the same. I'm due any day; my uncle needs his contracts and I have to keep my promise to my father."

"I understand," said Zekiel. A strange look came over his face. He made as if to move, then stopped, then moved again. Finally he nodded his head as though in answer to a question, picked up the restored fragments from the desk and held them out to Rand. "Here—take this with you."

"Oh no, sir," said Rand, holding up a hand to refuse the offering. "Now more than ever, it wouldn't be right for me to keep it. It's half your piece! Besides, it's alive now, and you need to—"

"Peace, boy," said Zekiel, the commanding tone of a master showing in his voice. "I do not offer it lightly, but because my heart tells me I must. We owe it to your uncle to let him see it for himself; if not for him you might never have come here, and a great opportunity would have been lost. Who knows? The sight of the living Word might motivate him to intercede for you with your father. Remember also that the Stone Tear that joined with yours was in my keeping, but it was not truly mine. I have never found a fragment of the Word; you have. But more than all these things, we must remember that what we have learned today changes everything. We must try to reunite more of the Stone Tears, and if we are to have any chance of that we must enlist the help of others who share our hopes. If I understand your uncle rightly, I think he might be such a man."

"But what of your friends at the other academies? Shouldn't they see it too?" said Rand.

"Of course," said Zekiel, "and in time they will. Let us consider the tablet on loan for now. If it comes to pass that you cannot return to the Academy, I can always arrange to visit you in Oakbridge and retrieve the piece on my way to show it to the others."

"Well, all right," said Rand reluctantly. "If you're sure."

"I won't claim to be sure of anything in this business," said Zekiel with a rueful chuckle. "Believe me, it isn't my natural inclination to let go of the greatest prize I have ever seen. But I am unable to shake the belief that this is the right decision for now." He offered the tablet again, and this time Rand took it.

"If you're going to catch a boat downriver today, we'd better get you on your way," said Zekiel. He stood and ushered Rand into the hall, where he unlocked the outside door again.

"Follow the hedge path back to the gate and you should have no problems," he said. As Rand opened the door and turned to go, the master laid a hand on his shoulder. "May the Speaker watch over you, lad. I hope to see you soon, either here or in Oakbridge."

"Thank you, sir," Rand said and slipped out through the door. He didn't look back for fear that the tears welling in his eyes would flow in earnest. He had thought that the life of a blacksmith was an unappetizing prospect before; now that he had seen the Academy and had a taste of all it could offer, his looming apprenticeship felt more like a death sentence.

Chapter 20

He makes his sun rise on the evil and the good,
and sends rain on those who do right and those who do not.

Rand followed the path between the hedge and the wall as he had done earlier in the morning, pausing at openings to confirm that no one was nearby. He reached the front gate unnoticed; from there it was easy to slip out onto Ridge Road without attracting attention.

He started down the hill, noting by the position of the sun that it was now late in the morning. He found it hard to believe that so much had happened with the day not yet half gone. As he looked westward across the river to the Hunter Range, he saw a mass of heavy rain clouds rolling toward the city. He quickened his pace, eager to reach the docks and find passage downriver before the storm arrived.

Before long, Rand came to Hornside Way. He started up the busy thoroughfare, but his progress was slowed by the midday throngs. He had not yet reached the Merchant Hall when the rain began to fall. By the time he reached Dock Street, it was coming down in blinding, windblown sheets. The way down to the docks was almost a river, gutters and drains being overwhelmed by the sudden downpour.

Rand waded down the hill carefully, holding on to every post, ledge, and cornice he could find to help him keep his footing. When he reached the docks, the wide promenade was deserted; the normally raucous crowds were huddled in overcrowded stalls or up against the buildings that stood behind them, waiting for the cloudburst to pass. He saw the schedule board in a gap between sheets of rain and slogged his way to it as quickly as the wind allowed.

The board was somewhat sheltered by a little peaked awning and since Rand approached it on the leeward side he was afforded some protection from the storm as he studied the postings. It would have been nice to travel with Captain Beck and the crew of the *Kelpie* again, but as Rand feared, there hadn't been near enough time for them to return from wherever their business had taken them on the riverways of Solethon. He saw that one of the barges he remembered from the dock at Kerrin, the *Dolphin*, was scheduled to depart downriver at noon. He peered out from the shelter of the schedule board and spotted the vessel at the northern end of the dock, ghostly through the twisting sheets of rain. He considered waiting where he was until the storm abated, but the *Dolphin's* departure time wasn't far off; besides, it would be easier to get settled now than to wait until the crowds were once again swirling across the docks.

When Rand reached the barge, there was no sign of the captain or the crew. He hesitated to go aboard without permission, but decided it was justified under the circumstances. He reached the door to the deckhouse and knocked. After a few moments the door opened a crack.

"What d'ye want?" demanded a deep voice in irritation.

"I need passage to Kerrin," said Rand, raising his voice above the storm. "Can you take me with you?"

"Hold," said the voice. The door slammed shut and Rand hunkered there in the stairwell leading down from the main deck, his back toward the blinding rain. After a long pause, the door cracked open again.

"Cap'n says ye can come in. Make it quick and mind the lads." The door swung just wide enough for Rand to slip through and he bolted in out of the storm. The unseen crewman slammed the door shut behind him as he stood there dripping and waiting for his eyes to adjust to the darkness of the hold. One small lamp hung from the low rafters overhead; after a few moments he could see well enough to understand why the man had said to "mind the lads"—the men of the crew were huddled amongst the cargo to get out of the rain. If he had moved farther into the hold without being able to see, he would have almost certainly stepped on various feet, legs, and hands.

"Cap'n's in the forward hold," said the sailor with the deep voice, a short man with a thick red beard. "Best go speak with 'im." Rand nodded and stepped carefully through the assembled bodies until he reached the passage forward. When he had slipped through to the other side, he found two more crewmen sheltered there; standing over them was a man who Rand thought must be the captain, judging by his silvery gray beard and long woolen coat. He peered at Rand with watery eyes.

"Lookin' fer passage, eh?" he said in a thin, high voice. "We're heavy loaded on this run, but I s'pose ye could come along if ye don't mind squeezin' in with the cargo. That suit ye?"

"Sounds fine, sir," said Rand. In his heart he wasn't so sure; neither the captain nor the crew of the *Dolphin* looked to be the equal of those he had known aboard the *Kelpie*, and he wondered if the journey might be tiresome in their company. He supposed, though, that the grim atmosphere might be mostly on account of the weather. Besides, he needed to get home before his time and money ran out, and this was the only boat that could get him there.

"As ye like, then," said the man. "I'm Captain Edvard. You can stow yer pack up there; we'll try to find somethin' softer than bare crates fer ye to rest on as we go." He indicated a narrow space between the rafters and the stacks of cargo along one side of the hold. Rand removed his pack and manhandled it into the small recess, then settled onto a row of crates below it that would serve as a makeshift bench.

The captain and his crew waited in silence as the rain fell heavily on the upper deck overhead. In a few minutes the initial blast of the storm had passed by; the captain rapped out a curt order and the crew stirred dispiritedly into action. Rand was left alone in the dim hold, listening to the muted calls of the men and the thud of their boots on the deck as they prepared to launch. He caught glimpses through a nearby porthole as they hauled the gangplanks aboard, cast off most of the lines binding the *Dolphin* to the dock, and unshipped the long riverboat poles from their racks along the sides of the deckhouse.

Tired of the stuffy atmosphere in the hold and wanting to get a last look at the city while the barge departed, Rand slipped out into the rain. The last lines were cast off and two polemen who stood in the bow pushed against the pilings of the dock to turn the prow of the boat out into the river. Rand leaned over the side to see what was happening at the stern. Polemen were dug in there to keep the barge from drifting downstream into the vessel berthed behind it. Two more men waited at the sweep for enough room to do their part.

As the prow turned into the current, the flow of the river pushed the barge around to face downstream. While the *Dolphin* maneuvered, Rand looked up and saw signs of renewed activity on the docks—now that force of the rain had abated, the city was returning to its busy pace.

Before long the polemen had the barge properly aligned in the current. Now the sweep was employed, and Rand marveled at how quickly the ungainly craft accelerated when the river was working with it rather than against it. He noted that the polemen had an easier job as well—since they no longer had to push against the current, they used their poles mainly to apply steering corrections from the forward sides of the upper deck, working in shifts of two instead of four.

Rand moved up to the bow now that the polemen were no longer stationed there. He took in all he could as they passed through the city, looking for things he might have missed when he rode upstream aboard the *Kelpie*. It was odd to think that he had only been here for a little more than a day; with all that had happened, it felt more like three.

In half an hour they were leaving the outskirts of the city behind. Rand decided that the view along the riverbanks was not worth standing in the chill of the autumn rain and went below. In his haste to get to the docks, he had had nothing to eat since his early breakfast at the inn. No one among the crew appeared likely to cook lunch for a passenger, so he dug into his pack and found the parcel that contained apples and hardtack.

As the day passed, Rand's initial misgivings about the *Dolphin* were justified. Captain Edvard didn't appear to be a harsh master, but he commanded the boat in a flat, perfunctory manner. The crew never sang or laughed—in fact, Rand couldn't remember seeing any of them so much as smile. The *Kelpie* had echoed with chanteys and lighthearted banter; in comparison the *Dolphin* felt more like a funeral barge.

Between the weather and the crew, Rand was grateful that the downstream passage was much faster than the one upstream had been. The barge pressed on into the early evening and made Kerrin that same day rather than tying up for the night along the riverbank. Rand paid the captain his fare as quickly as possible and went ashore, grateful to be off the boat and close to home. He had to be careful as he passed through the riverfront—it was late enough that revelers were getting rowdy among the dockside taverns. Soon he reached the Lantern House, where he found a warm welcome, a hot meal, and a soft bed—just as he had hoped.

A great oak tree stood beside a country lane southeast of Serenhorn, its limbs twisted and tangled by centuries of wind and weather. Its branches formed a canopy over a small hollow below, shrouding it in shadows deeper than the approaching night. There in the darkness the panther waited as its fellows arrived one by one—the wolf, the boar, the vulture, and the adder. These were the Others nearest to Serenhorn at the time of the Enslaver's awakening. Ancient and powerful servants of the Banished One, they radiated malice and left a scent of dread wherever they passed. Men seldom saw them as they moved through the world, but it was clear to those who crossed their path that they were not the natural creatures whose shapes they wore. They were too large, and the proportions of their limbs and features weren't quite right. When they moved their very substance shifted and flowed.

The creatures regarded one another silently. None needed to be told of the seriousness of the event that had drawn them together, or of the urgency with which they must now act. They never moved openly without dire necessity, but when such need arose they were swift, implacable, and ruthless. The night wore on until the time came when most mortals would be off the streets. In wordless agreement the Others emerged from the hollow and approached the city.

Tales were told long afterward of the terror of that night. The Others raced through the streets and alleys of Serenhorn, uttering unworldly cries in their eager pursuit of any trace of their foe. Even lying in their beds behind barred doors and locked gates, townspeople could hear the cries and feel the wave of fear that preceded the beasts wherever they went. A few guardsmen of the night watch were bold and foolhardy enough to stand and challenge them—their shredded remains were found the next day, along with a few people accustomed to being up late and caught in the Others' path.

The creatures scoured the districts of the city, coming together again at the focal point of the traces they had found—the gates of the Academy. Abruptly their demeanor changed from heedless violence to stealth and cunning. They dared not leave any overt evidence of the true focus of their attention; the school was a place where fragments of the Enslaver were kept, and the Banished One had gone to great lengths to cultivate scholarly indifference in the minds of men toward the Stone Tears. He did not want it disturbed by signs of supernatural intervention.

The adder was sent within the grounds of the Academy; it wound its way silently through the halls and pathways, drawn unerringly toward the Hall of Antiquities. There was no crevice large enough for it to enter though, and it was forced to circle outside in search of indirect clues to what might have happened. The strength of the Enemy's presence that would have accompanied a living portion of the Enslaver did not emanate from the place; the adder thought it sensed traces of such a presence moving away from the building, but they were growing cold and faint. After a time the adder rejoined the other beasts outside.

The Others considered what they had learned. A fragment of the Enslaver had passed through the city and entered the Academy. Something had happened within the Hall of Antiquities to restore and awaken a portion of the hated foe. This portion had left the Academy under cover of a heavy storm, leaving little trace of its passing. Nothing more could be learned at the school for the time being without unmasking themselves and extracting information directly from any mortals who had been involved. This would be a drastic departure from the subtleties preferred by their master, and in any case was not possible given the limits imposed on their activities by the power of their Enemy. Even such violence and audacity as they had employed this night had tested those limits, and would undoubtedly bear a price.

Reluctantly the creatures separated and left the city by routes that led to their respective haunts, where they would set aside their normal activities of incitement and temptation and work to find some sign of the missing artifact. One last ripple of fear followed in their wake.

Chapter 21

Be careful, and watch yourselves closely to not forget the things your eyes have seen or let them fade from your heart as long as you live.

Rand woke the next morning to find that the rain had cleared away in the night, leaving a sky of crisp autumn blue behind. He left the Lantern House as early as he could—the march back to Oakbridge would be uphill most of the way, especially where it climbed from the floor of Serenvale to the mouth of the smaller valley where his folk lived. He didn't want to be overtaken by nightfall and be forced to camp beside the road if he could sleep in his own bed instead.

Despite his best efforts, though, it was long after sundown when Rand arrived at the gate to the Porter estate and climbed wearily up the hill to the manor house. Mrs. Tanner answered the door. When she saw him standing there muddy and exhausted, her brow furrowed with a look of motherly concern; she gently took his arm and led him to a bench in the entrance hall, calling toward the kitchen for hot food and drink. Then she excused herself and went to find the master of the house.

When Bowin came to meet him, Rand was eagerly attacking a large bowl of broth provided by the cook. He was already feeling somewhat refreshed, and at the sight of his uncle he set the bowl aside and rose to greet him with an eager embrace.

"Uncle! You won't believe it—I've so much to tell you."

"Of course you do, Rand," said Bowin with a smile. "Come, let's move to my study where we can talk in comfort. Bring the soup with you. Mrs. Tanner, see to it that we're brought enough food to satisfy a hungry youth after a hard day's travel." The housekeeper nodded and went to the kitchen while Rand followed Bowin to the study.

When they got there Rand shed his pack, settled into a deep-cushioned chair, and told Bowin about his trip to Kerrin between mouthfuls of soup. He gave his uncle greetings from George Winter of the Lantern House, then told of the *Kelpie* and the voyage to Serenhorn. When he got to the part about the Merchant Hall, he remembered the contracts and rose to retrieve them from his backpack. As he was giving them to Bowin, Mrs. Tanner entered with a platter full of bread, fruit, cheese, and cold sliced beef. Rand thanked her and attacked the food with gusto while Bowin looked over the documents.

"Well done, Rand," said Bowin after reviewing the contracts. "We'll be well-provided for in the year ahead thanks to these. Now—what about the other matter? Did you find Zekiel? What was he able to tell you?"

This was the part of the story that Rand had been the most eager to tell, but now that they had come to it he felt strangely shy. How could he convey the wonder and delight he had felt as he learned the history of the Word? What would Bowin think of the living tablet? Where should Rand begin? In the end he decided that the best he could do was to tell it in the order it happened.

"I arranged to meet with Master Parma first, uncle, as you said I should. He was friendly, but I can't say I trusted him much. It appears that things in the field of antiquities are not as they were in your day." Rand told Bowin what Zekiel had said about Parma allowing the department to wither away, and included his own observations of some of the masters and the staff.

"You'll find many people like Parma in seats of power as you get to know the world, Rand," said Bowin grimly. "More clever than wise, they value knowledge only when they can turn it to their advantage in the constant effort to put themselves before others. They smile and flatter, but every gift they offer comes with a price and their hearts are empty of all but the craving for position." Rand nodded sadly and continued, telling of his first meeting with Zekiel and repeating the origin of the Stone Tears as well as he could remember it.

"So that's what the tablets were," said Bowin. "The scholars knew some of the tale when I was a student, but not nearly as much as that. Go on." Rand told him about the bazaar in Ramsgate and the Vokar document that helped open the way to translating the fragments. Bowin laughed appreciatively at the irony of finding a key to history in an old bill for lodging.

"So what about your own find, Rand?" he asked. "Was Zekiel able to tell you what it said?" Rand looked at his pack and back to Bowin. He tried to speak, but so many words tried to come at once that they clogged in his throat.

"What is it, lad?" said his uncle, leaning forward in alarm. Rand shook his head and held up a hand for patience. After a few moments he continued, relating with a quiver of emotion in his voice what had happened in the museum. As he told of the melding of the two fragments, Bowin's eyes grew wide with wonder.

"What on earth?" he whispered. "Legends springing to life in the waking world? I don't question that you believe what you saw, Rand, but I confess that I have doubts that it really was as it appeared to be. The old myths are entertaining and teach many truths, but you mustn't let yourself get caught up in them and start to think they are real in a physical sense." Rand nodded wordlessly; he could well understand Bowin's skepticism, but it was quite another matter to witness the Word come to life in your own hands. He knew the time had come for his uncle to see for himself. Turning to his pack, he searched within and found the drawstring bag containing the restored tablet. He rose and crossed to Bowin's desk, gave him the bag, and stood waiting to see his uncle's reaction to the living Word. Bowin paused a moment, curiosity and doubt warring with each other in his expression.

"Is this—you brought it with you? But why would Zekiel let it go?" he said.

"He thought you had the right to see it after helping me as you did," said Rand. Bowin nodded and carefully untied the strings. When he held the tablet and saw the symbols reshape themselves into the words of the Solethonian tongue, he gasped.

"I-I can scarce believe it! Yet here it is before me," he said. "So, this at least is no mere legend. But what does it all mean?"

"I think Zekiel would say that it means all of the tale is true," said Rand. "The empire, the tablets, and the message contained in the Word. He believes there really was a Speaker who gave us the Word, and that we should heed what it says." He was reluctant to continue, but felt he should be honest with Bowin. "And for my part, I am beginning to believe it also."

"Oh, my boy," said Bowin, shaking his head sadly, "I warned you—you mustn't let yourself be carried away by all this. Zekiel means well, but he is obsessed with the Stone Tears; he sees what he wants to see. You are young and excitable. Don't be too quick to give your devotion to anything that claims to hold all of the answers to life."

"I understand your reservations, uncle," said Rand, "but I cannot forget what I saw. You must admit that people's hearts are lacking, in need of help from something greater than themselves just as those of the ancient empire were."

"Perhaps," said Bowin. "But I have seen that hunger lead men into giving their allegiance to false promises and barren dreams. There are many who prey on the fond wish for a better world, Rand. Men like Parma often use such tools to manipulate others if greed and envy will not serve, but there are worse deceivers than his kind. There are zealots and mystics who will take away your possessions, your family, and even your very life in the service of their cause. Beware lest you fall under their spell."

"But you can't think Zekiel is a man like that," protested Rand.

"No, not he," said Bowin. "But I wonder if his years of searching and hoping have clouded his judgment. If he is not careful he may find himself given over to a fantasy; I would not have you follow after him."

"Then I fear you will not be kindly disposed toward his hopes in sending you the tablet," said Rand dejectedly.

"Oh?" said Bowin sharply. "What are those?" Rand told Bowin how Zekiel wanted him to enroll in the Academy and continue researching the Stone Tears, and how the scholar hoped that Bowin might help to make that possible. Bowin shook his head slowly.

"I would have been in agreement with Zekiel about what was best for your future before all this," he said. "But this is precisely the sort of dangerous enthusiasm I was warning you about. I don't know if I would have pressed your father to let you go, even if I felt it was right. With all this talk of gods and legends, though, I think it would be unwise to send you off on your own. You need to calm yourself and rethink these ideas of yours in the light of day. You need time to get over the shock and excitement of it all."

"Yes, uncle," said Rand, hanging his head in resignation.

"Don't take it too hard, lad," said Bowin kindly. "You are exhausted and overwrought. When you have rested and settled with your family again, you may see things differently."

"Yes, sir," said Rand. He had been through too much and simply wanted the trying day to end. Given the lateness of the hour and the long walk remaining into town, Bowin suggested that he sleep at the manor and return home in the morning. Rand readily agreed and was soon asleep in his usual guest room.

Chapter 22

Even youths become exhausted, and young men lose their balance.

When Rand returned home the next morning, he left the tablet with Bowin. His uncle had a strongroom for keeping valuables and Rand was more comfortable knowing that the artifact was protected; he also hoped that Bowin might look at it from time to time and become more amenable to the idea that the story behind it was true.

His mother greeted him at the door with a hug that nearly cracked his ribs. After telling her a few details about the trip, he unpacked his belongings and went out to the shop. His father smiled at the sight of him but quickly adopted his usual serious expression and plied Rand with questions. Had he been careful? Had he performed his duties faithfully? Had he spent his traveling money wisely? Once satisfied with Rand's answers, his father gave him a brief hug and told him to run along to the schoolhouse. He was determined that Rand not fall any farther behind in his schoolwork.

After school that afternoon, Eli fulfilled his promise and initiated Rand's official apprenticeship. There was a brief ceremony involving the hammer, the tongs, and the anvil. Then Rand's training began in earnest, immersing him in a world of blasting heat, clanging hammer, and hissing steam.

Rand was utterly spent as he sat at the table for supper that evening—it required conscious effort to lift the fork to his mouth.

He caught his father winking at his mother while they watched him eat; she put her hand to her mouth to hide a smile. It was nice that somebody found his condition amusing, he thought with a tinge of resentment.

Thus Rand's life fell into patterns both new and familiar. He was a one-week wonder among his fellow students because of his trip to the city, but once he had exhausted the stories he thought were safe to tell, their curiosity faded. Lyssa pretended that he wasn't even there and he gratefully avoided her as well. Sometimes, though, when he was telling a story about the world outside the valley, he would catch her listening with that strangely hungry look she had worn the day he recited the poem he had written for her.

Weeks went by swiftly and autumn passed into winter. Between the mental challenges of his final year at the school and the rigors of his apprenticeship, Rand spent less and less time thinking about the Stone Tears and the meaning of the Word. He still agreed more with Zekiel than with Bowin about their importance, but the thrill of discovery faded with time. It was unlikely that he could contribute anything more to their story; he was a young country boy in a small country town. Since Bowin had decided not to intervene, it looked as though he would stay in Oakbridge and become a blacksmith after all.

The winter doldrums were interrupted suddenly near the end of the year when a scandal captured the town's attention—Lyssa was pregnant. Her father was a member of the town's council of elders; he was furious, and insisted on an official inquiry. He discovered that Karl Morgan was the father of the baby, to no surprise on Rand's part. Karl had been earning respect among some in the community by his physical strength and bold self-confidence, but his indiscretion—and his failure to come forward voluntarily—brought embarrassment to himself, Lyssa, and their families. In the end he and Lyssa were compelled to marry quietly, disappearing from public life to a small cottage on the Morgan farm.

More bad news came after the turn of the new year, news that touched Rand closer to home. He returned from school one afternoon to find his parents seated at the kitchen table. His father looked bleak and his mother wept openly. He asked what was wrong; his father slowly stirred from his dark thoughts and told Rand the story. A messenger had brought word from the Porter estate that Aunt Cora was gravely ill after catching a chill from the winter cold.

Rand's mother moved out to the estate that very night to help care for Cora. Within days Rand and his father were summoned to see Bowin's beloved wife one last time before she died. They visited her room briefly as she lay pale and thin in the great canopy bed, her fever-wracked body concealed beneath layers of heavy blankets. Word came a few hours later to the sitting room where they waited with Bowin that she was gone.

Cora had been respected by all and loved by most in Oak Valley, but to Bowin she had been the center of life itself. He fulfilled the role of gracious host during the funeral and the visits of those who came to pay their respects, but Rand's mother confided to her family that when he thought no one was watching, Bowin moved listlessly through the house and stared into space as though his spirit had departed with that of his wife.

When the household matters of the estate had been looked after as best as possible, Rand's mother returned home. She was worried about Bowin but she knew that his grief must run its course; in the meantime, she had her own family to look after. Rand's father said nothing about Cora's death, but his usual manner of brusque intensity while training his apprentice grew quiet and somber.

Two weeks passed; Rand's family settled into the new realities of life without Cora. Rand's mother prevailed upon Bowin to venture forth from his empty house to share dinner with them in town. By the end of the meal he looked a little better for the company and he promised to come again soon; however, the following day brought events that dashed any thoughts of a return to normalcy in the Porter clan.

Rand was walking from his home to the schoolhouse that morning, picking his way carefully through the slushy snow banks that lined the street. He heard a growing clamor of rumbling wheels and jangling harness coming up the road behind him and turned to look. Two horsemen riding abreast appeared over the crest of the bridge where the road entered the town. They wore the livery of a noble house over chain mail shirts; armored helms protected their heads and swords hung from their belts. Behind them came a team of horses pulling an enclosed carriage that was painted black with gold trimmings. The driver was not equipped as a soldier, but he wore the same livery as the horsemen, dark blue with a coat of arms sewn in silver. The carriage rumbled up and over the arch of the bridge, followed by a second pair of armed escorts.

Such an entourage had never entered Oakbridge before as far as Rand knew. He hastened toward the carriage as it pulled to a stop in the middle of the road; a crowd of excited townspeople was already gathering. As he came close, one of the riders held up a hand to silence the questions being called out from the assembled onlookers.

"We seek the residence of Bowin Porter," he said in a commanding voice. "Where may we find him?"

"I'm afraid you've gone past it already, sir," called Rand. "His estate is about two miles back the way you came."

The soldier fixed Rand with a keen stare. "Is that so, lad?" he said. "And who might you be, to speak so confidently in place of your elders?" Rand was conscious of the eyes of the crowd on him; those who stood between him and the horsemen stepped aside and waited expectantly for his reply.

"I'm sorry if I spoke out of turn, sir, but I'm his nephew, you see—Rand Porter. My father owns the smithy over yonder." He pointed to his house, hoping he hadn't got himself into trouble. Abruptly a shade covering one of the windows of the carriage snapped up and a man wearing a peaked hat leaned out to peer at him.

"Come here, boy," he said in a tone even more commanding than that of the soldier. He was slight of frame and elderly, with a narrow, deeply lined face and large pale eyes. Rand approached cautiously.

"You say you are Bowin's nephew?" the man demanded. Rand nodded. The man looked him over carefully. "Are your parents at home?" Rand nodded again. "Fetch them while we turn this carriage around. We will have need of them also before this business is concluded."

"Sir," said Rand, summoning his courage, "may I ask who you are and what your business is?"

"So, you do have some boldness in you, don't you?" said the man with dry amusement. "Intriguing—as to your first question, I am Minister Dorian, chief advisor to Lord Falconer of Westmount. As to the second, your curiosity will be satisfied at the appropriate time. Now go and fetch your parents, boy, quickly! Driver, turn this carriage about!"

Rand slipped and stumbled back along the icy street to his house and found his father in the smithy; he explained as best he could that an important stranger had come looking for Bowin and wanted to see Rand's parents as well. Eli muttered an oath and set aside his hammer and tongs. While he marched outside to see what the stranger wanted, Rand went to get his mother.

When they joined Eli in front of the house, the carriage had just succeeded in turning around and was rolling up to them. Minister Dorian appeared in the window and looked them over.

"Well?" said Eli with a trace of annoyance. The minister frowned in return.

"I am the representative of Lord Falconer," he said. "As you may or may not remember, your brother's wife, Cora, was the former Lord Falconer's daughter. Her elder brother holds the title now. News of her untimely death has reached us only recently. This news, along with certain ... matters of state, makes it imperative that I speak with Bowin without delay. The issue at hand concerns the three of you as well. If you would join me, we can go at once." He leaned forward in his seat and swung the carriage door open. Rand caught a glimpse of luxurious upholstery on two facing benches that could accommodate four people with room to spare. He and his mother stepped forward, but his father raised a hand to stop them.

"I have a smithy to run, and my wife and son have their own work to do," he said with growing irritation. "We don't drop everything at the beck and call of a stranger, certainly not because he speaks for a noble. We are freemen here."

"That you may be," said the minister impassively. "However, you are still citizens of Solethon, and when business of the kingdom is at stake you are expected to make time for it." The apparent leader of the armed escort brought his horse around to face them. He moved one hand from the reins to the pommel of his sword. The minister turned at the motion and waved the guard back, but the significance of the soldier's reaction was not lost on Rand's father. He shook his head in disgust and gestured for his family to board the carriage.

The ride to Bowin's estate was silent. The minister looked straight ahead and Rand's father stared out the window next to him. Rand had no choice but to sit next to Dorian, which he felt put him in an awkward position given the hostility of his father. He was relieved that the speed of the carriage afforded them a short trip.

Rand pointed out the gate to the estate as they approached it; the minister called to the driver and the entourage turned smoothly off the main road. They pulled up in front of the terrace at the manor house, but the minister made no move to get out. The driver climbed down from his place and trotted up the steps to the door. He rapped the knocker sharply three times, then stepped back and stood in a stiffly formal pose. Mrs. Tanner answered the door with a look of irritation that quickly melted into surprise when she saw the driver standing there in his livery. He bowed crisply and spoke in a voice more suited to a parade ground than a porch.

"Greetings, good woman. Minister Dorian, chief counselor to Lord Falconer of Westmount, seeks audience with Bowin Porter, having also brought members of Mr. Porter's family."

"I see," said Mrs. Tanner, looking past him at the carriage and the horsemen. "Please wait here; I shall inform him at once." She disappeared within. Bowin appeared at the door moments later.

"What does Lord Falconer want with me?" he asked the driver. The man stepped aside and bowed toward the carriage. Minister Dorian took that as his cue and disembarked to stand at the foot of the stairs.

"News from Solaria has reached us in the last week," he said. "Together with the unfortunate passing of his beloved sister, this news places certain obligations upon my lord that require your co-operation, and that of your family." He nodded to the carriage.

"Hmph," snorted Bowin. "A great lot of cooperation I've ever received from his lordship. As for his beloved sister, it would have been more seemly for him to demonstrate that love while she was yet living. What does he think he can expect from me now?" Some of the staff employed by the estate had gathered by now to see the visitors. Minister Dorian glanced aside at them in irritation.

"My business is best discussed in private," he said to Bowin. "All will be made clear. Regardless, I have traveled through the night to see you. May I at least find a courteous welcome?"

"Of course," said Bowin, his expression softening. "Forgive me, sir. These have been trying times."

"Indeed," said Dorian with a slight bow. "I quite understand — may we proceed?" Bowin nodded and the minister turned to the carriage, waving for Rand and his parents to join them. Together the group followed Bowin into the house.

Chapter 23

Let us persevere as we run the race marked out for us.

They were ushered into a sitting room with a large stone fireplace. Two hired men had just finished building a crackling fire under Mrs. Tanner's supervision to chase away the winter chill. Refreshments were brought, and then the household staff withdrew to allow them to conduct their business.

"You are aware, Bowin, that Cora's father passed away and her brother is Lord Falconer now?" said Dorian.

"Yes," said Bowin. "Three years ago now, was it not? My wife was deeply saddened by her father's passing. Perhaps you will find it hard to credit, but I grieved as well. He was a man of honor and I had hoped that in time he and I would come to an understanding. With his son I am afraid there is even less hope of that."

"I am afraid I must agree," said the minister. "Older brothers can be even more jealous and protective of a dear sister than their father at times, and that was certainly true in Thomas' case. He has softened little since you appeared at Falconkeep all those years ago. Perhaps I seemed just as hostile when you met me back then, but you must understand that it was my duty to reflect their position. Philosophically I was opposed to Cora marrying outside of the nobility, but on a personal basis I have always found you to be a man worthy of respect. In time, Cora's father came to see that as well, but his pride would not allow him to admit it openly." Bowin considered this quietly. Rand's father cleared his throat in the silence.

"These matters are important to you, Mr. Dorian," he said, "and maybe they are to Bowin as well. What I can't see is why my family and I had to drop our business in the middle of the day and be dragged here under threat."

"What is this?" cried Bowin. "What have you done, Dorian?"

"Your brother and his family are required for the issues that concern us today," the minister replied. "It was not fitting for me to bandy words with him in the middle of the street and he was reluctant to accompany me. In the interest of time I asserted the authority of the royal court. The sergeant of my escort grew somewhat agitated as well, but I kept him in check."

"Minister Dorian," said Bowin sharply, "perhaps the new Lord Falconer's wits have been affected by assuming his father's title, but he is not the king, nor is our valley a part of his ancestral possessions. You had no right to coerce Eli in such a fashion."

"For the first part you are correct, of course," said Dorian. "But as for the second, I am afraid you are mistaken. I did not exaggerate when I invoked royal authority—I am here on a matter of state that falls under the jurisdiction of the Solethonian court."

"Then perhaps you'd best explain it to us," said Bowin grimly, "before there are any more misunderstandings."

"I would like nothing more," said Dorian. "That is, if your brother will allow me to continue?" He glared at Eli, who scowled but nodded.

"Very well," said the minister. "King Anthon has been seriously ill for months. His physicians are surprised that he has not succumbed before now; at the least, they are convinced that he cannot last much longer. When he passes, preparations will commence for a Royal Gauntlet to choose his successor." He paused to observe the effect of that news on his listeners; seeing that he had their full attention, he went on.

"As you may know, Solethon does not rely on hereditary succession to determine who will wear the crown. In order to maintain the strength of the monarchy, our kings or queens are chosen by the test of the Gauntlet. Each noble family contributes a contestant and the winner rises to the throne. It is not quite so simple as that, of course; few people outside of the noble houses are familiar with the finer points of the laws that govern the Gauntlet. These laws are the cause of my coming to you." Dorian rose and stood warming his hands at the fire for a few moments. Then he turned to face them as he continued.

"Has it ever occurred to you to question where noble houses come from? At first they consisted of the rulers of the fiefdoms that united to create our kingdom. The first king was chosen by a council of these lords, selected by mutual agreement as the best qualified among them. They were concerned lest the selected lord favor his own people at the expense of the others, so from the very beginning they decided to continue choosing future kings by this means rather than allowing the title to become hereditary.

"The number of lords grew quickly as the years passed. Noble rank was bestowed upon military heroes, favored advisors, those who accumulated great wealth and influence by their own efforts, and so on. Although every noble house was officially eligible for consideration, in reality the descendants of the original founders saw to it that the king was always chosen from among their own ranks. This bred a growing discontent among the newer houses; what is more, situations arose more and more frequently where even the older houses could not agree who should be king. The threat of outright civil war loomed; at last a solution was devised that was acceptable to everyone—the Royal Gauntlet.

"The Gauntlet gave every noble house an equal opportunity, and its challenges inspired confidence that the winner would be the best qualified to be king. Over time a complex system of rules grew up around it in response to the disputes that inevitably arose. For example, the high level of risk resulted in a decision that only unmarried nobles should participate, so as not to add the burden of bereaved spouses to the considerable cost of the undertaking. Also because of the risk, and furthermore for the sake of ensuring a long and vigorous reign on the part of the winner, it was decided that only young adults in the best of health would be allowed to compete. Nonetheless, the number of deaths and serious injuries remained high.

"Therein lay a problem. Some of the noble houses were eager to advance their fortunes, while others had a tradition of honor or a strong fighting spirit; such as these would choose to compete regardless of the cost. But many houses already had everything that noble status could offer—money, power, lands, and prestige. A turn on the throne had many advantages, but also many burdens. Was it worth the lives of their best and brightest heirs? More and more of the greatest houses felt otherwise, choosing not to contribute a contestant when a Gauntlet was declared. If the Gauntlet was to remain a means of choosing our king from the most worthy candidates, something had to be done to restore universal participation. The regulations that were devised to address this problem are the cause of my visit."

"How so?" said Bowin.

"First," said Dorian, pausing to fill a cup at the sideboard and take a sip, "a rule was created that sent a cold shiver through the noble houses—any family that failed to contribute a contestant would forfeit their noble status. The king at that time, Garon the Third, was from a house with a proud military tradition. He had no sympathy for those who would shrink from a challenge, or from their duty. He pushed the rule through with all the power at the disposal of the crown and he tolerated no exceptions. His successor was from a family more sympathetic to the needs of their fellow nobles, though, and some accommodations were made. If the heirs of a house were too young, that house was exempted until the next time. If they were too old, they were likewise excused, as long as there were women in the family who were still of childbearing age. Only if a house had no apparent means of producing a future contestant, or if they had an eligible heir but refused, would they lose their rank.

"Those who have tasted great power are jealous to keep it, though, and inventive in protecting it. The definitions of 'apparent means' and 'eligible heirs' were widened to include the extended families of the noble houses, then widened again to include those related by marriage. There was little controversy over the changes—noble families tend to marry less and produce fewer children than commoners, and why should the law punish those who were simply lacking in offspring? The real miscreants were those who could have competed and chose not to. All of which brings us to today."

"What are you up to, minister?" said Rand's father. His demeanor suggested that he had a suspicion of what was coming. Dorian returned to his seat and looked at them all quietly for a few moments before answering.

"Cora's death was a tragedy for us all," he said. "However, it poses a serious problem for the house of Falconer as well. She was no longer young, but she still might have borne a child. As the sister of the present Lord Falconer, she would have qualified him for an exemption. His own wife died in childbirth, and their only son was killed two years ago serving in the royal army. A Royal Gauntlet will be upon us any day now and House Falconer will fall from the nobility unless he invokes the final exception—producing an heir from a family related by marriage. That is to say, you." He lifted his arm slowly and pointed at Rand.

Several things happened then in rapid succession. Rand's mother cried out in alarm. His father bellowed in anger and rose from his seat. Bowin interposed himself quickly to prevent Eli from doing anything rash. Rand suddenly felt light-headed, and before he knew it he had tumbled from his stool onto the floor.

"Wait!" cried Bowin. "Control yourself, Eli; I will not allow this to happen. As for you, Minister Dorian, your lord has no right to take Rand against his family's wishes. I have friends among the best lawyers in Serenhorn. They will soon put a stop to this madness."

"I suggest you contact them at once," said Dorian, unmoved by their outbursts. "They will tell you the same as I tell you now—the rules of adoption for the Gauntlet do not require voluntary cooperation. Lawyers! Who do you think writes the laws that they wrangle over? The great houses do. I will wait at your village inn until you have had the opportunity to consult with your colleagues; then we will meet again to conclude this matter. Do not keep me waiting long—I would prefer not to call upon the local magistrate to resolve this matter, but I will if necessary." He rose and walked to the door of the sitting room, then turned to address them once more.

"If I were you, I would consider the possibility that this is a stroke of good fortune, not a calamity," he said. "You are in shock; you have not yet realized what this means. The Gauntlet is dangerous, but Rand is young, bright, and in excellent health. As part of his training he will be enrolled in the Academy of Serenhorn, the finest school in this province. If he survives the Gauntlet he will be the heir of our house and the next Lord Falconer. By extension, all of you will be members of a noble family with the privileges and resources that implies. Such will continue to be the case even if, fates forbid, he were to fall. But lest we brood too heavily on the danger, let us consider also its opposite—he may not only survive the contest, but even win it outright. In that case, Mrs. Porter, you will be mother to a king." They all stared at him in surprise, rendered speechless at the audacity of such a thought. Dorian turned and left without further hesitation.

Chapter 24

When the Speaker restored the fortunes of the holy mountain,
we were like those who dreamed.

Eli collected his family in brooding silence, stopping only to extract the strictest promises from Bowin that the matter would be resolved quickly. Bowin followed them onto the terrace and prevailed upon Eli to wait while he arranged for a wagon to take them back to town. The minister had taken his carriage and left, and it would have been a long walk through the winter chill. The wagon was made ready and they climbed aboard quickly. No one spoke as they rode along the road to home.

They arrived in the village at about mid-morning. Rand's father returned to the smithy, and his mother to her kitchen. Rand resumed the walk to school that had been so fatefully interrupted. When he arrived, everyone was eager to find out what had happened after he climbed aboard the minister's carriage; even Widow Liston was caught up in the excitement. Rand declined, telling them that he was not allowed to discuss the matter. In the end they let him be and returned to the lessons of the day, which he struggled to absorb without success. All he had to do to lose his concentration was glance out the window; down the street he could see the minister's carriage, parked in front of the inn like a crouching spider.

Bowin had told them that he would send a messenger on horseback up the royal post road to Serenhorn. The man should reach the city in a day's hard ride, deliver Bowin's plea to his lawyer friends, and return with their answer. Allowing a day for the lawyers to do their work and for resting the horse, the reply should make it back to Oakbridge sometime on the third day. All that the Porters could do until then was wait.

As the time passed, Minister Dorian's impatience made itself known. Rumors circulated about his low opinion of the food, the drink, and the service offered by the inn. Rand's father pounded the hot iron on his anvil with suppressed rage, sending sparks flying across the smithy. On the second day Rand tried to assure him that he would remain faithful to his apprenticeship come what may, but Eli refused to discuss it. Rand's mother tried to maintain a sense of normalcy in their home, but she often looked to be on the verge of weeping.

Rand's family sat down to supper on the evening of the third day in a somber mood. Only young Denny was unaffected, attacking his food with gusto and chattering about the latest rumors in town concerning the visitors. Since he had been at school during the meeting at Bowin's house, Rand's parents had decided it was best not to tell him the whole story. The quiet of the meal was interrupted by the thunder of hooves coming up the road at full gallop. The sound came to a stop just outside the house; Rand's father rose to look out the window.

"It's Bowin on Challenger," he said flatly. "Rand, take your brother upstairs—quickly." Denny pouted at being sent off, but he knew better than to try his father's patience. Rand hastened him up to their loft; they each sat on their straw pallets and listened, straining to hear what was happening below. In a few moments they caught the sound of the front door opening and closing, then the scrape of chairs as they were drawn up around the table. Rand's mother asked Bowin if he wanted something to eat; he declined. Rand's father was in no mood for social niceties.

"Well?" he demanded. "What did you find out?"

"I came here as soon as my messenger gave me his report," Bowin replied. "My lawyers are well-acquainted with the rules pertaining to the Royal Gauntlet. Serenhorn hosts a number of noble families, and situations like ours are not uncommon among them. Minister Dorian is correct—Lord Falconer has the right to claim Rand as his heir."

"Blasted nobles!" exclaimed Eli, pounding his fist on the table hard enough to make dishes jump. "Pigs, gorging themselves at the trough! We are nothing but fodder to them. I build a life, sire a son, train him up to enjoy the benefits of my labor, and that craven brigand comes to steal it all away. How our father would laugh at me now! After I endured so much to free myself from the yoke of the Porters, my son is to be made a pawn of something even worse. And wouldn't father have been enraptured at the thought of his fortunes joining with those of a noble house? That is, after all, why he was so keen for you to marry Cora Falconer in the first place."

"Enough of that!" cried Bowin. "I married her for love and nothing else; it is for love of her that I die a little more each day." Denny moved from his pallet to Rand's, shaken by the anger in the men's voices.

"Yes—I know that, Bowin, forgive me," said Eli. "She was a good woman. I did not mean to speak any ill of her. But what am I to do without Rand? He was to follow after me and take up the hammer in his turn."

"Eli, listen to me," said Bowin. "It's hard for the matter to be decided for us like this, suddenly and by force. But think about the broader view, if you can. It is unlikely that Rand would have remained a blacksmith, Lord Falconer notwithstanding."

"Is that so?" growled Eli.

"Yes," said Bowin. "Don't pretend you didn't see it coming. I have no children, and now my wife is gone. There is no one but Rand to inherit the estate and all that goes with it. Do you think he would have continued on here as before in light of that?"

"So if Falconer had not stolen him from me, you would have, is that what you're saying?" said Eli bitterly. "I have seen how you covet him, how you have contrived to influence him over the years. But he had a good life and honest work right here."

"No, that is not what I am saying," said Bowin. "It is not stealing to give a young man his birthright. He is a Porter the same as I, and for all your stubbornness, so are you. Have you no love for the house of your birth? Would you see our lands decay into ruin or be handed over to strangers?"

"Of course not," said Eli.

"That's not all," said Bowin. "You speak harshly of our father, and I know you have cause to. But have a care or you will look in your mirror and see him looking back at you. You had to summon all your courage and your will to gainsay him so that you could follow the calling of your heart. Would you now turn about and do to Rand what was done to you? Can you not see that he does not belong in a smithy for the rest of his life? Have you ever considered that the calling of his heart is not the same as yours?"

"You cannot know that," said Eli. "He is young and frivolous. It is not my work that he has no taste for, but work of any kind. My responsibility is to drive his foolishness out of him and make a man of him. Besides, he has already begun his apprenticeship without a word of quarrel."

"Yes, because he loves you and would break his own heart to please you," said Bowin. "Because he has a gentler nature and would not defy his father the way you did yours. Look at him, look hard and see him for what he is. He is not a craftsman like you—no, nor a man of commerce like me. He is a scholar and a dreamer. Given the right chance, he could outshine us all. Though I would not have chosen for it to come the way it has, what Lord Falconer is offering may prove to be that chance."

"Hmph," grunted Eli, then continued reluctantly. "What if you're right, then? Supposing Rand is not fit for my shop nor it for him, what do I do then?" Rand's mother had so far held her peace. She took advantage of the pause to speak.

"I think Bowin is right about Rand, dear," she said. "Do not let that fret yer heart o'er much. Think o' little Denny. He's been kept close under my wing, so young as he's been, and ye haven't seen much o' him yet. But he's gettin' older now, and I think ye'll find he's just like you. He likes to tinker with things and make them work, an' he's not shy o' getting' his hands dirty. He'll take to the forge like a fish to water, wait and see."

"Maybe," said Eli. "He did well as my helper while Rand was gone. I suppose it's little use to argue over it now regardless. Falconer has the law on his side. We'd better go make our peace with that minister of his before a company of soldiers comes knocking down our door." There was a scraping of chairs again as they rose from the table. Rand's father leaned his head up the stairs and called into the loft.

"Rand! Come down here. We're going to see that fellow at the inn. Denny, come help your mother clean up the table." Rand gave Denny a hug and ruffled his hair; Denny smiled uncertainly, then the brothers climbed somberly down the stairs together. Bowin and

Eli stood ready by the door in their winter cloaks. Rand took his from its peg and followed them out into the chilly darkness.

It was a short walk from the house to the inn, and a quiet one. As Rand trudged along behind the two men, he struggled to come to grips with all that he had overheard. He felt foolish for not realizing sooner that he was going to inherit his uncle's estate one day — after all, who else would? Perhaps it was a blessing that he hadn't had a chance to ponder that and get his heart set on it. Now he would be snatched away to an even larger inheritance, though one that lacked the joy of close kinship and fond memories. If that was not distressing enough, there was the unspecified threat that he might not live to inherit anything, along with the incomprehensible idea that he might somehow become a king.

As they approached the inn, one of the minister's escorts could be seen standing in the doorway. Rand supposed that he was posted there to keep an eye on the carriage. When he saw the Porters approaching, he turned and called into the interior; then he stood silently and nodded to them as they passed within.

The small common room was lit dimly by a single oil lamp hanging from the rafters overhead. Warmth came from a crackling fireplace set into the left wall. At the table nearest to the fire, the owner of the town mill was sharing a drink with the proprietor of the general store. The storekeeper had gained a reputation lately for overindulging in ale; most townsfolk attributed it to the unfortunate incident concerning his daughter Lyssa. Around the table next to them sat the other three members of the minister's escort; they were playing a game of cards. The minister himself was seated alone at a table on the right.

"Welcome, gentlemen," he said calmly. "Please join me if you would. I trust you have concluded your inquiries?" Rand, Bowin, and Eli took the offered chairs.

"My messenger returned an hour or so ago," said Bowin. "My lawyers in the city confirmed your assessment of the situation."

"As expected," said Dorian. "Very well, then, are we ready to discuss specifics?"

"Before we do, I have a question," said Rand's father. "When you've answered that, there's something I want you to understand."

"Of course," said Dorian with a sigh. "Do continue, Mr. Porter."

"I had a thought on the way over here," said Eli. "Since the rules of the Gauntlet allow a noble to choose an heir related by marriage, why can't Falconer marry a widow who has a child of the proper age? He'd have the choice of several in a city the size of Serenhorn, I'd warrant. For that matter, why not just adopt an orphan? He wouldn't even have to bother about a marriage then."

"You raise a fair point, Mr. Porter," said Dorian. "May I say it pleases me that you have been able to look far enough past your feelings, understandable as they are, to consider the matter logically. I will address the question of orphans first, since the answer is relevant to both cases. Noble houses are not allowed to adopt unrelated youths to serve in the Gauntlet because such a practice might one day come to be abused—they might twist the law to allow adopting such heirs even if they had eligible children of their own. They have already shown reluctance to risk their own children, which is what necessitated the participation requirements in the first place. Remember too that the purpose of the Gauntlet is to choose our ruler from the best sons and daughters in the land. It would hardly be fitting to recruit an army of street urchins to compete for the throne. The council of noble houses was concerned that such things might easily happen once the door was opened, so to speak."

"I can believe that," said Rand's father. "After this business I don't think they'd stop at anything if they saw an opening." Dorian reddened and pursed his lips, but he kept his temper in check.

"Yes," he said tightly, "I concede that there are unsavory persons of noble rank, just as there are in any station of life. As for marrying a widow with an eligible youth, this could also be done even if they had children of their own. In either case, the nobility desires to preserve the dignity of their position. Stretching the definition of family to include relations that already exist is one thing; actively acquiring new relations to serve a practical need would be crass. Some further clarifications of the law have been proposed to help those such as Lord Falconer who have neither spouse nor children, but the lawyers have been haggling over the details for years; nothing would be resolved in time to affect the approaching Gauntlet."

"Sounds to me that nobles and lawyers deserve each other," said Eli with contempt. "Very well, you've answered my question. Now here's the thing I want you to understand." He leaned forward across the table and stared hard into the minister's eyes. "I have accepted the fact that I cannot prevent this from happening. Even so, though Rand is doubtless little more than a convenience to your master, to me he is my firstborn son—my blood, my heart, and my legacy. He is to be treated as a true heir of Lord Falconer's house, not as a bumpkin to be used and discarded. He must be given every chance to survive the Gauntlet—training, equipment, and good counsel. I won't have Falconer throwing him to the wolves. So that I can know that he is treated well, he must be allowed to send a letter home every week. If I should learn that he is being treated otherwise, I will come to Westmount and dismantle the noble house of

Falconer with my own two hands." He flexed his thickly-muscled blacksmith's hands on the table in front of Dorian to emphasize his point.

"Your concern for your son is commendable," said Dorian, meeting Eli's stare unflinchingly. "Lord Falconer, hard man and proud though he may be, is a man of honor. He will do no less for Rand than he would for his own son."

"All right," said Eli with a sigh of resignation. "Now what?"

Dorian retrieved a valise from beside his chair and took out a document. "These are the articles of adoption," he said. "You will sign them to indicate that you understand the law and release all claim to Rand. I will sign them on Lord Falconer's behalf to establish that Rand is his duly recognized heir in all respects, and that all of the Porters are to be considered members of his house. Tomorrow, Rand will accompany me to Serenhorn where he will be enrolled in the Academy."

"So soon?" said Bowin.

"You might remember that you have kept me here three days already," Dorian replied. "I am responsible for many of Lord Falconer's affairs, not just this matter, and I have been away from my duties for too long. Besides, as Rand's father noted so forcefully, Rand needs every day possible to prepare for the rigors of the Gauntlet. The contest will begin as soon as the rivers thaw and the snow melts from the mountain passes. We are fortunate that these events did not unfold in the summer—in that case, Rand would have had only a few weeks to prepare while the court finished organizing the contest. Should we not proceed as soon as possible for his sake?"

"You've made your point," Eli said gruffly. He took the quill and inkpot offered by the minister and signed the document. Dorian did the same, then stamped it. Now that the debate was over, Rand decided he could risk speaking.

"What should I bring with me?" he asked the minister.

"Only the barest personal necessities and any mementos you particularly value, my lord," Dorian replied. "House Falconer may be impoverished in progeny at present, but by every other measure you will find it quite wealthy. I took the liberty of bringing suitable garments with me, as you shall see when you arrive here in the morning."

"Did you just call me 'my lord'?" said Rand in shock.

"Yes, my lord, I did," said Dorian, inclining his head in deference. "Now that the articles of adoption are signed, you are the heir of my master's house. You are second only to him in authority and respect among all of his family, officers, and retainers. Until you come of age, your authority will be circumscribed by that which he has entrusted to aides such as myself. But we all will accord you honor, and defer to your wishes to the extent that our duty allows."

"Oh," said Rand quietly. He felt light-headed as he tried to absorb the fact that with a stroke of a pen, he had become a "lord."

"Well, if his lordship is agreeable, I think it's time we returned home," said Rand's father and stood from the table. Rand was embarrassed by the jab, but he could imagine the hurt his father must feel. He stood also and nodded to the minister.

"I'll be here at sunrise then, Minister Dorian," he said.

"Very good, my lord," Dorian replied. Rand cringed inwardly, dreading his father's mood once they were back home. Bowin stood as well; as he turned away from the table he gave Rand an exaggerated wink and tipped an imaginary cap. Rand couldn't help smiling in spite of himself. He turned to go and Bowin gave him a pat on the shoulder. As the three Porters reached the door, the guard on duty there snapped to attention.

"Have a pleasant evening, milord," he said crisply, keeping his eyes focused straight ahead as they passed. Rand sighed. If his life from now on was going to be "milord" this and "my lord" that, he thought he might go mad. His father and uncle ignored the guard and they all passed through the door into the darkness of the winter night.

No word was spoken as they picked their way across the mud and slush in the street. The silence convinced Rand even more that he was in very deep trouble. His uncle started making a curiously constricted snorting sound; Rand was about to ask him if he was ill when Eli began to do the same. They came to a halt in the street. Rand looked from one to the other, trying to comprehend what had taken hold of them. Suddenly they both burst into roars of laughter. The fit passed after a few moments; they stared at each other and at Rand, gasping for breath. Bowin made a grand sweeping gesture down the road with his arm.

"After you, milord," he said, making a mock bow to Rand. Then he and Eli dissolved into whoops of laughter once more. This time Rand was carried away by it himself, in no small part from the sheer relief that they were not angry with him. The tide of hilarity grew in waves; they stood there in the middle of the road, arms around one another's shoulders for support as the convulsions shook them. The miller's wife came up the street, apparently on the way to drag her husband home from the inn and in a foul temper. She stared at the trio in disbelief.

"Really!" she huffed. "'Tis a sad day when drunkards stagger down the street of our fair town. At least my Richard keeps his revels inside the inn." Her false assumption shocked them into silence for a heartbeat. Then the absurd look of moral outrage on her face set them off even harder than before. She stalked away in frustration.

The three wore themselves out eventually and resumed their walk home. Rand's father wrapped an arm around his shoulders and gave him a rough hug. As he felt the sincerity in the embrace and reflected on some of the things that had been said in the last few days by Eli about the importance of his eldest son, Rand realized consciously for the first time in his life that his father loved him a great deal. They smiled at each other, continued on to the house, and went inside.

Rand's father hung his cloak by the door and went into the kitchen to tell his wife what had happened at the inn. Bowin stayed in the parlor and tugged at Rand's sleeve, motioning with his head for Rand to step aside with him.

"When I learned what the lawyers had to say," he said quietly, "I retrieved your—that is, your parcel, as it were, out of my strongroom and brought it with me. I knew then that things must unfold more or less as they have, and it occurred to me that you would be back in the city soon. You can return it to Zekiel if you like; in any event I believe you should keep it near you wherever you go." He pulled the familiar drawstring bag from somewhere within his heavy winter cloak and passed it to Rand, who tucked it into his belt and covered it with the edge of his tunic.

"Thank you for remembering it, uncle," he said. "Did you give its contents more thought after we talked about it last?"

"Yes, lad, I did," Bowin replied. "While I'm not about to run off and join a band of mystics on some mountaintop, I will admit that there are profound implications to your discoveries. After all, I was the one who told you that finding a Stone Tear was a sign of destiny, and look at what has happened this very day. Perhaps I should heed my own counsel a little more closely. Cora—" A shadow passed over his face at the mention of his wife. "Cora often chided me about that," he continued softly. Rand touched his arm in a gesture of silent support.

Rand's mother and father approached from the kitchen. When he turned, his mother rushed to him and embraced him, weeping and whispering his name over and over. He held her tightly and comforted her as best he could. Bowin cleared his throat and said that he needed to get home. At that, Rand's mother managed with some difficulty to compose herself and they all saw Bowin off. Rand retreated to the loft to find Denny waiting for him.

"Hullo, Rand. Went to see that old man at the inn, did ye?"

"Yes, we did," said Rand. "Do you know what it was about?"

"Are they takin' ye away?" said Denny, his eyes wide with alarm.

"It's not like that, Den. The old man is from Aunt Cora's family, where she grew up away in Westmount. They need my help, see, to do something only I can do. Since their family and ours are related on account of Cora being married to Uncle Bowin, I have to go and help them. You can't turn your back on family when they need your help."

"I s'pose not," said Denny. "B-but Rand, will I ever see you again?"

"Sure you will, pollywog," said Rand. "Because I'm helping them, we all get to be part of their family. They have a whole pile of money, even more than Uncle Bowin. I'll be able to come and go as much as I like, or send for you to come see me. It'll be grand, just you watch."

"I guess so," said Denny. Then his face brightened with a sudden thought. "Can I have a pony?"

Rand laughed. "We'll see," he said. "I haven't even got to meet them yet, and you'll have to check with Da." Denny appeared much reassured and they both went to bed. Rand lay long in the dark waiting for sleep to come as jumbled thoughts chased one another through his mind. What would their new living arrangements be? He knew that neither his father nor Bowin would be willing to leave their homes and move to Westmount, but they were all supposed to be part of the Falconer family now.

He also thought of Lyssa. How badly he had once wanted to show her that he was the more worthy suitor! Now he was a member of the nobility, with wealth, power, and prominence that he couldn't begin to grasp, and what good was it to either of them? She had fallen into disgrace, leaving him with no appreciative audience for his good fortune. Of course, it had been plain enough on that night by the willow tree that his affections for her were misplaced; injured pride, not unrequited love, had made him want to justify himself in her eyes. As he thought of the hard and colorless life that lay ahead of her now—especially in contrast to his own turn of fortune—he found himself moved by a measure of compassion for her; with that, he drifted off to sleep.

Chapter 25

The Speaker sends poverty and wealth; he humbles and he exalts.

Rand woke in the gray hour before dawn, as his body had long been trained to do. He chose his cleanest and least-mended clothes; the rest, he supposed, could be kept for Denny to wear when he was older. As for personal mementos, he could only think of three—the knife his father had given him, the gold royal wrapped in a note from Aunt Cora, and of course the tablet of the Word. He gathered them quietly so as not to wake Denny and went downstairs.

His mother and father were already eating breakfast at the table and a plate was waiting for him. They said little until the meal was almost finished; then his mother reached over and took his hand in her own.

"I'm sorry I carried on so last night; I'm not a wilting flower of a woman, as I'm sure ye know," she said with a brave smile. "I'm so proud of ye, me sweet boy—I knew there were great things ahead of ye. Proud not just o' what ye're goin' to be, though, but o' what ye've already become. Some o' the young folk hereabout've lost their way of late, but ye kept yerself true. Promise me one thing more, though."

"What's that, ma?" said Rand.

"Keep yer wits about ye in this Gauntlet o' theirs and come through safe. I know if ye use yer good sense and take yer time, ye'll be fine. Just don't let that Porter family pride take hold an' send ye chasin' headlong after all the others."

"Yes'm," said Rand soberly. She patted his hand and released it. Now it was his father's turn.

"I know there's much I don't have to tell you, son, because you've been raised to do things properly—you know to work hard, train hard, and study hard. I only want to remind you to listen closely and not get to daydreaming—you might miss something that makes all the difference when you're out there alone in the race. There's one thing they might not teach you that you should think about, though. It's just as important as where to go and what to do. You have to know the others who are racing with you. What can you learn by watching them? What drives them or makes them afraid? Who can be trusted and who can't? If you can learn those things, you're halfway home already."

"Yes, sir," said Rand. He hoped he could remember all of that when the time came that he needed it.

"Don't forget to write every week like I told that Dorian fellow," his father said. "Your mother will be counting on it. Now, you'd better get going—you don't want to be late for your first day of lording about." He let his stern fatherly countenance slip for a moment and winked in memory of their jesting the night before. Rand smiled gratefully in return and stood to go. His parents went to the door with him and they each gave him a final embrace. He took his thin, weather-stained cloak from its peg, trying not to think about how homely it looked. Then he was out the door and on his way.

Rand was gratified to see that the sun was still behind the eastern mountains when he stepped outside—he wanted to be prompt for the sake of Minister Dorian. The muddy street had frozen overnight and crunched under his boots as he crossed to the side where the inn stood. Looking behind and to the west, he saw a heavy wall of clouds rolling up the valley. It looked like they were in for some snow. One of the guards was posted at the door when Rand reached the inn, just as on the night before. He snapped to attention and saluted.

"Good morning, milord. Minister Dorian awaits your pleasure at the end of the hall upstairs." Rand nodded, wondering if there was some response that protocol required him to give. He suspected that he would be bumping into such unknown details rather often in the days ahead. He slipped quietly through the doorway into the common room. No one was there at this hour; he continued up the staircase. When he gained the upper landing, he had no trouble finding the minister's room—the last door on the right was open, with a pile of luggage stacked beside it in the hall. As Rand approached, the leader of the guards appeared with a trunk and set it with the others.

"Ah, welcome milord," he said cheerfully when he saw Rand walk up. "Go on in. We'll be ready to leave soon—my other two lads and the driver are getting the horses ready in the stables behind the inn." Rand passed by him into the room; he found Minister Dorian engaged in packing his clothing and personal items. The man looked up and smiled.

"Lord Rand! I see you keep your appointments—that is an excellent beginning." He looked Rand over. "Please understand that I mean no disrespect to the life you have known until now, but if you are to be the heir of a noble house, you are expected to look the part. I brought garments such as are worn by the young men of the Falconer family; while I was waiting for your uncle to consult with his attorneys, I engaged a local seamstress who was familiar with your sizes to alter them for you. They are hanging in that wardrobe."

Rand approached the wardrobe self-consciously and opened it. Within were clothes of a quality and elegance he had never seen before, except perhaps from a distance when he visited Serenhorn. He quickly removed his own simple things and dressed in the new finery.

He started with breeches of gray corduroy, soft but thick and warm. Next came high boots of polished black leather. Then he found a tunic of dark blue velvet; it was trimmed with silver thread and the stylized crest of a falcon was sewn over the left breast. Finally he donned a thick, heavy cloak of the finest gray wool; it clasped at the throat with a silver brooch that bore the same crest as the tunic. When he was finished, Dorian came over to inspect him.

"There you are, my lord! Now you look like the young gentleman you will become. If you don't mind, I think it is best to leave your old clothes here. I have an empty chest set aside for your personal items." Rand took the drawstring bag and the purse containing Cora's gold coin and placed them in the chest; it was small but sturdy, made from polished oak and bound with brass. However, despite its small size, Rand's two keepsakes were all but lost inside it; the thought of the small items rattling about loosely during the long journey was worrisome to him. He looked around the room and saw where he had stacked his old clothes.

"Minister, I know you suggested I leave them, but I think my clothes would be handy for filling up this chest, at least until we arrive," he said. He braced himself for a lecture.

"As you think best, my lord," said Dorian with a bow before returning to his own packing. Rand could hardly believe it. It appeared that the minister was serious about obeying his wishes wherever possible. He laid the clothing on top of his mementos, then showed Dorian the knife his father had given him.

"Would it be all right to wear this?" he asked.

"Of course, my lord," said Dorian, inspecting the weapon appreciatively. "It appears to be a well-crafted blade and should serve you well for traveling. I doubt you'd find better in the Falconer armory itself." Rand smiled and added the knife to his new belt before buckling it on. He was pleased that a small part of his old life could find a place in his new one. Dorian pointed to a looking-glass in the corner and Rand went to see how he looked. A stranger peered back out at him—he could only gape at himself arrayed so richly. The leader of the guards stepped in from the hall.

"We're just about ready to depart, sirs, if you'd like to go on downstairs," he said, then stopped at the sight of Rand. "Well-met, milord! You cut a fine figure as a Falconer, if I may say so."

"That will be all, sergeant," said Dorian dryly. "Take Lord Rand's chest with you as you go. We will be there momentarily." The guard hefted Rand's new chest from the bed and headed downstairs. Dorian waved for Rand to follow the man and began extinguishing the oil lamps that were scattered around the room. When Rand entered the hall, he saw that the carriage driver and the guards had been busy while he was changing clothes—the pile of luggage had been taken away. He went downstairs and ran into Mr. and Mrs. Weston, the owners of the inn, who were going about their morning routine. They were startled at first to see a wealthy young stranger coming down the stairs, and doubly surprised when they looked closer and realized who he was. He smiled shyly and waved, but they just stared without speaking. He stepped outside to break the tension.

The morning life of the town was in full swing by then—children passed on their way to the schoolhouse, the local businesses were opening, and townspeople were pursuing their errands. A handful of women had paused in their labors to watch the flurry of activity around the carriage as it was prepared for departure. Rand noticed that the passers-by were walking a little slower and by less direct routes than they usually would; they wanted to watch the goings-on as well, without seeming to.

"If you would, milord," said the driver, holding the carriage door open for Rand. He stepped fully out of the doorway of the inn. As he came into view of the onlookers, there was the same double reaction as he had received from the Westons. First they buzzed with interest at the sight of a noble young stranger in Oakbridge, then there was an outcry of amazement when they realized who he was. He gave a little wave again and climbed into the carriage, at a loss for what he could say in a few words to explain the situation. How could he explain it when it was as incomprehensible to him as it was to them?

Rand sat on the street side of the carriage—he wanted to get a last look at his home town before being whisked away into the unimaginable future. As he watched the children walking to school, he felt some regret to think that he would never finish his final year and receive Widow Liston's commendation as an official graduate. Some of the children paused to stare at the carriage and the soldiers; Rand was grateful that they could not see him clearly enough in the shadowy interior to recognize him. Presently the carriage door nearest the inn opened and Minister Dorian climbed in.

"There now, my young prince, we are at last ready to free ourselves from this quaint backwater and deliver you to your new life," he said. He leaned forward to open a small siding panel that was mounted in the wall behind Rand. "Driver! We are ready—onward, and make haste! The weather is closing in."

"Prince?" said Rand in disbelief.

"Ah, yes—you've had no time to learn that part of it, have you?" Dorian replied. "Ordinarily one associates that title with the child of a king, eh? But under the laws of Solethon, children of the king have no more claim to the throne than those of any noble house. Thus the heirs of noble houses are all granted the title of Prince or Princess. On formal occasions you will be addressed as Prince Rand of Westmount, while in day-to-day life you will be known as 'my lord' or 'Lord Rand.' The title of Lord Falconer is re-served for your adoptive father." There was a lurch as the driver flicked his reins and signaled the horses to start pulling. The armed escorts trotted along with them in pairs before and behind, just as they had when Rand first saw them arrive in town. He noticed that a light snow had started to fall.

"I do hope that the roads are not too soft," said Dorian as he looked out. "We need to reach the inn at Gathford before nightfall."

"Gathford? I thought we were bound for Kerrin," said Rand. "Are we not going to Serenhorn?"

"Of course we are," said Dorian. "We are not taking the river, though—too slow. It would also require a special ferry to transport our carriage. We will follow the royal post road that runs along the eastern side of Serenvale. It crosses this road at the base of the slope where your little valley begins. Gathford is the last stop along the post road before reaching Serenhorn. We will be in the city tomor-row if the roads allow."

Rand thought back to his trip to the river. He vaguely remem-bered seeing a road cross his own as he reached the floor of Serenvale, but at the time he hadn't realized what it was. It had been getting dark and he was in a hurry to reach Kerrin—he had assumed that the paths leading away to the north and south led to local farms. He hadn't even known there was a royal post, let alone a system of roads created for its use. Every time the minister opened his mouth, he revealed glimpses of a world that had surrounded Rand all his life but of which he was completely unaware.

The carriage picked up speed once it had pulled free of the spot where it had settled during the last few days. They passed Rand's house and he caught a glimpse of his mother standing by the kitchen window. He waved but he couldn't tell if she saw him. Then he had to brace himself as the carriage pitched up and over the bridge across Oak Creek. They rumbled over the wooden planks and on down the road beyond; Oakbridge soon disappeared behind a curtain of falling snow. Rand wondered when he would see it again.

Even in bad weather over a soggy winter road, the pace maintained by the carriage was impressive to Rand. They were approaching the gates to Bowin's estate in a matter of minutes, a distance Rand was accustomed to covering in a half hour on foot. As they drew near, Rand peered through the swirling flakes of snow; with luck he might catch a glimpse of the manor house. He found himself curiously hungry for each morsel of memory and familiarity now that everything was changing.

His attention was drawn away from the hillside just then by something closer at hand. A looming figure stood by the gate; Rand saw after a moment that it was a rider on horseback, hooded and cloaked against the weather. It waited like a statue as they approached.

Just as the carriage passed by, the figure pulled back its hood and raised a hand in a gesture of farewell. It was Bowin, seated on his old friend Challenger. Rand smiled and waved; he tried to think of something fitting to call out to his uncle, but the carriage was rapidly leaving the gate behind. Apparently satisfied, Bowin donned the hood of his cloak once more and turned his horse toward home. Rand sat back, wondering how long his uncle had waited there for them to pass.

"A capable man, your uncle," said Dorian. Rand turned to him—apparently he had been observing the silent exchange. "While I can understand the former Lord Falconer's reservations about his daughter marrying a commoner," the minister continued, "I think he gave Bowin less credit than he deserved—as does the present Lord Falconer, unfortunately. If you've had enough of the view, my lord, perhaps it would be best to close up these windows now."

"I'm sorry, sir, of course!" said Rand. "These clothes are so much warmer than what I'm used to that I hadn't given it a second thought." He looked and saw that there were heavy curtains tied into rolls above the windows. He untied the knots and Dorian did the same. In no time they had closed the carriage's interior off from the icy wind and swirling snow outside. Dorian unlatched a small compartment beneath his seat and rummaged in it for a few moments before withdrawing a small oil lamp and some matches. He fitted the lamp into a bracket beside one of the doors and lit it, careful of the shifting motions of the carriage as they rolled along.

"There, that will give us light and a small measure of heat as we go," he said. "On another matter, while I am pleased that you were raised to show respect and courtesy to your elders, it is not proper for you to call me 'sir,' my lord. One of your station would simply address me as Dorian, or minister."

"Very well—Dorian," said Rand. The minister nodded and settled his chin on his chest, closing his eyes for a bit of rest. Rand sat there quietly as the time passed, trying to grasp the significance of his new titles. Rand Falconer was the name of a stranger, not himself. Lord Rand was an unlikely impostor. Prince Rand—that was simply impossible, unthinkable. Yet here he was, with no choice but to accept the burden of it as best he could.

In the Citadel of Solaria, the Vizier set down his quill and gathered up the plans he had been working on. Preparations for the Gauntlet were going well; the previous contest had happened before he took up the mantle of his order, and he looked forward to his turn at testing the little princelings. He thought of the weather outside and smiled at its irony—on the one hand, the winter storm almost certainly spelled the final doom for Anthon in his last struggles for life; on the other, the falling snow would add to the delay before the Gauntlet could begin.

He heard a faint rustling and moved to open the grate for Garrak. The ancient bird emerged slowly into the room and shook snow from its ebony feathers. The Vizier uttered the phrases of their ritual greeting perfunctorily, eager for news. Soon they faced each other across the stone table.

"I have waited long for a report, Garrak. As I told you, without my scrying glass I am doubly in need of your eyes and ears."

"Yes, master," hissed the raven. "I was delayed by the storm; even so, I bring news. The Others are still deeply concerned by the awakening of the Enslaver and their inability to discover where the restored tablet went. The one who walks as a panther has kept watch over the commoner who seemed to be involved, but he has learned nothing—the boy has gone on about his unremarkable life. At least, that was the case until today."

"What changed?" said the Vizier.

"My own scouts have watched him also, as you commanded," said Garrak. "We were intrigued by the arrival of a nobleman's carriage in his village several days ago. According to a report just relayed to me by one of my swiftest messengers, the carriage departed this morning with the boy aboard."

"Indeed? I wonder what has attracted the attention of a noble house," said the Vizier. "Certainly it would not be anything like the Enslaver."

"Agreed," said Garrak. "All the same, forces gather about this boy. My observers were not certain, but it appeared that he was clothed in noble finery when he left."

"If they approached him more closely, could they sense aught of the Enslaver?" asked the Vizier.

"Nay, master. We of the lesser orders are not so keenly aware of it as the Others. Still, if we arranged a confrontation, we might learn more," said Garrak.

"See to it then," said the Vizier. "But have a care not to make it too unnatural. We must remain discreet for now. So—what news of the candidates for the Gauntlet?"

Garrak recounted what his agents had learned about the princes and princesses of Solethon—the bold and the quiet, the weak and the strong, the upright and the corruptible. Thus in the dark heart of the Citadel the rolls of the contestants grew, while outside the snowflakes fell, building slowly each upon the one before.

Chapter 26

For your ways are in full view of the Speaker,
and he examines all your paths.

Rand estimated that more than an hour had passed as the carriage swayed and bounced along the road. He dozed a little from time to time but it was difficult to sleep with Dorian snoring on the other bench. The carriage struck a deep rut and swayed heavily, rousing the minister.

"Wha? Hmmm, where are we?" he said as he came to his senses. He pulled back the edge of a curtain and looked outside. "How long has it been?"

"About an hour," said Rand.

"We have several more to go before we reach Gathford," said Dorian. "Perhaps you have some questions I could answer."

"Oh, yes," said Rand, "too many to count!"

"Then please continue, my lord," said Dorian with a smile.

"What will the Gauntlet be like?" said Rand. "Is it a race, or a test of combat, or perhaps of skill?"

"It is all of those things and more," the minister replied. "It will follow a course over rivers and up mountains, even beyond the kingdom itself. There will be tests of many kinds along the way. The course as a whole is a trial of speed and endurance. It starts and ends at the northern city of Willowberg, along the upper Solus River. The first contestant to return there alive will be named heir to the throne."

"If the nobles aren't willing to risk their lives in the Gauntlet, why can't they just hold back and take things slowly—protect themselves?" said Rand.

"There are judges and monitors following the contestants throughout the race," said Dorian. "Malingerers are disqualified from the Gauntlet and their houses stripped of noble rank, just as if they refused to enter."

"Is the course the same each time?" Rand asked.

"With small variations, yes," said the minister. "I am hardly an authority on the subject, never having competed in the event myself. As I understand it, the contestants race to the foot of the western high plateau, then climb to the top, which is the land of the Amhara."

"The Amhara? Who are they?" said Rand.

"A curious people," Dorian observed thoughtfully. "Their own traditions say that they came to the plateau shortly before the founding of our kingdom, migrating from far to the south. No one lived there at the time because of the cold thin air on the heights, although there is some evidence that people like ourselves lived there in the ancient past. The Amhara are dark-skinned and tall, spare of frame but tough as iron. Common folk often call them the Runners."

"Why?" said Rand.

"They have a strange custom," said Dorian. "Among them it is forbidden to ride a horse or travel in a conveyance of any kind. They run whenever they need to cover long distances, and at running they are gifted like no other people we know. They could not best a horse in a sprint, but on a long journey they can maintain a steady pace for hours, covering many miles in a day with little food or rest. That is one of the reasons why they are used by the court of Solethon as royal couriers."

"One of the reasons? What are the others?" asked Rand.

"They have a rigid code of absolute honesty and devotion to duty," said Dorian. "Doubtless they are as corruptible by nature as any mortals, but they ruthlessly purge untruth and faithlessness from their midst. Once an Amhara passes from childhood to youth, the telling of a lie is punishable by death. Breaking a promise might also warrant death depending on the circumstances, but would at least result in severe penalties."

"They sound like a very proud people," said Rand. "Why do they serve our kingdom—did we defeat them in battle?"

"A perceptive question, my lord," said Dorian with a nod. "I do not think anyone who knows them would care to face them in war. No, there is some other means by which they were induced to enter the service of the king, but I have no idea what it might be."

The carriage slowed suddenly and turned to the left. Rand and the minister both pulled back their curtains to look out. Rand was surprised to see that they had already reached the mouth of Oak Valley and were following the switchbacks by which the road descended to Serenvale. It had taken him eight hours to walk this far on his first trip to the city—today they had made it in less than two.

"Very good," said Dorian. "When we reach the bottom we will take the royal post road north to Gathford. The post roads are well-kept; we should make good time."

"I am glad to hear it," said Rand. "The snow is starting to cover the ground."

"You are correct, my lord," said Dorian. "It doesn't look more than an inch deep yet, but now that it is sticking, it will accumulate quickly. Fortunately we are well on our way. Now, where were we? Ah, the plateau. The Gauntlet crosses a portion of it and then continues through the Badlands to the Sentinel Range, where the course returns to Solethon. From there it follows the upper Solus River back to Willowberg. The first contestant to arrive will become the heir to the throne."

"I've been afraid to ask, but I suppose I can't avoid it any longer," said Rand. "Just how bad are my chances of survival?"

"The Gauntlet is a difficult and dangerous test, my lord," said Dorian carefully. "I do not know precisely how many contestants are injured or, well, killed. I hear the Badlands are the worst—the nomads have a rather violent reputation. I am sorry that I cannot tell you more."

Rand pondered all that he had learned as the carriage wound its way down the turns to the valley. He could feel it when they reached level ground again; he and the minister each pulled back a curtain so they could watch for the intersection with the post road.

"Looks like the snow is falling heavier," said Rand.

"I believe you are right, my lord," said Dorian. "It bodes ill for our journey, I fear." Rand looked at the road and saw that it was now completely covered by snow. He could still distinguish it easily from the untrod ground on either side, but that might change as the day wore on. What they would do if they could no longer perceive its course, Rand had no idea.

Once the road straightened out beyond the switchbacks, they reached the intersection with the royal post road quickly. Now that he knew to look for it, Rand could not understand how he had missed it on his way to Kerrin. It was enough to make him wonder what else he might have missed on his first trip to the city simply because he didn't understand what he was seeing.

Their progress was faster on the post road, just as the minister had predicted. They pulled up under a stand of trees to eat lunch and give their escorts a rest from riding unsheltered in the weather. Rand was impressed by the hardiness of the soldiers—they looked unfazed by the cold and snow. He reflected that he would need endurance not unlike theirs when he faced the Gauntlet. As they were preparing to get back on the road, the sergeant of the guard and the minister conferred quietly apart from the rest of the party. Rand could not hear what they said, but their expressions looked concerned.

When the carriage returned to the road, he could see why. The way was becoming increasingly difficult to discern under the deepening snow. It was marked by fences that ran alongside here and there, and as a royal road it had stone markers placed at intervals of a few dozen yards. Still, there was a risk of wandering far enough to end up in a ditch or a bog.

They pressed forward at a careful pace for another hour. Rand fell into a doze as he settled into the soft padding of his bench; he was roused suddenly by a call from the sergeant which was answered by the driver overhead. The carriage pulled to a stop. Dorian was reaching for the sliding panel to speak with the driver when there was a light rap on the carriage door. He raised the curtain and Rand saw the sergeant leaning over astride his horse.

"Apologies, minister and milord," he said. "I must strongly advise you to make camp until this storm breaks."

"We cannot press on?" said Dorian. "Gathford can't be far."

"In good weather, I would say another two hours," the sergeant replied. "In this blizzard—even if we don't lose the road—it would take twice that. Up ahead the road leaves these scattered trees and runs over open fields for two or three miles. The danger of losing our way is great and there is no shelter. Soon the snow will be deep enough to make the going hard for both carriage and riders, and as for visibility, well, see for yourselves." He pointed into the distance. Rand looked and saw that the heavy snowflakes blended into a featureless wall of white less than fifty yards away. "My soldiers are stout lads," the sergeant continued, "but they can't ride all day in weather like this. Their horses can't bear it either."

"Very well," said the minister reluctantly. "Find a sheltered spot as near the road as you can. We will make camp and see what the morning brings." The sergeant ordered his men to fan out in search of a good place to take cover. In a few minutes they returned with news of a stand of firs that lay a hundred yards ahead. The boughs of the evergreens would provide better shelter than the bare limbs of the oak and elm trees closer at hand. The driver of the carriage stirred his team to life; even the short pause they had taken made it difficult to get the wheels moving again. Nonetheless, they were able to reach the firs shortly.

The driver pulled the carriage up alongside the outer fringes of the branches; it would serve as a shield against the wind and snow. From one corner of it the soldiers ran a sheet of canvas to the trunk of the nearest tree, staking the bottom edge to make a lean-to. The horses were tethered in a line on the opposite side, and thus a kind of square was formed by the trees, the lean-to, the carriage, and the bodies of the horses, with the branches of the trees for a roof. In the center of this space the soldiers dug a pit and built a small fire. Rand thought it was as fine a camp as any could wish for.

There were still two hours of daylight left when they finished building the fire and settled around it. They watched the falling snow for a time in silence; then the driver hummed softly to himself. Before long he started singing aloud. The soldiers apparently knew the song, for they joined in the chorus.

Shining Shannon, smile for me
Afore ye cross the distant sea
Come ye back so e'er ye can
And leave me not a lonely man

She's gone, she's gone so far away
For I could never make her stay
I stand beside the stormy sea
And hope she will return to me

Now tidings come o' Shannon's quest
Her fame is risin' in the west
The south adores her hair o' flame
And eastern folk sing out her name

She's gone, she's gone so far away
For I could never make her stay
I stand beside the rollin' sea
And hope she's not forgotten me

Alas, my Shannon took a fall
She will not come home after all
The trackless depths beneath the wave
Are now her lover and her grave

She's gone, she's gone so far away
And no one now can make me stay
I wade into the heartless sea
To find her where she waits for me

The melancholy refrain died away and the men stared into the flickering flames. Rand imagined as he looked from one face to the next that each of them had his own tale of love lost and heart broken. He thought about his own dashed dreams of Lyssa and felt a silent kinship with them as the wind blew and the fire crackled. Many bonds could tie men together—laughter, battle, good fortune—but the memory of beloved faces and treasured voices when far from home was one of the strongest. Rand fell slowly into a light sleep, stirred occasionally by snatches of song as one of the men led out in another favorite tune. He came fully awake at dusk when the smell of cooking filled the camp.

They made a decent supper that night in spite of the fact that they had not brought provisions for camping along the way. There was cured meat that was savory when toasted over the fire, dried fruit, cheese, and some bread left over from their lunch. They would have little more than scraps for breakfast, but that was a problem for another day. They sang a few more songs when the meal was over and then it was time to settle in for the night. The sergeant gave his men orders for standing watch. Rand and Minister Dorian retired to the carriage, where the padded benches made decent beds, though somewhat short. The driver and the guards who were not on watch huddled together for warmth under the lean-to, wrapped tightly in their bedrolls. Save for the shifting of the horses and the crackling of the fire, stillness descended over the camp.

Chapter 27

I am sending you out like sheep among wolves.

Rand's eyes shot open. What was that sound? Something ghostly, distant. He held his rapid breaths to listen. It was gone, nothing left but cold and darkness. Had he slept at all? Probably—his bleary eyes proved it. The sound came again—a wolf howling far off in the night.

He looked over at Minister Dorian; the old man was propped on one elbow, listening. "Let us hope that they are not overly hungry tonight," he said. "Or if they are, that they hunt somewhere else."

The wolf cried again. This time it was answered by others; their cries were much closer. The minister cursed and clambered out of the carriage.

"Sergeant!" he bellowed. "Muster your men. Driver, see to it that the horses are firmly staked. Lord Rand, tend the fire—keep it built up as high as you can. Every man must have a weapon in hand." He paused and listened. Rand scrambled out after him and dashed to the fire pit. Dorian grabbed the sergeant's arm. "What of the sentry?" he asked.

"Gerrold!" cried the sergeant. "Gerrold, are ye out there? What do ye see?" The wolves howled again—many of them, from every direction. Rand's hands shook as he hastily threw wood on the fire. The pack must have crept near in the darkness and surrounded them, he thought. A man screamed somewhere out in the dark. Gerrold, Rand guessed. Then there came the mingled sound of growling beasts and a man's muffled cries of agony, followed by a terrible stillness.

Rand looked at the other men in the camp. He saw horror on every face. Were they about to die? It was unbelievable. He remembered his duty and continued feeding the fire, drawing his knife and gripping it tightly with his free hand.

The brief calm was shattered as something plunged in among the horses. They panicked, squealing, rearing, and kicking in terror as the unseen beast scratched and bit at them. In moments they had broken free from their tethers—two of them plunged forward over the fire pit and through the lean-to, shredding it. The others scattered away from the fire into the dark. Now the camp had lost two of its four sides. Rand looked from one man to another in panic. What was he supposed to do now? He turned to the sergeant, who spoke urgently but with confidence.

"Minister, Lord Rand—into the carriage and secure it as best you can. Driver, you take over the fire. My lads, swords up and look lively. We are men against beasts and we will stand!" He took a flaming branch from the fire and held it aloft as a torch, motioning for the other two guards to do the same. Rand and Dorian scrambled into the carriage and latched the doors. The window curtains were flimsy but Rand hoped they would appear solid to the wolves. By unspoken agreement he and Dorian left one window open on the inner side so they could see their comrades.

"Look," said the soldier nearest to where the horses had been. He raised his flaming brand higher. There in the trampled mud and snow lay the broken body of a wolf. It had paid the price for its attack.

"I like this not," murmured the minister to Rand. "Wolves are shy of men and fire. Spooking the horses was a clever tactic—one I would expect of men, not beasts." The driver took his position by the fire and began tearing strips of cloth from his cloak; after watching him wrap a strip around the end of a branch, Rand realized that he was making proper torches for the soldiers. Rand stared into the darkness beyond the fire. Clusters of eyes flashed briefly in the light and disappeared again.

The driver finished his torches and distributed them to the men. At a word from the sergeant, they all tossed the makeshift brands they had been using into the darkness on either side of the carriage. Rand glimpsed a welter of gray fur as the wolves scrambled away from the flaming missiles. Some of the beasts yelped in pain as they were struck and burned. From the deeper darkness beyond the outer side of the carriage there was a great yowl of rage.

"That was no wolf," said the minister.

Any further thoughts he might have had were drowned out by a chorus of howls that arose from the wolves in answer to the eerie cry. They abandoned stealth and surged forward to the attack. The soldiers stabbed and slashed desperately with their swords in one hand and swung their torches like clubs with the other. Two guardsmen blocked the gap between carriage and trees on one side; on the other side the sergeant and the driver did the same. During the first chaotic moments of the assault, it looked as though the defense might hold. Then Rand felt something bump against the underside of the carriage; he leaned his head out the window and looked down. A dark snout was emerging from between the wheels.

"Look out behind!" he shouted. "They're coming underneath us!" He tried to open the door so he could strike at the new enemy, but Dorian pulled him back. The struggling men shot hurried looks at the new threat, but before they could react, the wolf wriggled free of the carriage and lunged at the driver. Unlike the soldiers he had no armor, and only a long knife in place of a sword. Faced by attacking beasts before and behind, he fell and was quickly overwhelmed. One of the soldiers on the opposite side of the fire leaped to defend him but it was too late. Meanwhile his fellow guard stood alone and outflanked. A wolf made a running leap and latched onto his throat before he could block the attack. He staggered into the darkness and out of Rand's field of view.

The would-be rescuer and the sergeant now stood alone. They faced the wolves back to back beside the fire. Rand could see tears streaming down the young guard's face as he anguished over the deadly cost of his error. By this time, dead and wounded wolves littered the ground—the pack's numbers were thinned, but still the soldiers were hard-pressed. The remaining attackers circled and feinted, waiting for the men to tire or make a mistake. The sergeant looked around quickly for an advantage. Rand saw his expression change as he had an idea.

"Onto the carriage!" he shouted. He leaped and grabbed hold of the ropes that tied the luggage in place on the roof of the vehicle. The other guard did the same and soon they had scrambled up to stand on top. The wolves howled anew, furious at the temporary escape of their prey. They leaped upward with snapping jaws, but they could neither reach the soldiers nor gain purchase with their claws. The driver's bench at the front of the carriage represented a path of attack, but the men succeeded in defending it for the time being. Some of the wolves took to lunging at the doors on either side, trying to break through to the passengers within. Each time they tried it they were discouraged by a flurry of sword thrusts from above. It appeared that the defenders had achieved a stalemate.

Then the great yowl sounded again from the darkness, nearer and louder than before. The wolves had attacked the doors enough times that the curtains over the windows were shredded, allowing Rand to see in all directions. The wolves halted their assault and pulled back a few paces from the carriage. Though Rand could not understand why, they looked tentative, almost afraid. The strange cry sounded again and this time Rand saw it clearly—the wolves nearest the sound looked behind them and shied away to one side. He drew little comfort from their skittishness, though—whatever was making that sound, he knew he had no desire to meet it.

The soldiers raised their torches toward the noise, trying to throw light on the unseen enemy. Rand noticed that the falling snow had almost stopped; only a few flakes swirled through the night air. The rasping cry was repeated, slower and quieter but closer than ever. Rand thought he saw movement at the far edge of the torchlight, but then decided his eyes must be deceiving him. It looked as though a portion of night was flowing toward them, an extension of the blackness like a tongue.

As it came closer to the light, the form took shape and the illusion was broken. It was a great wildcat, black as coal and as long in the body as a horse. The wolves drew back from it but did not run. Though it terrified them, it was somehow their leader. It stopped about five yards from the carriage and blinked up at the torches with slitted yellow eyes, its tail twitching behind it. Then it lowered its gaze to the window where Rand crouched watching. It opened its mouth in a roar, showing great teeth set in a blood-red maw.

"My lord, do you still have your knife?" whispered Dorian.

"Yes," Rand whispered back.

"I think you are going to need it," the minister said. Rand tightened his grip on his weapon and held it before him without taking his eyes off the cat. The beast roared again and sprang at the carriage. As it did so, Rand got a fleeting impression of something unnatural—the way the limbs moved was wrong. The whole shape of the creature seemed to melt and flow like wax.

Whatever it was, it was solid enough. The force of its impact with the carriage threw Rand and Dorian back against the far wall. A great paw with three-inch talons snaked through the window to swat at Rand but fell just short. Rand saw the blades of the guardsmen jabbing downward repeatedly in an attempt to drive the cat back, but their attacks had no effect. The beast withdrew its paw and screeched at him through the window.

He lifted his knife once more and crouched low, putting himself in front of the minister. The cat clawed at the door, which cracked and splintered but did not break. It pawed through the window again and this time Rand knew he was within its reach. He slashed desperately at the swatting limb and felt the blade make contact. The paw jerked back and the beast screamed again, but differently this time—it was a cry of pain, not bloodlust.

Rand didn't understand how his knife could succeed where the swords of the guardsmen had failed. In a moment of instinct he lunged to the window and jabbed outward. The knife plunged into the shoulder of the beast and it roared in agony. Rand caught a whiff of something scorching and saw a wisp of smoke rise from the creature's fur. It braced its hind legs against the carriage and kicked off, leaping backward into the snow. The men atop the carriage were knocked off balance by the force of the kick and they tumbled to the ground. Their torches lay guttering in the snow; by the flickering light Rand could see the cat twisting and writhing on its back.

Now that the soldiers were within reach, the wolves sprang forward to renew their own attack. The men barely had time to retrieve and raise their swords; they succeeded in fending off the first wave, but they were backed up against the carriage and surrounded. The torches were completely out now—the only light came from the campfire on the other side of the carriage. Rand could see the exhaustion in the guards' posture. The cat had disappeared, but it looked like the wolves would have their victory after all.

"Hai! Hai!" yelled a powerful voice from the darkness. A tall shadow raced into the midst of the wolves and struck blow after blow with some kind of stave. The wolves yelped and whirled to face their new adversary. Thus reprieved, the guardsmen counterattacked with a burst of renewed energy. Caught between enemies, the wolves fell quickly. One or two slunk away into the darkness; the rest lay dead at the feet of the defenders.

"Who goes there?" called the sergeant to the dark figure. "We owe you our lives."

"Most welcome to them you are," said a voice in a strange and melodious accent. "I do only my duty just the same. I be a courier of the king."

"Well-met, courier, and thank you for your timely assistance," said Minister Dorian, emerging from the carriage followed by Rand. "What brings you here at night in such weather?"

"I ran until darkness hid my way, then sheltered by the road," said the courier. "I heard the call of the *aganint* and knew I must come."

"Aganint?" said Rand. "Do you mean the wolves?"

"If so I meant, then so I would have said, small-man," the courier replied. "Wolves be dangerous, but wolves be flesh. To hunt wolves I would not have come, save I knew they hunted men. To hunt the *aganint*, though, that is a sacred thing, for the *aganint* is not flesh but a spirit of great evil."

"Evil spirit?" snorted the sergeant. "You mean that black cat? It looked real enough to me; felt real enough too, when it knocked us off the carriage."

"To be not flesh is a far thing from being not real," said the courier. "Look where the *aganint* fell—where is its body? Where its blood, or trail?" They followed the gesture of his arm, visible against the snow in the dim light. Rand could see no trace of the beast, even though he should have against that light backdrop.

"Fetch your torches and rekindle them at the fire-pit," Dorian said to the guards. They fumbled on the trampled ground until they found the branches and took them around the carriage to the fire. As he stood waiting with the minister and the courier, Rand thought back to his conversations with Zekiel.

"Is an *aganint* something like a—well, like a demon?" he asked quietly.

"The same, small-man," said the courier. "How know you of demons?"

"I heard about them in a tale," said Rand. The courier started to ask another question, but at that moment the two guards returned with their torches. In the brighter light Rand could clearly see the courier at last. He was tall and thin, with a broad forehead, a proudly arched nose, and tightly curled black hair. His skin was deep brown, as were his eyes. He wore a sleeveless woolen tunic under a sort of harness made from interlocking leather straps, and short woolen breeches. His arms and legs were bare but he seemed unaffected by the bitter cold. The staff he had used to fight the wolves appeared to have been hastily fashioned from a tree branch; he had probably cut and trimmed it for the occasion.

The courier knelt and studied the tracks in the snow, motioning for the others to join him. They could clearly see the enormous paw prints of the cat approaching the trampled area of the fight, but there were none leaving it, nor the kind of furrows and drag marks that would be expected if the creature had crawled away injured. They saw the place where it had fallen and thrashed about after leaping away from the carriage—as the courier said, there was no sign of blood. The bodies and blood of the slain wolves nearby made a stark contrast.

"It's an eerie matter, there's no denying it," said Minister Dorian. "Nonetheless, we have work to do. The dead wolves should be dragged to a place well away from the camp lest they attract other hungry beasts. Then we must find and bury our fallen comrades. Sir courier, you have already done much for us and I know you have duties of your own; our numbers are much reduced, though, and we cannot be certain the danger is past. Will you accompany us to the next town?"

"Honor compels me so, and your need also," said the courier with a slight bow. The minister thanked him and the party went to work.

Fir branches were cut to serve as crude sleds for the dead wolves, which totaled fourteen when all were counted. Rand helped the sergeant and the courier pull them a couple of hundred yards away from the camp. It took three trips. When they were done they found the minister and the younger guard at work scooping out three shallow trenches. The guard who had fallen during the fight was laying just beyond the light of the fire. Gerrold, the sentry who had fallen first, was found over by the snow-covered road. He had received the wolves' undivided attention and the results were terrible; Rand staggered away from the sight and vomited into the snow. The sergeant came and helped him to his feet, patting him sympathetically on the back.

"'Tis a rum sight, lad, make no mistake," he said. "Don't fret that it got to ye—ye're not accustomed to it is all. Mayhap no man should be." Rand nodded his thanks and wiped his mouth with clean snow, then went back to help with the graves.

When their grim tasks were done, the battered and weary travelers gathered around the fire. Two of the horses had been found dead also; the rest had fled into the night. No one spoke of what they would do in the morning, but Rand feared that a long cold march lay ahead of them. He looked up across the fire and found the courier studying him.

"Small-man, 'twas you that struck the *aganint*, yes?" he asked.

"That's right; I slashed its paw, then I stabbed it in the shoulder," said Rand.

"A brave deed for an unblooded youth, small-man," the courier said. "Brave for true. What manner of blade carry you, that can strike an *aganint*?"

"I'd like to know that myself," said the sergeant. "We hacked at that thing with all our might and it didn't even twitch."

"It's just a knife my father gave me," said Rand, drawing it from its sheath to show them. "The blade is steel, which I gather is rare, but there's nothing unusual about it otherwise. My uncle said it was a Hamedan blade, whatever that means."

"Please to let me see?" said the courier. Rand nodded and passed it to him. "Steel, yes," the man said as he turned it in his hands. "Not Hamedan, though. Hamedans be masters of steel from most ancient times, 'tis true, but this blade be Amharic. From the old time, away south. My people made them and bound them with blessing, blessing to strike *aganint*. How came you by such as this, small-man?"

"My father received it as a gift from his grandfather, who traveled widely. He said it came from the south—I got the impression he meant Gawlian country."

"So it may be, small-man. Amhara exodus pass through Gawlian lands, oh so many years ago," said the courier. He passed the knife back to Rand. "Wield it you have with courage; keep it you should with honor." Rand was moved by the courier's praise. He knew little about the Amhara, but he was certain that they did not bestow it lightly.

The talk moved on to more practical considerations as the men discussed what to do next. They agreed that another attack was unlikely— *aganint* or no, the monstrous cat had somehow been the driving force behind the wolves. With it gone and the pack all but wiped out, the danger was past. In light of that, they might as well wait for daylight; after all the perils and labors of the night, dawn was only a few hours away. They would face the issue of what to do about the carriage and its cargo then. After assigning watches and rebuilding what was left of the canvas lean-to, they did their best to get some sleep.

Rand was awakened two hours later by a tugging on his boot. It was the younger of the two surviving guards, rousing him for his turn on watch. He nodded and crawled carefully out of the carriage lest he wake Dorian. They were keeping the fire low for the rest of the night; this served the dual purpose of preserving their dwindling supply of firewood and improving their night vision, but it robbed the camp of heat. Rand stamped his boots to improve the circulation in his numb feet and gathered the comforting folds of his new cloak more tightly around himself.

He looked around the little camp and saw that the courier had joined the two soldiers under the lean-to. He had watched the man produce a light, thin blanket from a sort of pack-roll strapped to the small of his back when they were all turning in. It looked as insubstantial a defense against the cold as his clothing, but Rand could understand how someone whose life consisted of running tirelessly over long distances would need to keep weight to an absolute minimum.

As if he felt Rand's gaze, the man rolled over and looked at him. After a moment he rose and approached Rand, gesturing for him to follow as he moved a short distance away from the others. Rand had misgivings but decided it was best to go along.

"Small-man," murmured the courier at barely more than a whisper, "tonight you spoke of demons. Where be you hearing this word?"

"From a teacher," said Rand. "He was telling me a story about—" He hesitated—how could he explain without revealing too much? "A story about something called the Stone Tears." At the mention of the ancient fragments the courier's gaze took on a frightful intensity. Rand was glad he had been cautious.

"Know you then the Stone Tears?" the courier said.

"A little, I suppose," said Rand as innocently as he could. "Pieces of an ancient book that fell from the sky, yes?"

"Yes, small-man, yes and more," said the courier. "You did strike the *aganint* well with Amharic steel, so now I tell you a true thing of my people. Our brother you are not, but our cousin maybe, so I tell you this one thing. The story that fell from the sky in tears of stone—it was to find this story and know it that the Amhara came from far away. But the king of the land where it lay was friend of *aganint* and he brake it. Amhara knew the story long ago, in the time of the old world. Story was lost when world was lost. So Amhara heard and Amhara came, but came too late." Great sadness was etched in the courier's face. Rand was tempted to tell him more of what he had learned, if only to ease his pain.

"What is your name, courier?" he asked. The man roused himself from his bitter reverie and smiled at him.

"Name, small-man?" he said. "Royal Courier has no name; has only message. Name be naught but extra weight." Rand smiled at the jest, though he could tell the answer was also the truth. He thought of another question.

"Why does the cold bother you so little, especially if your people come from the distant south?"

"Amhara people be a mountain people even then, small-man," the courier replied. "On the high places we live now, air be very cold and thin. It not feel so cold to us as to you when we come down here below. Couriers train to be extra hardy, too. Now, little cousin, good night." He nodded to Rand and walked back to his sleeping place. The rest of Rand's watch passed quietly, with nothing but tending the fire to break the boredom. He was glad to return to the shelter of the carriage and wake Minister Dorian for his turn.

Then he settled onto his bench and knew nothing more until morning.

Chapter 28

Do not be defeated by evil, but defeat evil with good.

It was a cold and miserable awakening for Rand when he was roused from sleep by the voices of the others. He had never slept out of doors before and he found the day's chilly gray welcome depressing. His body was stiff and unresponsive as he attempted to rise, and he noticed that his new clothes did not feel nearly as fine after being slept in.

"Morning, milord," said the sergeant as Rand climbed slowly down from the carriage. Fresh wood had been gathered for the fire and the man was building it up for some much-needed warmth. Rand sat gratefully near the fire pit and looked around. The sky was still overcast but the snow had stopped. It was almost a foot deep on the ground, though—they were going to have a hard time of it on foot today, especially if they tried to carry much of their luggage.

Good news arrived a few minutes later—the young soldier and the royal courier had gone out in search of game for breakfast and found something even better. They returned to camp leading two of the missing horses.

"By my beard, but that's some luck at last," cried the sergeant. "How did ye find 'em?"

"The courier here is the best tracker I ever saw," said the guard. "He found some prints in the woods and followed 'em right up to these two, huddled together under a tree. One's Gerrold's and the other's from the carriage team."

"Good," said Minister Dorian, appearing from the direction of the latrine they had dug the day before. "When we harness them together, the horse from the team will show the other what to do. He'll be a little awkward in the traces, but it will make shift to get us to Gathford."

They all pitched in to get the horses harnessed. None of them were very skilled at it, but the soldiers had helped the driver often enough that they were able to do a passable job. The sergeant and his remaining guard would ride on the driver's bench and steer the carriage while Rand and the minister rode inside as before. The courier would not ride at all, of course, but made ready to run along-side without complaint. They doused the fire and set out as quickly as they could, eager to leave the scene of terror and death behind.

"I'm glad he's willing to stay with us," said Rand to Dorian as he watched the courier trot easily along beside them. "He has a calm about him that I find reassuring."

"Indeed, my lord," said the minister. "The Amhara are an un-flappable people, and the Royal Couriers are selected from among their best. We are fortunate to have his company—even more fortu-nate that he came when he did."

"Do you think he's right—was that cat thing a demon?" said Rand.

"My first instinct would be to call that base superstition," said Dorian. "Upon reflection, however, it must be admitted that the whole affair defies a reasonable explanation. Why did those wolves attack us? There are plenty of farms nearby where they could have had a sheep or a cow with far less trouble. And what was a wolf pack doing under the command of a wildcat? Cats are solitary hunters, and aside from that, beasts of different kinds never hunt together. Demon or no, something unnatural was at work. I suppose we must simply accept it as a mystery for now. In any event, we should reach Gathford in two hours or so; a hot meal in a nice little inn will do wonders for our spirits."

Rand sat quietly as the carriage pushed on through the snow. He returned again and again to the memory of the cat as it looked at him. With its size and strength, it could easily have leaped atop the carriage and brought down the two guards. Once they were dispatched, the beasts could have dealt with Rand and Dorian at their leisure. Instead, the cat had come straight for him—he could not believe it was a coincidence. If the Word was real, so must be the demons that had labored with Vincitor the Mad to destroy it. They were real, they had found him, and they were angry. Rand was not optimistic about his chances for survival, even with an *aganint* knife at his side.

The Vizier had gone to bed with the breaking of day; he cursed aloud into the darkness when he was awakened by Garrak rapping at the grate. He was tempted to stay in bed and let the bird fidget in the ventilation shaft until nightfall, but he knew better than to indulge the impulse. It was not wise to test the patience of dark spirits, servants though they may be. He rose reluctantly and donned a robe before going to the study.

When he opened the grate, Garrak entered the room slowly. The Vizier was surprised—he had assumed that the visit must be urgent for it to come in the daytime. The raven was reluctant somehow as it walked across the stone floor and hopped at last onto the table. Something must have gone very wrong.

"What is it, Garrak?" he said, affecting an air of nonchalance he did not feel. The raven waited in silence for a time, looking about the study. He was about to reprimand it when it spoke.

"I bring tidings from the north, master. Strange tidings indeed."

"Go on," said the Vizier.

"I went to arrange a confrontation with the commoner boy as we had planned," said Garrak. "I caught up with his party along the post road to Serenhorn when they camped because of the weather. I then recruited a cooperative pack of wolves to attack the camp. Before we could proceed, I was... interrupted."

"By whom?" said the Vizier sharply.

"By the Other who first discovered him, the panther," Garrak replied. "He had followed the party ever since their departure, and insisted on leading the attack."

"But I gave explicit instructions that the confrontation must appear natural!" said the Vizier in frustration. "How is a beast from a land many leagues distant from our own supposed to appear natural, especially when leading a pack of wolves?"

"I understand, master," said Garrak, hanging its head. "I tried to dissuade the Other, but he was—he was most insistent. They are of a higher order; I was compelled to obey."

"I must consult my spirit-guides when we are through here," said the Vizier half to himself. "This sort of interference is intolerable! We must work together if we are to succeed. Well, that is a matter for another time—what happened?"

"The attack was going well, master," said Garrak. "The boy's party included an escort of four soldiers, and two of them were killed quickly. Their horses were driven off and the carriage driver slain. Many of the wolves had been lost but that was of no concern. I remained at a distance, listening for any talk among the humans that might tell us their purpose. They were trapped in and atop their carriage with nowhere to turn. I had already learned one thing—the old man who appeared to be in charge referred to the boy as Lord Rand."

"Lord Rand? I've never heard that name mentioned among the noble ranks before," said the Vizier. "So our farm boy is not just a farm boy after all—that or he has had some change of fortune. Continue."

"Our goal was to flush him out into the open where we could test him and see what manner of human he was," said Garrak. "The wolves were few by now, however, and the soldiers kept driving them back. The Other tired of the stalemate and moved to intervene."

"As I feared he would," said the Vizier.

"And I, master," said Garrak. "He was brutal—savage. He caught sight of the boy in the carriage and instead of dispatching the soldiers, he tried to rip the boy from his hiding place by tooth and claw. I wonder if his hatred of the Enslaver took mastery of him. The soldiers tried to drive him back with their swords, but the blows had no effect of course."

"Of course," said the Vizier.

"I could not see clearly what happened just then," Garrak continued, "but the Other drew an arm back from the carriage and cried out in what sounded like—sounded like pain."

"Pain? The spirit-kind do not know physical pain," said the Vizier in disbelief.

"Well do I know that, master," said Garrak, "It must have been another kind of pain. I did see what happened next, though. The boy appeared at the window of the carriage with a knife and struck the Other. The Other cried out again and leaped away. The torches of the soldiers failed and I could no longer see with mortal eyes how the battle fared. With my spirit-sight, though, I beheld the fate of the Other. He—he was banished, master."

"No!" the Vizier whispered.

"Yes!" cried Garrak in distress. "Cast into outer darkness, thrown from the earthly plane into shadow, from which he may not return in this age of the world."

"How could that be?" said the Vizier.

"It must have been the blade, master," said Garrak. "In former ages the thralls of the Enemy would sometimes bind power into an object that could be used against us. The knife must have been such, come down the years from the world of old."

"And this farm boy become 'lord,' this one who treats with the Enslaver, has such a weapon?" said the Vizier. "Much indeed gathers around him, Garrak. I think the Enemy has chosen him to oppose us in some way; we must deal with that. What happened then?"

"I do not know, master," said Garrak. "When the Other fell, I fled. I had to return here, to tell you this tale."

"I agree it was vital information, Garrak," said the Vizier, "but not so urgent that I wouldn't want you to stay and see how it all ended. What were you thinking?"

"I could not stay!" cried the raven in agitation. It fluttered and squirmed. The Vizier thought that it was edging away from him— but why? "I was compelled to come," it continued. "Compelled! To tell a tale that is to be finished by another ..."

"Another? What do you mean?" said the Vizier with growing unease.

"My part is finished; I must defer to one greater than I!" The bird squawked and bolted for the opening of the grate. Before the

Vizier could react, it had disappeared. A chill ran down his spine. Who or what was coming to see him?

The oil lamp he had lit after rising from bed grew dim. A kind of smoke appeared in the air, dark gray with a red glow at its core. The Vizier peered into the cloud; his mind raced through charms and protections that might ward off a hostile spirit, but there was no time. He saw something small and white in the center of the cloud, and after a moment he could tell it was growing larger. With a mind-wrenching shift in perspective, he realized that it was not tiny but very far away. Though the far wall of the room was only ten feet in front of him, the center of the cloud stretched into a limitless distance in an entirely different frame of reference

The object continued to approach; presently the Vizier could see that it was a human-like form, walking toward him through the cloud. He could do nothing but watch and wait. Soon it stood before him, a being of glittering white. Its skin was covered in very fine, iridescent scales. The face was elegantly molded but cruel, its only color found in blood-red lips and the burning coals of its eyes. It smiled at him, revealing razor-sharp teeth.

"Greetings, mortal," it said. The voice, like the face, was both beautiful and terrible. The Vizier's instincts screamed for him to flee, but he summoned his will and met the being's gaze.

"Are you—are you the one I serve?" he croaked. The figure laughed mockingly.

"A double-edged question. You will serve me, but I am not the one of whom you speak. He does not sully himself by treating with the likes of you. Be thankful that you will never see him face to face while yet you walk upon the earth."

"But my order has been allied with him for centuries," said the Vizier. "We seek the common goal—to free all life, all thought from the chains of the Enemy. Why would he scorn those who share his vision?"

"What are these childish ideals?" said the figure dismissively. "You know better than that if you would but use the meager crumb of wit that your kind possesses. Ours is not freedom of equality but freedom for strength to express itself. Each should rise as his power allows and supersede the lesser. Have you not been instructed so?"

"Yes, but—" The figure silenced him with a raised finger.

"If the strong rise and trample the weak, why then, he is the strongest and tramples all. How claim you common cause with such as him? If you embrace his truths, you become stronger and wiser, rising perhaps to master all your race. Yet even then you remain first among beasts, your throne atop the dung-heap. Forget not your place!"

"I understand," said the Vizier as humbly as he could.

"You most assuredly do not," said the fiend with a cold chuckle. "I look forward to the day of your... enlightenment. No matter— today, you answer to me. I am greatly displeased."

"How so?" said the Vizier, drenched with perspiration and struggling against his body's animal fear.

"The changelings that walk among you, the ones you call the Others—I am the captain of their host," said the being. "One of my faithful servants was cast down into banishment today. Your pitiful stratagems played a part in this, I deem."

"Not so, lord," cried the Vizier. "I merely set a trap to flush out a possible adversary. The Other chose to intervene. I did not ask for his help, nor did I want it."

"Help?" said the creature. "Still you persist in overestimating your importance. My legions do not help your kind. They do as they see fit, and as I command. You fumble clumsily toward a dim understanding of your opposition and my servant pays the price. Next time, do not be so stupid!" The demon's eyes blazed and the Vizier felt a burning agony in every nerve-ending of his body.

"I obey," he gasped. The sensation faded.

"Good," said the demon. "To ensure that things proceed more intelligently from now on, you will report directly to me. Take no action, give no command, without my leave. We must discover how this non-entity obtained a bane-blade and how we might neutralize his threat. Yet as events have shown, we must watch and listen, not strike untimely."

"Yes, lord," said the Vizier. "By what do I call you?" The demon laughed again.

"O-ho! I do not give my name so lightly," it said. "Names are power. Still, I suppose you must call me somehow. When you desire audience, you may refer to me as Lupus."

"By your command, Lupus," said the Vizier.

"That will do for now," said Lupus. "Until we speak again, do no more with the boy than watch. Your other duties should keep you busy enough." The figure turned and walked away into the trans-dimensional distance from which it had come. The red and gray fume folded in upon itself and disappeared. Exhausted, the Vizier collapsed across the stone table and covered his face with his arms as his body trembled uncontrollably.

Chapter 29

Those who do right choose their friends carefully,
but the path followed by the wicked leads them astray.

Rand's carriage picked its way along the buried post road at a slow but steady pace. The party soon reached the open grassland that had caused them to seek shelter the night before; Rand could see why the sergeant had advised them not to proceed. The wind had swept unhindered across the fields, sculpting the snow into twisted mounds and obliterating any sign of the path. In the absence of falling snow they were able to steer by the widely spaced marker stones; trying to cross in the midst of a blizzard, they might have gotten lost in minutes.

The drifts made the going even slower than before, but in time the road turned closer to the shelter of the foothills at the base of the valley's eastern wall, where trees were more closely spaced again. The snow was still deep but at least they had no trouble discerning where the road lay. After an hour or so they came to scattered farmhouses. Rand saw the ribbons of smoke rising from their chimneys and felt a flood of relief. They had passed through storm and terror, coming once more into lands tamed by men.

Before long the road led them down into a valley where a small river flowed from the mountains. A village about the size of Oakbridge lay spread out below them. Rand tapped the dozing minister on the knee and pointed.

"Ah, Gathford!" said Dorian. "Be of good cheer, my lord. Soon we will have a hot meal in front of us." The town looked like a confection under its fresh blanket of snow. The few people out on the street stopped to wave as the carriage passed, and a dog ran alongside the courier, barking and wagging with excitement. They pulled into the dooryard of the inn, a large circle where two other carriages were already parked. Rand took note of how the town was shaped by the frequent traffic that passed through, despite its small size.

The courier scuffled playfully with the dog for a few moments before sending it on its way. The man had kept pace with them all morning, and yet Rand saw little sign of fatigue in him as they left the carriage and gathered by the door to the inn. A stable boy came out to take care of their horses and Dorian walked over to speak with him.

"We'll need a fresh team if we can get it," he said. "These two are not well matched, and they've had a hard time of it besides. A driver and new mounts for my guards would be even better. We were attacked by wild beasts in the night."

"So I see," said the youth, inspecting the damage the demon-cat had done to the carriage. "We'll do what we can, my lords; maybe we can mend your carriage a wee bit too."

"Good lad," said Dorian. "We'll be waiting inside when you know something." The young man tipped his cap and began unharnessing the horses. The minister turned to address the royal courier.

"Sir courier, we offer our thanks again for your help in our great need, and for remaining with us this far. We have delayed you long enough, but will you allow me to buy you a meal?"

"Most welcome your thanks and your offer," said the courier, "but neither be needed. For the thanks, I helped gladly; for the meal, my keep is charged to the king where'er I go. Let us enter and be refreshed." Dorian nodded and they all went inside.

The common room was large and well-filled, Rand observed—more evidence of the busyness of the post road. The patrons showed interest in the arrival of the courier, but it was plain that they were accustomed to seeing members of his service. Dorian and the two guardsmen settled around one of the few empty tables. Rand was about to join them when the courier tapped his shoulder.

"Small-man, perhaps you break your fast with me?" he said. "I not be here long—must eat lightly and run far." Rand nodded. He turned to his companions and shrugged; they looked even more surprised than he was.

The courier led him to a small table by the bar that was apparently reserved for the use of the Royal Courier corps. As he sat, he felt a pause in the hum of conversation in the room. A quick glance around confirmed that there were many eyes upon the strange pair, but after a moment the other patrons returned to their own business with feigned indifference.

"One might think we sprouted wings and grew horns from our heads, eh, small-man?" the courier said with a chuckle. Rand smiled in return. "No matter," the courier continued. "If it not be offending you, I would ask a thing."

"Of course," said Rand. "Ask whatever you like."

"I look at you, you seem not one used to carriages and fancy clothes," the courier said. "How came you to be with these folk, and styled a noble yourself?"

"You see well," said Rand. "I was a commoner until two days ago. I've been adopted by a nobleman to serve his house in the Royal Gauntlet."

"O-ho! A new prince and a racer too," said the courier. "Fortune smiles on you many times, small-man. Is it always so?"

"Not until lately," said Rand. "My uncle warned me such things might happen, though, when—" He stopped himself.

"When what, small-man?" said the courier, observing him watchfully. Once again Rand felt the urge to confide in this man. He sensed a kinship between them—it was absurd in light of their vast differences, but he could not shake it.

"Last night you said we were like—like cousins," he said quietly, leaning closer so no one else could hear. "Can I trust you with a secret?"

"A courier betrays not," said the Amhara somberly. "Speak what you will."

"My uncle warned me that big changes were in store—for one who found a Stone Tear," said Rand. The courier's eyes grew wide.

"So, small-man, now things be clearer," he said. "'Tis a mighty thing came to you, and mighty things followed. 'Tis fitting that it be so. And now what say you? Having held it, do you honor what it once spoke?"

"I do," said Rand, "though I do not know all that it means."

"I called you cousin," said the courier. "Now I call you brother." He reached across the table and gripped Rand's hand. Rand smiled and returned the pressure. The innkeeper came to their table with bowls of hot porridge for each of them. They ate for a while before Rand decided to speak again.

"There is more to tell," he said.

"So I see upon your face," said the courier. "No place to say it here, though, and no time for me to listen. When you run the high country in the Gauntlet, I will run beside you. Tell me then." He finished his porridge and a cup of water, then stood to go. Rand nodded and watched him leave before taking his bowl and moving to the table with Dorian and the others.

"What was that?" said the sergeant, apparently speaking for the others.

"I don't know exactly," said Rand carefully. "I guess he wanted to know more about me. He could tell I wasn't born a noble, as I reckon anyone could."

"Not necessarily," said Minister Dorian. "You have acquitted yourself well so far, my lord. I think you will quickly adapt to your new place in life. What did he say as he left?"

"I suppose you could say we are friends now," Rand replied. The two soldiers burst out laughing at the absurdity of the idea, but were cut short by a stern gesture from Dorian.

"That is a rare privilege, my lord," he said. "To my knowledge there are few men in Solethon who could say the same of a royal courier. I think perhaps Lord Falconer has made a better bargain than he hoped." Rand looked at the table, wishing that the subject would change to something besides him. He was relieved when the stable boy came in and approached them.

"Good morning, gentle sirs," he said. "I've brought word from the owner of the stable. We can trade your two horses for a fresh team at little cost. He can get two more that're suitable for your guards, but with it bein' winter and all, they'll be priced rather dear."

"I understand," said Dorian. "We can accommodate that, if it's not too outrageous. What about a driver?"

"If you're agreeable, sir, I could do it," said the stable boy. "I'll cost you less than others would; you'll save money on the horses, too, if I use one to ride back on—it'd be the price to borrow rather than buy, if you take my meaning."

"Very good," said Dorian. "Make the arrangements. We want to leave as soon as the horses are ready." The boy bowed and hurried off. "What do you think, sergeant?" Dorian said to the soldier. "Should we send word to the city for reinforcements and wait here until they arrive?"

"I wondered the same meself, minister," the sergeant replied. "I think we'll be all right, though. We'll make Serenhorn before dark, and the country betwixt here and there is pretty well settled."

"I'll trust your judgment, then," said Dorian. "I'd rather not lose another day waiting for them here." They finished the meal and settled their bill. The stable boy came to collect them soon after; he acted as business-like as he could, but Rand could tell he was brimming with excitement to drive a nobleman's carriage into the city.

When they stepped into the dooryard they found the carriage waiting with the new team in place and expertly harnessed. Someone had scraped away the splintered wood on the door, tacked on reinforcing strips of wood trim, and covered the whole with a fresh coat of black paint so it would blend better with the rest of the carriage. The shredded remains of the fine curtains had been replaced with squares of plain cloth. They might not be stylish, thought Rand, but they were functional. He was impressed by the speed and quality of the work overall.

The stable boy climbed into the driver's seat and the two guards mounted their new horses. Rand and the minister took their places inside the carriage and the party set out onto the road. Everyone was in much better spirits than when they had first arrived in town. The weather was clearing and they went at a lively pace as they left Gathford behind.

Chapter 30

Do not be overly impressed when others grow rich, when the splendor of their houses increases; for they will take nothing with them when they die, their splendor will not follow them into the grave.

The houses along the way were closer together with each passing mile. The road left the foothills of the eastern mountains and bore northwest toward Serenhorn. They pressed on through villages that became larger and more numerous as they drew nearer to the city. It was just after noon when they came into the outlying districts and wound their way through the busy city streets.

Rand tied back the curtain over his window so he could watch their progress. He felt a strange shift of perspective to be rolling along inside one of the carriages that filled the avenues instead of trying to dodge between them. After a while he saw a signpost with a familiar name.

"Hornside Way," he exclaimed. "Are we going straight to the Academy, Minister?"

"No, my lord, but very nearly," Dorian replied. "The Falconer family maintains a house on Ridge Road just below the school. It is a convenient place to stay during visits to the city, and young Falconers live there while they attend the Academy."

"So I'll live there," said Rand. "Will there be anyone else?"

"Yes, my lord," said Dorian. "The butler, the cook, two footmen, and a contingent of guardsmen."

"What about you?" said Rand.

"I will visit when I can, but in the meantime I must return to Westmount and carry out my duties for Lord Falconer," said Dorian.

"My new father," said Rand cautiously. "When will I meet him?"

"Today, my lord," said Dorian. "He has come into the city to meet you and get you settled properly at the Academy. After that he must return to his fief and the affairs of state."

"Will he be happy to see me?" asked Rand.

"Lord Falconer is not a very warm and affectionate man, especially with the losses he has suffered in recent years," said Dorian. "You may not find him kind, but I think he will be satisfied when he takes the measure of his new son."

They moved along with the many wagons and carriages that clattered up Hornside until they reached Ridge Road and turned onto it. As they ascended the steep hill toward the Academy, the carriage titled back more and more, its forward progress slowing as the horses struggled against the grade. Rand looked from one house to another, making a private game of trying to guess which one would be his new home.

"There it is, my lord—the city house of the Falconers," said Dorian. He pointed to an imposing manor on the right that was built from blocks of granite. It stood three stories high, with bay windows that looked out over the city toward the river. Their young guard was the first to reach the gate in the wall around the property; he dismounted and opened it, allowing the stable boy to guide the carriage into a stone-flagged courtyard.

"Home safe at last," said Dorian with visible relief as the carriage pulled to a stop. "Come have a look at the place, my lord—I think you're in for a pleasant surprise." They climbed out and Rand followed the minister to the door. Before they could reach it, it was opened by a tall, heavily-built man in an immaculate uniform.

"Good afternoon, Gilbert," said Dorian.

"And a very good afternoon to you, Minister Dorian," said the man in a sonorous voice that carried a tone of austere formality.

"Gilbert, I have the honor of presenting to you Prince Rand Falconer of Westmount. My lord, this is Gilbert, your butler."

"My liege, welcome home," said Gilbert, bowing deeply at the waist. As he waited for the man to become fully upright once more, Rand's mind raced in search of a response that would make a good impression.

"I am pleased to meet you, Gilbert," he said, inclining his head in a slight bow. "I look forward to making my new home here after so gracious a welcome." Gilbert raised an eyebrow at Dorian before replying.

"You are too kind, my lord. Please enter, both of you." He stepped back and gestured for them to precede him. Rand moved forward into a richly furnished hall with a floor of intricate parquetry. Paintings, tapestries, and trophies covered the walls. A broad marble staircase stood immediately in front of him. As Gilbert closed the door behind them, Dorian started up the stairs and waved for Rand to follow. "Nothing on this floor but the scullery, the servants' quarters, the laundry—that sort of thing," he said. "The common rooms and the kitchen are up here. Bedrooms are on the top floor." Rand climbed up after him, his boots making a sharp clacking sound on the polished stone. Gilbert followed them a few deferential steps behind.

"Is Lord Falconer here?" asked Rand, half expecting that at any moment a grim and formidable man would appear to judge him and find him lacking. How was he supposed to prepare for meeting a brand-new father? It wasn't as though he could just trot up to the man with a cheery "Hi, da!"

"His lordship is currently away at the Hall of Justice," said Gilbert. "We expect him to return in time for a late lunch, after which he will accompany you to the Academy, my lord." Rand was relieved; at least he would have some time to clean up and learn his way around before he faced the man who had turned his life upside down.

The stairway brought them to a large hall as lavishly decorated as the one below. Rand could imagine dances being held here with distinguished guests in elegant costumes. Gilbert took them through a pair of paneled doors on the right into a dining room that reminded him of the one at Uncle Bowin's house; it had a long table with seating for a dozen people.

"The door there leads to the kitchen," said the butler, pointing across the room. Rand could hear the sound of pots rattling and smelled baking bread. He looked forward to lunch. Gilbert led them back to the main hall and across to a matching set of double doors on the other side.

"And this is the library," he said. Rand stood in the middle of the room and turned in a circle, impressed by the high, book-laden shelves on every wall except the western windows. There were desks for writing, and soft chairs and couches for settling with a good book or a quiet chat with a friend. Rand thought he could happily spend a lifetime in a room like this.

"It's wonderful!" he said softly.

"I'm pleased that you like it, my lord," said Gilbert. "It hasn't seen much use since Prince Marcus finished school."

"Was that Lord Falconer's son—the one who died in battle?" asked Rand.

"Yes, my lord. A fine young man—I wish you could have known him," said Gilbert, then caught himself with a start. "Of course, if he had lived, then you would not have been here to meet him. Forgive me, my lord—we all have certain adjustments to make."

"Yes we do," said Rand with a smile. "I am glad that your regard for him is still so strong. I only hope that I can do his memory credit when I run the Gauntlet."

"You'll do your best, my lord," said Gilbert with a bow. "Now, let us take you to your room. You'll want to refresh yourself before lunch."

They filed out of the library and up the nearer of two staircases that rose from the back of the main hall toward the front of the house; the staircases curved around the walls and met to form a landing on the third floor. As they reached the top they entered a smaller common room from which hallways lined with doors branched off left and right. Gilbert led the way down the south hall, the one on the same side as the dining hall below.

"You'll have this hall to yourself, my lord," said the butler. "I took the liberty of choosing a room with a nice view over the city, but if you prefer another, let us know. Lord Falconer's suite is down the other hall, as is the room we keep ready for Minister Dorian."

They walked to the end of the hall, their footsteps muffled by the thick carpet that ran its length. Gilbert opened the last door on the right. As Rand reached it and turned into the room, he came up short. Before him was one of the bay windows he had seen from outside; the curtains had been drawn back, revealing a view all the way to the broad Seren River and beyond.

"Is something the matter, my lord?" said Gilbert as Rand stared out the windows without moving. He stirred himself and turned to the butler.

"I'm sorry, Gilbert—no, I'm fine. It's quite a view."

"I'm glad you think so, sir," said Gilbert. Rand looked around the room. A large four-poster canopy bed stood against the right-hand wall. There was a wash-stand next to it and a brass bathtub filled with steaming water. In the left wall there was a fireplace where a crackling fire was going, surrounded by plush chairs.

"Ah, I see the footmen have carried out my instructions already," said Gilbert. "Excellent! I'll leave you to your bath, my lord. You'll find fresh clothing in the wardrobe there. If you need anything, just pull the bell-rope by the bed and someone will come in moments." He bowed to Rand and nodded to Dorian before leaving.

"A little different than what you're used to, isn't it, my lord?" said Dorian with a smile.

"I'll say," said Rand. "The grandest house I could ever have dreamed of living in was Uncle Bowin's, and this is both larger and richer than his."

"It's fitting you should mention Bowin here, my lord," said the minister. "He and Cora first met when she came to visit her brother at the Academy. After they became fond of each other, she would often come to the city to visit Bowin instead. He sometimes stayed the night in this very room while courting her. More recently it was used by Marcus while he was a student. But as for grand houses, my lord, while I grant you that this one is very nice in its way, it is quite small in comparison to your new ancestral home, Falconkeep."

"Falconkeep," echoed Rand. He remembered Dorian mentioning it back in Oakbridge. The name evoked images of spiraling towers and ancient battlements.

"Yes, my lord, the castle of the Falconers in Westmount," Dorian replied. "It was built as a fortress centuries ago, but over the years additions and renovations have transformed it into a luxurious residence. This house would amount to perhaps a tenth of its size."

"Are you joking?" said Rand.

"Quite serious, my lord, said Dorian. "With luck you'll have time to see it before the Gauntlet. Now, I will leave you to your bath while I find some refreshment of my own." He withdrew and closed the door behind him. Rand unclasped his cloak and laid it across one of the chairs by the fire. He shook his head as he realized that this was the first time he had removed it since putting it on in Oakbridge the previous morning. It had been a busy day and a half. He stretched and walked over to the bay windows, marveling again at the view. Then he explored the large wardrobe that stood to the left of the window. It was packed with tunics, breeches, cloaks, jerkins, doublets, shoes, boots, and slippers. He wondered how many of them he could wear before the Gauntlet began. Then he undressed and climbed into the bath, eager to soak in it before the water cooled off.

Rand felt much better once the grime of travel and terror had been washed away. When he had dried himself, he went back to the wardrobe and found some simple clothes that fit reasonably well. He was combing his hair in the mirror of the wash-stand when there was a knock on the door.

"Come in," he called as he put the finishing touches on his hair.

"Excuse me, my lord," said Gilbert as he entered. "Ah, good—I am glad to see you've had a chance to refresh yourself. We will be serving lunch shortly. Lord Falconer has returned and requires your presence in his salon." Rand swallowed and checked that his tunic was on straight. Then he took a deep breath and followed the butler out the door. They returned to the landing and crossed it to the hall on the other side, stopping at the first door on the left. Gilbert knocked and waited until a muffled acknowledgement came from within. He opened the door wide and stepped inside, striking a formal posture and speaking solemnly.

"Lord Falconer, I present to you Prince Rand of Westmount, your son." He stepped aside and bowed to Rand, gesturing with a sweep of his arm for him to enter. It was so similar to Bowin's jesting posture on the street of Oakbridge the other night that Rand had to fight off the urge to laugh out loud.

He entered the salon, a kind of combination sitting room and study. The sergeant of the guard was there, standing at attention before a desk; behind the desk sat a man that Rand knew must be Lord Falconer. He had broad shoulders and a military bearing, an impression furthered by the austere and functional design of his clothing. His long hair was red with streaks of gray and tied in a ponytail; he also had a short-trimmed beard that was more gray than red. Rand guessed him to be a few years older than his uncle Bowin.

"I gather you had a rough time of it last night, sergeant. How many men did you lose?" he said to the soldier.

"Three, my lord," said the sergeant. "Gerrold, Simon, and the driver, Mather. We might all have been lost if not for the help of a Royal Courier who happened by, and the nerve of Lord Rand—that is, the prince I mean." The sergeant nodded at Rand. Lord Falconer acknowledged his presence for the first time, leaning back in his chair and looking at him appraisingly.

"Yes, the prince. And here he is—join us, won't you, Prince Rand?" Rand walked over to the desk and stood beside the sergeant, doing his best to emulate the other's military posture.

"Now," said Falconer, "Sergeant Brooks here has just been giving me an account of the tragedy that befell your party last night. While I know him to be a worthy soldier, I find it hard to accept that a squad of my household guards could be so easily overcome by a pack of starving wolves. I must know if the losses we suffered were unavoidable or the result of inattention to duty. You were a witness to all that happened, and indeed your life was almost forfeit. What say you?" Rand glanced at the sergeant, who stood with his eyes straight ahead, then back to Lord Falconer, who regarded him impassively. He could sense that this was a test as much as it was a desire for information. He forced himself to look his new father in the eye and spoke carefully.

"Yes, my lord, I saw what happened," he said. "Sergeant, ah, Brooks assigned sentries to stand watches through the night before we turned in. The camp was secured as well as it could be under the circumstances. The wolves attacked without warning and showed unnatural cunning. When the horses broke loose, all was thrown into chaos, but the sergeant never lost his nerve. He and his men fought with courage and skill, risking their lives to save Minister Dorian and me." Rand fell silent and swallowed nervously. Falconer nodded thoughtfully and sat looking at Rand for a moment before replying.

"Very well, Lord Rand. Sergeant," he said, turning to Brooks, "I find the prince's report convincing enough; you may go. In the future, we must all remember that the world is often more dangerous than it looks."

"Yes, milord," said the sergeant. He saluted and marched from the room.

"As a point of protocol," said Falconer to Rand, "you should remember that it is more proper for you to refer to me as 'father' than 'my lord' or 'Lord Falconer,' except on the most formal occasions."

"Yes, sir—yes, father," said Rand.

"Don't be troubled," said Falconer. "We both have new habits to learn. Come, let's have a look at you." He rose and walked to the windows across the room, Rand following. "You're a healthy young man—good bones, strong back, and clear eyes," Falconer continued as he examined Rand in the daylight. "Quick of wit, too, when I put you on the spot, and well-spoken. Your parents have raised you well."

"Thank you, father," said Rand.

"Minister Dorian wasn't expecting much when he went to retrieve you, you know," said Falconer. "My sister was obviously fond of you when she happened to mention you in her letters, but we always thought she was a trifle too kind-hearted about people—not least the man she consented to marry. But Dorian reported to me that he was pleasantly surprised. Said you were bright, hardworking, and have a gift for making friends."

"That was very kind of him, father," said Rand. "I often made a fool of myself in his presence."

"Perhaps," said Falconer. "I think you have made a better start than we had hoped for. I imagine it was hard being taken from your family against your will." He paused and waited, obviously expecting a reply. Rand decided again that it was best not to shrink back. He met Falconer's gaze and answered frankly.

"Yes, father, it was. My da—my natural father and I have not always understood each other very well, but I am his blood and he is mine. He worked hard for my future; it was a bitter thing to see his hopes taken from him, both for him and for me. I feel for my mother's pain as well."

"So where does that leave us?" said Falconer. "Are we to be enemies, or do you think that you can accept what has happened and go forward?"

"I don't think it's my place to bear a grudge, father," said Rand. "When I heard about the death of your son and the danger to your house, I couldn't blame you much for doing what you did. Besides, there's something that came to light while my father and Uncle Bowin talked about it all—it's likely that my life would have gone differently than my father planned whether you came along or not. I don't think my inheriting the Porter family estate would have been much less of a shock for all of us."

"My thanks for your generosity of spirit," said Falconer dryly. "Well, you have been honest with me and I will be no less with you. I am not insensitive to the hardship on your family, and indeed I do this only out of necessity. My own son was more precious than life to me; his death was a grievous blow. To put another in his place is a desecration of his memory, and yet the laws of the Gauntlet leave me no choice. You are my son now under the law, and I shall treat you as my son in fact, but you cannot and will not take Marcus' place. You must understand that."

"Yes, father," said Rand. "I would not want you to love your son any less than you do. After all, how would I feel if I got a letter from home saying that my parents had found a boy to replace me?"

Falconer chuckled a little at that. "True enough, lad," he said. "Since we are on peaceful terms, let us have something to eat. After lunch we will go and see about enrolling you at the Academy."

The meal in the dining hall was a foreign experience to Rand. Gilbert orchestrated it like a general leading a campaign, directing the footmen as they kept a steady flow of soups, meats, breads, and puddings going between the kitchen and the table. Rand found his appetite to be enormous after the taxing journey and the light breakfast he had shared with the courier. Many of the dishes were new to him, but each tasted wonderful.

Minister Dorian joined them and Lord Falconer questioned him closely about the details of the wolf attack. Falconer dismissed the supernatural aspects of the wildcat and its disappearance; as a man of action he had no interest in legends. He became attentive, though, when Dorian spoke of the courier inviting Rand to dine with him.

"Well," he said to Rand. "You have made yourself a rare friend indeed!"

"Yes, father, but I didn't mean to," said Rand.

"Nonsense, boy," said Falconer. "You did no wrong. Learn all you can about the world, I say. Still, I would advise caution with the Amhara; they are fiercely proud and known to deal harshly with those who intrude on their privacy. I tell you, Dorian," he continued, turning to the minister, "the day will come when we have trouble with these Runners. They are too strong and too secretive; they are after something, and when they decide at last to pursue it, we will be in their path."

"I hope not to see that day, my lord," said Dorian. "As I told Lord Rand, I fear it would be costly to oppose the Amhara in war. Yet I must say that you are probably right."

The two men went on to speak of practical matters concerning the administration of the Falconer fiefdom until the conclusion of the meal. Dorian excused himself and Falconer instructed Gilbert to prepare a carriage for the trip to the Academy.

"We could walk there in the time it would take to ready a carriage," said Rand in surprise. "It's just up the hill."

"Of course we could," said Falconer. "We must arrive there in a manner appropriate to our station, though, Rand. Noblemen do not walk through the gate like beggars in search of alms."

"I see, father," said Rand. "I should have known better."

"You will by the time we're through with you," said Falconer. "Now go fetch a cloak from your room. I'll expect you at the front door in two minutes."

Chapter 31

Those who flatter their neighbors are laying traps for their feet.

The carriage they took to the Academy was an open two-seater pulled by a single horse. One of the footmen drove them and they made the trip in only a minute or two. Rand had to admit to himself, though, that it was a very different feeling to roll into the courtyard of the school in grand fashion rather than to walk through the gate in the shopworn clothes of a blacksmith's son. He was about to climb down when Lord Falconer gestured for him to wait. The nobleman sat looking forward with an expectant air. News of their arrival apparently spread to the headmaster's office, for soon Master Parma's aide, Matthew, hastened out to them and spoke with great deference.

"Lord Falconer, we are honored that you grace us with your presence! Please come inside where we may show you proper hospitality." The young man was practically beside himself. He bowed to Rand in passing, but gave no sign that he recognized him.

"I assume Parma is available to meet with us?" said Falconer as he climbed from the carriage.

"Of course, your lordship, of course!" Matthew bobbed his head up and down like a chicken pecking at its feed, thought Rand, doing his best not to smile. The aide ushered them into the echoing hall where Rand had once sat on a bench and endured the doubtful scrutiny of both students and masters. This time Matthew parted the crowds peremptorily and took the guests directly to the headmaster's office.

Parma was not there when Matthew showed them in and bade them to be seated. The aide rushed off, grabbing hold of hapless students and shouting orders at them as he went. In moments the guests were being plied with refreshments by harried youths. Before Rand and Falconer could decide whether they wanted anything or not, Matthew returned with Headmaster Parma.

"Lord Falconer, my sincerest apologies—I trust you were not kept waiting long?" said Parma breathlessly as he bowed. Rand marveled at the changeability of the man; on his previous visit he had found that Parma could be solicitous, flattering, condescending, dismissive—almost anything but genuine or trustworthy. This time he was positively obsequious, and Rand found it to be no improvement.

"Not at all, Parma, we've barely had time to warm our chairs," said Falconer. "We're here to see about enrolling this young man."

"I see, yes," said Parma, bobbing up and down in much the same way as Matthew had done earlier. Then he looked closely at Rand for the first time. A hint of hardness crept into his expression. "Wait, now—I have an excellent memory for faces. This boy visited us a couple of months ago; wasted his time visiting one of our more... eccentric instructors, then returned the next day uninvited and created some sort of stir. I still haven't been able to get to the bottom of it. Forgive me, your lordship, but I fail to understand why he would be in the company of one as distinguished as yourself. Are you his benefactor in some way, perhaps?" Lord Falconer stood and gestured for Rand to do the same. Then he stepped toward the headmaster with a firmness that made the other flinch unconsciously.

"I know nothing of these matters, Parma, but I'm sure they are of no importance." He turned and pointed to Rand. "This is Prince Rand of Westmount, my lately adopted son and heir. He will be competing in the Royal Gauntlet this year, representing House Falconer. I believe the Academy has a training program for competitors?"

"My apologies, my lord—and to you, Prince Rand," said Parma, bowing to both of them. "I was unaware of these momentous events in your family; please forgive my impertinence. Lord Falconer, you are quite correct. Rumors have reached our ears of King Anthon's declining health, and we have taken steps to reinstitute the accelerated training program that has been used on similar occasions in the past. As your heir, Prince Rand is of course welcome to participate."

"That's more like it," said Falconer. "I assume he can start tomorrow?"

"We have not yet completed the preparations for the program, my lord, but of course there will be some clerical details of enrollment to occupy his time tomorrow," said Parma smoothly. "Having finished those, he may avail himself of all that our campus has to offer until training begins."

"That sounds adequate," said Falconer. "I will instruct my agent at the bank to deal with your office in regard to payment. I'll be checking up on things here regularly, Parma, and I'll consider it a personal favor that Prince Rand is well taken care of. You understand?"

"Perfectly, my lord," said Parma, bowing again.

"Until tomorrow then," said Falconer. "Come, Lord Rand—let us return home."

They swept out of the headmaster's office into the anteroom. Matthew jumped up from his desk and escorted them to their carriage, attempting various pleasantries along the way that Lord Falconer barely pretended to hear. He and Rand said nothing until they rolled out of the gates.

"Well, that was ... nauseating," Rand observed.

"As good a word as some I might use," said Falconer. "Dealing with their kind is one of the drawbacks of your new position, Rand. They are easy to recognize—treating all below them with contempt and all above with fawning and flattery. Engage with them when you must, but never trust them, and ruthlessly weed them out from the ranks of those in your own service."

"I will, father," said Rand.

"As you move in the circles of nobility, you will meet many who do not see the wisdom in that," said Falconer. "They take pleasure in flattery and servility, surrounding themselves with vipers like Parma and rabbits like his secretary. But hard times come upon all men, Rand, even nobles—in the hard times, the rabbits run and the vipers bite their masters. What is more, a house of rabbits and vipers is visited by such times sooner and more often."

"Yes, father," said Rand. With that, the carriage reached the gate of their house.

It was late in the afternoon when they arrived home; less than an hour later, Lord Falconer and Minister Dorian took their leave of the city and set out for Westmount. Rand felt conflicting emotions as he bid them farewell—on one hand, he was relieved to have a respite from his new father's scrutiny. On the other, the two men were a significant portion of the people he knew in his new life; he felt more alone without them. Lord Falconer was a hard man just as

Dorian had warned, but Rand knew from their brief association that he could learn much from the nobleman. As for Dorian, Rand had grown rather fond of the old minister during their journey together. He hoped they would see each other often in the coming months.

When he returned to his room, Rand saw that the oak chest Dorian had provided for him was sitting at the foot of his bed. He was seized by a sudden anxiety—in all the chaos of the last two days, he had not checked that the tablet of the Word was safe. It took him a moment to undo the latches and open the lid. Part of his mind whispered that the demon-cat had somehow stolen it away, and that the creature's sudden disappearance was thus explained. Another suggested that the courier had helped himself to it while Rand slept, as payment for his aid.

At last the lid opened. He frantically tossed aside his old clothes and swept his hand back and forth across the bottom of the chest until his fingers closed over the drawstring bag. He lifted it out, checked that his bedroom door was closed, then took it over to the bay windows and opened it. The tablet slid into his waiting palm and he breathed a sigh of relief. Once again he read the mysterious words, then he returned the stone to the bag. He resolved to keep a closer eye on it thereafter.

As he finished tying the bag shut, a gust of wind rattled the window panes; it drew his attention to movement in the street. A traveler was plodding up the hill, concealed beneath a hooded scarlet cloak trimmed in black that furled and flapped in the wind. The figure continued steadily on until it disappeared from view. Rand wondered if it was a student bound for the Academy.

He cast about for a place to hide the tablet and finally settled on putting it back in the chest, then hiding the chest behind some hanging cloaks in the wardrobe. Once that was done he sat on the edge of the bed and collected his thoughts for a moment. It dawned on him that this was the first time since he had said goodbye to his parents that he was free to do as he pleased. There was no journey to take, no appointment to keep, no serious old men giving him orders or demanding explanations—just a quiet room with a crackling fire.

Rand laughed and hopped up from the bed. Here he was, alone in a mansion with a staff of servants at his command and more riches than he could enjoy in a lifetime. Tomorrow he would have to get started at the Academy, but what would he do tonight? Why, anything at all! He decided to begin by exploring the library downstairs.

It felt like only minutes had passed when Gilbert found him there browsing among the shelves, but when he glanced out the window, Rand saw that night was falling. The butler announced that supper was ready; at the mention of food, Rand discovered that he was very hungry. He followed Gilbert to the dining hall, where he was greeted by the strange sight of a lone place-setting waiting there on the long table.

"Is there no one else dining with me?" he asked.

"No, my lord," said Gilbert. "Your father and Minister Dorian have left, as you know, and we have no other guests staying with us at present."

"What about Sergeant Brooks?" said Rand.

"My lord, the guard detachment has its own mess in the barracks," said Gilbert. "Common soldiers do not share meals with those of high station. An officer might, but we have none assigned here."

"I see," said Rand and took his seat. "I don't suppose you or any of the others…"

"Unthinkable, my lord," said Gilbert with a severe expression. "Please, enjoy your meal and allow us to serve you. You'll become accustomed to it in time." Rand nodded; the footmen appeared shortly with the first dishes and the food was even better than what he had been given for lunch. There was an almost hypnotizing quality to the rituals by which items were brought, served, eaten, and removed. Gilbert guided him with an occasional discreet cough and gesture toward the proper utensils at the appropriate times. Without seeming to, the butler was teaching him how to eat like a nobleman; Rand was grateful for the help. The meal was quiet, lonely, and often unfamiliar, but he supposed there was nothing to be done about it.

As he was finishing his dessert, it occurred to Rand that there was one thing he missed more than any other—the sound of his mother's voice across the table. In fact, it would have been a relief to see or hear any woman at all. His mother, his teacher, and the other women and girls of the town had been a constant presence in his life, but since embarking on his new course he had entered a world of nothing but men. He supposed the cook might be a woman, but Gilbert would frown on him hanging around the kitchen to chat with her. He hoped that he would have some female instructors at the Academy.

When the meal was over, Rand decided to explore the house. One of the footmen gave him an oil lamp—it was now completely dark out and the mansion lay in shadows. He returned to the library and discovered that there were more rooms on the far side of it, including a music room, a sitting room, and a sort of museum or armory. Then he climbed to the top floor and wandered through unused bedrooms where the furniture lay hidden under protective sheets.

One of the rooms appeared to have been furnished for a woman. Had it belonged to Lord Falconer's late wife? Maybe his sister Cora had stayed there. Rand tried to imagine the two of them as children, running through the halls and sliding down the banisters. Then his mind's eye saw Cora as a young woman, descending the stairs in an elegant gown while the dashing Bowin Porter waited below.

The thought made Rand feel closer to his beloved aunt, but also made her recent death all the more painful. The intense weariness of the last few days came over him in a wave; he went to his own room, where he found the covers on the enormous bed turned down and a clean nightshirt laid out for him. He dressed for bed and climbed in; the mattress and bedding were more comfortable than any he had ever experienced, and he floated off to sleep as if on a cloud.

Chapter 32

But I, with shouts of grateful praise, will make offerings to you.
What I have vowed I will make good. I will say,
"Salvation comes from the Speaker."

Rand slept through the night like a stone. In the morning, Gilbert had to physically shake him to awaken him, then reminded him that he was going to start at the Academy that day. Rand washed up and dressed as quickly as he could. He was just pulling on his boots when a footman came to tell him that breakfast was ready.

The meal was every bit as elaborate and satisfying as those that had come before it. Rand finished as quickly as he felt he could without doing an injustice to the efforts of the cook. When he stood from the table, Gilbert told him that the small carriage he had used the day before was waiting for him in the courtyard. Rand protested that he was perfectly happy walking, but the butler insisted that doing so would bring reproach upon the Falconer reputation. Not wanting to cause a scandal on his first day at the Academy, Rand relented for the time being.

As the carriage rolled up the hill, Rand stared at the back of the footman's head, resisting the urge to toss something at it just to break the rigors of decorum. They arrived in the courtyard of the Academy before he could make up his mind one way or the other. There were three other carriages parked there among the morning crowd of students bustling to their various lectures. The other privileged students looked at Rand appraisingly as he stood to disembark; he knew that he must be a mystery in their close-knit social circle. He smiled and nodded pleasantly, but they chose not to respond. When he climbed down from his carriage, Matthew was waiting for him; the aide had made time to attend to him personally, which Rand considered a bad sign.

"Listen, footman—er, what is your name?" said Rand to his driver.

"Coleman, milord," the footman replied.

"Coleman, then," said Rand. "Why don't you come for me about three o' clock this afternoon? That should give me plenty of time for—for whatever it is I'm supposed to do today."

"As you wish, milord," said the footman and started the carriage on its way home. Rand turned to Matthew. The secretary stared at him coldly, looking around to see that no one was listening before he spoke.

"I should like very much to know how you managed it," he said.

"Managed what?" said Rand.

"To come here as the poor relation of a merchant the first time, and return as the heir of one of Serenvale's most prominent nobles the next," said Matthew.

"It's simple," said Rand with a bitter smile. "All you have to do is arrange for your beloved aunt to be the sister of the prominent noble, then suffer through watching her die before her time, and finally, manage to be ripped away from your family and forced to call a stranger your father—all so you can enjoy the privilege of running in a race that may kill you. Does that sound like a lark?"

"I suppose not," said Matthew, looking down. "Anyway, we'd better get you enrolled; come on." He led the way into the building without stopping to see if Rand followed. Rand suspected that he could cause Matthew a lot of trouble for his lack of courtesy and deference, but he decided he didn't want to play that game. He preferred knowing what people truly thought of him, good or bad.

Matthew took Rand to the administrative area as before, but entered one of the offices at the side of the hall instead of going to the end where Parma's suite was located. The room had four small desks arranged in a grid; it reminded Rand of Merchant Hall on a much smaller scale. He noted with interest that someone wearing a crimson and black cloak was sitting in front of one of the desks; it was the stranger that he had seen in the street the day before, he thought. The hood of the cloak was raised, obscuring the wearer's appearance.

"This is the office of student records," said Matthew. "The clerks will formally induct you into the Academy. When they are finished, cross the hall to the bursar's office; there you will sign for the fees owed by Lord Falconer and be issued your academic robes." He took Rand to a clerk that was not currently occupied with a student. "I present to you Prince Rand of Westmount; he will be enrolling in the Royal Gauntlet program." The clerk looked up from his records.

"Welcome, my lord," he said. "If you will have a seat, I'll be with you in just a moment." Matthew bowed to Rand in the merest suggestion of civility and left without a word. Rand sighed and sat in the offered chair. He turned to his right and looked at the red-cloaked stranger.

"Hullo, friend," he said cheerfully. "I saw you go past my house on Ridge Road yesterday. Are you a new student too?" The stranger slowly removed the hood and regarded him with a cold stare. He must be a younger boy even than me, thought Rand, for he was rather small. His glossy black hair was cut just below his ears and a splash of freckles across his nose gave color to otherwise pale skin. His eyes were dark brown and relatively large in his fine-boned face. When he spoke, Rand received a shock.

"I do not call anyone friend lightly," said the stranger, and by the timbre of the voice Rand realized that it was a girl. The short hair had misled him. "Are you following me about the city, or do you always keep a catalog of those who pass by your house?"

"Sorry, miss—it was the cloak," said Rand. "It's easy to recognize and hard to forget."

"You find it so hideous, then?" said the girl sharply.

"Oh, no—I think it's grand," said Rand hastily. "I've just never seen one like it."

"You aren't likely to, either," she said with lessened hostility. "I designed and made it myself. It's one of many things about me that the people of this fair city find ... unusual."

"I know what that's like," said Rand with a grin. "The first time I walked into this place, they looked at me like I had three heads. My name's Rand."

"Yes, Prince Rand—I heard it when you came in."

"Oh," he said. He tried again. "What's your name?"

"It isn't 'miss,' I'll tell you that much," she said archly. When he looked away in consternation, she relented. "Oh, very well, if it means so much to you—I am Lady Jen, Princess of Lochinvale."

"Pleased to meet you, Lady Jen," said Rand.

"Yes, I'm sure you are," she said with a lightly mocking smile. He sighed inwardly; apparently she was determined to needle him indefinitely.

"Where's Lochinvale?" he asked pleasantly, refusing to let her get the best of him.

"You've never heard of it? Thank goodness you're here for an education, then, before you suffer a fatal attack of ignorance," she said disdainfully, her stare meeting his in a battle of wills. He burst out laughing, which appeared to catch her off guard.

"You're right," he said. "The sum of what I don't know could fill an ocean. If you would subtract this one item from the burdensome total, I would be in your debt."

"I suppose I have an obligation to help the less fortunate," she said with a grudging smile. "Pay attention, then; Lochinvale lies in the high eastern valley where the East Horn of the Seren River rises. The valley is filled with scattered lakes and the town lies where three of the largest ones come together."

"It sounds like a beautiful place," said Rand.

"You cannot imagine how beautiful it is," said Jen with a touch of sadness. "Especially in comparison to this fly-blown sewer."

"I know what you mean," said Rand. "On my first visit I came up the river by boat; the smell of the water wasn't the worst stench I've ever known, but it came close." She showed a measure of satisfaction with his agreement.

"So, Prince Rand of Westmount," she said, "what is your ancestral home like?"

"Well," he said, uncertain how to explain, "I guess that's part of my vast supply of ignorance—I have no idea what it's like." She glared at him in annoyance, but as he continued to look at her with perfect sincerity, she laughed.

"Why, I think you're serious!" she cried. "But you can't be. How is that possible?"

"It's simple, really," he replied with a smile. "I've never been there."

"What? Why not?" she said, speaking for the first time in a tone not of mockery or hostility but of genuine curiosity.

"Lord Falconer of Westmount was a distant relative of mine, one I didn't even know I had," said Rand. "He needed an heir to serve in the Gauntlet and I was the only qualified relation he could find. His aide showed up about a week ago to tell us the news, and here I am. I only met him yesterday before lunch and he left before supper."

"Typical," she said with distaste.

"What do you mean?" he asked.

"Only that we have something in common after all, Prince Rand," she said enigmatically. Before he could ask what it was, the clerk who was helping him interrupted politely to let him know that it was time for them to go over his enrollment papers together. Lady Jen finished her enrollment and departed before he could continue their conversation.

Rand left the records office once the paperwork was finished, crossed the hall to the door marked "Bursar," and went in. Lady Jen was not there; he found that disappointing, then was surprised at himself for being disappointed. Why did he want to see her? She was insulting, argumentative, and abrasive. Still, he had to admit that she had a sharp wit, and he relished the memory of the few times he had managed to pique her curiosity or make her laugh.

The bursar instructed him to sign a bill for tuition, fees, materials, meals, and a set of student robes. The bill would be taken to Lord Falconer's bank for payment, as Falconer had arranged with Parma. Rand asked for instructions about the robes; the bursar explained that students wore their usual clothes underneath and were expected to be in uniform at all times except during physical training. Two sets were provided so that one could be worn while the other was laundered. If Rand was planning to remain at the Academy that day, he should don his robe immediately, for he was now officially a student.

Rand was only too happy to comply, removing his cloak and donning the robe in its place. It was made of gray linen with a single stripe of blue cloth on each sleeve near the wrist, and had a hood for protection from inclement weather. He thanked the bursar and left, exiting the administration area into the main hall. A group of students collided with him when he emerged unexpectedly into their midst. One of the boys shoved him back roughly.

"Watch where you're going, scrub!" he declared contemptuously. Rand's first instinct was to shove back, but he saw that he would have a fight with the whole group if he tried it. He stood where he was and gritted his teeth. The boys laughed and moved on down the hall, calls of "scrub!" floating back over their shoulders. Rand collected himself and turned toward the rear of the building. Somewhere in the smaller corridors that branched off of the main hall was the exit that would take him by the shortest route to the Hall of Antiquities. He couldn't wait to see Zekiel again and tell him all that had happened.

Matthew had led the way before, and Rand soon discovered that he didn't remember the proper turns. He tried asking a passing student for help but she muttered something about "pathetic scrubs" and kept walking. Finally he came across a master who impatiently but expertly directed him to the proper door. He slipped out into the brisk cold of the winter morning and passed through the lightly traveled grounds of the school like a specter through a graveyard. He reached the Hall of Antiquities and entered the dimly lit exhibit hall, noting that few footprints other than his own had marked the snow before the entrance.

Rand wound his way through the display cases until he reached the hallway where Zekiel's office stood. He could see flickering lamplight spilling into the hall from the old scholar's open door. It motivated him to quicken his steps.

"Who's out there?" said the familiar rumbling voice. "No lectures until tomorrow. If you're here to vandalize my exhibits, I'll teach you a lesson about respect for history that you won't soon forget!"

"No vandals, Master Zekiel," said Rand as he came up to the door. "Just a friend from out of town." He found the old man sitting behind his desk with a scattering of maps spread out before him.

"Rand! Is that you? The robes make a good disguise—I should have thought of that the last time you were here."

"I have to wear them, Master Zekiel," said Rand with a grin. "It's required once you enroll at the Academy, you know." The teacher's bushy eyebrows shot upward in shock.

"Enrolled? How could that be?" he said, rising from his chair and coming to embrace Rand in a bear-hug before stepping back to inspect his uniform. "This is most welcome news. Did your father have a change of heart?"

"Actually, I've had a change of fathers," said Rand. They both sat down and he told Zekiel about Lord Falconer and the Gauntlet. The scholar shook his head in amazement.

"I suspected that you were in for some surprises after the discoveries we made here," he said. "Nothing quite this drastic, though. Speaking of our discoveries, do you have the tablet with you?"

"Yes, it's hidden at my new house," said Rand. "I can bring it tomorrow if you like."

"I'd be encouraged if I could see it again," said Zekiel. "Sometimes the events of that day feel like only a dream. I would have been by your village to visit you and retrieve the tablet long before now, but I was never able to make the trip."

"Why not?" said Rand.

"Parma," spat Zekiel. "He keeps cutting funds and hedging me about with restrictions. I couldn't very well explain the real reasons for the trip, so he disapproved my modest request for a travel allowance. When I declared my intention to pay my own expenses, he hinted that I might return and find my position filled by someone else. Gave me a lot of chaff about it being improper for masters to abandon their duties in the midst of the academic schedule, as if he gives a copper for anything I do while I'm here. He probably thinks I'd be an embarrassment to our school if I visited the other academies—that, and he takes a perverse pleasure in finding excuses to deny me something I want."

"My new father made him jump when we spoke with him yesterday," said Rand. "Maybe I can get Falconer to pressure Parma on your behalf."

"That's kind of you, Rand, but it wouldn't be wise," said Zekiel. "Parma will play the lackey for any wealthy noble, but one patron's voice only carries so much weight. Lord Falconer would have to rally the opinion of several prominent families to his cause if he wanted to push Parma into reversing himself—I doubt your father would care enough about what I teach to take the trouble." Rand nodded—Zekiel was probably right. They continued talking and

Rand told him about the Royal Courier and the attack of the demon-cat.

"A supernatural creature?" said Zekiel in alarm. "Describe it to me—include every detail you can remember." Rand told him everything he could recall about the black cat. Zekiel looked grim. "Something happened in this city the night after you left, Rand. Most people saw nothing and heard only rumor. Those who experienced it first-hand and survived try to forget it, pretending that all is well. Because of what happened with the tablet, I thought there might be a connection and I quietly gathered as much information as I could. Your tale confirms my worst fears."

"How?" said Rand. "What happened?"

"After nightfall on the day you left, Serenhorn was ravaged by an attack of strange beasts. At first I thought that fright and confusion had clouded the eyes of the witnesses, for the reports described very different creatures. As I reconstructed the times and places of events, I realized that there must have been several of them running amok in the city at once. Each beast was of a different kind, but they had things in common—they were much larger than normal animals of their species, their forms were distorted or misshapen, and they were unnaturally vicious. One of them was a great black wildcat with yellow eyes."

"No," breathed Rand, his eyes wide.

"I'm certain of it," said Zekiel. "There were four beasts, perhaps five. They raced through the streets bringing terror and slaughter wherever they went. Eleven members of the city guard died trying to stop them. But they didn't come merely to sow death and chaos; they were looking for something."

"How do you know?" asked Rand.

"By retracing their movements I determined that they must have entered together by the south gate," said Zekiel. "From there they spread out across the city, but their paths slowly converged on a single location—here on the hill where the Academy sits."

"They attacked the Academy?" said Rand.

"No, and that is perhaps the strangest thing of all," said Zekiel. "They simply stopped for a time. Then they left the city as swiftly as they came. Given your experience, I would venture a guess that they were after the tablet and lost interest when they discovered that it was no longer here." Rand whistled quietly—what would he have done if a pack of such creatures descended upon him? The Amharic knife would probably not be of much help then, and if the tablet had remained with Zekiel, the old man would have been completely defenseless.

"I guess something was protecting you when it prompted you to send the tablet with me," he said.

"Indeed," said Zekiel. "We are in over our heads, lad. We thought to learn the secrets behind old legends, but now those legends are alive all around us, contending with one another while we are caught between them. I have been giving the matter much thought; if the Speaker and the Shadow are at war here in our world today, then I think it would be wise to choose a side and declare my loyalty."

"Do you think it would matter—would they notice, I mean?"

"The history surrounding the Word tells us that it was a saga of the Speaker reaching out to his creation, making a way for us to know him again," said Zekiel. "If that is true, then perhaps choosing a side is the point of the entire affair. I do not know how we were meant to demonstrate that choice, but I am going to try." He stood and straightened his robes, then spoke solemnly to the air. "I, Zekiel

Jacobson, choose to be on the side of the Speaker and his Word. I believe his Word is true, and I will do my best to discover it and share it with all people. Furthermore, I will oppose the purposes of the Shadow and his servants by all possible means."

Rand shifted uncomfortably, his thoughts going back to Bowin's warnings against being drawn too much into Zekiel's obsessions. Part of him wanted to join the old man's declaration, but he just couldn't bring himself to go so far. Zekiel stood there quietly for a few moments, as if listening. There was no clap of thunder or flash of blue light this time, but he smiled and nodded.

"Well, that's done. I've doubtless bitten off more than I can chew, as the saying goes, but I'm tired of living by half-measures. Speaking of living, you should go to the refectory and eat—they're about to serve lunch."

"What about you?" said Rand, though the mention of food did make his stomach rumble.

"I try to keep out of sight these days," said Zekiel. "I have a store of things here for dining at my desk. But you need to go and get a fresh hot meal, and meet some of your fellow students. We can see each other tomorrow when you bring the tablet. Come in the morning; I have a lecture in the afternoon."

"I will," said Rand. They shook hands and he took his leave.

Chapter 33

Though one may be defeated, two can defend themselves.
A cord of three strands is not easily broken.

Only when he stepped out into the cold did Rand realize that he had no idea where the refectory was. He was about to go back in and ask Zekiel for directions when a bell tolled somewhere to his right. The area around the Hall of Antiquities was as secluded and untraveled as ever, but in the distance he could see students emerge from a handful of buildings and move toward the sound of the bell. He guessed it was coming from the refectory and set out to follow the others.

They led him to a long, low building located close to the north wall of the complex. When Rand entered, he found himself in a dimly-lit space filled by a double row of long trestle tables and bench seats. Some students were already seated with trays of food. Rand peered into the far recesses of the hall and spied a line of students at one end; that must be where they got the trays, he thought, and walked over to join them.

He reached the back of the line and greeted the student in front of him, receiving a noncommittal grunt in reply. Others soon lined up behind him and he let himself be carried along in the queue, watching closely to see what he should do. First each student took a wooden tray from a stack against the wall, then they presented it at a window where it was laden with a bowl of stew and a hunk of bread. Mugs of water stood on a counter beside the window.

Rand got his tray and took it to the window like the others; he was a little intimidated by the blank unhappy stare of the man serving the food at the window, but apparently it was nothing personal. He took his mug and walked down the aisle between the tables. Most of the seats near the food line were already full. Rand smiled and nodded to the other students as he walked along, hoping to build a little familiarity with his future classmates; most of them either ignored him or regarded him with cold silence.

When he reached a part of the hall where the crowds thinned, he saw one student ahead that sat alone. He thought the diner looked familiar and walked that direction. As he got closer, he saw that it was Jen—he hadn't recognized her at a distance now that she had exchanged her red cloak for the gray robes of a student. He smiled and hastened to join her.

"Hello again, Lady Jen," he said cheerfully as he set his tray down and settled on the bench.

"Leave me be or I swear I'll—oh, it's you," said Jen, stopping her outburst as she looked up and recognized him. "Excuse me, Prince Rand—I do not wish to appear rude, but I prefer my own company." She rose and left him sitting there, unable to think of a suitable response. He ate in melancholy silence and left to explore the Academy library.

Rand returned the next day with the living fragment of the Word as he had promised Zekiel and spent the morning among the exhibits of the Hall of Antiquities with the gruff master, learning about the history of his people. When the lunch bell rang, he went again to the refectory. Jen sat alone at the same table. Unwilling to let her snub of the day before go unchallenged, he walked up to her table and stood within her field of view until she was forced to acknowledge his presence. She sighed and lowered her spoon, turning to regard him with a look of irritation tinged by a kind of sadness.

"Though you may not be my enemy, Prince Rand, still for your own sake you should dine elsewhere," she said. "I am thrice-cursed, and you would not want to be the same by association."

"Enemy? Thrice-cursed? What do you mean?" said Rand, contriving to sit and place his tray on the table as a natural part of listening to her answer.

"In the first place I am a scrub," Jen replied. "The lowest of the low."

"I've been called that twice already," said Rand. "What does it mean?" Jen raised her arm and pointed to the sleeve of her robe.

"See this? One stripe," she said. "It marks us—brands us, if you like." Rand looked confused. "Have you not noticed the robes of the others?" said Jen. Rand shook his head. "Just when I thought there might be some hope for you," she sighed in exasperation. "Look—there are four ranks among the students, one for each year at the Academy. The number of stripes on your sleeve tells anyone at a glance what rank you are." Rand looked around and saw for the first time that students did indeed have different numbers of stripes on their sleeves, and that they were gathered with others of the same rank.

"First-years are scrubs," Jen continued. "Second-years are tyros, third-years are bloods, and fourth-years are tops. Each rank ignores or abuses the ones below and curries favor with the ones above. Good training for life in the real world, I suppose, in a nasty way. Anyway, as I said the scrubs are at the very bottom, huddled miserably together and trying to be as invisible as possible. The tyros make a great show of abusing the scrubs—they're a little giddy from no longer being at the bottom, you see, and they know their way around well enough to work things to their advantage. They try to form alliances with the more prominent bloods as errand-runners or informants. The bloods are the worst—so close to the top of the heap they can taste it, with lots of suppressed anger to release and plenty of experience in how to take it out on others. The tops really don't care; they have nothing left to prove, but they torture the others once in a while just to keep their hand in and prove they haven't gone soft."

"Sounds perfectly beastly," said Rand. "So you're a scrub; I am too, so why should I care?"

"That's only the first black mark against me," said Jen. "I'm also a dayfrog."

"A what?" said Rand with a laugh.

"A dayfrog," Jen repeated. "That's what they call the students who live off-campus and only come during the school day. Like frogs, you see—hopping in and out. In their eyes you aren't a real member of the Academy if you don't live in the dormitories."

"I live down the road in my new father's city house," said Rand. "So I guess I'm a dayfrog too. What else?"

"I'm a prank," she said glumly. Her expression contrasted so starkly with the silliness of the word that he wanted to laugh, but he was able to maintain a straight face as she continued. "You see, among all the other means of grading and belittling their fellow scholars, the students have the issue of class. The nobles instinctive-ly separate themselves from the commoners, of course, but even within their own circles there are distinctions based on whose fami-ly is wealthiest, or most influential, or has been noble the longest."

"I see," said Rand.

"I told you before that we had something in common," said Jen. "I was not born a noble either, Rand—I was adopted for the Royal Gauntlet the same as you, and in the eyes of the other noble students that makes me an unseemly bastardization of all they hold dear. As one of the silken darlings deigned to explain to me, someone like me is a prince without an 'e,' as in elegance, etiquette, esteem—therefore I am only a princ. And since the very existence of my kind is a cruel jest, I am more properly called a prank."

"But that's three for three," said Rand. "Here I am—a scrub, a dayfrog, and a prank. Not sit with you? How would I dare to sit anywhere else? In fact, I think we need to form an alliance for mutual protection." He grinned at her encouragingly; she smiled slowly in return.

"Perhaps you're right," she said.

"You just watch—before we're through, we'll be the exclusive club that everyone is clamoring to join," said Rand. "I barely know you and I don't yet know any of them, but already I can tell you're worth ten of them on their best day." She looked down, embarrassed by the praise. Not wanting to let the positive spirit of the moment slip away, he raised his mug with an exaggerated flourish. "To the pranks!" he toasted. She smiled again and reached for her own cup.

"To the pranks," she agreed and clinked her mug with his.

Having established some common ground, Rand and Jen found it natural to eat lunch together often in the days ahead. Soon Rand felt sufficiently at ease with her to inquire more deeply into her history.

"So you were adopted too," he said one day in between spoonfuls of stew. "What's your real family like?"

"My father runs a fishing boat around the Clover Lakes," said Jen. "That's what we call the three lakes that flow together at Lochinvale, for on a map they look like the leaves of a clover. He used to let me come with him on the shorter runs—I learned how to sail, steer, tie knots, and anything else I could. I was good at catching fish, too. What about you?"

"My father is a blacksmith and my uncle owns a large apple orchard," said Rand. "I had just started my apprenticeship when—you know, when all this happened."

"What about your new father? What do you think of him so far?" asked Jen, keeping her attention on her plate and her voice neutral.

"He's all right, I guess," said Rand. "Very serious and very busy, but he's taken good care of me so far and he seems to be a wise man. I think I can learn a lot from him if I get the chance. What about yours?"

Jen sat quietly for a moment, chewing on a piece of bread. Then she raised her eyes to Rand's and spoke with a quiet bitterness. "My new 'father' is a fat, drunken pig." Rand stared in shock; Jen continued heedlessly. "He had no children because no self-respecting woman would marry him, and because he is too busy exhausting himself with prostitutes to bother about finding a real wife. Our family knew he existed, but we stayed as far away from him as possible. He inherited his title and the fortune that came with it when he was still quite young—too young to bear it well, as it turned out."

"If that's true, don't you think your opinion of him is overly harsh?" said Rand.

"Do you think so?" she replied, bristling. She was about to say more, then paused and took a breath. "No matter—if I have been uncharitable toward him, he has already managed to exact a little revenge for my ... ingratitude. His house is not a prominent one, and so they never maintained a home in the city. He contrived to save money on my fees at the Academy by securing off-campus lodgings. I am the mistress of a leaky, unfurnished row house in a once-fashionable neighborhood that has fallen into disrepute— much like the noble family I represent. I am also the cook, the housekeeper, and the rat-catcher."

"Rat-catcher?" said Rand with a twinge of alarm. He hated rats.

"Yes," said Jen with a teasing tone. "Princess Jen has no human subjects, but she presides over a veritable kingdom of rats."

"That's awful," said Rand.

"Yes, it is," said Jen. "But it gives me purpose—I am determined to survive the Gauntlet so that I may live to stand beside my dear father Lord Wilhelm's grave, and after that perhaps succeed in restoring some dignity to my adoptive family's name."

"That's a—a powerful motivation, I suppose," said Rand, still struggling to understand the strength of her hatred for the man. Perhaps she just needed someone to treat her nicely for a change. "Listen, I'm going to spend some time in the library after lunch. I'm guessing you still don't have any real classes for a while, same as me. Why don't we see what we can learn together about the Gauntlet?"

"That's very kind of you, Lord Rand," said Jen. "I'll be busy for a while, though. Can I meet you later?"

"If that's what you'd like," said Rand. "You can find me there until three."

"Until I see you, then," she said and rose from the table.

Rand watched her go as he chewed thoughtfully on a mouthful of bread. She made for an unusual friend, he thought, but a friend nonetheless. He pondered the fact that he had known very few friends in his life. Other than casual playmates when he was younger, his best friend was his Uncle Bowin. Now he had Zekiel too, but no one his own age, let alone a girl—until now. He hoped that the looming Gauntlet would not dampen their friendship by forcing them to compete with each other.

Shortly after he enrolled at the Academy, Rand had renewed his acquaintance with the librarian, Master Atticus. Atticus surprised him by remembering him from his previous visit and was pleased when he learned that Rand would now be a student. On this particular day he helped Rand find books on the history and landscape of Westmount and Lochinvale. Rand took the stack to a table and began the considerable task of familiarizing himself with the domains of the Falconers and Wilhelms.

Time slipped by unnoticed in the soft quiet of the library. Rand was deeply engrossed in an account of war against a band of pirates that had terrorized the Clover Lakes about eighty years ago; slowly he became aware that someone was standing in front of his table. He looked up to find Jen regarding him with amusement.

"My, you do get buried under your load of ignorance, don't you?" she said. "I was beginning to wonder if you would ever come up for air."

"I find it easy to lose myself in tales of the past," he said with a smile, rubbing his face to clear his mind. "Do you know what time it is?"

"Just before three," said Jen. "Am I too late to accept your offer?"

"Not at all," said Rand, feeling a little self-conscious as he stood from the table. "Let's go see what Master Atticus can show us about the Gauntlet." Together they approached the librarian's desk. Rand introduced Jen, and then told Atticus what they were looking for.

"Hmmm," he mused while stroking his beard. "We do indeed have a few volumes on the subject, but I'm afraid they fall into one of two categories, neither of which will be of much use to those who must face the test themselves. You have the annals, which meticulously record the names, houses, ranks, and finishing order of the contestants—as dry and dusty as the covers that contain them. Then you have the memoirs and heroic tales, which are not at all dry, but sadly are composed mostly of exaggerations and bald-faced lies."

"How are we to learn anything helpful, then?" asked Jen.

"I suppose the best source would be someone who had experienced it in person," said Atticus. "Preferably someone trained in the rigors of academic inquiry and objectivity."

"Where would we find someone like that?" said Rand. Jen nudged him and nodded toward Atticus, who arched his eyebrows and smiled mischievously.

"The lady has guessed my meaning," he said. "What would you like to know?"

"When did you run in the Gauntlet?" said Rand in disbelief.

"I know you find it hard to imagine as you look at me now, but you must remember that the last Gauntlet was run some forty years ago," said Atticus. "Anthon was the winner, of course. I was the heir of a minor noble house, and so I competed along with him and all the rest."

"What did you have to do?" said Jen.

"Much the same as you will, I expect," said Atticus. "The path of the contest has become a matter of tradition over the years. First there is an examination that will test your grasp of the kinds of basic knowledge that a ruler of our land must have. As you leave Willowberg Academy afterward, you will face a challenge of combat, followed by a labyrinth. Once beyond that, you will race on foot to the river and swim across the treacherous spring floodwaters. On the far bank you will employ horsemanship, galloping through farmlands and leaping hedgerows on a chase to the foot of the western high plateau. Then you must negotiate a treacherous climb up the escarpment onto the plateau itself."

"The homeland of the Amhara, isn't it?" said Rand.

"Yes," said Atticus.

"The Amhara?" said Jen, looking from Rand to Atticus in confusion.

"The people who provide us with the Royal Couriers—the ones called the Runners," said Rand.

"Oh," said Jen. The look on her face betrayed her consternation at Rand knowing something about the wider world that she did not. He couldn't help feeling a little satisfaction in that.

"They will be waiting there to serve as guides for the next leg of the race," said Atticus. "Then you must do as the Amhara do—run along the cliffs and over the hills of the high plateau until you reach its northern end. The air is thin and the way is long. You must strike a balance between running too fast and collapsing or running too slow and falling behind."

"What comes next?" said Jen.

"At the northern end of the plateau, you must climb down cliffs that are as challenging as the ones you ascended. When you reach the bottom, you will be within the Badlands. Then the Gauntlet becomes a test of stealth and cunning, for the path leads across the nomad wastes to the Sentinel Range and the headwaters of the Solus River."

"What alliance does the king have with the nomads?" said Rand. "I thought they were enemies to all."

"None, and they are," said the librarian with a wry smile. "It is perhaps the most deadly part of the Gauntlet. A casual observer might glance at a map of the region and think the task to be simple—the most direct route from the north edge of the plateau eastward to the Sentinel Range is not long. However, the nomads of the waste hate us passionately, and never more so than when we violate their territory for the sake of our contest. They will soon realize that a Gauntlet is being run; when they do, they will be waiting with sharpened blades along any likely path. The only way through is to use your wits to slip past them. In the midst of that, of course, you will have to deal with the heat, the sand, and the lack of water."

"Sounds simple when you put it that way," said Jen with a sardonic grin.

"Do the nomads kill anyone they capture?" asked Rand.

Atticus looked around the library, then motioned his audience closer before answering in a conspiratorial whisper. "When you go through the training program, your instructors will tell you so. It was true enough in times past, and they maintain the fiction that it remains the case in order to keep contestants on their toes and flush out cowards before the race begins. But there's another reason, I suspect, which is tied to the reason why the nomads no longer kill all their captives."

"What's that?" said Jen, unconsciously whispering as well.

"The nomads have learned over the years that a noble family will pay handsomely for the safe return of a beloved heir," said the librarian. "Thus the tribes will usually take contestants hostage rather than kill them. There's a mercenary quality to the situation that the nobility would rather not be associated with, so they cover it up as best they can."

"You said the nomads don't kill all of their captives," said Rand. "Does that mean that they still kill some of them?"

"Unfortunately, yes," said Atticus. "An individual band of nomads might be particularly ruthless or excitable. Furthermore, if the contestant fights back and spills any nomad blood, they will want revenge. If the contestant's family can't or won't pay a high enough price, the nomads may slay the hostage as a warning to others."

"I don't like the chances of adopted heirs like us under those circumstances—in my case particularly," said Jen. Rand patted her shoulder in a way he hoped was reassuring.

"Since we're speaking of the dangers of the race, what are the prospects of making it to the end?" he said. "I asked Lord Falconer's aide when he was telling me a little about the Gauntlet, but he didn't know."

"Not so grim as some of my comments must have made them sound," said Atticus with a kindly tone. "The Gauntlet is not designed with the intent of killing the participants. It varies from one race to the next—perhaps one contestant in ten actually dies."

"Actually? As opposed to what?" said Jen.

"As I said, the Badlands and the nomads are the deadliest threat in the race," said the librarian. "Most of the deaths occur in that stage. The total fatalities would probably be higher but for other factors."

"Such as?" said Rand.

"A small number fail the examination at the beginning. Another one out of ten, maybe two, lose heart before making it to the Badlands," said Atticus. "Officially, abandoning the race would cause their family to forfeit nobility; in practice, the judges on the course exercise some discretion on this point. They get to know the competitors rather well over the course of the race, you see—if a contestant has striven to the utmost and simply has no strength left to go on, the judges may be lenient. The largest portion of those who fail, though—perhaps another two out of ten—consists of those who suffer a serious injury. Most of them heal well enough after the Gauntlet is over."

"Most of them," said Jen doubtfully.

"Some are maimed for life, unfortunately," said Atticus. "Still, it's better than dying. Taken together, about seven out of ten reach the Badlands stage. I cannot say for certain, but I imagine that the reason so many of those slip past the nomads is a matter of sheer numbers. The desert-dwellers can't be everywhere at once, and while they are—well—dealing with one quarry, others go free. Most of those who pass the Badlands finish the race—more than half of all who start, usually."

"Hmmm, so I get at least an even coin-toss between finishing on the one hand, and death, dishonor, or crippling on the other," said Rand. "I guess that's better than some chances in life. What happens after the Badlands?"

"When the racers cross the Sentinel Range, they come into fertile, wooded lands," said Atticus. "The headwaters of the Solus River rise there. Each contestant must build a raft or boat of some kind from the local timber and use it to navigate downstream to Willowberg. The first to return to the city square is the winner."

"How long does all this take?" asked Jen.

"The examination, the combat, the maze, and the sprint to the river take up the morning of the first day," said the scholar. "Depending on how well the river crossing goes, you could start the ride on horseback to the plateau by noonday. It's important to reach the escarpment before nightfall, for the climb would be impossible in the dark. Those who reach the top on the first day usually sleep there before running across the plateau, which requires perhaps two days. Crossing the Badlands can be unpredictable—you must take care to avoid the nomads, but if your progress is too slow you will run out of water. It usually takes two or three days. Longer than that and the contestant is rarely heard from again. Once through the Sentinel Range it takes about a day to build a suitable river craft, then another day to reach Willowberg. The winner usually finishes in eight to ten days."

"What happens when the winner arrives?" said Rand. "Do the others stop then?"

"No, that is not allowed," said Atticus. "All entrants must finish the Gauntlet if they are able. It is to their benefit to press on, no matter how long it may take them."

"How so?" asked Jen.

"In the first place, contestants are not given any knowledge of where they stand in the race until they reach the finish," Atticus replied. "No matter how far behind they believe themselves to be, there is always the chance that they are ahead. Even if they are not, fortunes change often in the Gauntlet—one may falter and another gain much ground at any time. In the second place, simply finishing the Gauntlet is an accomplishment that will bestow honor upon them for the rest of their lives. A hero's welcome awaits all who reach the end, though only one wins the crown."

"Our thanks, Master Atticus, for your patience with our many questions," said Jen. "I believe we are much better prepared to face the Gauntlet now than we would have been otherwise. Now, if you both will excuse me, the afternoon is passing into evening and I have a long walk home." She turned and strode toward the exit. Rand caught up with her and touched her arm. She stopped and turned to look at him questioningly.

"I don't like the thought of you going back to that dump by yourself," he said. "Why don't you come to my house for supper? It's just down the road."

Jen regarded him at length before replying. "I suppose that an evening of sitting alone in a drafty house with a one-copper candle and throwing bricks at rats can wait until tomorrow," she said.

"I'm glad you reminded me of the time when you did—I might have left my poor footman sitting out in the cold waiting for me," said Rand.

"Your footman?" she said, raising her eyebrows.

"Yes, the one who drives my carriage," said Rand.

"Ah, your carriage," she said with an exaggerated air of mock amazement. He laughed.

"My dear Princess Jen, I'm afraid you'll just have to find it in your heart to forgive me," he said. "Through no fault of my own, it appears that I have become disgustingly wealthy. I don't know yet exactly how wealthy I am, but from what I've seen so far, I'm pretty sure it's disgusting."

She grinned and gave him a playful slap on the arm. "All right, all right—I guess I'll have to forgive you this time," she said. "Just try not to let it happen again." Rand waved to Atticus and led the way out into the main hall. Watching them go, the librarian smiled and shook his head.

Chapter 34

When you help those in need, do it secretly.
Then he who sees all secret things will reward you openly.

Coleman was waiting in the courtyard with the carriage when they came outside. Rand introduced Jen and lent her a hand while she climbed into her seat.

"I thought you said your house was on Ridge Road," said Jen as they pulled away from the door.

"It is," said Rand. "Just down the hill."

"Then what on earth do you need a carriage for?" said Jen.

"I tried to tell my butler that, but he insisted that if I walked to school it would shake the very foundations of the nobility," said Rand.

"Butler?" cried Jen, rolling her eyes.

"Guilty again," said Rand. "I told you it was disgusting. To avoid any more unpleasant surprises, I'll get the whole roster out of the way now—I have a butler, a cook, two footmen, and a unit of guardsmen from my father's private army."

"All that just for you?" said Jen. "Are you that hard to take care of?"

"I am a bit of a slob," said Rand impishly. "Really, though, it's more for the house than for me. They keep the place ready for Lord Falconer, and I get the impression that he and his aides come to the city fairly often."

They arrived at the house and the other footman, Bertram, opened the gate for them; the horse clopped into the cobblestone courtyard to stop before the front door. Gilbert appeared as Coleman was helping Jen down from the carriage. Rand wondered how the butler always knew when to open the door.

"Welcome home, Lord Rand; I trust your day was a pleasant one," said Gilbert. "And who is this charming young lady?"

"She's one of my fellow students, Gilbert," said Rand. "This is Princess Jen, Lady Wilhelm of Lochinvale. She's going to be in the Gauntlet, same as I am."

Gilbert smiled and bowed deeply to her. "Welcome, Lady Jen," he said. "You grace our house with your presence. Will you be joining us for supper this evening?"

"Lord Rand has kindly invited me to dine with him, yes," said Jen.

"Splendid, my lady—please come in," said Gilbert. "I will allow Lord Rand to show you the way while I go to inform the cook." He disappeared through a side door that Rand supposed must lead to the kitchen by a back stairway somewhere. Rand led Jen up the grand staircase to the hall on the second floor. She tried not to show it, but Rand could see that she was impressed by the place.

"You're absolutely right—it's disgusting," she said, putting on a mock grimace. Rand shrugged and stared at his feet, pretending to be ashamed. He looked up at her and they both laughed.

"If you think this is bad, wait until you try the food," Rand said with a chuckle. He showed her the library and the rooms beyond, then the third floor and some of the dusty, unoccupied bedrooms on the way to his own chamber. He ducked his head in quickly to make sure it wasn't a mess before giving her a quick tour, showing her the bay window and how he had seen her pass in the street. Finally he led her back down to the library. Jen found a set of checkers and a board in one of the dim corners of the room; they played two spirited games before Gilbert came to tell them that supper was ready.

When they entered the dining room, Rand was glad to see that the places had been set across the corner from each other at one end. He could chat with Jen almost as if they were around his table back in Oakbridge. They took their places and the rituals of serving began.

"They take eating so seriously," whispered Jen to Rand as she watched Gilbert and the footmen move through their precise choreography.

"Imagine what it's like to eat here alone," said Rand. "It would be unseemly for them to chat with me, so the only sound is the clatter of plates and silverware. I burped at breakfast this morning and it was like a thunderclap in the room." Jen burst out laughing at the thought. The sound echoed as loudly as the burp had done, making Rand laugh in return. Then they were laughing at each other's laughter, and it took them a few minutes to compose themselves. The servants went on about their duties as though nothing had happened. As the courses came and went, Rand told Jen about his family and the town of Oakbridge, and she told him about the lakes and life with her little sister.

"Lady Jen, may I ask you something?" said Rand as they were finishing their dessert.

"Why don't we just be Jen and Rand?" she said. "After all, we're just a couple of pranks."

"All right then—Jen it is," said Rand. "You saw all those empty rooms upstairs; why don't you stay here with us? I hate the thought of you living in a run-down old house full of rats while I sit here in luxury. Besides, it's lonely here for me too." Jen stared at him with a frozen expression. Abruptly she rose from her chair and backed away from the table, shaking her head. Then she took a deep breath and regained her composure.

"Please excuse me, Gilbert" she said to the butler. "Rand, may we speak privately?" She left the room without waiting for him to reply.

What have I done? Rand thought. He excused himself and followed hastily after her. She wasn't in the central hall; he borrowed an oil lamp from a nearby wall sconce and crossed to the library.

He found her standing by the tall library windows, staring out into the winter darkness. He closed the doors behind him and went to a table near the center of the room, setting the lamp down on it and waiting there. When she did not turn or speak, he cleared his throat and took the initiative.

"I'm sorry if I offended you," said Rand.

"Are you?" Jen replied, turning to look at him with a raised eyebrow. "Not half as sorry as I am, for now I find I must explain myself, and in so doing relive things that I have tried hard to forget. You see, I had the privilege of staying in my new father's ancestral home for a few days before coming here. Over the years he has turned it into a reflection of himself—cluttered, dirty, and rank. He's too cheap to pay a proper staff to maintain the place, and the only servants that are willing to stay in his employ are almost as bad as he is." She paused and took a deep breath before continuing. "On my second night there, he drank himself half-blind and decided to celebrate my adoption by coming to my room and inviting himself into my bed. I was able to discourage him with a well-placed kick before he could pin me down. I spent the rest of the night hiding in a hayloft in the stables."

"Oh, Jen," said Rand as horror, anger, revulsion, and sadness roiled within him. She saw the pity in his eyes and struggled to fight back tears in her own.

"Don't look at me that way—I won't have it!" she said sharply. "I refuse to be poor little Jen, the bruised flower. If I let his foulness overcome me, it will be as though he had succeeded that night after all. But it is I that will overcome him, and anything else this world throws at me."

"I believe you," said Rand sincerely. "What happened after—after that? You said you were there several days."

"When I ventured back into the house the next day, he pretended nothing had happened. Given his condition, he probably had only a vague memory of what he had done, although I noticed he walked with a limp for a while—he must have had some idea of where the pain came from. I managed to bribe the housekeeper into giving me a key to the lock on my door, and that put a stop to any more night-time surprises. Wilhelm shipped me here to the city as quickly as arrangements could be made."

"In this house, you alone would have the key," Rand said and left it at that, clasping his hands tightly behind his back to steady his nerves while he waited for her to reply.

"I have no doubt of that, Rand," she said, mustering a smile for his benefit. "Please don't misunderstand me; your offer is very kind and I don't doubt your motives. I still need some time, though, before I will feel comfortable sleeping under someone else's roof again, and that's not all. Wilhelm put me in that house to teach me a lesson, to show me my place and my value to him. If he hears that

I've fled to nicer lodgings, he might see it as some kind of victory. I mustn't allow that."

"At least I understand your contempt of him a little better now," said Rand. He shrugged and gestured around them. "If you change your mind, the empty rooms will still be here."

"I know, Rand," said Jen. "Thanks. Well, quite a full day we've had, isn't it? I think I'd better get home and rest."

"Will you at least let Coleman give you a ride home?" said Rand.

"I guess I can accept that," said Jen. "Rats aren't the only vermin that come out at night in this town." Rand nodded and left her there to find Gilbert and ask him to arrange for the carriage and driver.

"Tell Coleman to remember the way to Lady Jen's house," he said quietly to the butler. "I have an idea I want to discuss with you after she leaves."

"Very good, my lord," said Gilbert, and went to find Coleman. Rand returned to Jen and escorted her downstairs to the hall by the front door. They chatted for a while until Gilbert came to tell them that the carriage was waiting outside. Rand walked her out and bid her good night.

As soon as the carriage disappeared through the gate, Rand went in to speak with Gilbert. He explained how Jen was forced to live in a run-down, leaky house without furniture.

"We have rooms full of unused furniture here, Gilbert," he said. "Could we not spare some for Lady Jen's sake?"

"I find it most distressing that a young lady of her stature is living under such deplorable conditions, my lord," said Gilbert. "I think we could gather enough items to give her a proper bedroom suite at least."

"That would be wonderful, Gilbert, thank you," said Rand. "I would like to do a little more than that, but I don't know if I have the, well, that is, the money to do it, or the authority for that matter. I want for nothing here, but I don't know if I have any cash resources, if you see what I mean."

"Ah," said Gilbert. "Things have progressed so rapidly these last few days that many details were not explained to you. You are aware that because of your youth, agents of Lord Falconer such as Minister Dorian and I have a sort of guardianship over you in most matters?"

"Yes," said Rand. "Minister Dorian explained that to me."

"As part of my responsibilities, my lord, I am to disburse a maintenance to you each month," said Gilbert. "It is for your personal expenses—gifts, entertainment, leisure travel, and so forth. Minister Dorian indicated that it should be the same as the amount given Lord Marcus when he was a student at the Academy, that is, ten a month."

"Ten coppers," said Rand, somewhat crestfallen. "It won't be enough to repair the whole house, but I guess I can buy some shingles for the holes in her roof and nail them up myself."

"Coppers, my lord?" said Gilbert, stifling a burst of surprised laughter. "I am afraid you misunderstood me. The maintenance is ten silver crowns." Rand's eyes widened; he tried to repeat the words, but no sound came. Ten crowns? But that was a hundred coppers. Still, though it would do for buying some lumber and nails, it might not be enough to hire tradesmen to do the work properly. Then he remembered something that he had been carrying with him since his first visit to Serenhorn—Aunt Cora's good-luck piece, the gold royal. He had been keeping it as a personal memento of her, and because he had no idea what to spend it on.

But now that he thought about it, he was sure she would approve of him using it to help a young woman in distress. He pulled it from the purse around his neck and showed it to Gilbert. He told the man how he had come by it and what he hoped to use it for.

"I want to hire some carpenters to go in and patch the place up a little—shore up anything that's in danger of collapsing, fix holes and leaks, that sort of thing. Maybe I should get a mason, too, so Lady Jen can have at least one working fireplace."

"Very good, my lord," said the butler. "I will make preparations tomorrow."

"One more thing," said Rand. "Lady Jen is a good sport and all, but she's been a bit proud and stubborn in the short time I've known her. If we could get everything ready quietly and do the work while she's at school, we'd avoid any arguments that might arise."

"I understand, my lord," said Gilbert. "Leave it to me. I will inform you when everything is ready."

Chapter 35

Unless the Speaker builds the house, the builders labor for nothing.

Rand visited Zekiel's office the next morning to discuss the tablet, as they had arranged during his previous visit. Together they marveled once again at the revelation that the Word had somehow been embodied in a man; they puzzled also over the passage on the reverse side of the tablet, which spoke of a man in prison being freed by a servant of the Speaker. Rand lamented the fact that they had been unable to learn more.

"What if other academies and museums possess Stone Tears that can be joined? We have to find out!" he said, pacing impatiently in Zekiel's office.

"I know," said the master. "I wanted to go in person to see for myself if such would prove to be true, and to convince them by showing them our own results if they doubted me. I fear there is danger in trying to inform them by letter—both of failing to persuade them and of attracting the attention of enemies. Now that Parma has hedged me in here, I am afraid that I have no choice but to risk it. We must press forward by correspondence."

"How long will that take?" asked Rand.

"Perhaps a week for the letters to reach the others," said Zekiel. "After that, it depends on whether they will believe us. What we really need is to gather all the known fragments together in one place; that would be the best hope for finding more of them that match. I don't want to suggest that at first, though—my colleagues need time to adjust to the idea or they will resist out of habit."

They talked about it for a while before deciding that Rand should keep the tablet hidden at his house in case any agents of the enemy came looking for it again. When lunchtime arrived, Rand met Jen in the refectory; he was careful to give no sign of his plans for her house. After they bid each other farewell, he rushed home to join Gilbert in the preparations.

The butler handled things with an organizational skill that showed why he was in charge of a nobleman's house. He sent Bertram the footman to hire carpenters and procure the supplies they would need for the job; Coleman was dispatched to lease a house across the street from Jen's, where they could stockpile everything and be ready to descend on her home as soon as she left for the day. Meanwhile, Gilbert and the cook, Mrs. Orton, had spent the morning selecting surplus pieces of furniture from the vacant rooms of the mansion. The only trouble they encountered was finding a bed that wasn't part of a set; they were still trying to decide what to do about that when Rand arrived. He was about to go and buy a new one when they found a very nice single-sized canopy bed stored away in the attic.

Gilbert met with Sergeant Brooks to ask for his help, and the soldier was only too happy to give his men some exercise. They loaded the chosen pieces into a heavy cargo wagon, one of the vehicles kept in the stables at the back of the property. Shortly before they finished loading, Coleman returned with the news that a suitable house had been found and that Bertram was already having lumber delivered there for the next day's work. Rand went along with the cargo wagon to help unload the furniture; Gilbert and Brooks protested that it was unnecessary for him to stoop to manual labor, but he insisted. The project was his personal gift to Jen—he wouldn't feel right about it if he didn't take part.

Before dawn the next morning, Rand waited in the rented house with Coleman, Bertram, the guardsmen, four carpenters, and a brick mason. As soon as they saw Jen leave for school, they swung into action. It was easy to gain entry to the house through an unsecured rear window, whereupon they unlatched the front door and started moving everything across the street. Without their livery and armor, the soldiers passed easily enough for hired laborers. Rand was wearing the old clothes that he had packed in his chest from Oakbridge; dressed as a commoner, he blended right in among them. He shook his head sadly when he saw the little nest that Jen had made for herself in the least decrepit of the upstairs rooms—a bare straw pallet on the floor for a bed, an empty apple crate for a table, and a pole propped across two broken hat-stands for hanging her small collection of clothing.

The work went quickly with so many hands, and Rand helped wherever he could. Holes were patched in roof, floors, and walls. Weak timbers were shored up and the little fireplace in Jen's room was made whole again. They swept and scrubbed years of dust from the floor once it had been repaired, then placed the furniture. If not for the cracked and stained plaster on the walls, Rand could almost imagine that it was a room fit for a noble young lady.

It was early afternoon by the time they were finished. Rand bid the workers goodbye with heartfelt thanks, then re-latched the front door and slipped out through the back window. He circled around and sat on the front steps to wait for Jen to come home, doing his best to dust off his clothes and clean the grime from his hands and face in the meantime. She arrived less than an hour later, walking down the hill from the busy thoroughfare above with her attention on the ground in front of her. She gave a little cry of surprise when she reached the steps and looked up to find Rand sitting there.

"Rand! What on earth are you doing here?"

"I had some work to do in town today," said Rand. "I decided to stop by and say hello when I was finished."

"I wondered why I didn't see you at school today," said Jen. "From the looks of you, it must have been hard work indeed. If you aren't careful, people are going to start thinking you're still a commoner."

"If only it were true," said Rand with a smile.

"I suppose I have your driver to thank for telling you how to find me," said Jen. "Well, since you're here, I might as well give you a tour of my castle." She nudged his leg aside with her foot and climbed the steps to the door. Rand followed and stood waiting while she unlocked it with a rusty old key, struggling to keep a straight face. She led the way in, not yet noticing anything while she spoke to him over her shoulder.

"Here it is," she said with sarcastic cheerfulness. "Watch out for the huge hole on the right." She turned to gesture at the floor, then stopped in confusion. The gaping hole had been replaced by fresh floorboards, expertly joined with the undamaged remains of the originals. Her attention was drawn to one change after another—the braces supporting the sagging staircase, the boards nailed over the cracks and holes in the walls, the dirt and debris that had been cleared away.

"What—who?" she said, turning slowly in a circle. Rand could contain himself no longer.

"Surprise!" he exclaimed, throwing his arms up in a dramatic gesture. She stared at him with wonder, then understanding came over her face.

"Rand! How dare you come into my house without my permission?" she shouted in outrage. She took a step toward him and slapped him stingingly across the cheek. "This is a—a violation! What will Wilhelm do if he finds out about this?"

Rand reeled back, rendered speechless by the fury of her reaction. She stormed up the stairs, exclaiming angrily at each new discovery. Then she suddenly fell silent. Rand followed cautiously after her, rubbing his cheek. He found her standing in the center of her room, turning slowly around as she stared at the elegant canopy bed with its fresh linens, the dressing table, and the wardrobe where her clothes were hanging neatly. A little fire glowed invitingly in the mended fireplace and scraps of lumber left over from the day's labors were stacked neatly beside it for firewood. She heard his footsteps and turned to him.

"Oh, Rand," she whispered, her jaw trembling and tears welling in her eyes. Without warning she rushed at him. He braced himself for another attack. To his amazement, she wrapped her arms around his neck, burying her face in his shoulder.

"I'm sorry," she said. "Thank you, thank you ever so much." He held her as she clung to him, her body wracked by sobs. After a few moments the spasms subsided and she stepped back, wiping her eyes.

"Well," she said, looking away from him, "that was quite a scene, wasn't it? It's just that I—it's been so long since I felt, you know, that anyone really cared. I'll never forget this, even if Wilhelm has me thrown in jail until the Gauntlet."

"I'm glad you like it," said Rand. "I couldn't let a friend live like that, especially a lady like you. Don't let yourself fret too much about Lord Wilhelm; we were careful that nothing would show on the outside. Probably the only changes a passerby could see are the new shingles on the roof, and they're not really visible from the street level."

"I don't know why you went to all this trouble, especially after I turned down your offer to live at the manor," she said, looking him in the eye again now that she had regained some of her composure. "I suppose you'll be holding it over my head forever, expecting me to be nice to you and all." A trace of her devilish smile crept back into her face.

"I think I know a way you could repay me, if you're interested," said Rand. "It's something I've been thinking about while working today."

"Oh? What is it?" said Jen. She sat in one of the new chairs near the fire, and he did the same.

"As you're so fond of saying, we're just a couple of pranks," he said. "We didn't ask for all this noble bosh. Now, I don't know whether they allow it or not, but as I see it, we don't owe them a thing in this Gauntlet of theirs, so if it's outside the rules I don't really care."

"If what's outside the rules?" said Jen.

"Contestants helping each other," Rand replied. "Let's agree to look out for each other during the race; I don't know about you, but I know better than to think I have a chance to win the crazy thing. I just want to get back alive, and I want you to do the same. It may not work, what with their judges and monitors and whatnot, but if there's ever a time that I can keep you out of harm's way, I will. Not outright cheating, mind you, just helping each other survive."

"So, pranks against the world, is it?" she said, staring into the fire thoughtfully. "I like it, Rand. I want to live through the Gauntlet too, and there's no one else I would trust to stand beside me." She fixed him with a look of mock disdain. "Just try not to slow me down too much, will you?" He laughed.

They sat there enjoying the warmth of the fire while she peppered him with questions about how the secret renovations had been done; then he took her on a tour of the repairs. The carpenters had even done their best to stop up any likely rat holes, but Rand knew better than to think they had gotten them all. When night fell, they bought hot bread and sausages from a street vendor up on the main avenue and ate beside the fire in her room.

"Well, I'd better get home before Gilbert sends the troops after me," said Rand when they were finished. Jen nodded and they went downstairs in the empty dark of the house. She opened the door and stood holding it wide for him; as he moved to leave, she put her hand on his cheek.

"Thanks—I mean it," she said. He nodded and squeezed her hand in reply before stepping outside.

"See you at school," he called cheerfully, turning and trudging up the hill. As he went, he thought about the warmth of her hand on his cheek and how it had felt to hold her while she wept. Something turned over in his heart. He pushed the feeling aside and marched all the more vigorously, not wanting to behave like a fool.

Chapter 36

Do you not understand that in a race all the contestants run,
but only one wins the prize? Run in such a way as to win the prize.

Rand was awakened early the next morning by the sound of bells ringing throughout the city of Serenhorn. He threw a robe over his nightshirt and ran downstairs to find out what was happening. Gilbert and Sergeant Brooks were standing by the front door.

"Good morning, my lord," said the butler. "The sergeant here has just dispatched one of the men on watch to go and inquire after some news. We should know something in a few moments." Rand nodded and went to one of the tall windows that stood on either side of the door, peering out into the pre-dawn darkness. He didn't expect to learn anything by it, but it gave him something to do. Soon he saw one of the guardsmen trotting up the stairs.

"It's the king," the soldier said when he entered. "A courier arrived from Solaria just this hour. King Anthon is dead."

"That does it, then," said Rand. "As soon as the weather warms up, I'll be running in the Gauntlet."

"I'm afraid so, my lord," said Gilbert. "We'd better get you ready for school as quickly as possible. No doubt you'll have an eventful day there."

"Luck to ye, lad—I mean, my lord," said Brooks and patted him on the shoulder. Rand smiled and nodded, then dashed upstairs to get dressed.

When he came back down, he found that the cook had managed to prepare a simple breakfast for him. He polished it off quickly and went to the courtyard, where his carriage stood ready. He looked at the sky and estimated that it was still a good hour before dawn.

"The Academy can't have done much about the news yet, Coleman," he said as he climbed into his seat. "Let's retrace the path that Lady Jen would most likely take to school and see if we can pick her up. Today of all days she'd appreciate being given a ride."

"Very good, milord," said Coleman and started the horse into a brisk trot. Rand leaned over the side of the carriage and peered into the pre-dawn mist that floated through the streets. They were more than halfway to Jen's house when he spotted a slight figure in gray robes emerging from the fog ahead of them.

"Ho there! Lady Jen!" he cried. She froze momentarily in surprise, then walked over cautiously to see who had called. When she recognized Rand, she quickened her pace and climbed aboard.

"You think of everything, don't you?" she said once she was seated. "Watch out—if you keep this gallantry up, I'll come to expect it." Coleman guided the carriage to the next intersection and used the open space to turn around, then set out for the school.

"Nonsense," said Rand. "It's just that I know how slow you are, and I'd hate it if I had to repeat all the news to you when you finally decided to show up."

"Ah, just looking out for yourself," said Jen with a grin. "I should have known. Well, thank you anyway."

"So you heard about the king?" asked Rand.

"Yes," said Jen. "One thing about neighborhoods like mine is that gossip travels very quickly."

"I find myself wondering about Anthon," said Rand. "I've never seen him or even heard anything about him, good or bad. Yet here we are, about to compete to replace him. It's as if he didn't matter at all, and that can't be right."

"I guess the one who sits on the throne doesn't matter all that much when you think about it," said Jen. "The laws, the nobles, and the people go on regardless. It must take either a very good or a very bad king to make a difference."

"Or queen," said Rand, nudging her with his elbow.

"Be careful what you wish for," said Jen. "Queen Jen might just make you her personal court jester, since you find yourself so amusing." She paused and spoke more seriously. "Actually, my chances aren't very good; I looked it up in the library and there have only been two queens since the Gauntlets began."

"Probably because girls are so annoying," said Rand. Jen elbowed him sharply in the ribs.

They reached the intersection of Hornside Way and Ridge Road and turned up the hill. In a few minutes the carriage rolled into the courtyard of the Academy, which was abuzz with activity. Jen and Rand got out and joined the milling crowd of students and masters. The door to the administration building opened and Headmaster Parma emerged. He climbed onto a stone bench and spoke in a voice that carried strongly over the crowd.

"My fellow members of the Academy, your attention please! By now most of you have heard the tragic news—his majesty King Anthon has left us, succumbing at last to the lingering illness against which he struggled bravely for so long. Do not fret for the safety of our great land in these troubled times. In accordance with our law, the king's sage and faithful advisor, the Royal Vizier, will act as regent until a successor is chosen." He paused to survey the crowd before continuing.

"Which brings me to matters that directly concern us here at the Academy," he said. "As you know, we have several among us whom fate has chosen to rise to the challenge of this dark hour — those who will participate in the Royal Gauntlet to select our new sovereign. We have been diligently at work on our training regimen to help prepare them for this heavy responsibility; now the training must proceed forthwith. The candidates are to assemble in the main lecture hall by the chiming of the hour; I will address them then. If any of them are not here present, please seek them out immediately and let them know. In conclusion, let us all show them a token of our respect and our gratitude." Parma led the crowd in a round of applause, which garnered only a halfhearted response; he didn't notice, having turned to go as soon as he started clapping.

"Here we go," said Rand to Jen as they filed into the building with the other candidates. Rand had never been to the main lecture hall before and was surprised to discover that it occupied most of the interior of the administration building. There were seats for perhaps five hundred people; the group of candidates looked pitifully small as they trooped down the sloping aisles to the first few rows at the front. Faculty members were milling around on the raised lecture platform, settling into the row of seats that stood along the back wall. Rand smiled when he saw Zekiel among them. The master caught his eye and gave him a wink. Beside him, Jen cleared her throat.

"Friend of yours?" she asked.

"Yes, actually," said Rand. "That's Master Zekiel of the Antiquities Department. If you haven't met him I'll have to introduce you. He's an expert on ancient history."

"He looks like ancient history himself," said Jen with a smirk. Rand was about to protest when a side door opened on the platform and Parma entered. The headmaster walked to the lectern and cleared his throat; the masters who had not yet taken a seat scrambled to do so.

"Distinguished princes and princesses of the realm, welcome," said Parma in his most unctuous tones. "Our Academy is honored to be entrusted with the task of preparing you to seek your destiny in the Royal Gauntlet. Nineteen candidates have enrolled with us in Serenhorn this year, one of the largest groups we have ever hosted for this purpose. Over the next few weeks we will devote our best efforts to giving you every opportunity to succeed." He turned and gestured to his assistant Matthew, who rolled forward a wheeled blackboard that displayed a series of topics.

"The Royal Gauntlet is a many-faceted challenge," Parma continued. He used a long pointer to indicate the subjects one by one. "There will be trials of speed, balance, dexterity, endurance, and skill. You will be tested on your knowledge of history, your valor in single combat, your horsemanship, your capacity to think on your feet, and your ability to survive under harsh conditions. We will train you in each of these areas to the extent that time allows. Regardless of how much progress has been made, when the call goes forth to assemble at Willowberg you must comply. Since time is of the essence, the program will begin this very day." He paused to let that sink in.

"You will train together as a group," he continued. "We will drill you in academics in the mornings and athletics in the afternoons. Good luck to you all, and be confident that our fondest wishes go with you. My assistant will now give you the specifics of your schedule."

Parma nodded to Matthew and left the podium, exiting by the door through which he had entered. The secretary reeled off a list of times and places for each subject, introducing the instructors as he went. Rand couldn't keep up very well, but he realized that he could follow the others from one class to the next until he knew his way around better. Matthew concluded by handing out paper copies of the schedule and everyone rose to go. Rand followed, trying to ignore the fluttering in the pit of his stomach.

The days that followed were exhausting both mentally and physically. Classes started at first light and athletic training ended when darkness fell. Rand had to force himself to eat a light supper before collapsing into bed each night and falling asleep as soon as he closed his eyes. Each morning he had to rouse his cramped and aching limbs by sheer force of will.

After the first week, his body toughened to the point where the physical strain was easier to bear, but the mental challenge of the academic classes was relentless. It didn't help that he and Jen were two of the youngest candidates. They had to keep up with upperclassmen as well as young adults who had already graduated from the Academy and were serving in places of leadership appropriate to their noble status.

His respect for Jen grew as he watched her press on through the challenges. She was one of only three young women in the program, and the only one who prospered. The other two were accustomed to lives of society and fashion, having been born into noble families. One of them was earnest enough, but she had not led a physically active life and the toll of the athletic training on her was tremendous. The other treated the entire affair like a lark, alternating between flirting with the older boys and sulking over being forced by the rules of the Gauntlet to participate. Several of the young men were no better—they enjoyed various parts of the program according to their talents, but by their demeanor they made it clear that they did not take the Gauntlet seriously.

As for himself, Rand was soon grateful that he had spent the last part of his former life as an apprentice blacksmith. Working with iron and hammer had put some muscle on his spare frame and now he felt its benefits. He thought he would excel in the academic subjects after being the best student at his village school, but he was soon overwhelmed by the pace. Jen proved to be a lifeline for him, coming to his house on their one day off each week to review subjects with him in the library of the manor. Meanwhile the days grew longer and snow flurries gave way to rain, silent reminders that their time was running out.

The death of the king had brought changes to the Vizier's life as well. The one he found most irritating was that he was compelled to abandon his nocturnal habits—his duties as regent could not be performed in the middle of the night. He was sitting on a chair in the throne room, discreetly positioned close enough to the dais to give himself an air of authority but not so close as to suggest that he was usurping the king's place. He struggled to stay alert while ministers and supplicants came and went with their droning voices and petty concerns. Privately he reflected on the wisdom of being an unseen power behind the throne; from that position, one was free to choose the affairs of state in which to meddle. A regent had no such luxury.

There were some compensations, however. The Vizier was able to keep a tight rein on the Royal Gauntlet without the restraints of subtlety or secrecy. He was just finishing the authorization of funds for toughening some of the obstacles on the course when one of his personal agents appeared at the edge of the crowd of courtiers and gave the signal for a private meeting. The Vizier finished imprinting his seal on the bills of appropriation and announced that he was taking a brief recess. He stood and walked behind the throne to a private audience chamber, followed by the agent.

"What news?" he asked when the doors were closed.

"Someone's creating a stir among the antiquities departments at the academies," said the agent, handing him a letter. "Copies of this were sent to all of them by the master at Serenhorn. As you know, the antiquities master at the Academy of Solaria is a friend of ours; he gave me his copy as soon as it arrived."

"The old fool!" laughed the Vizier as he read Zekiel's letter. "We thwart him at every turn, so he responds by declaring his intentions openly. I couldn't have asked for better if I had instigated it myself. Go now," he said to the agent. "I will deal with this personally." The man bowed and slipped out quietly.

The Vizier was about to return to his seat and issue a decree when he was brought up short by the thought of Lupus. The demon cared little for the mundane affairs of state, so long as an effort was made to maintain a general atmosphere of oppression and discontent. In a matter concerning the Stone Tears, however, the Vizier must consult him before taking any action. The Vizier muttered an oath and called for the sergeant at arms, instructing him to announce that audiences would be suspended indefinitely. He then retired to his private chambers to call upon the spirit world.

As on the first occasion and each one since, Lupus approached the Vizier's room across the planes of reality from a distant realm of fire and smoke. The glittering white being with the blood-red lips regarded the Vizier with casual contempt.

"Why have you called me?"

"Master Zekiel at the Academy of Serenhorn has revealed his plans," said the Vizier and read the letter to Lupus.

"So he admits that he was instrumental in awakening the Enslaver—interesting," said Lupus.

"This is the excuse I need, and now I have the authority to act on it," said the Vizier eagerly. "As regent I can order royal troops to confiscate all known fragments of the Enslaver. I can say that I am acting to preserve them from irresponsible meddling that could jeopardize their safety."

"You could," said Lupus. "You could also post notices advertising that you are a servant of the Banished One, and write a sign across the mountains in letters of fire proclaiming that the Stone Tears are somehow important. Fool! Have we not labored for centuries to lull these ignorant mortals into spiritual slumber? Now that this doddering fossil is attempting to rouse them, will you add your trumpet to his?" Lupus made no move, but an unseen force struck the Vizier across the face hard enough to knock him to the floor.

"These simpletons do not yet know for certain that you traffic in dark arts," the demon continued. "All they see is mystery and hidden power. Give that power a smiling face; embrace this Zekiel's project and pledge the support of your vast store of knowledge. Play the gracious host and insist that a gathering take place here in the capital so that your resources may be brought to bear. Thus the doubts that he and any sympathizers may have will be allayed; they will bear their little treasures to you willingly and lay them at your feet."

"Is that not dangerous?" said the Vizier. "What if there are more fragments that may join and awaken? The power of the Enslaver would only grow."

"That is where we must rely on you, unfortunately," said Lupus with distaste. "You will have to employ subterfuge to ensure that the fragments cannot join. I will teach you how to make a certain resin, transparent when dry, which you will apply to the edges of the Stone Tears once they are within your reach. It will prevent them from bonding even if they match. It cannot adhere to them for long—nothing can—but it will do so long enough to thwart the scholars for a day or two. When the old man's claims fail to materialize, you can discredit him, gently and regretfully of course."

"What if he brings the awakened portion as evidence?" said the Vizier.

"That would be a stroke of fortune too good to be hoped for," said Lupus. "If he brings it with him, an unfortunate accident will befall him on the way to the capital. He and his party will be set upon by ferocious beasts and destroyed. The inert Stone Tears from his collection will be found and added to the others, but the living fragment will be irretrievably lost."

"And if he comes without it?" asked the Vizier.

"Then conduct the sham experiment as I instructed you. When he is discredited, seize upon his failure as evidence of fraud against both the kingdom and the cause of knowledge itself. Throw him into your deepest dungeon and keep him there until after the Gauntlet. I gather that you are hard at work to secure a proper winner for that contest?" Lupus paused and the Vizier nodded vigorously.

"Good," the demon continued. "Once the new ruler is crowned, he or she will be our instrument to unleash a new age of bloodshed, war, and sorcery upon the earth. The trial and execution of the old fool will serve as its inauguration. Thus will we stamp out this new stratagem of the Enemy before it may properly begin."

"I can hardly wait," said the Vizier, his face twisted into a mask of malice by the strength of his lust for the coming darkness.

"I know," said Lupus. "The new ruler shall be our instrument, but you shall be our prophet and priest. The blood of the ignorant will fill your communion cup; the screams of their torment will be the anthem of your sacraments. If you wish to hasten that day, be diligent in your tasks." Lupus withdrew and passed back into the realm from which he had appeared. The Vizier refreshed himself and returned to the throne room, where the courtiers remarked among themselves about the new enthusiasm he brought to his duties.

Chapter 37

No discipline is enjoyable at the time, but painful. Later, however, it grows a harvest of right living and peace for those who have been trained by it.

Rand was in the fourth week of his training program when he received word that Zekiel wanted to see him. Once the exhausting afternoon of riding lessons was over, he walked gingerly across campus to the Hall of Antiquities, mindful of his saddle sores at every step. He found Zekiel in the exhibit hall by the display case that contained the Stone Tears. The master was removing the two remaining fragments from their mountings and wrapping them in cloth.

"Master Zekiel, what's happening?" said Rand with a twinge of concern. "I came as soon as I could."

"Don't be alarmed, lad," said Zekiel. "I have news to share—tremendous news! There has been a most unexpected response to my letters. Replies came from my peers, of course, some interested and others not, but then I received a letter from the Royal Vizier himself. He has taken a personal interest in our discoveries, and has sent forth a call to all who possess Stone Tears, inviting us to gather them together under his sponsorship for a full investigation!"

"The Royal Vizier?" said Rand. "Headmaster Parma said that he was acting as the regent; who is he, exactly?"

"He is the king's closest advisor, specializing in knowledge of the arcane and the mysterious," said Zekiel. "His order has held that post for centuries, studying the heavens and the secrets of the past in a quest for wisdom. Rarely do they intervene in any matter not directly concerning the throne, and rarely does a king of Solethon make a momentous decision without seeking their counsel."

"He certainly sounds like someone who could help us," said Rand. "But what will you do about it? I thought Parma wouldn't let you leave."

"I don't think even a smirking windbag like Parma would dare to contravene the Vizier," said Zekiel. "I am going to attend the meeting regardless, even if it means—" He was interrupted by the sound of the door opening again. Rand looked across the exhibit hall and saw that Parma himself had entered. The headmaster spotted them and came their way.

"Ah, Master Zekiel!" he called cheerfully. "And a good evening to you, Prince Rand. Zekiel, I just received a proclamation from the royal court. The Vizier has summoned all masters of antiquities to the capital for a symposium. Did you know of this?"

"I only just received word of it myself," said Zekiel cautiously.

"Excellent—then I trust you know all about it," said Parma. "This is quite an honor, Zekiel, and reflects well on the Academy."

"Am I allowed to attend then?" said Zekiel.

"Allowed to attend?" said Parma incredulously. "My dear fellow, you are too modest—the Vizier and I have worked together in the past, and with my copy of the proclamation he sent a personal note explaining how you yourself are the inspiration for the gathering. Allowed to attend, indeed! Why, I will be sending you with a generous stipend and an armed escort for your safety on the road; furthermore, you will ride in the best carriage that can be hired for the purpose. Can you be ready by tomorrow morning?"

"Of course," said Zekiel, obviously shocked by Parma's change in attitude.

"Very good," said Parma. "I'll go make the arrangements. A pleasant evening to you both." They wished him a good evening in return and he left as suddenly as he had arrived.

"This is it, my boy," said Zekiel. "I'm returning from the wilderness at last. With the Vizier's support, not only will every academy bring its collection, but even the private collectors will not dare to refuse. We'll never have a better chance to show the world that the story of the Word is true."

"It's an amazing opportunity," Rand agreed. "I'd better go get the tablet."

"I've been doing some thinking about that," said Zekiel. "As much as I want to show it to them, I can't forget about those beasts, those—what did the Royal Courier call them?"

"*Aganint*," said Rand.

"Yes, the *aganint*," said Zekiel. "You managed to fend off one of them, but we know there are more. My heart tells me to beware going abroad with the living fragment while they are after it. Besides, if we find another pair at the symposium that can join, a live demonstration will be far more convincing."

"I see," said Rand. "I only wish I could go with you."

"By rights you should, lad," said Zekiel. "Unfortunately, your training for the Gauntlet is more urgent just now. Once you've discharged your duty in that regard, we'll be able to work together again." Rand mustered a smile for Zekiel's benefit and followed along to help him pack for the journey. When he was done, he went home to supper and bed; for the first time since he began training, sleep was long in coming.

Rand found it difficult during the first few days after Zekiel's departure to concentrate on his studies. Though he knew it was impossible at so great a distance, he half expected to hear the echo of distant explosions as more Stone Tears were joined and brought to life. In time, however, the all-consuming demands of the training program swallowed up his attention again. Thus it was a shock when one day he realized that two weeks had passed with no news from the symposium. Wary as he still was of Parma, he decided that no one else was likely to know what was happening in Solaria. He went to the headmaster's office as soon as training broke for lunch.

"The headmaster is unavailable at present," said Matthew when Rand appeared in the anteroom, standing and putting out a hand to stop him. "I suggest you make an appointment if you think you must see him, though I doubt he will find time in the midst of his important concerns." Rand stared at Matthew's rude, self-important expression and felt a rising anger. He had been reluctant to exercise the prerogatives of his new station in life, but now he realized that he could make use of them when dealing with people like the secretary. Recalling Lord Falconer's observations about vipers and rabbits, he decided it was time to see how fast this rabbit could run.

"You will remove your hand from my noble person and you will not touch me again without my leave," he growled, shoving Matthew so that he fell back into his chair. "Furthermore, you will address me as 'my lord' or 'Prince Rand.' If you show disrespect to me again in these ways or in any other, I will have you flogged, do you hear me?" Matthew nodded, his eyes wide with fear. Rand turned without further delay and opened the door to Parma's office.

He didn't see the headmaster at first when he entered the room. Then he heard a noise coming from the windows behind Parma's high-backed chair; the man was bent over a large black bird that sat on the sill. A draft of wind came through the open window and slammed the door shut behind Rand, making both Parma and the raven jump and turn toward the sound. Parma shooed the bird out the window and closed it.

"Prince Rand, you startled me!" he said, gathering his composure and sitting at his desk. "I was just chasing that bird out of my office—he flew in while I was enjoying the spring breezes for a moment. Ah, hmm, while I am of course ever at your service, it is quite irregular for you to visit unannounced. But no matter—what can I do for you?"

"I am sorry to intrude on you, headmaster—I know you are very busy with the affairs of the Academy. But I am eager for news of Master Zekiel and the symposium; in truth, so much time has passed that I'm a little worried. I hoped you might have heard something." Parma's expression hardened as Rand spoke.

"I see," he said grimly. "I have indeed received a report from the symposium, Prince Rand. Please come and sit. I did not want to share such news with you while you are in the midst of training for the Gauntlet—I feared that it would upset you and distract you from your duty. Since you have sought me out, I suppose I have no choice." Rand crossed the room and sat, a feeling of dread rising in his heart.

"It pains me to do so, but I must remind your lordship that I discouraged you from associating with Master Zekiel when we first met," Parma continued. "Now it appears that my apprehensions were justified."

"What happened?" said Rand. "Did he meet with—with some mischance on the road?"

"Oh, no, nothing like that," said Parma. "He arrived in Solaria as scheduled, although perhaps it would have been better if he had not. His claims were put to the test before his assembled peers and the Vizier himself, and were proven false."

"But how?" said Rand. "I mean, what claims were they?"

"Apparently some of the old fragments that he and others of his kind collect were supposed to be capable of joining together, with remarkable effects," said Parma. "Suitable fragments were found among those brought to the symposium, but none of the promised manifestations occurred when they were combined."

"Oh," said Rand, his mind racing as he tried to understand why the fragments had failed to react.

"That was a poor enough reflection on Master Zekiel, not to mention upon me and the Academy," said Parma. "But matters became worse—he claimed to have a sample of the effects he described, but could not produce it. The Vizier was embarrassed and not a little angry that the resources and authority of his position have been misused for a kind of hoax."

"Zekiel would not lie about such things; you must know that," protested Rand.

"Perhaps not intentionally," said Parma. "Nonetheless, he has given his thoughts over to these matters to an unhealthy degree for many years now—I fear to the point of corrupting his reason. He has not so much tried to deceive others as he has deceived himself. Regardless of why it happened, the fact that it happened under the sponsorship of the royal court makes it a very serious offense. The Vizier had no choice but to take Master Zekiel into custody until a formal inquiry can be made."

"When will that happen?" said Rand. "I—I would like to speak on his behalf, if I may."

"I strongly advise you to reconsider any further association with the man," said Parma sternly. "I concede that he meant no harm, but you must recognize that he has influenced you with false hopes and empty myths. I prefer to let the matter drop where you are concerned, including your involvement in the strange incident that apparently set all of this in motion, but if you persist I will have no choice but to speak with your father about it. If nothing else, you run the risk of being tainted by Zekiel's disgrace—you might even face legal repercussions yourself if he is found guilty. In any case, the investigation cannot proceed until after the Royal Gauntlet is complete; the Vizier will be much too busy overseeing that contest to spare attention for other matters, as will you."

Rand saw that any further argument would only make his position more dangerous. In retrospect it was harder than ever to understand why Parma had chosen to support Zekiel's trip; now the viper had turned back onto its old track, biting Zekiel and threatening to bite Rand. He did his best to appear repentant and abashed.

"I understand," he said with his head bowed. "Thank you for telling me what happened, headmaster. I guess I should get back to my training."

"I think that would be best, my lord," said Parma. "I am sorry to be the bearer of such distressing news, but I urge you not to let it weigh upon you. It really had little to do with you, and you must focus on the Gauntlet." Rand nodded and excused himself. When he came out of Parma's office and closed the door behind him, Matthew glanced up, then stared resolutely at the work on his desk. Rand cleared his throat and stood waiting.

"Good day to you, my lord," Matthew said at last, still looking down as his face reddened.

"And to you, Matthew," said Rand and left, trying not to smile.

Rand was grateful that he had athletic training for the remainder of that day—he would have been in poor shape to concentrate on academic subjects while he was so worried about Zekiel, and the exercise gave him an outlet for his anxiety and frustration. When evening came, he headed for the front gate, trudging along with a heavy heart. As he approached his carriage he discovered that Jen was there waiting for him.

"Oh, hello," he said, trying to appear his normal upbeat self.

"Don't 'oh, hello' me," she said. "What's gotten into you? You've been mooning around all afternoon like you just lost your best friend."

"That's just it, Jen," said Rand sadly. "I really may lose my best friend—but it's a long story and I'm very tired."

"So am I, but tomorrow's our day off," said Jen. "I can spare a little time for a long story. Besides, I thought I was your best friend. Who else would you tell your troubles to?"

"You're my best friend now," Rand said with a smile. "Before you came crashing into my life, though, Master Zekiel and I went through some amazing things together. I owe him a lot for what he taught me and the kindness he showed me, and now he's in terrible trouble. If you really want to hear about it, I guess you'll have to come over for supper tonight. It really is a very, very long story." Jen didn't say a word; she simply turned and climbed into the carriage. Rand sighed and did the same.

When they had finished eating, Rand told Jen to meet him in the library; meanwhile, he went to his room and retrieved the tablet of the Word. During the meal he had decided to tell her everything—she was stubborn, temperamental, and merciless with her barbs of wit, but she was also true to the core. He knew he could trust her with any confidence; besides, if Zekiel should be lost, someone else besides himself had to know the story of what they had learned.

When he had retrieved the drawstring bag from his room, Rand joined Jen in the library and they settled into comfortable chairs. He began with the tale of finding the Stone Tear, then repeated as much of the history of the tablets as he could remember. When he told her what happened when he fitted two of the fragments together, he wasn't surprised to see disbelief creep into her expression. He brought forth the living piece of tablet and gave it to her. She admitted that its properties were impressive and that the message it displayed was intriguing, but she was still skeptical about the significance of it all.

Rand had expected no more and pressed on, telling her about the attack on the city by the *aganint* creatures and his own encounter with the demon cat. He showed her his knife and offered to summon Sergeant Brooks to confirm his account.

"That isn't necessary, Rand," said Jen. "I don't know if I believe everything you're telling me, but I know you believe it. I don't win many friends with my, ah, candor, but it does help me to recognize honest people when I see them. You are one; if you were not, I wouldn't be your friend."

"Thanks," said Rand. He continued, telling her what had happened to Zekiel in Solaria.

"Now you know the whole story," he concluded. "I only wish I knew what really went on down there, and that I could help Zekiel somehow."

"There is one way that you could help him," said Jen, her eyes growing wide as a thought came over her.

"What is it?" he said eagerly.

"No, forget it," she said. "It's—it's too ridiculous."

"Tell me!" he pleaded.

"Very well, but don't laugh at me since you insisted on hearing it," she said. He nodded and she went on. "Until now, we have spoken only of ways to help each other survive the Gauntlet. You would have the power to secure the safety of your friend, though, if you won the race—if you became the new king."

Rand was barely able to keep his promise and restrain his laughter. "You're right—it's ridiculous," he said. "Have you seen who we're up against? I can name a half dozen in our class who could beat me hopping on one leg, not to mention all the candidates from the other schools."

"I know," said Jen. "But as I said, it's the one way you can spare your friend, and maybe spread these ideas that are so important to the two of you. Besides, you shouldn't think so little of yourself— you're not the tallest or the strongest, but you're pretty fast. You have an able wit, too. And there is one advantage you have that no other contestant can boast, at our school or elsewhere."

"What's that?" said Rand.

"Me," Jen replied with a mischievous grin. Never had Rand valued her friendship more than at that moment. Once again he felt that strange movement deep within himself, and once again he willed it away before it could overwhelm him.

"Well, then, you might as well start calling me 'your majesty,'" he said and smiled in return. "How can I lose?" She laughed and tossed a cushion at him. He caught it reflexively and set it aside.

"All right," he said. "If we're going to win, how do we do it?"

They explored the possibilities over the next hour without coming to many conclusions. They simply didn't know enough about the details of the Gauntlet to make specific plans. Neither of them wanted to cheat, that much was certain. In the end they decided that the easiest places to help each other would be on the climbs up and down the Amharic plateau, the crossing of the nomad wastes, and the final race down the river to Willowberg.

"I have an idea for the river," said Jen. "It's something an old trader on the Clover Lakes told me about when I was just a little girl. I don't know if the story was true; I'll do some digging and see if I can learn more."

"What is it?" said Rand.

"I'd rather not say anything yet," said Jen. "It may just be a tall tale."

By then it was getting late and they decided to get some rest. This time Rand prevailed upon Jen to stay in a spare room, since she was going to spend the next day studying with him anyway. After they had said goodnight and he was dressing for bed in his room, he discovered that he was relieved to have told her the story of his involvement with the Stone Tears. A large part of his life that had been walled off from her was now open, no longer excluded from their friendship. It eased the burden of his worries for Zekiel as he drifted off to sleep.

Chapter 38

*No one who puts a hand to the plow and thinks better of it
is fit for service in the kingdom of the Speaker.*

The grueling training regimen at the Academy continued for another five weeks. Then a morning came when Rand arrived at school for his first class of the day and was told to report to the main lecture hall instead. The scene reminded him of the day King Anthon's death was announced—the handful of candidates clustered together in the front rows, the masters muttering to one another on the platform. The reenactment was completed when Parma entered through the side door just as he had done before. He came to the podium and waited for quiet.

"Honored contestants, princes and princesses of the realm, a momentous day is upon us. The word arrived from the capital early this morning—the Vizier has declared that the time for the Royal Gauntlet has come." He paused for emphasis before continuing. What a windbag, Rand thought, impatient for the headmaster to get to the details.

"We here at the Academy have done all we could to prepare you for this day, and you have distinguished yourselves by your own efforts," Parma said. "Now, however, the time for preparation is past and the day of your destiny has come. Accordingly, the Gauntlet training program is now suspended. You will have a week to report to the race marshals in the town of Willowberg. We here in

Serenhorn are closer to Willowberg than many of the Academies; nevertheless, I urge you to make arrangements at once for travel by the swiftest means available. All journeys bear a measure of uncertainty, and anyone who fails to report by the deadline will be disqualified, with the corresponding consequences to his or her family. I know I speak for the staff of the Academy and the citizens of the kingdom themselves when I bid you good fortune in this great contest. With highest regard and fondest hopes, you are now dismissed." He bowed to the students; behind him, the faculty rose and did the same. With that, the meeting was over.

"This is it," said Rand to Jen. "We'd better get back to the house and ask Gilbert how to get to Willowberg."

"We?" said Jen, lowering her voice and casting wary glances at the other contestants as they rose to leave. "Are you sure that's wise?"

"I think they've noticed that we're friends by now," said Rand. He hadn't told her about it, but he had endured many jests and innuendos in the boys' changing rooms regarding Jen. More than once the banter had fallen to a level where he felt obligated to put some of his new combat skills to the test. Those trials of honor had not always ended in victory, but he had succeeded in making his point.

"I suppose you're right," said Jen. "Some of the others will probably travel with their friends too."

"Undoubtedly," said Rand. "Besides, it's pranks against the world, remember?" Jen smiled and nodded.

"One good thing about this surprise is that Coleman won't be back for us until nightfall," Rand continued. "We can skip all the nonsense with the carriage and go straight home." They edged away from the others and slipped quietly from the hall.

It took them only a few minutes to walk down the hill to the manor house. Gilbert set things in motion immediately when he heard the news.

"An exciting day, my lord," he said, speaking to them in between bursts of orders to the rest of the staff. "We'll ready the overland carriage for you, along with an escort of course. Your fastest route will be along the West Horn of the Seren River. There's a pass through the Hunter Range that leads from the West Horn's headwaters to the Solus Valley on the other side. The only other way I know of is to go down Serenvale to the end of the Hunter Range, then up the Solus Valley to Willowberg from there. It could be done by riverboat in a few days, but it would be a close thing with little chance for rest."

"Overland carriage?" asked Rand.

"Yes, my lord," said Gilbert. "One suited for longer journeys, like Minister Dorian's that brought you here. The light two-seater you've been using is considered a city carriage—convenient for short trips, but not built to withstand the rigors of the open road. By the way, there's an advantage other than speed to taking the road along the West Horn."

"What's that?" said Rand.

"You'll pass through Westmount and have the chance to visit Falconkeep, your true home," said the butler. "You should reach it by nightfall tomorrow. You and Lady Jen will find it a memorable place." He was about to say more, then stopped and smiled enigmatically at them before calling after a passing footman. "Bertram! There you are; please accompany Lord Rand to his room and help him pack for his trip. My lady," he said, turning to Jen, "Coleman can run you home to get your things if you like; it will take us a while to make everything ready here."

"That would be lovely, Gilbert, thank you," she replied. She nodded farewell to Rand; he followed Bertram upstairs.

The footman disappeared into a storage closet and emerged with a large trunk designed with the traveling gentleman in mind. He wrestled it into Rand's room and stood it on end. The two halves opened like a set of doors—the left-hand side was a kind of mini-wardrobe with a rod for hanging clothes, while the right resembled an elaborate chest of drawers, with many cunningly crafted cabinets and trays for storing accessories. The top swung up to reveal a mirror for grooming.

Bertram helped Rand choose suitable clothing and other useful items for the trip; as he did so, he explained the purpose of some of the more obscure implements, many of which Rand had had no opportunity to experiment with during his short and busy tenure as a nobleman. While the footman was occupied with stowing these things away, Rand retrieved the nondescript bag that contained the fragment of the Word from the chest he had hidden in his wardrobe. When Bertram went to the wardrobe to get more clothes, Rand slipped the bag into one of the drawers in the trunk.

There was a clamor of activity outside. Rand went to the bay window and looked into the courtyard below. A carriage similar to Minister Dorian's, blue and silver instead of black and gold, had been brought out of the stable and parked there. The family crest of the Falconers was painted on the door. Two grooms appeared with a team of horses and set to work harnessing them to the vehicle.

Rand heard a heavy thump behind him and turned to see that Bertram had closed the trunk and was busy snapping the many latches into place. Since Coleman was out with Lady Jen, Bertram consented to letting Rand help him haul the heavy luggage down-stairs. When Gilbert saw them he shook his head in disapproval and ordered a passing soldier to take Rand's place. Left with nothing to do until Jen returned, Rand went to the library and selected a hand-ful of books and charts that they could study while they traveled.

Less than a quarter of an hour later, he heard a clatter in the courtyard and looked out the library window; Coleman and Jen had arrived in the town carriage. Once Jen's single well-worn trunk was hoisted up and secured atop the overland carriage, the expedition was ready to depart. Coleman would be their driver, as he had been so often before. Rand bid goodbye to Gilbert and the household staff, then shook hands with Sergeant Brooks and raised an arm in salute to the rest of the escort. Then he and Jen climbed into the car-riage and got settled for the trip.

The memory of their ambush by wolves still fresh in his mind, Brooks insisted on taking seven guards with him this time instead of three. That left only three behind to stand watch over the manor house and the surrounding grounds, but under the circumstances they all agreed that the risks on the road were of primary concern. Now the sergeant guided the escort into formation and sounded the call to move out. Gilbert and the assembled members of the house-hold shouted good wishes after them as the caravan passed through the gates and out onto Ridge Road.

Rand expected the streets to be astir with activity as his party and the rest of the contestants set out for Willowberg. He was sur-prised and somewhat humbled to find that life was going on as usual in Serenhorn that day. After all, he reflected, what were nine-teen young nobles amongst a city of tens of thousands of people?

"How do you suppose the others are going to make it to Willowberg?" he asked Jen.

"Most of them will probably take the river," she said. "If they don't know about the pass through the Hunter Range, they'll assume that they have to go south around the mountains. Some of the hardier ones may try to gallop down Serenvale and back up the Solus Valley on horseback, but unless they had the foresight to arrange for a string of fresh horses along the way, their mounts will tire quickly."

"So we might have an advantage," said Rand.

"A small one," said Jen. "Some of the others probably know about the pass we're taking, for one thing. Then there's the school in Willowberg itself, of course—Great Northern Academy. The candidates there have probably been training on some of the actual obstacles that make up the first part of the Gauntlet."

By this time they were plodding along Hornside Way toward Merchant's Hall. At the next intersection, they turned left and made for the river. Rand leaned out the window to look ahead and saw that they were approaching one of the massive stone bridges that connected the three districts of Serenhorn. Traffic was heavy in front of them as it funneled across the link between the east and west sides of the river, but Sergeant Brooks did not hesitate to use noble privilege.

"Make way for Lord Falconer! Way for the prince!" he shouted in his throaty parade-ground voice. Seeing that his demand was backed by a cadre of mounted soldiers, people quickly complied. The looks on their faces spoke eloquently of their resentment, though, and Rand retreated back into the shadowed recesses of the carriage with a pang of embarrassment. People in distant hamlets like Oakbridge had no experience with the demands of the ruling classes; as such he had never given any thought to how burdensome those demands could be to common folk.

"I wish he hadn't done that," he said. "We're not in that big of a hurry."

"You are a peer of the realm, Rand—at least your father is, and you are acting on behalf of his house," said Jen. He looked at her and saw that she was observing him carefully. "Your business is more important than theirs, by definition," she continued.

"How so?" said Rand. "They all have a living to make and families to feed. If anything their business is more important than mine, since it appears that I don't have to earn my keep at all any more. In fact, if I understand it right, most of my family's wealth comes from the work of people like them. I saw hatred in their faces and I don't fault them for it."

"Nor I," said Jen. "I'm glad you see it that way. Remember that we're in the Gauntlet to win it now, to save your friend. If by some chance we do win, you can't just pardon Zekiel and then abdicate the throne. You'll have to rule Solethon for years to come, and I hope you'll think of the welfare of ordinary people the way you do now."

"Zekiel," sighed Rand with concern. "I hope he's holding up all right. I spent so little time with him and yet he opened my eyes to so much. Even what we're talking about now plays a part in it."

"What do you mean?" said Jen.

"In the time of the lost empire, men sought the Word because they could see all around them that life was not as it should be," said Rand. "If you pay attention, you can see the same is true again today. The nobles pushing people aside, the people hating them in return—it's all part of some disease we carry inside of us."

"I find that easy enough to believe," said Jen, and Rand saw a shadow of bitterness pass over her face. "Lord Wilhelm may be one of the most debased men I've ever known, but he was always able to find plenty of friends to join in his revels. I must confess I find it harder, though, to credit that this ancient book of yours holds the cure."

"I understand," said Rand. "We need to know more about it, and now that Zekiel is beyond our reach, we'll have to find that knowledge ourselves."

"Fine, then," said Jen in a tone of mock relief. "I was afraid we'd get bored with nothing important to occupy our time." Rand rolled his eyes and made as if to tear a double handful of his hair out in exasperation. She laughed and playfully kicked his foot.

Rand glanced out and saw that they were now climbing the arch of the bridge. On the river below, a barge was passing underneath them; he wondered if it might be the Kelpie and smiled as he considered what Captain Beck might think of what he had become. A smaller craft slid swiftly by downstream, reminding him of his competitors in the Gauntlet and making him impatient to leave the city traffic behind on the way to Willowberg. He felt the carriage shift as it passed over the peak of the bridge. Thinking that they must have left the disgruntled commoners behind by now, he decided it was safe to lean out the window again. Jen did the same on the other side.

There was a less crowded feeling to the streets and buildings on the west side of the river. For one thing, the waterfront lacked the decaying, disreputable atmosphere of the central docks where Rand had come ashore on his first visit to Serenhorn. At the next intersection they came to a broad avenue that paralleled the river. Sergeant Brooks led the company onto the wider road, headed north. They made good headway—the traffic was light compared to the throngs on Hornside Way. Soon the road reached the point where the East and West Horns converged into the Seren River. There the road angled to the northwest, following the southern bank of the West Horn.

The urban landscape thinned out; before long they passed through the western gate and left Serenhorn proper behind. Shops and homes gathered near the skirts of the city like children around their mother, but before the sun reached midday the expedition had left these behind as well. The party stopped for a picnic lunch by the side of the river, allowing the horses to graze and drink their fill.

When the horses were sufficiently rested, the column set out on the western road once more. They passed farms, orchards, vineyards, and country estates. Every square yard of the fertile, gently sloping valley was allotted to some particular purpose. From time to time the road passed through a village or market town. As night approached, they stopped at a large inn where Rand and Jen were treated like heroes for being contestants in the Gauntlet. They were embarrassed by the attention but happy to learn that none of their fellow participants had been seen going that way.

Chapter 39

You are my strength, I keep a lookout for you;
you, Speaker, are my stronghold.

By the middle of the afternoon on the following day, they came to a part of the valley where the crest on the side of the carriage was recognized by the farmers and townsfolk they passed. Many of these people touched their caps or foreheads in a gesture of respect, and a few called out a cheerful greeting.

"You're quite an important figure in this corner of the kingdom," said Jen with her characteristic teasing. "Still, I look forward to meeting your new father. House Falconer apparently enjoys a reputation somewhat better than my own House Wilhelm. When my lord passes by, the gestures and calls are of a less complimentary nature."

"Lord Falconer is a serious man, but a capable and honorable one from what I've seen," said Rand. "You'll like him."

"But will he like me?" said Jen. "I'm not much of a courtly lady."

"He strikes me as a man who is more interested in people's substance than their appearance," said Rand. "I think he'll understand you very well."

"He won't mind at all that I'm ugly, is that it?" retorted Jen sharply.

"Of course not!" said Rand in consternation. "I mean, that's not what I meant. No one could think you ugly—that is to say, you're very..." he trailed off awkwardly.

"I'm very what?" said Jen, regarding him intently.

"Nothing—he'll like you, that's all," said Rand. He turned away to stare out the window, conscious of his face turning hot with embarrassment. He was relieved when Sergeant Brooks chose that moment to appear beside the carriage, matching its pace and leaning low in the saddle to speak with them.

"Your pardon, milord—I thought you'd like to know that we're nearing the castle now. You can see it yonder." He pointed up and to the right of their present path. Rand leaned out of the window and looked, shading his eyes with his hand against the glare of the afternoon sun.

"Do you mean that thin spire there?" he said. "The one rising from that flat-topped mountain?"

"That flat-topped mountain is the castle, milord," said the sergeant with a smile. "The spire is its watchtower." Suddenly the scale of the scene fell into place for Rand, and he couldn't help gaping. The dark mouth he had taken for a cavern was the castle gate; the niches scattered across its face were windows, not natural crevices. His mind struggled to encompass the size of the place. It occupied the entire summit of the mountain on which it stood, as though springing from the natural rock itself. Now that he knew what to look for, he could tell where the sloping sides of the mountain ended and the vertical walls of the keep began, but the effect of its first impression lingered.

"So that's Falconkeep," said Jen, her voice coming to him over the top of the carriage from where she leaned out the window on her side. "I do hope they can spare a room for us." Sergeant Brooks chuckled at her jest and shook his head as he trotted forward to re-take his place at the head of the company. Rand sank back into his seat inside the carriage, gripping the edge of the window to steady himself as he absorbed the idea that the massive fortress was his home. Jen plopped down beside him and smiled.

"You'd better get used to it, my friend," she said. "We can't have you dumbfounded every time you find out how wealthy you are or we'll never get a word out of you." He shrugged his shoulders and looked out at the castle again. In a few minutes, they were approaching a new village. The sliding panel at the front of the compartment opened and Coleman's voice spoke to them from the driver's bench.

"Westmount, milord—the principal town of your family's domain."

"Well, well," said Jen. "Your own town, too. Do you think we can get a discount at the shops?"

"Oh, leave off," said Rand in irritation. "I suppose your new father has no fiefdom of his own?"

"Even in their heyday the Wilhelms were a lesser house, Rand," said Jen. "Not so old or so grand as the Falconers. Most of their wealth consisted of a fleet of trade barges that ferried goods around the Clover Lakes and down to Serenhorn. They had some land as well, it's true—a few acres of pastures and crops around the manor house. But the present Lord Wilhelm gambled away what was left of the boats and had to sell off most of the land to pay for his lavish debaucheries. I'll be lucky to keep the house long enough to have a chance at rebuilding the family's fortunes, if I survive the Gauntlet."

She was interrupted by Sergeant Brooks' booming voice as he announced the arrival of Prince Rand in his ancestral village. Westmount was about the size of Kerrin, with shops and town homes lining a busy main thoroughfare and branching out along several side streets. It was tucked up against the lower slopes of the Hunter Range at the western verge of Serenvale. At the sergeant's announcement, people all along the street stopped and turned to look.

"Hail Prince Rand!" someone shouted, and others took up the cry. Rand didn't know how to respond; he mustered a smile and waved at the crowd as the carriage rolled on. He wasn't surprised in the least to hear bursts of stifled laughter coming from the seat behind him, but he chose to ignore them.

The road curved to the right and crossed over the West Horn on a stone bridge. The river had become narrower as they drew near its mountain source, and here it was narrowed further by passing through a deep gorge. As a result the bridge was not a very long one, but the town came to an abrupt end on the near side. On the far end, Rand saw that a heavy iron gate blocked the road, guarded by soldiers in Falconer livery. The party came to a halt while Sergeant Brooks rode forward to identify himself.

Once the proper phrases had been exchanged, the guards opened the gate and waved the travelers through. As the carriage pulled even with the men, they saluted. Rand raised a hand in acknowledgement but if they saw it they gave no sign, standing at attention with their eyes fixed straight ahead. It was apparent that Lord Falconer set a high value on discipline.

The road rose steeply and turned back and forth in switchbacks across the southern face of the mountain topped by Falconkeep. The peak stood apart from the mass of the Hunter Range to the west, commanding unobstructed views in every direction. Midway up the slope there was a second gate obstructing the way. The party went through the same procedure as before and continued on. As the carriage swung around the corner onto the last switchback,

Rand saw that they were approaching a final gate. This one was much larger than the others; it was flanked by heavy stone columns and topped by a stone arch and parapet. There were four guards this time instead of two. They were very thorough, even opening the doors of the carriage and peering within to assure themselves that nothing was amiss.

When the guards were satisfied, the expedition proceeded through onto the small plateau that lay before the walls of Falconkeep. A trumpet sounded from the watchtower high above. In response to the signal, the heavy portcullis that blocked the entrance to the castle rose. Brooks led them through an echoing stone passage and into the open courtyard of the keep. It was spacious enough to hold the carriage and its escort with room to spare, but the towering walls overhead made it appear smaller than it really was. Most of it was in shadow this late in the afternoon; Rand guessed it would only be fully illuminated when the sun was near its zenith.

Rand was still taking in the surroundings when he felt Jen rise from her seat and heard her open her door. She climbed down into the courtyard before he could react.

"I guess we've arrived," he muttered to himself and followed suit. A great door on the far side of the courtyard swung open and two footmen trotted down the steps. Behind them came a familiar figure.

"Minister Dorian!" exclaimed Rand with delight, happy to see a familiar face in such intimidating surroundings. The somber old administrator smiled in spite of himself at his young master's enthusiasm.

"Welcome home, Prince Rand," he said. Rand hurried forward and clasped his hand warmly. Dorian looked past his shoulder and stared. Rand turned and saw that Jen was approaching.

"Minister, I'd like you to meet Princess Jen of Lochinvale," he said, gesturing for her to come forward. "She's to compete in the Gauntlet also; we met at the Academy."

"My lady," said the minister, bowing to her with great ceremony. "Gilbert mentioned you in some of his regular household reports. It is an honor to meet you."

"Then I gather that his reports did not predispose you against me," said Jen with a laugh that carried a tinge of anxiety.

"Most assuredly they did not, my lady," said Dorian. "He spoke well of both your deportment and your efforts to help our new heir in his studies. However, if I may say so, he failed to convey what a winsome young lady you are in person."

"You are too kind, sir," Jen replied, blushing and making a little curtsey. As he observed the exchange, Rand found himself blushing also, though he could hardly understand why. Dorian ushered them up the steps and through the great iron door into the keep.

As Dorian had told Rand when they first toured the Falconer mansion in Serenhorn, Falconkeep had been converted over the centuries from an austere fortress into a luxurious residence. Yet behind the finery, the raw-boned strength of its original purpose remained. Walls were thick, rooms and passages were high and narrow, and any part of floor, wall, or ceiling not obscured by later adornment was made from cold, unyielding stone.

Dorian led them through echoing greatrooms, down shadowy halls, and up two spiraling staircases to the third floor of the keep. He described the names and uses of the areas they passed, but the flood of information was more than Rand could absorb; he was too occupied just looking at the place. It was both richer and more austere than the city house had been. Great wealth and long occupancy had filled it with a tightly-packed collection of furnishings and heirlooms that adhered to no design Rand could perceive. It was an active house, though, not a museum—footmen, maids, military officers, and civilian administrators like Dorian came and went as the visitors passed by, absorbed in their unknown duties.

The third floor of the keep was quiet—Rand saw no one as Dorian led them down a deeply carpeted corridor. It was more brightly lit than the lower floors as well, for they were high enough now that the windows in the rooms they passed caught more of the light from the setting sun. Dorian stopped about halfway down the corridor and rapped at a heavy double door. Rand had an eerie sense of time repeating itself as he recalled his first meeting with Lord Falconer, standing in the hallway of the manor house in Serenhorn while Gilbert the butler knocked at his adoptive father's door to announce him. He looked at Jen and smiled encouragingly, but she didn't respond.

Brisk footsteps could be heard approaching from the other side of the door. It opened inward abruptly and at first Rand was unable to discern the figure that stood there, silhouetted as it was against the light from the windows across the room. When his vision adjusted, he saw a man about forty years old wearing what must be a uniform of the Falconer militia. He was compact of frame and erect in his bearing, with close-cut hair and a narrowly clipped moustache.

"Ah, Captain Reichart," said Dorian. "May I introduce Prince Rand Falconer and his guest, Princess Jen Wilhelm."

"An honor, my lord and lady," said the captain, bowing crisply and snapping the heels of his boots together with a sharp click.

"Captain Reichart at your service. I am the officer of the household guards, chief of security, and Lord Falconer's aide de camp, second in command of his forces under Commander Timmons. Please come in." He stepped back and bowed again.

Jen hesitated, so Rand led the way into the room. Lord Falconer was leaning over a large table near the windows, gesturing to a map spread upon it as he spoke with two other soldiers. When he noticed Rand approaching, he turned and took stock of the visitors.

"Dorian!" he cried. "What strays have you collected on our doorstep today?"

"A curious pair of vagabonds, my lord," replied Dorian with a twinkle in his eye. "They have a rather ill-favored look about them. 'Twas pity made me take them in, I confess—mark it down to my well-known softness of heart."

"They do look somewhat shopworn," said Falconer, circling around Rand and Jen with his arms crossed behind his back as though he were inspecting his troops. "One might almost think they had been engaging in vigorous exercise—most inappropriate for children of privilege, don't you think?"

"Oh, disgraceful, my lord," Dorian agreed with a sad shake of his head. Falconer stopped in front of Rand and fixed him with a stern look. Then he broke into a laugh that was shared by Dorian and the soldiers who had been looking on. He motioned to the door and his advisors filed out, official business concluded for now. He clasped arms with Rand in greeting.

"Welcome home, lad," he said. "It's good to see you again. I can tell by the look of you that you've been training hard for the trial that awaits you. I only wish we had time to introduce you properly to your ancestral home here, but of course you have more urgent business for now."

"Yes, my lo—I mean, father," said Rand. "This place is amazing, though. I would like to see it all, and get to know the people here. It will have to wait, I suppose."

"It is a double-edged blade indeed," said Falconer. "The very errand that brings you to this house and makes it your own is the one that calls you away too soon. But such is the cost of duty, one which will grow for you from here onward. It is the price that a true noble pays for the privileges he or she enjoys. Speaking of she, I have been ungallant, gabbling away with you while a princess stands waiting." He turned to Jen and bowed, taking her hand and brushing it with his lips as he did so. She curtseyed in response, smiling in a bashful way that Rand found both surprising and amusing.

"You also are most welcome, Lady Wilhelm," Falconer continued. "Our halls are too rarely graced by a noblewoman's presence of late, especially such a fine young lady as you." Jen stiffened a little at that and looked down.

"I thank you for your kindness, Lord Falconer," she said quietly. "Yet I would not have you think more highly of me than you ought. You and your house are esteemed greatly among commoners and nobles alike. House Wilhelm is—well, not of the same cloth, as it were, nor am I a natural child of its lineage any more than Rand is of yours." Rand was moved as he looked at her standing there downcast and subdued. Falconer considered her for a moment before answering with a surprising gentleness.

"Please, Lady Wilhelm, favor me with your countenance." Jen lifted her head reluctantly and looked him in the eye.

"That's better," he continued. "Do not value your name or yourself so lightly. I have had the displeasure of meeting the present Lord Wilhelm at the gatherings where the nobles of Serenvale conduct their business and pursue their revelries; I am not surprised that he is burdensome to you. But I also knew his father, and I count that as a privilege. We served together in the Third Vokar War, where he used his skills as a boatman to command the barges that ferried our troops across the Copenag River to the field of battle. When the struggle fared ill for us, he organized the retreat, taking his barges again and again into the thick of the fray on the enemy shore until every man that still lived had been carried to safety. He was pierced by a spear as he helped to push the last barge away from the bank. If not for his valor and skill, our forces would have been trapped against the river and destroyed."

"An honorable end," said Jen, her head held higher and her shoulders lifting. "I had not heard of this before."

"I owe him my life, as do hundreds more," said Falconer. "If we had not lived to fight other battles, the armies of Solethon would have been greatly weakened; we may have lost the war in the end. I think perhaps it was for his sake that the noble houses were reluctant to censure his son—a failing that has allowed him to sink lower than he might otherwise have done."

"I see," said Jen. "I had believed that a long and thankless struggle lay ahead of me to bring even a scrap of honor to the name of Wilhelm. Perhaps my task is more one of honor restored than of honor wrung from naught but disgrace."

"What you have said is proof of the second thing I would tell you," said Falconer. "I entreated you earlier to think better of yourself as well as of your name. You display courage and nobility of spirit by your determination to redeem your adoptive house. Add to that the nimble wit and dedication you have demonstrated during your training for the Gauntlet, attested to by the mentions made of you in the reports from my staff in the city, and you are clearly a young lady of substance who would be a credit to any noble house. I am very pleased to meet you in person, and more pleased still that you are friends with my son."

As Falconer spoke, Jen's expression brightened until she was smiling. Her eyes glistened as though she were on the verge of tears.

"I thank you again for your kindness, my lord," she said with a quaver in her voice. "Your words mean more to me than I can express. I have been fortunate to have a friend like Rand, but never more so than now that our friendship has brought me to your house."

"In my house you will always find welcome," Falconer replied. "Indeed, I am sure you will find welcome in any noble house of the realm. When you have discharged your duty in the Gauntlet, I trust you will visit us again."

"Gladly, my lord," Jen replied.

"Excellent," said Falconer. "Why don't the two of you join me on the battlements? I can show you a little of the lay of the land while we yet have light."

Lord Falconer took Rand and Jen up past the fourth floor of the keep and onto the broad walkway atop the walls. They were on the south side above Falconer's office. The town of Westmount lay spread out below them, separated from them by the West Horn of the Seren River. The water glowed white in the deep shadows of the gorge below as it foamed over rocks and rapids.

"Our fief stretches from the crest of the Hunter Range in the west, runs down this valley, and stops about twelve miles to the east," said Falconer. "My ancestors chose this mountain to build their fortress because it allows us to see most of the district at once and it is easily defended. You can see down there how a road continues westward out of town along the southern side of the gorge. It leads to the mines up in the mountains."

"Mines?" said Rand.

"We really must find the time to educate you about your new family," said Falconer with a shake of his head. "We earn a little income from surplus crops in their season and we have a few hundred head of sheep and cattle, but most of our wealth comes from timber and mining. We pull several tons of iron and copper out of these mountains every year. The miners sometimes find a little gold and silver, but not enough to live on."

"So the people in the village work the mines?" asked Rand.

"Yes, and the lumber mill," said Falconer. "You can see it there on the far side of town. Herdsmen care for the sheep and cattle, and tenants work our fields. Not everyone works for us, of course. There are freeholders with their own farms and all the merchants and tradesmen who service the town."

"Those who run the shops in a nobleman's town are not necessarily free," said Jen. "I have paid close attention to the idle chat of my classmates at the Academy, hoping to learn what I could about this noble life that was thrust upon me. I gather that many nobles own every shop and stable in their domains, or else own the land under the shops and charge stiff rents. Between the rents and the price of the goods, they contrive to squeeze most of the meager wages they pay to their tenants back into their own coffers."

"You speak the truth," said Falconer. "I find no honor in such practice, but some lords believe it to be their just due. The Falconers did not follow that path, though perhaps it was not from higher principles. Our house has always been active in military service; commoners in our militia who win honor on the field of battle are traditionally granted freeholds in reward. Such a grant might be a tract of land or a franchise for a business in the town. We have to take good care of our miners and loggers, too. Their work is difficult and dangerous; if we did not pay them well and treat them fairly, they could flee to an easier life elsewhere. Taken together, our fief has grown over the years into a patchwork of tenants, laborers, and freeholders with plenty of wealth for all to share."

"I am glad to hear that there are ways to rule an estate with justice," said Jen. "Perhaps I could learn more about the methods of your house and apply them to my own."

"Minister Dorian would be delighted to tutor you in the minutia of administering a fief," said Falconer. "In fact, I imagine the difficulty would lie in getting him to stop." He laughed heartily and his young guests joined in.

"You'll take the mining road into the mountains tomorrow," he continued. "It goes up beyond the mine heads to a narrow pass at the crest of the range, then it descends into the Solus Valley. Not many people travel that way, but my miners keep the road in good repair as far as the border of my lands at the top of the pass."

"How long will it take us to reach Willowberg from here?" Rand asked.

"You should make it in three days at the most," said Falconer. "Come with me. There's something I want to do for you." He turned and trotted down the steps to the interior of the keep. Rand and Jen looked at each other questioningly before following him.

Lord Falconer led his young guests all the way down to the first floor of the keep, which was dedicated to the practical functions of the fortress. In addition to the kitchen and the laundry there were stables, a smithy, and an armory. Falconer took them to the latter. It was adjacent to the smithy since most of the articles kept there required metalwork of one kind or another. An armorer and his assistant were at work over an anvil, attaching a shoulder guard to a breastplate with rivets and strips of iron.

"Good afternoon, Henry," said Falconer to the armorer. "This is Prince Rand, my lately adopted heir, and his friend Princess Jen." The thin, balding old man looked at them over the rims of his spectacles and nodded in reply. He turned the pieces of his project over to his assistant and wiped his hands on a rag before bowing to the visitors.

"M'lord, m'lady," he said in a high, reedy voice. "'Tis an honor to have ye with us."

"Henry, these two will be running in the Gauntlet in a few days' time," said Falconer. "They can only afford to stop with us for the night and then they must be off to Willowberg. Do you think we could fit them with scout harnesses by then?"

"Aye, 'twould be just the thing," said Henry. "Mayhap we can cobble up some good soft boots, too, fer the runnin'."

"Excellent," said Falconer. "Measure them now so you can begin the work at once."

"Aye, m'lord," Henry replied with a nod and snapped his fingers impatiently. His assistant hastened to bring him a measuring tape, then took up a slate and chalk to jot down measurements as Henry called them out. They worked their way around Rand quickly, collecting sizes for his waist, chest, shoulders, and feet.

"Yer pardon, m'lady," said Henry to Jen as he turned to her when they were done with Rand. "We've no time to wait for the seamstress to come, but I swear by me life we'll be naught but proper to ye." His discomfort was evident in his averted gaze and shuffling feet.

"I have every confidence in you," said Jen reassuringly. "Please, do whatever you must." Henry proceeded to take the same measurements as he had with Rand, but with a great deal more care.

"What is a scout harness?" Rand asked Falconer.

"It's a wide belt with shoulder straps that incorporates a light pack," said the nobleman. "The belt has storage pockets for useful items, and the pack is designed to lie flush against the small of your back, tapering off as it rises toward the shoulders so as to add as little bulk as possible to your frame. The pack and the pockets are waterproofed as best as possible. Army scouts have to travel lightly and quickly. Quietly, too, so there's no metal in the making of the harness."

"It sounds a lot like the gear of the Royal Courier I met," said Rand.

"Much the same," Falconer agreed. "The pack is a little larger than what they use, for unlike them you won't be able to stop at an inn for most of your meals. Speaking of meals, let us repair to the dining hall. Supper will be served shortly, and you could use some refreshment after your journey."

That evening they enjoyed a banquet such as Rand had never known before. Lord Falconer's elderly aunt and sole surviving relative, the Lady Roberta, joined them, as did five officers from the Falconer militia in their best dress uniforms. Each diner had a servant standing behind his or her chair, ready to anticipate the slightest wish. A quartet of musicians played near a fire that roared and crackled in the largest fireplace Rand had ever seen. Lord Falconer led the table conversation by formally introducing Rand as his new son; everyone toasted his health and wished him well in the Gauntlet. Seized by the spirit of the occasion, Rand stood and took up his own glass.

"To the Lady Wilhelm," he declared, gesturing toward Jen, who shot him a dirty look which he cheerfully ignored. "She is a steadfast friend and a true princess. May she come through every trial and bring honor and prosperity to her house." The toast was heartily seconded around the table. Rand smiled and sat, whereupon Jen gave him a swift kick in the side of the leg. She sighed and stood in her turn.

"To our host, the estimable Lord Falconer," she said and raised her glass toward the head of the table. "May we all profit from his example." Again the others voiced enthusiastic agreement.

The meal continued with lively conversation all around. Rand and Jen fielded questions about their training from Lord Falconer and his people; in their turn, they asked about the doings and history of the Falconer domain. As time passed, Rand felt the effects of a large meal and a long day's travel. He noticed Lady Roberta starting to nod sleepily as well. Lord Falconer recognized their fatigue and brought the occasion to a close, sending servants with Rand and Jen to lead them to their rooms.

After his way had separated from Jen's, Rand and his guide overtook the Lady Roberta just as she reached the door to her suite. She turned and saw them coming, beckoning Rand to pause and speak with her.

"Good to have you in the family, my boy," she said with a twinkle in her startlingly blue eyes. He smiled and made a little bow. She glanced at the footman who served as his guide and motioned Rand closer.

"Has the wind ever spoken to you?" she whispered. He looked at her in confusion and she continued. "No matter; I thought by the look of you that it might have. It speaks to me sometimes. Heed me, lad—if it speaks to you, listen!" She winked conspiratorially and waved him onward, turning and limping into her drawing room slowly on her aging joints. He didn't know what to make of her strange advice, but the footman coughed discreetly and motioned for him to follow. He nodded and went on to his room.

Chapter 40

Why do the kingdoms conspire, and their peoples form vain plots?

The Royal Vizier sat at his favorite stone table, presiding over a meeting of his chief agents and allies. Only the need for complete privacy could have prompted him to violate the sanctity of his chambers with the presence of outsiders. Now that the gathering was in full swing, however, he found that he derived a certain satisfaction from playing the host at a council dedicated to the culmination of his plans.

"So there we have it," he said as a silent acolyte distributed copies of a roster of names. "These are the most promising candidates we've been grooming while waiting for Anthon's death. I have my personal favorites, of course—Prince Uthor, the ruthless and fratricidal boor who would gladly march forth in one war of conquest after another; and our budding sorceress, the lovely Princess Jylla with her hair of copper, who would popularize the practice of the dark arts at every level of society." He tapped the list in front of him and smiled wolfishly.

"You have not been idle at your labors elsewhere," he continued approvingly. "We have Prince Neglin, who styles himself a future statesman while practicing deceit and self-enrichment on a scale that would beggar the imagination of a master thief. He could set our neighbors against each other and expand the dominance of

Solethon without drawing a single blade. There is also the refreshingly uninhibited Princess Aurelia, who would gladly promote a greater devotion to personal freedom in our kingdom and abroad by encouraging the exploration of unfettered sensuality. Moreover, we mustn't forget young Prince Loran, the idealist. At first blush his hatred of corruption and oppression might seem a threat to our designs, but his zeal to purge the nobility of its sins would eliminate many of our more obstinate rivals and concentrate great wealth and power in the hands of someone who feels perfectly justified in using it regardless of the blood he might shed."

"A rich harvest indeed, master!" hissed Garrak the raven, perched atop the table at the Vizier's left hand.

"How do you plan to improve their chances?" asked the headmaster of the Solaria Academy.

"Sheppard here, whom many of you know as the sergeant-at-arms of the royal court, is serving as the Marshal of the Gauntlet this time," said the Vizier. "I will let him address that."

The sergeant, short but thickly built and bearing the scars of many battles, stood from his chair at one end of the table. "At the Vizier's urging, this running of the Gauntlet has been so ordered as to be the deadliest in centuries," he said. "The pits and traps of the obstacles at the start in Willowberg have been fortified with sharpened stakes. The river crossing passes through treacherous rapids to drown the weak or unwary. The mounts provided for the hedge-jumping gallop to the high plateau will be skittish and ill-tempered, eager to bite and trample any rider who gives them a chance. Such chances will come often, for the tack will be of poor quality, with an unfortunate tendency to break under strain. I could go on, but you can imagine the rest." He smiled grimly and sat down.

"But how will our favored candidates pass through these dangers?" pressed the headmaster.

"There will be many opportunities for the managers of the course to steer them clear of the worst risks," said the Vizier. "For example, we will see to it that their horses are well-tamed and their saddles secure. Some dangers will be unavoidable, though, such as the river crossing. Do not forget that we want a winner that is strong and competent as well as useful for our plans. We will clear the way, but one of these five must rise above all others and seize victory on his or her strength alone."

"Won't such wholesale bloodshed foment unrest among the noble houses?" asked the chancellor of the exchequer, a heavy, turtle-like man known for his caution.

"You forget that most of the Gauntlet takes place beyond the view of spectators," replied Sheppard. "The families gathered at the finish line may raise an outcry when they realize that most of their beloved heirs will never come stumbling home, but by then one of our candidates will be celebrating victory and taking the crown. He or she can move quickly to quell dissent."

"Very well," said the Vizier, rising from his seat. "All is prepared, and each of you understands his duties. Go to your posts; I will leave for Willowberg tonight."

The other members of the ad-hoc council rose from the table and slipped out of the Vizier's chambers one by one. When all but Garrak had left, the Vizier turned his attention to the raven.

"How go matters with regard to the Enslaver and the Others?" he asked.

"Little news," said the bird. "The spirit planes are quiet since you imprisoned the old scholar and confiscated the known fragments. The farm boy who appears favored of the Enemy has done nothing but prepare for the Gauntlet like the rest. He is presently en route to Willowberg."

"I think we should see if the Others can ambush him before he gets there," said the Vizier. "He may be nothing more than a nuisance of happenstance or a bit of misdirection on the part of our enemy, but I dislike loose ends. My order believes it is best to strike first when in doubt, a policy that has yielded satisfying results over the centuries."

"A blow struck in darkness is as likely to injure you as your opponent," chided a gratingly familiar voice. The Vizier spun around to find Lupus observing him from his customary dimensional portal. "Remember, my servant, that you attracted my attention in the first place by meddling in the affairs of my beast-walkers," Lupus continued. "Have you forgotten your place again so quickly?" A flicker of heat rippled along the Vizier's skin, a fleeting reminder of the searing pain that the being could inflict with the slightest effort of will.

"No, master Lupus," he answered quickly. "I will never forget your—your lessons. I would have consulted you before taking any action, just as you commanded."

"I doubt that," said Lupus drily. "But since you have not yet acted on your ill-conceived notions, I suppose we will never know what you might have done. Regardless, my point stands—to strike at this boy without knowing where he figures into the Enemy's plans is rash. That mistake has proved costly to us in the past, and we will not repeat it."

"Yes, lord," said the Vizier.

"Besides, if your underlings do their jobs, the princeling should fall during the race along with the other surplus contestants, should he not? We have found that we are less likely to attract intervention from the Enemy when we approach indirectly, creating conditions of hardship which apply equally to many mortals at once. Singling them out for special attack tends to draw out special defensive measures in response."

"I see," said the Vizier.

"Now leave trying to strategize in realms you do not understand and be off on your journey," said the glittering white fiend. "If you don't make haste, you will be late to your own little Gauntlet." With a chilling laugh, Lupus withdrew his presence from the room.

The Vizier swallowed his pride and anger and went about packing for his trip. When he was done, he sent Garrak to fly ahead and gather information on the doings of the Gauntlet contestants. Before climbing into his private coach and speeding off into the night, he made time for a visit to the cells deep in the bowels of the Citadel.

He ordered a guard to throw open the door to Zekiel's cell, bursting into the tiny space before the old man had time to recover from the deafening clang. The scholar blinked and squinted against the light of the lamp that the Vizier hung from a hook in the ceiling. The Vizier took a stool from one of the guards and ordered them to wait outside with the door shut before sitting by the iron bed where Zekiel lay chained.

"Do you know who I am?" asked the Vizier after waiting silently for the prisoner's eyes to adjust to the light.

"Yes, my lord, of course," said Zekiel. "You are the Royal Vizier. I have hoped against hope that I might speak with you and plead my case. There has been a dreadful misunderstanding!"

"Indeed?" said the Vizier, affecting to stroke his chin thoughtfully. "I am here now. You may make your statement if you wish."

"Thank you, my lord," said Zekiel with a look of dawning hope that the Vizier found delightfully pathetic. "I do not know why my demonstration failed at the symposium, but I assure you that I acted in good faith. I am a seeker of truth, not a charlatan. On the contrary, my peers find me to be rather too direct in my honesty for their liking."

"I would like to believe you, Master Zekiel," said the Vizier. "Certainly your description of your colleagues' opinion of you is consistent with what they have said during my investigation of the matter. But there are other issues that concern me at least as much as the possibility that you are a fraud."

"What issues?" said Zekiel.

"For one, there is the question of just how dangerous your experiments might be, to yourself and to us all," the Vizier replied. "You claim that you witnessed the awakening of great power. What if you did? The greater the power, the greater the danger. Did you even once consider that? It is my responsibility, my burden, to know something of the arcane matters of the spirit world. That realm is fraught with risks that are not to be taken lightly. Are you familiar with those risks? Did you take even the most elementary precautions against them?"

"Well, no, my lord, not as such," said Zekiel with visible discomfort. "But everything we know of the history of the Stone Tears tells us that they represent a power of goodness and hope."

"Then your history is one-sided," said the Vizier. "I know of the legends that you and like-minded scholars have uncovered. But my order is an old one, and we have heard other versions of the tale. This power who gave our forefathers these tablets is vast and ancient. Ever it seeks to dominate us, to bend our will to its own and subvert our destiny to its purposes. What hope or joy is there for man in that? We are not perfect, of course, but we are free. If you succeed in rebuilding the tablets, you reforge chains that will place all mankind in a much deeper bondage than that which you have endured briefly in this cell."

The Vizier watched as perplexity and concern warred across Zekiel's face. At last the scholar settled into a firm resolve.

"No, my lord," he said calmly. "I do not dispute that such tales are told, but I say they cannot be true. I have tasted the great power of which you speak, and in its presence I have found only goodness and truth. Indeed, I have pledged my loyalty to that power, and from that pledge I will not waver."

"That much at least I believe," said the Vizier with a quiet more threatening than any bluster. "When I arrived here, I asked you if you know who I am. You said yes, but you were mistaken. I do not merely collect the tales of the danger of your Stone Tears—I am he who tells them, and he of whom they are told. I do not speak in philosophical generalities of the chains forged by the power you serve; it is my order that has labored in darkness to prevent those chains from being forged anew. Long ages ago, the forebears of my order played a part in breaking those chains in the first place."

"What do you mean?" said Zekiel, his voice betraying a growing doubt and dread. "The histories say that the Word was shattered by the last ruler of a lost empire, one named Vincitor the Mad."

"Do not dare to name him so in my presence!" hissed the Vizier, lurching forward as if to strike the old man before catching and composing himself. "You speak ill of what you do not know; he is properly called Vincitor the Magnificent, one of the great heroes of our race. As for me, can you not guess even yet? Even the slanderous tales you have heard make a passing mention of an order of priests that assisted the great one in his sacred quest of liberation. A single member of that priesthood survived the craven, profligate vengeance that was unleashed by the Enemy when his bonds upon our race were broken. He withdrew into the shadows and passed down his legacy across the leagues and the centuries, always from one teacher to one pupil in an unbroken chain, an order that emerged to offer its aid and counsel when the old prejudices had at last died away. A score of years ago, that legacy passed down to me. Fool! The one you thought to impress by remaking the tablets is the bearer of the heritage of those who laid waste to an empire to destroy them!"

Zekiel sat back in silence, staring at the Vizier as he absorbed what he had been told. When at length he replied, his voice was steady and sure.

"Then why haven't you slain me?" he said. "If your cause is more just and your power the greater, what stays your hand?"

"You are quite the direct one, aren't you?" said the Vizier. "Very well, I shall be equally direct. You are still alive because I am saving your trial and execution for a special occasion. They shall be the first state ceremony hosted by our new sovereign when the Royal Gauntlet is complete. Whoever he or she may be, I will be the true power, as one of my order has been for generations. In spite of your treasonous allegiance to the Enslaver, I grant you the honor of inaugurating a new age of freedom and power for your people by the sacrifice of your flesh and your blood."

"Perhaps," said Zekiel. "Nevertheless, the power you disdain has thwarted you thus far, and may do so again."

"Thwarted?" said the Vizier with a chuckle. "Say rather that your master has shown his hand too soon and is about to have it cut off. You had a small success or two, but that only drew my attention. You are already in my power, and as for this peasant boy who has trotted along at your heels—oh yes, I know all about him—he shall be one of many who never return alive from the Gauntlet."

The Vizier watched with satisfaction as the old man's bravado dissolved into horror and despair. Zekiel sank back onto his bed, his face drawn and ashen. The Vizier stood and took the lantern from its hook.

"Speaking of the Gauntlet, it is past time for me to go and set it in motion," he said. "I leave you to imagine the boy's fate as you spend the next several days here in the dark, awaiting your own." He left the cell and ordered it sealed once more. He summoned the chief jailor and ordered that the prisoner's rations be reduced to the bare minimum for sustaining life. Then he went to his waiting carriage and departed for Willowberg in high spirits.

Chapter 41

I lift my eyes to the mountains—where does my help come from?
It comes from the Speaker, the Maker of heaven and earth.

Having retired early the night before, Rand woke before daybreak; he was eager to set out for Willowberg. At the sound of him climbing out of bed, a servant appeared and bustled around the room to make everything ready for his use—lighting lamps, filling the wash basin, stoking the fire, and laying out his clothes. Before Rand finished yawning and rubbing the sleep from his eyes, two more servants appeared and filled a tub with steaming water. He had thought the staff of the manor house in Serenhorn was impressive, but the service at Falconkeep was almost frightening in its speed and efficiency.

As Rand was drying off after his bath, a kitchen maid rolled in a hot breakfast on a serving cart that was large enough to serve as a table on wheels. He hastily wrapped his towel around his waist but the girl kept her eyes on her work and appeared oblivious to his state of undress. He supposed that the staff were trained to take no notice of such things; still, he was relieved when she finished laying out the meal and retreated with a little curtsey.

By the time Rand dressed and ate his fill, the eastern horizon outside the windows of his room was bright with the approaching dawn. He emerged into the hallway to find a footman waiting to guide him downstairs to the armory.

"Master Henry is waiting to fit you with your new boots and harness," the man explained. As they turned to leave, a pair of servants hastened into Rand's room and began packing his luggage. He shook his head and hurried after the footman.

When he reached the armory, Rand found that Jen was there already. She wore the boyish, utilitarian tunic and trousers that the girls in the Gauntlet program had been instructed to adopt during training at the Academy. After all, skirts and petticoats would hardly do for swimming rivers and scaling cliffs. Not having seen her dressed that way outside the training grounds, he was suddenly reminded of the day he met her and mistook her for a boy, hidden as she was within her hooded cloak. He smiled at the memory.

"Keep your mirth to yourself," said Jen, misunderstanding his expression as she stood with arms extended while Henry buckled her harness.

"Please believe me, I would never treat you as a laughing matter," said Rand in a nettling tone. Before the verbal sparring match could escalate further, Henry's assistant descended on Rand to fit him with his own scout harness.

Despite Henry's repeated tuttings, cluckings, and apologies, the fit and workmanship of both Rand's harness and his shoes were excellent. He found it hard to believe that they had been made in less than a day. When the fitting was over, the gear was packed into a canvas bag for the journey to Willowberg. As if summoned, a servant appeared to take the bag and usher them to their carriage. Jen excused herself to go and change out of her athletic attire.

Lord Falconer was waiting in the courtyard with the carriage and the escort. He signaled Rand to join him.

"Captain Reichart will be in command of your troops on the way to Willowberg," he said, indicating the officer Rand had met when first arrived at Falconkeep. Reichart was pacing back and forth among the soldiers, noting deficiencies in their uniforms and equipment while making sure they understood his expectations for the journey.

"Is Sergeant Brooks not coming?" asked Rand, looking for the grizzled veteran among the men who sat at attention on their horses.

"He will be returning to Serenhorn," said Falconer. "I suppose you have become accustomed to having him nearby, but his primary responsibility is to command the guards at our city house." He paused and looked toward the main door into the keep. "Well, here's a surprise. Aunt Roberta has come to see you off; she seldom walks outdoors anymore."

Rand turned to look and found that another surprise lay in store for him. Lady Roberta was leaning on Jen's arm as she came. Jen was wearing the crimson and black cloak that Rand had been thinking of just a short time before. Her hair, which had grown longer since they first met, was pulled back from her face by a silver band. She wore a dress of fine gray cloth that was visible beneath the open front of the cloak; combined with the headband, it gave her a look of simple elegance.

Jen flashed a suspicious look at him and Rand realized he was staring. He quickly shifted his attention to the ground. It was a strange thing to realize only now, despite their growing friendship and the times his heart had been moved toward her, that she really was a rather beautiful young woman. The pair walked up to him, forcing him to look them in the eye again. Jen spoke first; she looked awkward—hardly the response Rand expected to his gawking.

"I know I'm overdressed," she said hastily. "Lady Roberta insisted on giving me the headband and I couldn't refuse. Then we had to find a dress to match."

"Don't fret, dearie," said Roberta. "As I told you, you look lovely. Isn't that right young man?"

Rand fumbled for something to say as the two women looked at him expectantly. "Well, you know—I'm not much of a judge of such things. But, ah, if you must know, I think you look grand. The headband, that it—it's very nice."

"There, you see?" said Roberta. "Now into the carriage with you my dear; I thank you for propping me up thus far, but I can make it back on my own." Jen curtseyed and climbed through the carriage door, giving Rand a puzzled look as she passed him. Roberta put a hand on his arm and drew him close.

"Remember the wind, my boy," she whispered. "And take good care of that girl—she's not as tough as she wants the world to believe."

"Yes, my lady," Rand replied. As she turned to go back into the keep, Lord Falconer cleared his throat and motioned for Rand to step aside with him.

"It's time to get you on your way, Rand," he said. "I'll follow soon. The heads of the noble houses all turn out to see the Gauntlet, of course." He paused and eyed Rand appraisingly for a moment. "You aren't a fool, are you lad?"

"I hope not, father," said Rand apprehensively.

"There are some matters in which a young man must heed his own counsel," said Falconer. "However, I would hazard to say that only a fool would let a girl like that slip through his fingers."

Rand was uncertain how to reply to such an observation. He nodded noncommittally and climbed into the carriage as quickly as he could; he didn't want to give anyone else an opportunity to offer their advice. Once within the carriage, though, he discovered a new vexation.

Normally Rand would have shared the forward-facing bench with Jen. Such an arrangement allowed them both to have a better view of the road ahead. However, her comely appearance and the comments of his elders made him too keenly aware of her as a young woman this time. After an awkward pause, he elected to sit across from her in order not to be forced into close proximity. But then he found he couldn't avoid looking at her, which was even worse than being close to her. He sighed in frustration and moved to sit beside her after all, careful not to come in contact with any part of her or her clothing.

"What on earth is wrong with you?" Jen hissed in exasperation. She stared at him as though he was an oddity in a traveling show.

"Just nervous about the trip," said Rand, trying to sound light-hearted. "My mother used to scold me for having ants in my pants."

"Please keep your ants to yourself," said Jen crossly. Rand pantomimed scratching at imaginary ants all over himself. Her severe expression crumbled into a smile. He smiled back, feeling that the tension was broken at last.

Captain Reichart shouted the order for the column to depart. This time there would be no mistaking that the heir of a prominent noble house was going abroad. Two squads of four lancers rode with pennants in the Falconer colors streaming from the heads of their lances. They formed the head and tail of the procession. Between them and the front and rear of the carriage rode two groups of ten soldiers—counting the captain, there were twenty-nine horsemen in all.

Even Rand's untrained eye could tell that these troops were of a higher caliber than the household guards who had escorted him before. The men held themselves proudly erect, carrying better weapons and more equipment. Every piece of metal in their gear gleamed brightly and not a strap or buckle was out of place. Surrounded by such a company, Rand sensed the reality of his situation more deeply than before. He truly was the prince of House Falconer, and very shortly he would be required to carry the full burden of that title and bear it well.

The gates down the length of the switchback road to the valley stood open. Apparently the rigors of Falconer security did not apply to outbound travelers, at least not on such an occasion as this. The horses of the escort stepped smoothly down the steep ramps with the carriage rolling along in their midst.

When the company reached the bridge at the base of the mountain, trumpets rang out from the town across the river. A wave of sound rolled toward them as scores of people began to shout. Rand leaned out the window and tried to see what was happening—it sounded like a riot. When his head popped out of the carriage, the shouting intensified. Belatedly he realized that it was directed at him. He pulled back abruptly.

"Rand! Prince Rand! Falconer, long live Falconer!" people shouted, the words tumbling over one another in a torrent of enthusiasm. Rand stared at them uncomfortably. He waved as cheerfully as he could, but inwardly he found the display deeply troubling.

Once across the bridge, the column continued south to where the road turned east toward Serenhorn. Another road branched off from the main street at the apex of the curve and climbed westward into the foothills of the Hunter Range. Rand had not really noticed it the day before—his attention had been focused on Falconkeep across the river. When the foremost pikemen turned onto it, he realized it must be the road to the mines and the high mountain pass.

The crowd had known the company would follow that route, of course, and had taken up position along it. Once the incline grew steep and the last buildings of the town were left behind, however, the throngs thinned away. As the rearguard of pikemen passed the turn, the unseen trumpets sounded a fanfare of farewell.

"I'm glad that's over," said Rand, rubbing his face with his hands. "There's something—I don't know, indecent about it. I'm just a boy; what have I done to deserve their praise?"

"Your humility contains a seed of presumption," said Jen. "It's not really about you. They honor what you represent. Your house protects them from enemies, enforces the law, provides employment, and probably even fixes the roads. You are the symbol of the power that makes their world."

"But that's just it, Jen," said Rand. "You hit upon the root of what troubles me. They treat me, or the Falconer name if you like, as though I'm some great power but I'm not. It would be bad enough even if there were no great power at all—the Falconers don't make the earth, the weather, the mountains, or the river. For people to act as if we control their destiny makes fools of them and a wicked fraud of us. But it's even worse than that, for I have come to believe there is a great power—the Speaker who gave us the Word. I would think that he does not appreciate people giving his due to others, and I would not want to answer to him for accepting it willingly."

"That's taking the matter rather seriously, don't you think?" said Jen. "It was only a harmless celebration. People enjoy having something to get excited about."

"I know," said Rand. "I suppose it bothers me because it's the other side of a bad coin. On the one side we have a strong impulse to ruin the good things in life. On the other, we take things that are not great and make as if they are. Look at your own Lord Wilhelm—he despoils everything that life granted him, and yet because of his title people are expected to treat him with deference."

"Very well," said Jen, her mouth curling in distaste. "You've made your point. Let's not spoil the trip by mentioning him."

"Sorry," said Rand and fell silent, watching out the window as the carriage climbed.

The road wound along the creases between the ever-steepening hills. Westmount disappeared behind the first curve they passed; from there on, the road itself was the only mark of human presence until they reached the first mine head.

That mine and many of the others they passed appeared to be abandoned, the ore long-since removed. Several of the mines at higher elevations were active, though, and the men working them paused to watch as Rand's column went by. Having worked as a smith, he wished he could stop and observe the process of obtaining the ore that provided the raw materials for his trade.

Soon the road took them above the foothills and into the mountains proper. The way narrowed and grew steeper. Instead of staying down in the creases between slopes, it sometimes traversed the sides of the peaks, affording Rand and Jen all too clear a view of the steep drop-offs a few feet from the wheels of the carriage.

As mid-day approached, the road entered a narrow cleft between two of the highest peaks that Rand had seen so far. Captain Reichart called out for the column to halt. He trotted back to the carriage and dismounted, handing the reins of his horse to the carriage driver.

"My lord and lady," he said, executing one of his crisp bows. "If you would care to stretch your legs with me, there is a sight worth seeing a short distance up the road."

The two passengers were only too ready to escape the confines of the carriage and stand on solid ground for a while. They disembarked and followed the captain past the double line of knights and pikemen. Rand soon felt the strain of the thinner air on the heights, but it was crisp and bracing also. Not long after they passed the head of the column, the road ahead of them disappeared over a crest. Reichart stopped and turned to his charges.

"The rise there marks the boundary of your domain, my lord," he said. "Walk ahead a little and see what lies beyond."

Rand gave Jen a playful wink and they walked up the road together, They reached the summit of the mountain pass and stood silently as if by unspoken agreement, taking in the vista that lay before them.

The road descended in a gentle slope for a few dozen yards, then dropped sharply out of sight. The shoulders of the peaks on either side fell away just as abruptly and the tops of the lesser mountains below were low enough that they did not obstruct the view. Thus Rand could see far into the great valley beyond.

This was the valley of the Solus, laid out like an undulating ocean of green in the bright midday sun. It felt inadequate to call it a valley at all, so wide did it stretch to the north, south, and west. He supposed that the brooding mass on its far side must be the plateau of the Amhara. In the nearer distance he could catch an occasional glint of sunlight along the silver ribbon of the Solus River itself.

"Now that's a sight," said Jen. "Pity your adoptive great-great-however many grandfather didn't build Falconkeep up here."

"Maybe I'll have it moved here when the Gauntlet is over," said Rand. "Might teach these nobles a thing or two about adopting any old shirt-tail relative that comes to hand. There's no telling what we might do."

"I can certainly testify that you have a talent for surprise renovations," Jen replied. It caught Rand off guard. She had never spoken before of the day he had secretly hired craftsmen to repair her dilapidated townhouse, nor of her uncharacteristically warm show of gratitude. He turned to look at her and she flashed him a shy smile before walking back to their carriage.

"Let's get going," she called to him over her shoulder. "We don't want to be on these mountain roads after dark." Rand followed, catching up in time to join her in thanking Captain Reichart for showing them such a spectacular vision. They climbed back into the carriage and the party moved on.

The slopes on the western side of the Hunter Range were heavily forested in comparison to the east. Whoever held sway over this region did not appear to have any commercial operations or settlements established in the remote reaches of the mountains. The travelers saw no one on the road, which was in rough condition from disuse.

Rand felt rattled and bruised from the ride over the cracked and rutted paving when they came at last out of the mountains into the lower foothills. Afternoon was passing into early evening by then. Captain Reichart called them to a halt as they entered a valley where broad swaths of trees had been felled on either side of the road. Rand heard voices and leaned out the window to see what was happening.

A camp or temporary village lay along the road ahead. From the stacks of lumber and piles of sawdust scattered about, it was clear that this was a logging operation. A group of men had come out to meet the column and was talking with the captain. After a few minutes Reichart rode back to the carriage.

"These laborers are serfs of Lord Vardon, master of this fief," he reported to Rand. "They were uneasy at first to see an armed force from a neighboring lord appear on their back doorstep, so to say, but they took heart when I explained our purpose."

"Did they say whether any other contestants have come this way?" asked Rand.

"I asked them about that, but apparently they've seen no one else," said Reichart. "They did tell me that there's a village ahead with a decent inn, and that we can reach it by nightfall."

"Let's move on, then," said Rand. "I look forward to a hot meal and a clean bed."

"Very good, my lord," said Reichart, saluting crisply and trotting back to the head of the column. He gave the order and they got under way.

"Well, this is interesting," said Jen as Rand waved to the woodcutters who stood watching.

"What do you mean?" said Rand, turning to find her regarding him with an enigmatic smile.

"You're beginning to fit into your new station very comfortably," said Jen. "Captain Reichart is the trusted aide of a prominent nobleman and a hardened veteran. You hardly know him, and at your present age and experience his role is more that of your keeper than your servant. Yet you just gave him an order as naturally as if born to it, and he accepted it without hesitation."

"I didn't think of it that way," said Rand. "I was almost thinking out loud. But I guess you're right—it was an order, after a fashion."

Jen patted his hand. "Don't waste much thought on it," she said. "You must become accustomed to taking the initiative if you are to be a nobleman—or a king."

Despite her advice, Jen's mention of his possible future had Rand thinking rather a lot as they traveled on. He peered into his own soul in search of a sign that the qualities of command and rulership were developing there, but in the end he had to admit to himself that he had no idea what he was looking for. The expedition reached the village at sundown as promised; after a plain but satisfying meal he went to his private room for a restless night's sleep.

They made good time across the valley lowlands on the next day and reached the royal post road that ran beside the Solus River. Reichart contrived to find roads that led them through Lord Vardon's lands without taking them near his keep, avoiding the pomp and protocol that attended an official visit between noble families, not to mention any tension that might arise between rivals in the Gauntlet.

The party progressed even faster on the carefully maintained post road, covering several more miles by the end of that second day. It took one more day to reach Willowberg after that, pressing on straight up the valley. Now that they were on a major thoroughfare, they encountered several of their fellow competitors. Some traveled in parties like their own; a few galloped past alone on hard-pressed steeds; others were pushing slowly up the river in gaily decorated barges.

It was twilight on the third day out of Westmount when the Falconer contingent entered the tree-lined avenues of the aptly named Willowberg. Captain Reichart led the column directly to prearranged lodgings at one of the grand hotels located right on the city square. Rand and Jen scarcely had time to exit their carriage before members of the hotel staff surrounded them and bustled them upstairs to their rooms. Rand stripped off his clothes and tumbled gratefully into bed.

Chapter 42

Blessed is the one who keeps going under trial because,
having endured the test, they will receive the crown of life
that the Speaker has promised to those who love him.

Rand smelled coffee, bacon, and fresh-baked bread. He stretched and felt soft, fine linen against his skin. His sluggish thoughts struggled to catch up with the present as the last shreds of a dream about working in his father's smithy evaporated. Such a luxurious bed—he must be in the manor house by the Academy. No, he had left on a journey. Falconkeep? Wrong again—that was miles and days ago. Willowberg—the Gauntlet! He snapped his eyes open and sat up abruptly, all fatigue banished in a blood rush born partly of fear and partly of excitement.

He discovered that the breakfast he had smelled was sitting on a tray next to his bed. Muscles sore from travel protested as he reached to take hold of it and pull it onto the bed beside him; one bite, though, and all other sensations were pushed aside by appetite.

Hunger satisfied, Rand cleaned up, got dressed, and left his room. The suite thrummed to the bustle of people coming and going. He spied Jen perched on a stool by the window, managing somehow to look bored and besieged at the same time. He dodged through servants and furniture to reach her.

"Morning, lazybones," she piped wryly. "Glad you decided to come out of your cave and see what all the fuss was about. I'm not sure you've heard yet, but they're having this odd little festival called a Gauntlet in a few days. I thought we might toddle over eventually and have a look at how we're going to die."

"I can't think of a more fitting companion for such a morbid pursuit," he said, offering his arm.

The town of Willowberg buzzed with activity; the broad, stone-paved avenues of the affluent district where their hotel stood were jammed with the carriages of the noble houses. Rand looked up and down the street, uncertain which way to go. With her usual bold pragmatism, Jen caught a passing footman by the arm and inquired as to the direction of the local Academy. The man tipped his hat and gave her a crisp, precise description of the route.

"Better stay close," she jested with Rand as they went on. "You'll be lost without me."

The Academy of Willowberg stood on a long, grassy slope overlooking the river. It had an open, inviting feel compared to Serenhorn. The buildings were of brick rather than cold, hard granite, and the walls were short and decorative, without the fortress-like air of Rand's school.

Its appearance was changing before their eyes, however, as laborers swarmed over the grounds. The slope below the school had been sectioned off with fencing and trenches were being dug. Further down an area had been enclosed by high walls of wooden planking.

Rand and Jen picked their way through the crowds within the campus, familiarizing themselves with the hall where they would sit for the examination that made up the first stage of the Gauntlet.

They noted the roped-off paths that led from the hall to the slope with its as-yet-unknown challenges. Beyond that, there wasn't much they could do, but Rand felt better for having made the effort to learn what he could.

The appointed day arrived sooner than Rand expected, the intervening time having passed in a kind of sustained chaos that diverted his attention first one way, then another. He was roused out of sleep by Minister Dorian, who had arrived with Lord Falconer the night before, rapping on the door of his room.

"Best be at it, my lord," he declared with a businesslike formality that Rand had not heard since the first hours of their acquaintance. He waited until Rand lifted his head and made eye contact, then nodded crisply and withdrew.

Nerves at the edge of nausea and a surge of energy in his blood chased any remaining cobwebs from Rand's mind and he tumbled out of bed. He put on light woolen breeches and tunic, good for staying warm even after soaking in the river crossing, then buckled on the custom-fitted scout harness and slid his feet into the flexible but tough racing boots. He made sure his Amharic blade was securely on his belt and other useful items for the contest were tucked in their appropriate pouches. His Stone Tear went into the hidden pouch on a cord around his neck. A glance in the mirror confirmed that he looked every bit as scared as he felt, but he knew that further delay would be no use. For Zekiel, he told himself firmly, and strode into the parlor of their suite.

Jen eyed him from the hall doorway, her impatience clear on her strained face. Lord Falconer paced in the center of the room like a caged beast, whirling as if to pounce when he caught sight of Rand.

"At last! To the carriage, boy; at this pace they'll disqualify you and banish my house before the race even begins!"

Falconer, Jen, Rand, and Dorian hastened downstairs and bundled into the waiting carriage. An escort of Falconer's guard stood ready, arrayed even more richly than before. At a nod from the carriage driver, they trotted briskly into the busy boulevard.

The streets of Willowberg were festooned with banners and pennants, the heraldry of the great Gauntlet. Rand spied other parties in the livery of noble houses and tried to count them, but gave it up as the ebb and flow of the traffic made it impossible to keep track. He looked at Jen, wishing they could speak as friends and encourage each other as they had done in quiet hours of the last few months, but she sat in the opposite corner of the carriage from him. Such reassuring familiarities would be out of place in the presence of the two older men.

They arrived at Willowberg Academy and pressed into the crowded courtyard. A major domo in official garb did his best to organize the throng, calling through a speaking trumpet. With a skillful mix of courtly words and commanding tone, he made it clear that each party was expected to drop off their contestant swiftly and make way for those still arriving.

Dorian prodded Rand and Jen out of the carriage. Lord Falconer stepped out with them for a brief final word.

"Lady Jen, take heart and trust to the strength within you," he said as he bowed and kissed her hand. "Rand, I'll give you this much—you have never shrunk from what was asked of you. Remember the fates of two families rest on your best efforts now. Get to it—and come home safe." He clapped Rand gruffly on the shoulder and climbed back into the carriage. The Falconer procession wheeled about crisply and moved out of the courtyard, leaving the two youths stranded in the chaos.

Rand looked at Jen, who was shifting her weight nervously from foot to foot. He gave her a slow, exaggerated wink and she smiled in spite of herself. She punched his arm.

"Come on, blacksmith. Let's go show these highborn tosspots a thing or two."

"After you, fishwife." They laughed and joined the crowd of contestants that waited at the doors of the Academy's great hall.

Carriages came and went in a steady stream and the number of milling young people grew. Hard-eyed race marshals watched over them, putting a stop to any nervous or high-spirited antics with barely a word. The carriages dwindled in number as the minutes dragged on. A somber quiet descended on the contestants now that the hour was at hand.

The clock tower in the central square of Willowberg tolled eight o'clock. As the last stroke reverberated, trumpeters sounded a processional. Two marshals pushed the tall doors of the hall inward. The crowd of contestants streamed forward.

Rand's eyes struggled to adjust to the dim light as he followed Jen into the foyer. Attendants directed them through a row of doors into the hall proper, where they filed down the aisles and took places at the desks awaiting them.

When they were settled, Jen's eyes grew wide and she nodded toward the stage. Rand looked and saw court officials seated in a line across the front, looking out over the crowd. Their royal regalia was imposing, but not as much as their fixed expressions of accustomed authority. In the center of them sat a mysterious figure completely obscured within a heavy, hooded black robe. The frame was motionless, but powerfully built, and even in its plain appearance it radiated a dominance that superseded the nobility to either side.

The contestants had all found a seat. A marshal stepped to the rostrum.

"Esteemed candidates, I bid you welcome to the Royal Gauntlet. And now, I give you his excellency the Royal Vizier."

The robed figure stood slowly and came forward. He pulled back his hood, revealing a shaved head, an arched nose, piercing black eyes, and a face tattooed with swirling arcane symbols. His voice was deep and rumbled with a curious mixture of good-humored intimacy and veiled threat. Surrounded by stiff, formal old men, his animal energy was both intimidating and magnetic.

"Yes, welcome candidates—welcome to the crucible in which you will be refined by the fires of adversity, until the pure metal of royalty is revealed." He flashed a wolfish smile. "Many of you have no doubt been coached as to what you can expect during this trial. You anticipate a few tests of knowledge and skill, mixed with some arduous but otherwise uninteresting athletic displays." His face grew stern. "If so, you are gravely mistaken. This is no country fair or palace masque. The prize is not a golden bracelet or an apple pie. You are contending for the crown of this realm. The tests before you will be much the same as you have heard of from the past, 'tis true. But I believe they have become too soft—soft as the weak and over-privileged houses from which you yourselves have sprung. So I have undertaken to strengthen them. The dangers within these trials will be real, and the penalties for the clumsy, the slow, and the dull-witted will be most severe.

"Beast-handlers will be following after you, ready to unleash their pets if you dawdle behind the pace. Pit traps will be spiked. Mazes lead to nasty ends for those who choose their path unwisely.

If you lack the courage or the strength to go on, you may of course call upon any of our race marshals and withdraw. But if you do, your house will be banished from the nobility. If you die or suffer incapacitating injury, we may allow your family to retain noble status, provided your efforts were otherwise satisfactory."

The Vizier paused to allow the contestants time to absorb his words. Then he spoke more gently. "Of course, we will begin with a less dangerous challenge. You will take an examination on the history, geography, and governance of Solethon. As soon as you finish, you may begin your race. If you fail the exam, you are disqualified and your house forfeits."

He nodded and returned to his seat. Marshals fanned out among the contestants, distributing folios of exam questions. When they were finished, one of them rang a bell and called for the test to begin.

Rand opened his folio, took quill and ink-pot and tackled the first question. How many academies were there in Solethon? Seven. Next: What year was the first Gauntlet run? Year of the Realm 187. And another question, and another. He was confident of the first few answers, but on some of the later ones he had no choice but to hazard his best guess. When he finished the fiftieth and last, he looked up to see that a dozen or so of the others had already left. Happily Jen was still with him, working on her last page.

A nearby marshal saw him put down his quill and quickly took his folio. The man gave it to an examiner for grading and motioned for Rand to come to her table and await her verdict. By the time he reached the front of the hall, Jen had finished as well and was on her way down the aisle to join him.

His examiner took only a few minutes to flip through his folio and score his answers. She made a notation and closed the cover. He tensed for the verdict. She regarded him gravely.

"You answered forty-one correctly," she whispered so that he alone could hear. "Not an exemplary performance, but sufficient. You may continue." She pointed to a side door and Rand shuffled toward it on legs made unsteady by relief. Jen trotted up behind him.

"I made forty-eight," she whispered with excitement. "How about you?" He told her with a grimace. She nudged him and smiled.

"All the same, we both made it through. Let's go!" She led the way into a short hallway. When they stepped out the door at the other end, they emerged into the bright morning sunlight, blinding after the dim interior. The families and friends of the contestants sat in wooden bleachers facing them across a grassy field, cheering and waving as their representatives appeared.

Rand searched the crowd for the Falconer banners and saw them along the lowest benches toward the left. The gateway to the next challenge was in that direction, so Rand angled his path to pass nearby. Jen followed his lead.

Lord Falconer himself leaned over the rail as they approached. He spoke quickly. "Well done, but mind your steps, both of you. My men in the high benches can see ahead. Some of the first racers have already been badly hurt."

Rand nodded and turned to go on. There was a wall of striped canvas across the path, with an opening in the center. Jen hurried through it and he followed.

Marshals greeted them grimly and handed them each a quarter-staff. As they advanced they came to a deep trench spanned by large logs. The logs were spaced about eight feet apart, and the far end of each was guarded by a soldier with a quarterstaff of his own.

"Choose a path and step forward," said the senior marshal. "You must defeat the opponent blocking your way to pass to the next challenge. If you fall you may try again—if you are able." He faltered on the last words. Rand stepped forward and saw why. The bottom of the trench was studded with sharpened stakes. There were patches of bare earth where a falling contestant might land safely, if they were both nimble and lucky. One boy who had not been enough of either was being helped out of the trench just then, his leg streaming blood where it had been pierced.

Rand looked to the other end of the trench and fought the urge to vomit. The marshals had not yet had time to remove the body of a girl who had fallen squarely on a pincushion of stakes. Her body was run through in three places. He had to tear his gaze away from the sight of her lifeless eyes staring skyward from her gore-crusted face.

He took a deep breath and readied his staff as he approached a log. The training program at Serenhorn had included combat drills with staves; he supposed this would be the final exam. The soldier at the far end grinned and stepped forward from his side, knees flexed and staff at the ready. Rand saw Jen approach the log of her choice, the one just to his right.

Rand found that the soft soles of his running boots gave him a good feel for the rough bark of the log as he stepped onto it. He made a preliminary swat with his staff. The soldier blocked easily, then hooked under the end of Rand's staff and twisted. Rand loosened his grip so that the staff, rather than his body, flipped to the side, then swung it back to himself and retreated a step. The man's counter had been fast, smooth, and treacherous. This would be even harder than he feared.

Jen had exchanged testing blows with her opponent and stepped back as well. Behind them, two more contestants arrived and chose logs of their own. One was a tall, barrel-chested man in his early twenties, his expression hard and contemptuous. The other was a girl with long, curled locks of deep red hair falling over her shoulders, brilliant green eyes and an unnervingly secretive smile.

The powerfully built prince wasted no time. He stepped forward so quickly that the soldier at the far end of his chosen log had to hurry to meet him. He flung his staff directly at the guardsman's face, then used the moment of distraction to seize the other man's staff with both hands. The two wrestled briefly for control of the weapon. Then the young racer heaved and lifted the soldier bodily off the log and flung him aside. There was a sickening crunch. The victorious candidate roared in triumph and leaped to the far side of the trench.

The red-haired girl had stepped onto a log as well. Her opponent sneered at her slight frame and casual stance, but her amused smile never wavered. She held forth her staff at an angle with a two-handed grip, not unlike a sword. As the soldier swiped at it with his own, she uttered an eerie cry in a language Rand had never heard. The air seemed to darken and crackle with unseen energy. When the staves made contact, the one held by the guardsman shattered into long splinters. He was pierced by them wherever his skin was exposed, but she and her staff were unharmed. He lost his balance and fell, managing to hook his arms over the log in time to dangle precariously from one side. She laughed lightly and stepped over him, tossing aside her staff when she reached the other side.

Rand took all of this in within the space of a few seconds while he prepared to face his own guardsman again. He knew that further delay would risk the displeasure of the marshals; he hefted his staff and stepped forward.

Jen was ahead of him and he could glance quickly at her without taking too much attention away from his own opponent. She and her adversary cycled through a handful of standard attacks and blocks, taking each other's measure. Rand did the same. Nothing he tried seemed likely to give him a chance for victory.

Without warning, Jen responded to a counter-thrust from her opponent by dropping her staff and grabbing his. She had no intention of wrestling with him as the warrior prince had done. Instead she pulled the staff past her twisting waist along the path that the soldier had jabbed it. The added momentum surprised him and he toppled forward. He fell from the log, but managed to twist and land on bare ground.

Rand's guardsman caught sight of his falling comrade and flinched involuntarily. In a moment of inspiration, Rand took advantage of the distraction and thrust his pole between the man's legs. He levered it sideways against the log and the soldier toppled over. His armor spared him from skewering himself on the stakes, but he looked badly shaken as he rolled to the bottom of the trench.

Rand reunited with Jen on the far side and they exchanged looks of strained relief. A marshal directed them to the entrance for the next challenge, which led through a high hedge. They came into a rectangular area surrounded by holly bushes that had been trimmed into walls ten feet high. The burly prince was gone, but the auburn-haired young woman stood waiting to one side. She regarded Rand with an arched eyebrow and a teasing smile.

"Princess Jylla of House Connell," she greeted him with a slight bow of her head. "And you are?"

"Prince Rand of Falconer," he replied, clearing his throat as he seemed to have trouble with his voice for a moment. "This is Princess Jen of Wilhelm," he added, turning hastily to his friend. Jen looked irritated and he wondered why.

A marshal stood beside an opening in the hedge across from where they had entered. A whistle sounded somewhere ahead and the marshal told Jylla to proceed. He called Rand and Jen over after she had left.

"You are entering a maze. At each spot where the path divides, there are arrows marked with the names of the kings of Solethon. The correct path to the exit follows the names in order from the oldest to the most recent. There are fewer paths than there are kings, so there will be gaps in the order and you must remember which comes next in spite of ones that are skipped over.

"Choose with caution, for the Vizier's policy of heightened challenge dictates that wrong turns lead to unpleasant surprises. Also, you will not want to move too slowly. Every few moments, a section of the floor behind you will drop. Wild boars roam the tunnels beneath, and we have put them in a foul temper for the occasion. Each contestant runs the maze alone. Milady, since you finished the combat challenge first, you will be the next to go."

Rand looked at Jen and she returned his anxious expression. He forced a smile and gave her a nod of encouragement. Another prince passed the log challenge and joined them, then the whistle sounded for Jen. She did not risk another look at Rand, plunging quickly into the maze. He watched her retreating figure until she turned a corner and was gone.

Rand paced restlessly while the marshal repeated his instructions to the new arrivals. His shoulders hunched in tension as he waited for the roar of beasts and the screams of a girl being torn apart. Seconds passed without any sign of disaster, and yet each seemed slower and more unbearable than the last. Dim sounds of struggle and commotion mingled with a far rumor of the spectators, but the maze remained silent.

Finally the whistle sounded—the maze was clear. The marshal waved Rand forward. He dashed along the first path, nervous energy making his feet fly. He turned the corner to the left as Jen had done and found himself treading on a wooden lattice-work that flexed just enough to remind him that it would give way on command. A divider slid from the hedge walls he had just passed and locked into place, sealing off his retreat. The hourglass was draining now.

He hurried forward and found his first pair of plaques, each with an arrow and the name of a king. Neither of them was the founder of the kingdom; the skipping of names on the royal roster had begun even at the start. Which was first, Ezra or Gordon? He was almost sure it was Gordon, but that sign pointed left, toward the side of the maze where he had begun. Ezra's pointed ahead toward the far side.

As Rand hesitated, the first section of floor fell behind him. A hungry boar squealed eagerly. Rand winced and followed the path for Gordon. When he had run far enough that he knew he must be close to where he had started, the path turned right and doubled back on itself. Soon a sliding partition closed behind him and he came to another signpost. He had chosen correctly.

Thus he continued, choosing Harald over Julia, William over Simon. Sometimes he was confident in his choice; other times he had to wager his life on the most likely name as the trap doors fell close behind. Then he burst unexpectedly from the stifling green walls and stood blinking in the sunlight. He was through.

Chapter 43

I have seen something else in this world: The race is not always to the fastest or the battle to the strongest, nor are the wise well-fed, or the brilliant rich, or the educated well-respected; but time and chance happen to them all.

A nearby marshal shouted and gestured impatiently for him to get moving. Ropes marked off a path down a long, grassy slope to the bank of the river. Far ahead, Rand thought he could see the slim, graceful form of Jen sprinting along. He flexed his shoulders to settle the straps of his scout's harness, then his feet to stretch the soft hide of his boots. Then he started down the hill in an easy lope, letting the fall of the ground do the work as he stretched his legs forward to cover long spans with each bounding step.

In those evening planning sessions that now seemed so long ago and far away, huddled together in the library of the Falconer city house in Serenhorn, he and Jen had agreed that they would do their best to stay close to each other—at least as much as they could without arousing suspicion. If they were separated, the one ahead would find excuses to delay until the one behind could catch up. At the bank of the river below, Rand could see Jen employing that strategy now. She had stopped to remove and re-lace her boots.

Rand skidded to a stop as close to her as her dared. He bent to tighten his own laces. Neither of them looked at the other, but he heard a sharp hiss from her and cocked an ear to listen as he worked.

"Listen to a lakeman's daughter," she whispered. "Swim almost straight upstream or you'll be swept far down by the spring flood. I've seen it happen to some already while sitting here." Rand risked a slight nod of acknowledgement without raising his head or looking her way. Jen rose and sprinted for the river, splashing into the water until it was up to her knees, then plunging forward with arms outstretched and head pointed into the current.

Moments later he rose from his crouch and followed. As he ran to the water he observed her technique carefully. Her progress toward the far bank was slow but steady, and she was losing hardly any ground to the current at all.

Then he was at the edge of the water and plunging forward with great high-stepping strides. The water was shockingly cold even through his woolen leggings. When he was up to his knees, he knew it was time to make his headlong leap while he still had leverage for a good push-off.

The shock of the icy spring water numbed his skin almost instantly, but a dull, throbbing ache began to spread through his body. He could feel it sapping his strength and he pushed on, straining to get across the mighty river before it overwhelmed him. Swish, swish, swish went his arms and legs through the dragging, clinging water. It gurgled and stopped up his ears, slapped at his eyes. His lungs ached as they struggled to seize enough air to keep him moving. He began to fall into a senseless rhythm, as though sleep-walking.

A foot thudded against something unyielding, then the other did too. He tried to kick it away but it would not move. Groggily he realized that it was the river bottom. He had reached the shallows on the far bank. With an effort that seemed almost greater than the swimming, he thrust himself shoreward on the numb, toppling posts of his legs.

"Keep moving until you're warm," a sharp whisper hissed at him as he sensed a figure passing close by. He wiped the river water from his eyes and saw Jen pacing back and forth along the river bank, swinging her arms and legs to force the blood back into her extremities.

Rand followed her example, careful not to trace a circuit too close to hers. The woolen clothing prescribed by Lord Falconer was working its magic, trapping his body heat though still sopping wet. He worked at squeezing the water out of his sleeves and leggings as he marched around. At the same time he looked back along the river to see how the others were doing.

Those who were trying to go straight across the river were being swept far downstream by the rampaging current. In the distance Rand saw a curved low bank where the river turned back toward Willowberg. It appeared to be acting as a catch-basin for the swimmers who had been carried away. He could make out several figures clustered there, flapping about to warm and dry themselves just as he was doing.

"Oi! Off with you to the horses now, afore we loose the dogs!" A sneering ruffian with the armband of a marshal pointed to a marked path leading west from the water's edge. Rand, Jen, and two other contestants scrambled to comply.

They broke out of the low thickets that lined the river and found that the path ended at a paddock fenced in with fresh-hewn timber. More than a hundred horses waited within. Rand couldn't help wondering how many of them were, even this early in the Gauntlet, waiting for riders who would never arrive.

Two stable hands directed the contestants to horses and held the reins while they mounted. Once again, Rand and Jen contrived to hold back while the other two youths climbed into the saddle first. There was no Gauntlet marshal with the stable hands for the moment, and thus little risk. Once mounted, they trotted out a gate at the far end of the paddock and found the markers for the next stage of the Gauntlet.

"Ride, princelings! Ride for the Great Wall!" A portly sergeant sat by a fire, waving a greasy leg of lamb toward the west. Rand had to admit that the Great Wall was aptly named. Even through a haze of some thirty miles, the gray rugged cliffs stood tall and clear, dominating the horizon north and south. Willowberg lay closer to their northern end, and the marked path ran due west toward a sort of bay formed by a great promontory that jutted out into the plain.

"Steady now, and mind your jumping," Rand said to encourage Jen. Horsemanship was one of the few parts of their Gauntlet training that had come easier to him than to her. Remembering the lessons, he led off with his roan at a trot and she followed on her bay. Since they were following a clear country cart-path, he took them up to a canter. As his confidence in his mount grew, he looked over at Jen and made a rolling motion with his hand. Her mouth tightened a little, but she nodded. He spurred his horse into a gallop and she did the same. After all, he thought, this was a race—a race to save a man's life.

Back at the corral, the race marshal returned from the latrine in the bushes and took note of the horses that were missing. He called the stable hands to him.

"So they're off, then, like I told ye?"

"Yes, sir."

"And ye watched fer the young pair, the boy and the girl?"

"Aye, sir—made sure they got the special horses." The stable hand touched his nose and winked.

"Sure it was the tallish ginger lad with the slight brunette, then?"

"Wha-er, well…" the stable hand darted his eyes to his mate and cleared his throat. The other jumped in.

"Why surely, squire, 'twas the ginger lass and the short brown-haired lad that you said to watch for. That's who came first, and that's who we gave 'em to."

"What? Are ye daft?" The marshal cuffed the two in a rage. "The master sergeant will have us all in irons! An if'n it comes to it, to save my own hide, what done no wrong, I'll see to it that the Vizier himself hears your names!" The stable hands both turned pale at that and craned their necks to the west, wondering what had become of the riders.

Rand exulted in the feel of the cool morning wind as it swept over him, drying his river-soaked clothes and whipping his hair. He heard laughter and turned to see Jen riding high in her stirrups, gripping her reins in one hand as she lifted the other to sift the whistling air through her fingers. So far the marked course had led them over two fences and a low hedge, and they had guided their horses over them without trouble.

The joy drained from Jen's face and she pulled back on her reins. Rand slowed his own horse and looked ahead. Another fence ran athwart their path, and there seemed to be some commotion gathered around it. Rand's heart sank as he began to grasp what he was seeing.

A horse was sprawled over the fence rails. The top rail had snapped, as had at least two of the beast's legs. It writhed and whinnied in agony. Just over the fence lay a red-haired girl, still tangled in the saddle that lay partly on top of her. Something in the angle of her back and neck, the absolute stillness of the way she lay there, made Rand certain that she would never move again.

A second horse circled farther ahead, eyes rolling in fear, rearing and shying first one way and then another. A voice cried out in agony from the tall grass about twenty feet beyond the fence. Rand dismounted and tied his horse to the fence rail a safe distance from the crippled animal and ducked through to search for the source of the voice. Jen followed and dashed ahead of him. They found the second rider—a dark-haired young man in his early twenties— clutching at a badly broken leg and gritting his teeth. Jen fished some leaves from a pouch of her scout harness.

"Chew on these—they're not strong enough, but they're better than nothing." The prince nodded his thanks as he did his best to follow her directions. His breathing slowed and his face took on a grayish cast.

"That's more the shock of the injury than the leaves," Jen commented quietly to Rand. "If we can't find help soon, he may not make it."

"Can you tell us what happened?" Rand asked as he did his best to arrange the saddle and horse blanket so the rider could lean against them.

"Saddles...gave way. Felt a little loose after the hedge back there—then, just gone. Both went flying. The girl?" Jen shook her head. The man groaned and lay back.

Two marshals galloped up to them. "We'll need a litter for this one, quickly!" said the senior man and the other rode off again to fetch more help. "You two—knock down a fence rail and get going. This is our job. Yours is to race."

They did as he said, making a gap in the fence and walking their horses through it. As they mounted, the marshal drew his sword and slashed the throat of the horse with the broken legs. Rand looked away quickly from the gouts of blood and hoped that death would come swiftly to the poor beast.

All sense of adventure and exhilaration was gone as they resumed their ride. When they were far from the scene of the disaster, Jen spoke.

"Seen bad riding accidents before—tack gets old, horse steps in a rabbit hole. But two different saddles at once? That's no accident."

"You're right—impossible. But why? Who?"

"I don't know. This whole race is wrong. Too dangerous every step. It's supposed to be a test, not a deathtrap."

Sobered by the thought, Rand focused on riding his horse carefully as they negotiated the long miles of the course marked out before them. Pasture and cropland, orchard and country lane passed beneath their thundering hooves, punctuated by hedges and fences as before. Thankfully they came across no more deadly tragedies.

They were obliged to slow their pace now and then so that they would not exhaust the horses. When the sun crept close to its zenith, they stopped by a stream to eat a small meal while their mounts grazed and drank.

"The highlands seem no closer than when we started," said Rand as he gestured toward the line of cliffs in the west.

"I know," Jen stretched as she peered into the distance, trying to loosen sore muscles. "It's odd that we haven't seen any others since we came upon...those two. Well, let's go on before every prince in the realm gallops on by."

Almost as if in answer to her puzzlement, they soon met with another racer once they had resumed their ride. He stood beside his horse, tugging at the bridle and shouting for it to move. The animal stood with its head stooped low, legs quivering and flanks lathered with sweat.

"He'll be lucky if that beast moves more than a furlong before nightfall," Jen called to Rand as she glanced over her shoulder. "What comes of foolish haste." Rand nodded and resolved to be even more attentive to the limits of his own horse.

Miles and hours slipped by in what began to be at least as great a test of patience as of skill. They passed two more riders who had missed a jump along the way. The first incident had injured the horse, while the second seemed to have been worse for the rider; thankfully, neither was as severe as the double tragedy early in the day.

By midafternoon they had left closely settled lands behind and were able to gain some speed. Fences and hedges gave way to rolling hills clad in long grasses. Weathered gray stones were scattered about thinly, like the stumps of old rotten teeth. Ahead, the dark line of highlands had at last begun to draw noticeably nearer, revealing their true nature as looming, forbidding cliffs.

Rand rehearsed the briefings from their training days in his mind. Their route would take them to a bay formed by a large outcropping that ran northeast from the main body of the plateau. Somewhere close to where it joined with the larger mass, they would scale the steep slopes to the lands above, arriving in the domain of the Amhara for their first camp of the Gauntlet.

By the time they had followed the route markings to the designated spot for the climb, the westering afternoon sun had passed behind the high country, leaving the bay in twilit shadow. The loose, sloping piles of rock that had crumbled down from the cliffs were moist and slick.

Rand slowed and nodded slightly for Jen to proceed, still trying to be discreet about their teamwork lest it draw unwanted scrutiny. As he guided his weary horse along the last few meters of its journey, he spied movement against the face of the cliff. The red-haired mystic was swinging from ledge to ledge, working her way upward along the guide ropes with the poise and grace of an acrobat. Then his attention was drawn to movement higher up. The husky young noble who had forced his way through the combat test by sheer power earlier in the day was using the same approach to mountaineering, pushing upward with his muscular legs until he reached the edge, then hauling himself up and over with a single mighty heave of his arms.

Jen trotted up to the marshals who waited where the guide ropes were anchored. When she dismounted, one of the men led her horse to a corral that filled the very end of the bay. As Rand rode up, he peered into the shadows and counted about a dozen horses. Not bad, he thought. They had already left over a hundred of their competitors behind. If they could stay near the front of the pack, Jen's special rafting trick, whatever it was, might be enough to tip the balance.

Rand dismounted and stretched a little to shake off the soreness of the saddle before approaching the ropes. There were three of them, spaced about five feet apart and knotted every yard of their length to provide hand and footholds for the climbers. He was relieved to see that the face of the escarpment was sloped and uneven rather than sheer and vertical.

"Best get at it, yer lordship!" The nearest marshal was a young man not more than three years older than Rand. He tried to mask his contempt for the spoiled dandy he believed Rand to be with an unconvincing leer of a smile. "Night be fallin' soon, an' ye don't wanna be dangling from the ropes when it does."

Rand looked up and saw that Jen had made about twenty feet of vertical progress already. He selected a rope other than the one she was using, not wanting to disturb her balance as he found his footing. He was about ten feet into his climb when the rope to his right shook with a rapid rustling sound. He looked up. Jen was now about thirty feet higher than him. He traced the path of the rope above her and saw that she was about to negotiate a tricky section where an overhanging ledge would force her to pull herself up knot by knot, climbing the rope itself rather than using it to climb the steep slope. She caught his eye and pulled the rope taut with her hands, bracing her feet wide apart against the stone.

Rand took the hint and shifted to the rope she was using, taking up the stance she had shown him. He made a great show of wiping his brow on his sleeve and taking a sip from his water-skin with his free hand, all while subtly anchoring the rope for Jen. In a few minutes she was up and over the ledge.

Thus they worked as a team while staying far enough apart to appear independent. Sometimes she would brace the rope from above; others, she acted as a scout, shaking another rope to steer him to an easier route up the cliff. His weight and lower position, meanwhile, gave him chances to anchor for her while he took a breather.

The first hundred feet went quickly and brought them up out of the shadowy cleft into the warm afternoon sun. The second hundred required conscious effort and more frequent pauses for rest. The sun was outpacing them, plunging them into shadow once more. The final fifty feet were a sore, aching struggle in deepening gloom, ever mindful of the consequences of a fumbled grasp or careless footing. Jen's was no gymnastic flip over the final ledge, nor did Rand heave himself upward with a mighty thrust. They struggled slowly over the lip that marked the end of the climb. As Rand reached level ground, he found Jen flat on her back, gasping like a fish. He was only too happy to follow her example, and they lay there watching the stars come out as dusk descended.

A marshal ambled over to them. "Mandatory rest stop for the night. Food by the campfire yonder. See me for a tent when you're ready." Having finished his stock speech, he went to the edge of the cliff and whistled. And answering whistle drifted up from below. The man began pulling up one of the ropes and coiling it neatly.

"Are no more allowed to climb?" asked Jen.

"Not until daybreak. Any stragglers that reach the cliff tonight will sleep below. We don't want anybody getting ideas and trying the ropes in the middle of the night."

"How many have made it this far?"

"See for yourself." The marshal jerked a thumb toward the fire as he finished coiling the first rope and started on the second.

Rand followed Jen at a discreet distance, toward the flickering light and the sounds of a group taking a meal together. He felt the weight of the miles he had crossed and thought he might go straight to bed, Then the smell of roast mutton and pan-fried potatoes changed his mind most emphatically.

Eleven other contestants showed in the flicker of the firelight as he got closer. Jen was joining them already. A man in an apron handed her a large wooden bowl and spoon. She nodded her thanks and sat on an empty log round, murmuring greetings to the others.

"So this is it, eh?" Rand observed as he reached the group. "I would have expected more to keep up so early in the race." The burly young man wiped grease from his full beard and laughed, shaking a leg of mutton for emphasis as he spoke.

"Ha! Weak, all of them. They do not have the wit or will to rule, and so they fall away, as it should be."

"We must not be over-confident, Uthor," said Jylla. Rand sat as the camp cook handed him a portion of food. The red-haired conjuror continued, "After all, some of the stragglers may catch us up come the morrow. There are elements of chance that may have delayed them thus far."

"If you wish, you may see it thus, Jylla," answered Uthor with an impatient wave of the mutton chop. "For myself, I expect to build on each advantage I gain by my skill and the mistakes of others—I don't intend to give any ground back."

"Very well, Uthor. We will see what awaits us in the challenges to come. Now, friend—Rand, wasn't it? I suppose you were the last to make the climb today." Rand looked up from his food in surprise when he realized Jylla was speaking to him, and found himself looking directly into her large green eyes. He found her attention strangely unnerving.

"Um, yes, I was—they pulled up the ropes after I reached the top."

"Welcome to our little company. I think we will all know each other better in the days to come—those of us who can keep the pace, that is." She laughed lightly to soften the bluntness of her words. Her voice had a high, musical quality that was as exotic to Rand as her fine features and her long red curls. He smiled and nodded. He glanced toward Jen and saw her regarding him with an unreadable expression. It made him feel awkward, and he turned his attention back to his food.

Conversation continued around the circle. The other young people spoke of how cold the river had been, or of how close they had come to being caught by a trap door in the hedge maze. As Rand listened, he did his best to take stock of them. While on the surface they might seem to be an ordinary collection of bantering young adults, it was clear that the tests of the day had brought strong contestants to the front of the pack. These were bright, confident people in prime condition.

It wasn't long, though, before they began to excuse themselves and retire for the night. It had been a long day and the fire only did so much against the spring chill. Rand handed his bowl back to the cook and walked past the fire to a tract of level ground where rows of small one-person tents had been set up. A steward beckoned him.

"You can have the second one in this row, m'lord. We have had far fewer guests than we expected, sorry to say." Rand nodded and pulled back the flap of his assigned tent. The light was dim this far from the fire, but he could see a smooth, dry floor of the same thick canvas that the walls were sewn from. There was a pallet of soft cushions covered by a woolen blanket. He crawled in and lay down as soon as he could get his boots off. He was asleep in moments.

Chapter 44

How welcome on the mountains are the feet of those who bring good news.

The next day, he awoke to the smell of frying bacon. He had thought he was hungry the night before; his appetite this morning was overwhelming. As quickly as he could dress and freshen up, he hastened to the fireside. A marshal paced around the ring of log seats with his arms crossed behind his back.

Rand grabbed a portion of bacon, eggs, and bread. Jen was already seated. He sat a few spots away from her, careful not to make any obvious gesture of greeting. Before long the last members of their little group had turned up. The marshal stopped pacing and cleared his throat.

"Now, then, milords and ladies. Welcome to the second day of the Royal Gauntlet. You may already know that this part of the course is an endurance run on foot. Your path follows the crest of the promontory northeast to its end, then doubles back to the northwest until you reach the place where you will climb down from the plateau and face the challenges of the northern wastes. How long this journey takes depends entirely on you, but you will not face it without guidance.

"I'm sure you know of our royal couriers, and that their people call this severe land their home. They are the best runners in the world. One of them will accompany each of you, serving as your guide and imparting as much of their skill as they can. We'll sound a horn to call you to assemble at the starting point a little while from now. It's there on the far side of the tents."

"Excuse me, marshal," said Jen. "What of the others—the ones who didn't make it this far?"

"The horn will also be their signal to start climbing the cliffs below, milady. They won't be as well-rested or well-fed as you, but they won't be too far behind all the same. Remember that."

Rand finished his breakfast quickly and stepped away from the fire to run through the stretching exercises he had learned during the training program at Serenhorn. As he considered the test before him, he took note of the cold thinness of the air and the way it sapped at his vigor. Just as they had with the horses, he and Jen would have to resist the urge to hurry, rationing their strength. Seeing the others clustering casually here and there and chatting, he thought he could risk moving within earshot of his friend.

"Hello, Jen—ready for the day?"

"Sure you want to waste time talking to me? Princess ruby-locks is just over there!"

Rand was shocked. "What d'ye mean?"

"Hmmph! Just about fell over yourself when she spoke to you last night. And staring at her like a starving man eyeing a fresh loaf of bread."

Rand tried to answer, but the words all seemed to jam together. All that came from his mouth was a confused mumble. Jen gave him a knowing sidelong glance. The odd tableau was shattered by the sounding of the horn.

The contestants hastened to the starting line beyond the tents. The marshal waited there with a loosely grouped gathering of Amhara. Rand's pulse quickened at the sight of these mysterious outlanders, only one of which he had ever met before. All those weeks ago, the courier had said he would run the high country with Rand. Was he serious? If so, would he be here?

Rand searched the faces of those who were turned his way. None of them wore the outfit of a Royal Courier, but then they were not delivering messages here. Perhaps that one?

The man turned from chatting with another of his people and glanced at Rand. He gave the briefest of winks and looked away again. Rand's heart leaped. He was here! He had remembered his promise and he had come.

Other Amhara had begun to mingle with the racers, offering their help and pairing off. The courier waited for a few moments, then moved toward Rand, looking over the other contestants as though sizing them up. He stopped by Rand casually, seemingly at random.

"So. small-man—the Speaker ordains that we meet again." He pitched his voice low, speaking quietly. Rand did the same.

"I'm glad you could come. It's good to have the help of a friend."

"Friend, small-man? Say not so. I claimed you as brother, and by that I stand."

"Thank you... brother. One thing I wanted you to know about—"

"Yes?"

Rand was careful not to look or gesture to where Jen stood. "The girl with the brown hair—she is a friend. Her name is Jen. She does not know if she believes as I do, but she listens and tries to help."

"Hmmm. Such is the seed from which truth will often grow, little brother. Wait here—I will send my clansman to her." He strolled back to where other Amhara were still gathered and spoke briefly to another man. The man's eyes widened, and then he nodded emphatically. The two came back toward the racers. Rand risked a look at Jen, who looked back as if to ask what on earth was happening; Rand gave a quick nod that he hoped would be reassuring and looked away again.

The marshal cut through the general activity with his parade-ground voice. "Now that you all have a guide, I'll send you off in the order that you reached the top of the cliff yesterday. Prince Loran, you first. And go!"

The other pairs shuffled into their proper order. The marshal started them about a minute apart. The courier quickly gave advice to Rand.

"Step lightly, with knee bent to soften the blow of each step. Likewise, think of sliding level over the ground, not up and down. Save strength an' motion. Do not swing arms or clench fists. Hold hands still with elbows bent, about chest height. Let thumbs rest lightly on fingers, as if carrying a flower petal you wish not to bruise. Breathe in through nose, out through mouth. Full, slow breaths."

Jen and her guide started. Rand and the courier were the last ones left. He squinted into the morning sun, watching her progress until she disappeared around the first bend in the road.

"Off with ye, then," the marshal waved them forward. Rand nodded to his unlikely ally and they began. He practiced the advice he had been given and found it helpful.

"I will speak to guide you as I may, little brother. Best you be silent except at need. I have more breath from long practice." Rand nodded. The courier was keeping them at a slow and steady pace, but Rand could already feel the effort of keeping his legs moving.

"Soon as we be well out of sight, my clansman will slow until we travel together. Then we can work as one to help you an' your friend as best we may."

After about ten minutes, Rand saw Jen and her guide ahead. Sure enough, the distance slowly closed. The courier and his relation greeted one another briefly in their own speech and they continued on.

"When strength be failing you, we walk for a time and then go on," said the courier. "This way we be always moving, an' the land go by." So they did, and the road led them on as the sun rose up the morning sky.

After about two hours had passed, the Amhara called them to a halt. "Stay on your feet and keep moving about. Here we take water at a fresh stream by the road, and a little food to refresh us." The guides shared small tin cups which they all used to dip cool draughts from the stream, and bites of a paste made from dried berries, nuts, and roasted grain. It was satisfying and Rand felt some renewal of his strength.

"This is your courier friend, I take it?" said Jen. "His kinsman knows little of our tongue, but he knows how to run."

"They are the best, no doubt of that. Jen, listen—that girl Jylla is nothing to me."

"Oh, save it—"

"No, listen! She has a flirting way, 'tis true, but I had a taste of that once and I want no more of it. I only watched her closely because there was something odd about her and I wanted to know what it was. You are my friend, you know all my secrets and my hopes. We are a team, and I won't let anyone come between us."

Jen nodded, but she kept her eyes on the ground and did not smile. Their guides announced that it was time to go on and they returned to the road. They continued through the morning, stopping every hour or so to refresh themselves. Having hung back a little to join forces, they had seen none of the racers ahead of them. About the time that the sun was approaching its zenith, the Amhara declared that it was time to take a longer rest.

As they sat and took turns sipping water from the tin cups, Jen's guide began to speak earnestly to the courier in Amharic. The courier turned to Rand.

"He is asking how I came to call you brother, and what you know of the Stone Tears. I confess it is hard to explain the events of those days to one who was not there." A thought struck Rand and he reached for the hidden pouch that hung about his neck. Jen guessed what he was about to do and seized his wrist.

"Are you sure that is wise?" she whispered fiercely.

"Call it instinct, I guess. These people revere the Tears, and we need their help." He gently pulled his hand free and continued, opening the drawstring bag and pulling out the cloth-wrapped living fragment. "I never had the chance to show you this, did I? It was the thing you said we could speak more of when we ran together." He briefly explained what had happened in the antiquities room at the academy in Serenhorn. The courier took the bundle and unwrapped the cloth. His eyes widened and his fingers trembled as he touched the joined piece.

"It speaks to me! In the words of my people!"

"Look, Jen!" Even from where he was seated, Rand could tell that the characters had transformed into a new alphabet of curving, many-branched runes. The courier turned and carefully handed the fragment to his kinsman. The other man cried out in wonder; as he read the tablet, tears began to stream down his face. He looked up at Rand and reached out his arms, motioning for him to come closer. He seized him in a powerful embrace. After a time he released the youth and carefully pressed the fragment back into his hands. He turned to the courier and spoke swiftly. The courier nodded.

"My kinsman believes we should change our plans, an' I agree. Ahead along this road there is another that runs to a special place in the hills to the north. We must spare a little time to go there."

"Why?" Jen was guarded.

"Under the shadow of the hills, we find a great, deep cave. There we make a place of safety if evil should come our way. There also we gather together what Stone Tears we have found. We must see if more can be made to speak."

"What about the race? Rand's friend may die if we do not find a way to win."

"We need not tarry overlong there. 'Twill be close to time for night-time rest when we get there, an' we can leave a little early come the morning. The little roads along the hills will be some shorter than this main cliff road we follow now, so when we come back to it, we may not have lost any time."

"But surely we must stay on the course! The marshals will know if we do not pass their checkpoints."

The courier smiled slowly. "Ah, but you see, small-lady, the Gauntlet be long, an' our land be high an' cold. Solethon not have marshals to spare for every mile. So, for this running part, they make Amhara guides the marshals." He tapped his own chest for emphasis. Rand burst out laughing; Jen shook her head in a show of disapproval and disbelief, but as she ducked to hide her expression, he saw that she was smiling.

By a kind of unspoken consensus, the question seemed settled. They finished their mid-day break and rose to continue, taking time to warm and stretch their recently unused muscles. The day's efforts were definitely taking their toll, but Rand was pleasantly surprised at how well he and Jen were holding up. Evidently the weeks of training at the academy had given them some benefit.

They returned to the road and resumed the loping pace set by the Amhara. After about an hour the courier signaled for a halt. "This be our turning," he said, pointing northeast. The vague outlines of collapsed walls showed where a town had once stood at the meeting of the ways. Beyond them, a smaller road snaked between rising hills until it was lost among them.

"Was this a town of your people?" asked Rand.

"Oh, no, small-man. Those who came to see the Word were not many when set against so large a land as this. We have grown since, but not to fill it that much more. We have towns here an' there, where we found good water or good fields, but 'tis a wide country. Mostly we settled at the northern edge, where we stood an' saw the blue fire. To west an' south of here, there be some mighty cities once, all dust an' ruin now. Not places for the living, so we passed them by."

The little party set out on the inward way, their pace slowing as they climbed the steepening grade. Soon they were compelled to walk more than they ran. The sun moved into the west until the road was fully overshadowed by the surrounding hills. Rand hoped they would reach the underground sanctuary before darkness overtook them. This empty land was unsettling. No trees broke the skyline of the hills. What few signs of habitation appeared along the road were ruins like those back by the main clifftop road.

Chapter 45

Those whose hope is in the Speaker will renew their strength.
They will fly up like eagles; they will run and not grow weary,
they will walk and not be faint.

Rand felt emptied of every reserve of strength; when he looked at Jen, he could tell by her dulled expression and open mouth that she was at least as exhausted as he felt. There were no stars overhead as yet, but the sky was turning the darker blue that presaged their appearance.

"How far?" he gasped to the courier. The man could not help smiling at his distress.

"Not quite ready for the courier's life, small-man? No shame in that; you an' Lady Jen run well today. Our goal be not far. We can stay to walking now." He whistled to his kinsman and signed that they should slow. Around the shoulder of the next hill, as stars began to appear above them, the lights of distant lanterns glowed.

"This be the holy place of which I speak," said the courier.

"Holy?" asked Jen.

"It mean, oh, I s'pose, good an' clean, special. Set aside to the Speaker an' his ways."

"Oh."

They walked toward the lights, grateful for their help in seeing their footing. On either side, Rand could see houses with standing walls and whole roofs, flickering lamplight visible through the windows. With these signs of human habitation and community, a weight of anxiety he had not realized he was carrying slid from his shoulders.

They came close to the large, lamp-lit opening in the side of the hill. Two men stood there, one on each side of the door. One of them called a challenge and the courier answered. The guards looked at each other doubtfully and one rapped on a small door set into the larger portal. He spoke with someone not visible beyond the door, then turned and waited, watching the visitors carefully.

Rand and Jen looked at each other, shifting from foot to foot in apprehension. The courier and his kinsman were impassive, content to wait quietly. It wasn't more than a few minutes before the small door opened and an older man stepped out. His frame was as spare and straight as the courier's, but deep lines were etched around his eyes and gray hair was sprinkled through the black. He beckoned for them to approach.

"Well, now, this is a sight worth interrupting my dinner for! A royal courier brings two lowlanders to the very doorstep of this holy place—lordlings in a Gauntlet, no less! What tidings do you bring?"

"Perhaps be better we show than tell, old father, away from others," said the courier.

The man regarded them intently for a few moments, then nodded and stepped back through the door, motioning for them to follow. They stepped through in single file. Rand looked around the lamp-lit space. The roof curved high overhead in an arc from the floor on one side to the floor on the other. The passageway was at least thirty feet across and stretched into the depths of the hill beyond sight. The floor was a smooth gray stone that seemed to be all of a piece. Down the center of the tunnel, two parallel ridges ran. They appeared to be made of metal. Indeed, so did the walls, though Rand could scarcely credit so profligate a use of such valuable material.

"Now, what will you show me?" said the man. The courier nodded to Rand, who carefully unwrapped his tablet fragment and handed it to the elder. The man stared and uttered a great cry of amazement in his own tongue. Then he switched back to Solethonian.

"What is this? Are some of the Stone Tears in our speech as well?"

"Watch carefully, sir, as I look at it," said Rand and stepped close. He turned the fragment so it faced him directly and saw the characters reform into Solethonian. The elder gasped.

"Ah, I see! As the ancient tales told us, the ones that drew us here—a living Word! And how did it awaken?" Once again Rand told the story of that day in the Serenhorn Academy museum: blue lightning, thunder, and the fateful discovery.

"So what you be thinking, courier, an' you bring him here?"

"Old father, I be wondering, what if some of the stones we have found can be made to speak again?"

"Hmm, well-thought. Think you there be time to study on this in the morrow? These children be much tired, I would say."

"Sadly, they must race as early as they can to make up for our sidestep here—may we look now before they take their rest?" The elder nodded and clapped his hands. Two younger men appeared and took up lanterns, leading them down the arched main corridor. Still the twin ridges of metal ran down the center of the passage and off into the gloom ahead of them. In time they came to another great wall or door that sealed the passage.

Their guides turned aside to a door set into the left side of the main corridor. The group followed through, then the elder motioned for the visitors to wait. Rand watched as the two young men moved through the surprisingly large room. Other lights flickered into being as they moved, lighting candles as they went. The light grew, and Rand saw that they were on a kind of broad terrace. In front of him stretched a long desk that had an angled backing decorated from one end to the other with strange emblems, symbols, and inset devices. On the table surface, there were a few ornate stands, and on each of these there was a Stone Tear.

On this long, curving desk he saw more Stone Tears than in the Academy museum in Serenhorn—maybe more than Zekiel had recounted in collections across all of Solethon. As he stepped forward to look closer, he saw beyond the desk. The room descended in steps or terraces like the one where he stood. There were eight levels, and each had a desk like the one before him, with a like number of Stone Tears on display.

"This is—how?" Rand trailed off and turned to the elder in helpless confusion. The man smiled and nodded.

"You have heard, I t'ink, how came the Amhara to this place?"

"Yes—you heard about the tablets, the ones in the old kingdom, before they were shattered."

"True—an' so far as this had we come to see them, when the terrible day came. Far into the sky rose the pillar of blue flame. An' then, as the storm pass, down came the Stone Tears. We knew not what they signify then, but we knew the place we hoped to see was gone. So we stopped an' bided here. Stories began to come with the pass of time, as the fleeing people came over the wasteland. Then we knew the stones for what they were. We foun' this ancient place an' gathered in all the tears we could find. Read them we could not, but we sought them across this high forsaken land, doing them honor an' keeping them against a day when they might speak again."

"What would you have me do?"

"Help us—show us what you did, an' help us look to see if mayhap it can be done again."

"Rand." Jen tugged his arm and nodded her head for them to step aside and confer. He wondered why, but her glare made it clear that she had reason enough.

"Excuse us, sir," he said to the elder and they moved to the side of the room.

"We are in a race, remember? To save your friend—looking for matching pieces could take long. And if we succeed? From the way you described it, it sounds dangerous. This blue fire that destroyed the old empire—what if you somehow set it off again?"

"We'll just have to mind the time, and try to search quickly, no more than we can do before bed tonight. As for the danger, you give me pause there. I hadn't really thought of that. It did knock us flat the first time. We may not find any matches, but if we do, maybe not join more than two at a time?"

Jen glanced toward their waiting hosts. "We could spare a little time, as you say. Just mind what you're about. I… I have to admit that a part of me would like to see it for myself."

"Let's try it, then." They returned to the waiting men. "I don't know what we may find, sir, but I'll try—at least until we must have our night's rest."

"That is well," said the elder. "Please, proceed as you like."

Rand began to walk along the next terrace down, his attention hopping from one fragment to the next. "Did you ever play with picture puzzles when you were little?"

"A few," said Jen.

"I remember that it was always easiest to match the edge and corner pieces first. That's how I found the first pair." The two racers and their escorts fanned out through the hall, looking for such fragments.

"Let us bring together such as we find, that we may try them one against another," said the elder. The others nodded and continued searching. What a scene we must make, thought Rand — shadowy figures quietly rustling through a man-made cavern whose ceiling vanishes into darkness, hovering over the glow of a score of lamps as they peer at small, mysterious objects. The passage of time was difficult to measure, but between the seven of them it did not seem to take very long. Rand had found one small piece with a straight edge. Jen had done better, finding two — one of which was a corner.

The others were finishing now. The elder motioned for them to join him in the wide space at the bottom of the room. He directed his aides pull a table that sat against a side wall into the center of the area. On it they each laid out their pieces.

"Now, brother, approach and see as you might." The elder smiled at Rand and gestured to the table. Rand stepped forward and searched among the pieces by both sight and touch. They had gathered twelve in all. After a few minutes he found two that had similar outlines along one edge, but on closer inspection they seemed to be mirror images rather than a match. Rand hesitated a moment, then groaned in frustration at his own lack of insight and flipped one of the pieces over. Now the edges appeared to be a perfect match.

"I think I have one. Everyone stay back from me and brace yourselves. If it's anything like the first time, there will be a pretty big bang." He picked up the two fragments and moved close to the far side of the room, careful to keep the stones separate.

When he got there, he paused. His intention had been to face the wall and try to shield the others; Jen, however, had said she wanted to see it for herself, and these Amhara had waited for generations for something like this. He turned to face them all and braced his back against the wall.

"Well, here we go." He raised the two fragments and slowly fitted them together.

The Vizier settled comfortably in Willowberg, given the limitations of the place. He did miss the privacy and solidity of his suite nestled deep in the stone pile of the citadel in Solaria, but with reports flowing in from the Gauntlet, both official and unofficial, doing business in a more open environment had its advantages.

He soon found himself wishing for privacy for different reasons. He had had little contact with Garrak and the network of familiars since coming north—it would not do for the uninitiated to see him carrying on conversations with uncanny beasts. Though it was after dark and most people had left the sumptuous villa that he had secured for the contest, he was perturbed when the raven came fluttering down the main entryway toward him with no regard for subtlety or concealment.

"Alarm! Alarm!" he squawked. The Vizier darted anxious glances around the area, but the few visible figures were distant and appeared to take no notice. The bird landed heavily on the polished floor and skidded to a clattering stop.

"What is it now?" the Vizier hissed as quietly as his anger would allow.

"Master! The Others are enraged! The Enslaver stirs again. You must speak to—to the one you know of, at once!"

"Faugh! The Enslaver again? Why must it interfere now? Very well, we will go to my private chambers, such as they are." He held out his forearm and Garrak perched there, struggling to keep his balance as they marched quickly down the hall.

The Vizier burst into his apartments and slammed the door shut. As he turned the key in the lock, he felt a prickling unease emanating from behind him. He spun around to find that Lupus had wasted no time in appearing from his distant realm.

"Ah, priest! I trust that this audience does not unduly inconvenience you?"

The Vizier knelt and lowered himself in a posture of obeisance, glancing up only fleetingly into the demon's glittering ruby eyes. "Certainly not, oh deathless one! What do you require?"

"I and my servants are perturbed. It seems that more fragments of the Enslaver have awakened this night. Did you not assure me that you took steps to prevent this from happening again?"

"I did, milord. I gathered all known fragments in the kingdom into my keeping and treated them to prevent them from joining. They are hidden deep in my chambers under the capital. No one goes there without my knowledge!"

"In the capital, you say? This complicates matters."

"What do you mean, milord?"

"My servants sensed the awakening in a very different direction. It occurred somewhere on the high plateau to the west."

"That is far beyond my sphere of control—almost beyond my ken. The Runners hold sway there, and no one ventures there but them. I did not know that they possessed fragments, but it appears that they do. I like it not that this would happen in the very time of the Gauntlet."

"The commoner that we have encountered before—where is he?"

"Running the Gauntlet as we speak. He eluded the first few traps we set for him, but to the best of our knowledge he did so by happenstance, not by guile."

"So it often seems when the Enemy is at work. He prefers subtlety even more than we do. Is the boy in the highlands now?"

"I have not received an update about him since the trap of the horses failed yesterday. If he made good progress from there, he may be on the plateau."

"I tire of the limitations of your flesh, vizier. I think it is time to gather my special servants and send them in force to address this matter. It may prove costly, but the awakening of the Enslaver is danger enough to justify the risk."

"May Garrak accompany them, so that I will know what happens?"

"He may. Careful priest—you may find yourself closer to the line of battle than you would like."

Chapter 46

In the wilderness prepare the way for the Word;
make straight in the desert a highway for our Speaker.

Rand groaned and rolled over, clinging gratefully to the solidity of the floor beneath him. Blurred fogs of light and dark wavered before his eyes. Sounds came to him in hollow, distant echoes, as if his head was under water. An acrid tang was in the air.

Many hands touched him, lifting him to his feet. His vision began to clear. The Amhara surrounded him, chattering excitedly in their native tongue. Jen's face swam into view. "Rand! Are you all right?" He nodded wordlessly, willing his mind to function. There was something important he was forgetting.

The fragment! He cried out, unable to produce more than a hoarse croaking. He fell back to his knees and began to search the floor. The Royal Courier appeared beside him and placed a gentle hand on his shoulder.

"Fret not, my brother. See? Here it is."

He placed the Stone Tear in Rand's hands. Rand blinked and focused carefully. As before, he saw words plainly engraved in the glossy stone.

"For the Speaker loved all that he had made so much that he sent the Word into the world, so that anyone who believed the Word would not come to nothing, but know never-ending life."

"Jen! Have you read this?" She knelt beside him.

"Yes, I did steal a peek while you took your little nap. Never-ending life... Rand, have you considered the possibility that what happened here is more important than what we've been doing in the Gauntlet?"

"My heart is torn between the two. But I think we need Zekiel's help to deal with this business, and we need to win the Gauntlet to save him. One is tied to the other."

Jen nodded. Rand turned and handed the awakened fragment to the elder. The man read it, and tears welled up in his eyes until they spilled down his weathered cheeks.

"Never-ending life! All this time we have held these words, silent and hidden in the depths of the mountain. If only we had known!" He passed the table to his aides, who exclaimed joyfully at its message.

"Now we have seen it, an' now we know—the Word can live an' speak again. We will see whatever pieces here may yet join together. But as for you, you have far to go an' much to do. Rest now. When you go with the morning, go in peace. We will remember you always. Brother courier? There is food an' beds for you all back by the outer door."

"Yes, elder. Come, friends—I t'ink we all sleep well tonight." They made their way out of the room of the Stone Tears and back down the tunnel, into a side room that had a table with bowls of food, and a door to another room where cots had been prepared for them. After a quick supper, the courier's prediction proved true. It had been a full day, and the racers slept harder than ever before in their lives.

Rand felt as though he had only just closed his eyes when the courier woke them the next morning, and his body longed to stay in the cot. Still, he knew there was no choice but to rise and face another day of the Gauntlet. They ate and drank a light but fortifying breakfast, then left the odd cavern before the sun had risen above the eastern horizon. Rand's muscles were stiff and sore, protesting every step, and he could tell from her wincing that Jen felt it too, but the courier assured them that the best remedy was to get moving again. They headed out of the Amhara village by the eastward road.

"We meet again with the cliff-side highway not far ahead, an' the little distance we have trimmed should make up for the time we spent stopping by the holy place," said the courier. Rand and Jen were working too hard on just keeping their legs moving to do more than nod.

They rejoined the main road and went on, the day passing much the same as the one before—running, walking, resting, and running again. They met no other racers ahead and were overtaken by none from behind. They reached the eastern end of the promontory and turned back to the west. Not long after, night fell and they laid out their bedrolls to sleep as well as they could on the hard earth.

The westward leg went on for two more days of the same, though Rand was pleased to discover that his body was responding to the extended strain by getting tougher and able to do more. Midway through the first day after the turn, they came upon a female contestant who was lying beside the road, her guide trying to apply aid to her leg. Apparently the exertion had been too much for it.

"I met her at the camp after we climbed the cliff," said Jen. "Princess Aurelia."

As night approached on the second westward day, they saw campfires ahead, close to the edge of the plateau. The courier slowed as they neared the camp. He stopped to speak quietly with a fellow Amhara who was serving as lookout, then turned to the young contestants.

"This be the end of the running, small-man. An' so I take leave, to return to my duties. 'Twas a pleasure to run wit' you both." He put a hand to his chest and bowed.

"Thank you, courier," said Jen. "It was an honor to have you for our guide."

Rand did his best to emulate the courier's bow. "It was good to see you again. I hope it won't be the last time."

"I be here an' there, small-man, here an' there," the courier replied with a grin. "You never know when I turn up!" He bid farewell to the lookout and slipped back into the darkness, along with his kinsman who had been Jen's guide. Rand and Jen followed the lookout into the camp.

It was almost a mirror image of the one they found when they climbed up to the high country. As a Gauntlet marshal explained while they ate their supper, the difference was that they would be climbing down in the morning, and not into a lush pastureland like they had passed through on their way to the plateau. This was the southern edge of the great barrens—the wasteland, thought Rand, that the refugees had crossed from the old empire where the Word had been broken.

In the morning, Rand and Jen ate a quick breakfast with the two other racers who had been in the camp when they arrived. Other than that, they had little sense of where they stood in the Gauntlet. Rand tried to make casual conversation with the marshal about how many had already passed this way, but the man saw through him and laughed.

"Oh, no, milord, not so easily as that! If ye want to know how ye rank, ye'd best race fast enough to pass all an' count 'em as ye go!" Jen laughed along with the others, and Rand smiled in spite of himself. The marshal gathered them at the edge of the cliffs.

"Look ye there—see the two peaks wit' the risin' sun shinin' betwixt 'em? That's yer next goal. Mind ye don't take too long getting' there, or ye mightn't get there at all!" Then he led them to the climbing ropes and the other two racers descended in the order they had arrived. Going down was much faster than climbing up had been.

Rand had entered the camp last, so the marshal gave Jen leave to begin her descent before him. He did his best to keep from staring after her, looking off to the distant hills that marked their goal, then checking his gear. He did spare a look when the marshal noted that the first runner had reached the desert floor. Then the man slapped him on the shoulder and sent him off.

Remembering his drills at the Academy of Serenhorn, he fell into the rhythm of pushing off, rappelling, and choosing the next landing spot. It flowed like the verses of a well-remembered song. The rising sun called forth the flinty smell of the barren rock and sand below as he approached the bottom. Faster than he would have expected, his feet touched the ground. He disentangled himself from the ropes and started jogging to the northeast, toward the distant marker of the two peaks, though as yet he could not see them over the surrounding hillocks of bare earth.

He reached the crest of one such hill and saw the landmark, adjusting his course a little to the south. As he reached the sandy hollow at the bottom of the hill, he jumped when a rock bounced off of his left foot.

"Glad you decided to show up," said Jen, grinning from her seat against a large boulder. "That hill should screen us from any prying eyes behind. We can team up again."

This improved Rand's spirits tremendously. Once again they shared little stories from their former lives to pass the time as they trotted along at the best pace they could maintain without exhausting their strength. When they needed to, they stopped to catch their breath and take a sip of water along with a morsel of the nut and berry mix favored by the Amhara.

"There aren't any roads across this waste—not even trails. I wonder why?" Rand mused during one stop.

"There wasn't much about this land in the library at the Academy, but I did run across one odd mention. Some believe that it was once at the bottom of a great sea, and that the clifftops of the land now ruled by the Amhara were really coasts."

"But if that was true, wouldn't most of Solethon be underwater too? Are we all fish people?" Rand gaped his mouth open and closed like a fish. Jen laughed and punched him lightly on the arm.

"I always knew there was something fishy about you! Well, I can't say it all makes sense, but if half the stories Zekiel has been telling us are true, the world has changed a lot over the centuries—more than once, I imagine."

Rand's mood shadowed abruptly. "Speaking of him, we'd better keep at it if we have any hope of helping him." They resumed their run.

They kept up a strong pace as noon approached. Suddenly, Jen held up her hand in warning and they crouched low. As they ceased their own noise-making, Rand could hear shouts and the scuffling sounds of a struggle. They crept forward, Jen first since she was smaller, pressed close against the side of the little hillock of dried ancient mud on their left. Jen put a hand on Rand's knee and they stopped.

He took the risk of leaning forward over Jen's head until he could see what she saw. The scene was a confused jumble of flailing limbs and scuffling dust at first. As he watched and sorted it out, he recognized one of the contestants who had started before them in the morning. The youth was crouched defensively in the center of a flat space, surrounded by figures wrapped in robes the color of the dusty ground. He spun one way and then another, trying to keep them all in sight while they jumped and jerked and feinted in and out.

Rand was torn between the instinct to escape and the urge to help a fellow contestant in need, but as he wavered, the inevitable happened. While the racer faced one way, a figure behind him tossed a net over him. Then the pack closed in.

Rand's frozen indecision was interrupted by something moving out of the corner of his eye. A small dust devil spun in the mouth of a crease that led away from the scene of the fight, but still roughly toward their distant goal. He tapped Jen's shoulder and pointed— she nodded. They scrambled away while the attackers were still focused on their captive. The little whirlwind moved ahead of them, changing course along one gully and then another. Moved by instinct, Rand kept following it until at length it dissipated. Now that they had put some distance between themselves and the ambush, they chose a relatively sheltered spot and stopped to breathe and collect their wits.

"I ill liked leaving a countryman to the wolves like that, Rand, but we must remember—he was our competitor, and his capture helped us avoid the same end to our race."

"I know." Rand shivered as he remembered facing real wolves on a snowy night halfway to Serenhorn. A gust of wind kicked up a puff of grit that made him duck his face to protect his eyes. As he did so, he thought he heard a kind of soft whisper: *Rand...*

"What?" he said to Jen.

She looked at him in confusion. "I didn't say anything."

Afternoon passed into dusk as they pressed on, moving more slowly now and seeking cover wherever they could find it. Rand was thinking it would soon be time to find a spot to sleep.

A shadow passed overhead and he heard a slow, heavy flapping sound as of large wings. He glanced around swiftly, but in the fading light he could not find the source of the sound. Suddenly a fiery pain sliced along his upper arm. He stumbled to one side and turned. Oily black feathers buffeted him and he felt talons ripping at the front of his leather jerkin. He cried out to warn Jen and thrust upward with his left forearm while fumbling with his right hand for his knife. Jen shouted angrily and kicked at Rand's attacker from behind. It turned toward her, giving him the time to seize his blade and a chance to see his enemy.

It was some kind of ungainly carrion bird—a vulture, but oddly shaped and enormous, with a body the size of a small child. The stench of decay surrounded it. As it heaved itself up into the air with a mighty thrust of its wings, Rand saw an odd shifting in its outline that sent a cold shiver of recognition through him.

"Jen! Get behind me! It's... it's one of them!"

"What!?! We'll do better to attack it from two sides!"

"It's not normal! It's an, uh, *aganint*! A demon-thing in animal shape—my knife can hurt them, but other weapons can't. Please, trust me!" She looked doubtful, but she shuffled behind him as the vulture screamed and swooped on them again. He grabbed for the thing's outstretched talons with his left hand as he slashed with the blade in his right. It buffeted him with its wings and wheeled aside.

Again and again it attacked, the deepening dark making it harder for Rand to see its movements before it crashed into him. His hands and face were stinging with scratches from the thing's claws. Finally he seized hold of a talon long enough to prevent the beast from swooping away. He thrust the Amharic dagger into its breast, and as he had hoped, the thing melted away, trailing an angry wail.

"What—where?" gasped Jen, turning and searching rapidly in all directions. Rand slumped to the ground.

"Banished, back to whatever dark pit it came from. It's the blade, blessed by the Amhara long ago to fight such creatures."

"You're bleeding—how badly are you hurt?"

"Not... not badly, I think, I'm more scratched and bruised than anything."

"Let me tend those wounds before they get infected. Who knows what kind of filth that thing had on its claws?"

Jen took a little water from her water-skin and used it to wipe away the blood and grime from his wounds. Then she took a small glass bottle from a pouch and began to apply ointment to them. It stung and smelled terrible; he flinched away.

"Hold still! This is a salve used by the fishermen I grew up with, when ropes burn their hands and hooks snag in their flesh. It will protect you and help you heal." Rand did his best not to move and let her work. As she finished applying the salve to each wound, he realized that both the sting of the injury and the pain of her touch eased. When she had treated all the cuts she could find, she put the bottle away and shook out the blanket from her bedroll. It was then that he noticed the stars were out.

"No fire tonight, I think. Between bandits and monsters, we don't want to attract any attention. Here, lay down." She helped him shift over onto her blanket, then she took the one from his own harness.

"We'll have to be warmth enough for each other." She settled beside him and drew his blanket around them.

"You have a healer's touch. Thank you," he murmured. Uncertain if he should, but feeling it was the natural thing to do, he placed his arm around her shoulders. She rolled to face him and placed a hand on his chest.

"You're making a habit of rescuing me. I should be thanking you," she said quietly. He reached and gently brushed a strand of hair away from her face, then softly traced the outline of her cheek with his finger.

"Jen..." he whispered.

"Yes, Rand?" she whispered back. He moved his face closer and lightly brushed her lips with his. He paused, his heart thumping like a hammer on the anvil in his father's forge.

She touched his lips with hers. Then she kissed his cheek and turned over, snuggling against him and laying her head on his outstretched arm.

"Good night," she sighed quietly. He rolled onto his side facing her back, and with his other arm he enfolder her, drawing the blanket close around them both.

He thought back to his two encounters with Lyssa, a time that seemed so long ago now. Those moments had been full of excitement, an intoxicating thrill of desire and discovery, but there had been no tenderness, no sense of companionship. This young woman beside him might not have dazzled or beguiled him, but she made him feel strong and whole in ways he had never known. He wondered how he could sleep with his heart so full, but after the labors, fears, and struggles of the day, he drifted off quickly.

In the Vizier's chambers in Willowberg, unseen forces flung papers and furniture around with reckless abandon. The Vizier huddled on the floor with his arms over his head, waiting for the storm to pass.

Though outwardly cowering before his master's rage, inwardly he felt a growing sense of confidence. Lupus' behavior was a sign of weakness. Powerful he might be, ancient, wise, and cruel, but he was not accustomed to being thwarted and it did not sit well with him. He had lost a second servant at the hands of the young upstart, and this time he could not blame it on the Vizier.

Chapter 47

Floods cannot snuff out love, nor rivers sweep it away. If one gave all of one's wealth for love, it would be completely disregarded.

Bright sunlight streamed across the wasteland and penetrated the thin covering of Rand's eyelids. He groaned and rolled away from the light, then slowly opened his eyes. Memories of the night before came back to him. He slowly pushed himself up on one elbow and looked around.

Jen sat cross-legged nearby, busy making a little meal out of their meager trail rations. At his movement, she looked up at him and smiled. Rand was surprised to see that she looked self-conscious.

"Good morning, milady—no, I should say, good morning, dear friend." Did she actually blush a little at that?

"My hero," she said with a cavalier grin. "Here, eat something." She leaned over and handed him a few chunks of flatbread and cheese. He reached to take it and allowed his fingers to caress her hand as he did so.

"All right—let's be clear-minded about this." She spoke seriously, but not unkindly. "You are my true friend, proven time and again. I am glad that you feel for me, and I have come to be fond of you myself. Agreed?"

"In every detail."

"But here and now, we cannot afford distractions. We have to finish this Gauntlet foolishness, and find a way to win, if we are to save your friend."

"You speak the truth as always," he said around a mouthful of food. He climbed to his feet and brushed away some of the dust on his breeches. He reached down and waited for Jen to take his hand, then pulled her to her feet.

"I want you to know, though," he continued, "no matter how far we run, or how many we fight, being with you makes my heart glad. Please, before we turn our faces back to our labors, let's have one moment…"

She kept her eyes on his, then gave the slightest nod. He leaned close and they shared one kiss, brief but tender.

"I have had another thought I would like to act on," he continued. "Once, after we had joined those first pieces at the Academy, Zekiel decided to make a declaration of his belief in the Speaker and his desire to take action. I was reluctant to follow his example then. With all we have been through and the message revealed to us in the cave, I think it's time I did the same." He stepped apart and spoke to the distance, trying to find a way of addressing the unseen.

"I believe in the Speaker and his living Word. I will try my best to serve them and learn more of them." He faltered, a little embarrassed and not sure what else to say. Jen came to him and took his hand with a smile.

"I'm sure that's fine, Rand, and—and—I agree."

Then they busied themselves with rolling up and bundling their blankets. Having no tents, no fire, nothing but what little they carried, they were ready to go in no time.

"There's the pass we're bound for," Jen pointed to the east. Trying as before to keep low and quiet, they began their march.

No tribesmen or beasts appeared to threaten them as they scrambled along. As the sun rose higher, wind kicked up great clouds of the ochre dust into the air. They wrapped cloth around their faces to keep from breathing in too much of it. They could not be sure they were still on course, but from time to time Rand thought he heard a whisper that was more voice than wind. Convinced now that this was no trick of his imagination, and remembering what Aunt Roberta had said to him, he always turned in the direction from which it spoke. When they stopped for a brief morsel at midday, Rand mentioned that the dust storm must be protecting them, obscuring any signs of their passage. It was hard to judge when only brief gaps appeared through the murk, but the hills in front of them looked a good deal closer. By the time the shadows in the dust began to deepen, Rand started to hope that they might reach the pass by nightfall.

"Another stage completed," noted Jen with satisfaction. They were striding up a rising slope into the shadowed valley between the peaks. To Rand's relief, they broke above the dust storm at last, and the hard-scrabble dirt and rock of the waste was changing into a spongy turf. As they crossed into the mouth of the pass, they saw a pennant and a tent in the midst of the valley floor. Rand hung back and let Jen march forward, wanting to maintain the impression that each acted alone.

"Ho, ye tuckered racer!" Rand heard a marshal greet Jen as she reached the tent. He sped up to a jog, to better play the eager competitor.

"Ah, and a motley hound at yer heels!" said the soldier as Rand trotted up. "Well, ye'd best stop here for the night, though there be no fine accommodations. I've a little plain food, water, an' tents to sleep in behind yonder pavilion." They availed themselves of the bread and fruit, cheese and dried meat that were laid out on a table. As promised, there were little one-man tents behind the larger one used by the marshal. Rand looked around and saw that the man was still watching into the oncoming dusk for any more racers.

"No one else here," he whispered. Jen nodded.

"I don't know if that means we're ahead or behind," she said with a little shrug. "At least we're not crowded." They gave each other a wave and crawled into the little tents to sleep.

In the morning, they cleaned off as much of the dust as they could from their desert crossing, then took a little breakfast. One other racer had come sometime in the night. The marshal gave them their instructions before starting them off in the order they had arrived.

"Traverse this valley east and down into the lowlands. Soon enough, ye'll find the beginnings of a stream. Follow it along and ye'll reach the next stage."

Jen left first, before the morning sun had reached the floor of the wide-mouthed pass. Since Rand had only been a few steps behind her, his turn came soon after. He nodded to the young man who had come in the night, who looked scuffed and bruised from his journey. That reminded Rand of his own cuts from the fight with the vulture-thing. How did his own face look, he wondered?

He jogged along the lightly-worn dirt track through the dew-soaked grasses of the valley floor. It seemed Jen was a good ways in front of him now. After he had run long enough to warm up his muscles and start to feel winded, he came to the eastern mouth of the pass and started down. He was back in the valley of the Solus now, where the land was green with spring and trees began to appear. Suddenly, Jen arose from behind a thicket to join him.

"And so we follow the same road again, Lord Rand."

"So it would seem, Lady Jen." She laughed as he made a sweeping bow.

"I think we will be testing what rules there may be about cooperation from here on."

"How so?"

"If I understand the course of the Gauntlet correctly, we are approaching the final challenge, followed by the final stage. Somewhere along the stream ahead, we will come to a place where we must build our own water craft, then take them down the Solus River back to Willowberg and the finish."

"All right, what then?"

"It is time for the advantage I spoke of on that day in your library in Serenhorn. We will make a kind of boat that I heard of long ago when I was a young girl, but it will take both of us to make it and to pilot it. The pretense of us racing separately will have to end."

"I will not miss it. I'm proud to race beside you."

"Very well, let's see if you can!" With a laugh she broke into a jog and he scrambled after her.

They soon reached the stream that they were to follow. The grass was lush and trees grew even thicker along its banks. Rand was surprised that he had missed green and growing things so much after only two days spent crossing the wasteland.

As noontime approached, the stream gathered together with others and widened into a river. It continued to flow east and a little south toward the great Solus. Jen tugged at Rand's sleeve and pulled him into the shadow of a large oak.

"In that clearing up ahead—I think that's our next stop." There was a wide space surrounded by trees, the grass cropped short by grazing sheep. Along the edge of the water, Rand saw clusters of supplies—lumber, rope, and canvas. A pair of marshals were having lunch at a table.

"Time to put my little scheme to the test." Jen walked on and Rand followed. The marshals saw them coming and one stood to greet them.

"Welcome, milady and milord. This is your final challenge. By the water's edge you will find supplies suitable for building a raft. When you are finished, you will ride it down to the Solus and on to Willowberg. Each stack of supplies is the same and should have all you need. One stack per contestant, and you may not borrow from the other stacks."

"Good sir marshal, may I ask a question?"

"Of course, milady."

"If I chose to use things other than the supplies offered, would that be allowed? I would keep to what could be found nearby."

The marshal looked to his comrade, who shrugged and continued eating. The first man frowned in thought.

"If you limit yourself to what grows here naturally, I suppose that would be acceptable. The Gauntlet is a test of resourcefulness and ingenuity as well as strength and endurance."

"Thank you, sir. And my fellow racer here—can we combine our efforts if we wish?"

"That may be another matter, milady. We want no tricks."

"Surely not, sir. It is only that the craft I seek to build will take two to make and two to pilot. We have become friends along the way and would like to help each other."

"This would be most unusual." The marshal paced back and forth as he considered it. "Still, the forging of alliances is another useful skill for a leader. I propose this—I will observe your work. If I judge that you are abusing the spirit and intent of the Gauntlet, you must stop immediately and go back to making each your own raft from the supplies provided. No argument from either of you. Agreed?"

"Agreed."

"Very well—please begin."

Rand followed her across the clearing, his mind racing. He waited until they were away from the marshals.

"Now may I know what we are doing?"

"Looking for a tree with about ten feet of straight trunk that's clear of branches, two feet thick if possible. Birch would be best." They found a good candidate about a third of the way around the clearing.

"We're going to strip off the bark and form it into a long, thin boat. To do it properly would take days and involve shaping many different pieces, but we will do a simple one that we can finish quickly."

"What's the advantage?"

"It's fast, light, and easy to maneuver. Trust me! Now, give me your dagger and hoist me up on your shoulders."

He held her as steady as he could while she scored a cut around the trunk. Then she made the start of a vertical cut down to where he could easily reach it. He took over from there and continued the cut until it was near the ground. While he worked at this, she took her own small knife and dug up strings of root from a nearby spruce.

When he was done cutting a line around the base of the trunk, she got back up on his shoulders and used the tip of his blade to pry up the bark and begin peeling it back. Again, when she had worked it low enough for him to continue, she had him let her down.

The marshal who had spoken with them watched from a few paces away. When he saw the bark peeling away from the tree, he murmured with interest. While Rand worked, Jen continued to collect roots. When she felt she had enough, she snapped off two branches and stripped them of twigs, making two sticks a couple of feet long.

At last Rand succeeded in peeling the bark completely off the tree. The inner surface was sticky with sweet-smelling sap. They had been at work for a little more than an hour.

"All right, now—at the end, fold the edges up until they meet. Press the bark flat together and use the tip of your dagger to drill holes clear through. I'll do the same on the other end." As Jen went to her end, she stopped and used the two branches to prop the upper edge of the bark apart in the middle. By this time the second marshal had joined the first to see what they were up to. Rand could hear them commenting quietly to each other.

"Now, use the roots as cords to lace the end together through the holes. Make it as tight as you can. The sap will help to seal it." When the ends were done, Jen drilled holes about three feet from each end and used them to lash the branches permanently in place as cross-braces.

"Now our bark canoe is done!" The project had taken less than three hours. While they worked, the young man from the previous stop had arrived and started making a raft from the provided supplies. Jen turned to the marshal.

"Are you satisfied, sir?"

"I have seen nothing out of order. I doubt how well this... thing can carry you, but that is your choice."

"May I choose one pile of supplies and take a few things from it?"

"You may."

Jen found that a couple of oars were included for each raft and took them. She also took the square of canvas and cut it into strips, using them to line the floor of the canoe. "Don't want to get stuck to all that sap."

She showed Rand how to hoist the canoe onto their shoulders using the cross-braces. Together they carried it to the river. They greeted the young man who was busy lashing together planks to form the deck of his raft. He paused and scrutinized the canoe, then shook his head and turned back to his own project. Rand saw that another racer had arrived by now and was sorting out a raft of her own.

Jen found a good spot to lay the canoe into the river, its side pulled tight against the bank. "I'll hold it steady while you climb in—one leg at a time, kneeling behind the back cross-brace." He did as she said, slowly and with a few wobbles.

"Good! Now, dig the blade of your oar into the earth and use it to hold the canoe still." He did, then she climbed in on her knees just behind the front cross-brace.

"All right—when we need to steer, you can use your oar as a rudder. When we are running in the clear, we can both paddle for speed. We always paddle on opposite sides with every stroke, to help even out our motion and keep us going straight. Ready?"

"Yes, captain!" That earned him a smile. She nodded and he pulled up his oar. She used hers to push off from the bank, then dug into the water to help get the boat moving. He carefully followed her example. Soon they were into the main current and picking up speed.

"Hurrah!" Rand couldn't help shouting as he felt how eagerly the canoe sliced through the water.

"Aim for where the current flows fastest!" shouted Jen over her shoulder. Soon they were moving at about the pace of a brisk jog, and with a much more sustainable amount of effort. As they slipped along the tributary, Rand had the chance to practice steering with his paddle, and Jen demonstrated how to stroke with the least effort and resistance. He started to feel like he was getting the hang of it. Then he noticed that his knees were wet.

"Hey! We're leaking!"

"Don't worry! These quick-made canoes aren't sealed as well as the fully crafted ones, but the seepage isn't bad. We can always stop and dump it out if it gets too wet."

Before Rand could worry too much, they came to the confluence with the Solus River. Following Jen's directions, he kept them closer to the bank until they were well into the larger waterway, so as to avoid the turbulence of the currents merging together. Then they eased back into the main flow and gathered speed.

The afternoon sun sank lower and filtered through the trees on the western bank, dappling the water. When they had been going for a couple of hours, Rand tapped Jen on the shoulder and pointed to a gravel bar where they pulled up to eat trail rations, stretch their cramped legs, and dump a few inches of water out of their boat. He inspected the root lashings at bow and stern, and they had remained tight. He turned to Jen and caressed her cheek, which earned him a smile in return.

"This was a great idea, Jen! Let's see who we can catch!" They launched back into the river and continued.

Chapter 48

By me kings reign and rulers issue decrees that are just.

Splash and paddle, roar of water and song of bird, onward they went. The afternoon was passing, but the light was still good so they pressed on. They came to a stretch of rapids and had to carefully pick their way through the rocks, Jen often rising up on her knees to spot the path ahead.

"Look there!" she shouted, pointing about a hundred yards downstream. The current gathered into a deeper channel on the right side, fast and narrow. A raft had tried to drive through the widest gap between a row of sharp rocks that jutted up from the river like teeth, but it had run aground. Planks and rope lay in a tangled mass with the rushing water foaming around them.

"We'll pass by there in the smaller gap!" She pointed and Rand switched from paddling to steering. As they swiftly drew near the wreck, he saw a figure thrashing in the midst of it, struggling to pull some of the pieces together and get them to pass through the gap. Doubtless he hoped to float along with them to a spot downriver where he could lash a smaller raft together out of what he had left. As they came closer, Rand saw that it was Uthor. He looked up and saw them too. He shouted violent oaths and threw a broken plank in their direction, but it splashed harmlessly nearby. Then the slender canoe shot like an arrow through the gap and they were past.

They did not spare the breath to talk about what they had seen, focusing instead on staying in the heart of the current and keeping up a steady pace with their paddles. Nevertheless, as the minutes passed, Rand thought over what he knew about the other competitors. As far as he could tell, Uthor had been near the lead all through the race. How close were they to the front after passing him?

Late afternoon was swiftly turning into evening. Rand dared not think too much about the aching in his arms or the cramped muscles in his folded legs. Thankfully Jen pointed out the seepage in the bottom of their boat and nodded toward a sandy spot where they could pull over to rest and pour out the water.

They renewed their vigor with the last of their trail food. Then, with many a stretch and groan, they climbed back into the canoe and went on. The sun had slipped behind the highlands where they had run with the courier. The sky was still bright, but finding their way on the river would be ever more difficult as darkness gathered over the water.

They came around a long bend and stared in confusion at a scene that played tricks with their eyes. Red, green, purple, and gold light sparkled on the surface of the water. It flowed through the air like ripples on the surface of a pond, then fanned out in rays like sunlight bursting through a layer of clouds. As their eyes adjusted to the bursts of light, they could see that something was silhouetted against the glare. At a signal from Jen, they backed water to slow their approach.

The shape proved to be a raft, with a mast and sail rigged. As they drew closer, they could hear strange humming and hissing that accompanied the lights. Jen pointed—Rand could see a figure on the raft, gesturing swiftly. Over the unearthly sounds, they could hear chanting.

Jen began paddling to one side to steer them around and past this strange apparition. Rand followed her lead. He soon discovered that the surface of the river was broken by dark, up-reaching fingers—the bare branches of dead trees that had been swept downstream by the spring thaw. The raft had become entangled in their embrace. The figure onboard was visible now in the glow of the strange lights—it was Jylla. As she chanted and waved her arms, the multi-colored streams of sparks burst forth and struck her sail.

The canvas bulged and the ropes strained, but still the raft was unable to break free. Rand looked down and saw that the current had carried them into the thicket as well, but the canoe's narrow beam and shallow draft allowed it to slip through the barrier, slowed but not stuck.

The red-haired mystic gave an angry shout and clapped her hands together. A shaft of blue light struck the sail. It burst into flames and the rope braces snapped. The mast fell forward, and the fire began to consume the entire raft.

Jylla collapsed in exhaustion with a cry of despair. Her face in the firelight was streaked with sweat, her shoulders heaving as she gasped for breath. Rand wasn't sure if she was even aware of them as she stared into the flames. They slipped free of the last of the branches and left the eerie scene behind. As their bedazzled eyes adjusted once more to their surroundings, they saw that evening had passed into twilight.

"Should we stop until daylight?" Rand asked.

"I would, but I do not want to stop anywhere near that... that witch."

"Nor do I. I wonder, too, if Uthor may have broken through his log jam and contrived to come after us."

"Onward, then; but carefully, and look sharp."

So they continued down the river. As the last pale light of day faded from the horizon, the moon rose and helped them see their way. Then once more, light appeared around a bend. It was no unearthly rainbow, though, but rather the familiar glow of torches and lanterns. They flickered along the docks of a town.

"Willowberg! Rand, we're nearly there!"

A thrill shot through him and he found renewed strength. Together they paddled, pulling through the water as fast as they could. At first there was no one in sight. Then a watchman called, followed by another and another. Soon figures could be seen gathering in the torchlight.

Suddenly, Rand's tumbling thoughts turned up a question he had not considered, and he knew he needed to answer it. He backed water and slowed the canoe.

"What are you doing?" Jen twisted around to look at him in angry disbelief.

"We need to choose—who wins?"

"What?!?"

"There is only one winner—one who crosses the finish first and takes the crown. We only have moments to decide and—well, you might think I'm crazy, but in my bones, I know it should be you."

Her face was a study in visible thought; first, anger at his stopping them. Then, comprehension of the weight of his reason for doing so. Finally, shock at his conclusion.

"Don't be a fool! That would be grand, wouldn't it? Queen Fishwife the Homely!"

"Would King Blacksmith be any better? Who was a better student at the Academy? Who is sure and decisive? Who—who knew about canoes? Maybe neither of us was born and bred to rule, but in my heart I know that you'd be better at it than me."

She shook her head and looked toward the docks, where the crowd was growing. It was all too much and time was too short.

"Besides, you're wrong," he continued. "You may be a fishwife, but there's nothing homely about you. You—you're my heart."

She gripped his hand, and tears sprang from her eyes. A shuddering sigh escaped her, then her shoulders straightened.

"Very well, Lord Rand. But you'd better be with me all the way in this, or my first royal decree will be off with your head." A hint of a smile played on her lips and he laughed.

"Yes, your majesty! Now, let's get this won!" They turned back to their rowing.

Scattered cries turned into the full murmuring of a crowd. By the time they pulled alongside the dock, it was thronged with people, and many eager hands reached to help them up. Rand took care that Jen was lifted first, so there would be no question of who had won.

Shouting and smiling people pressed them on every side. Then suddenly they drew back. Along the broad boulevard from the city square, the Vizier and other royal officials approached solemnly.

"Whosoever has won through fire and flood, toil and terror, sand and sword, let them stand forth to claim their prize" the Vizier's voice rang out with the ritual words that signaled the resolution of the Gauntlet. He rapped his staff once, sharply, on the flagstones.

"I am here!" answered Jen, stepping forward. The Vizier's eyes flickered with a surprise that he quickly masked.

"Declare yourself!" he called, rapping his staff again.

"I am Lady Jen Wilhelm of Lochinvale!"

"Well met, Lady Jen, and well was your Gauntlet run. Rest now from your labors. Come morning we will depart for Solaria, where your investiture as queen shall be fulfilled." He bowed, then turned and began walking back to the square, giving directions to the officials for the next day's journey.

Now that the formal conclusion of the Gauntlet was complete, well-wishers crowded around Jen again, asking about the race, offering congratulations. Rand stayed close without truly being at her side. As she responded to the crowd, she looked his way from time to time, flashing him a little smile that let him know she was aware of and thankful for his presence.

The crowd thinned as people sought their lodgings, hoping to rest before the journey to the royal city. Rand felt a heavy hand on his shoulder and turned to face the imposing figure of Lord Falconer.

"So, boy—you did your part, and finished well. Our title is secure. My thanks."

"Yes, father."

"We will see what we can make of you in days to come. For now, I think a bath and a good meal are in order. What say you to that, Lady Jen?"

"Oh, yes, a bath would be heaven!"

"Back to our apartments, then."

The crowds continued to disperse. As Lord Falconer led the way through the night, Jen took the opportunity of relative privacy to slip her hand into Rand's. He almost stumbled, so great was his surprise. His heart raced as he leaned close to her.

"My dear friend," she whispered. "Thank you for being near." And so they walked, not releasing their grasp until they arrived at their rooms.

Chapter 49

Beautiful in its heights, the joy of the whole world,
is the city of the Great King.

Rand had thought it impossible to sleep given the excitement that surrounded them. His bath was relaxing, though. When he climbed into bed, the weariness of the race he had run crashed over him in a wave—he slept before he even knew it was upon him.

In the morning there was a whirlwind of activity as Lord Falconer's party packed up for the processional to Solaria. They had barely finished a simple breakfast before a footman of the royal court appeared to collect Jen. As he watched her go, with a regretful glance back at him over her shoulder, Rand realized that he should have expected something of the sort. All the same, he had been looking forward to riding with her and speaking to her about the unknown yet amazing days to come.

Lord Falconer and his party were perfunctory in their dealings with Rand as they finished arrangements for their part in the processional. He had performed the task for which he had been needed, he would receive the rewards he had been promised, but he was still a stranger to them and would perhaps never be seen as a member of the family.

Footmen and valets and assorted functionaries completed their tasks in good order. Lord Falconer nodded brusquely for Rand to follow him and they boarded the family carriage for the passage to

Solaria. Other noble houses were on the move, richly appointed conveyances jostling for position. Slowly and with much shouting, the carriages filtered out of the avenues of Willowberg and onto the post road south along the Solus River. Rand looked sharp and caught glimpses of the glittering royal carriage at the head of the procession. He wished he could catch sight of Jen, wave to her, and let her know he was with her in spirit if not in body.

The morning gave way to high noon as the train of carriages rolled on. Rand was thankful that they were yet in the damp and cool springtime. He imagined that so many wheels and hooves would have created choking clouds of dust when the roads dried under the summer sun.

On the fourth day, the procession arrived at the city of Solaria. Long had the hours seemed with little to do but stare silently at the passing countryside. Rand passed some of the first day telling Lord Falconer and Dorian of his adventures during the Gauntlet, but once he had satisfied their curiosity, there wasn't much more for them to talk about. He contrived to play games of cards or dice with Dorian now and then, and the man would sometimes share his knowledge of the places they passed. Each night was spent in rooms suitable for wealthy travelers. When they at last came within sight of Solaria, though, any idea Rand may have had that he knew what to expect from the capital of the kingdom was quickly dispelled.

Tucked between the broad westward curve of the Solus River as it turned toward the sea, and the looming escarpment that marked the frontier of Gawlia, Solaria spread farther than he could see. Fashioned from blocks of stone carved from the cliffs, sturdy structures fronted by thick columns and pierced by ornate arches rose layer upon layer. But as impressive as the buildings were, they faded into the background compared to the throngs of people who had gathered to greet their queen-to-be.

The people wore their most colorful clothes, waved pennants, and tossed flowers in the path of the carriages. Joyous shouts moved like ocean waves through the crowds, echoing from the stone canyons of the streets.

"Strange that they should give such a greeting to a girl they know nothing about," mused Rand.

"'Tis more for the crown than the wearer that they cheer, Lord Rand," said Dorian. "Not to mention, one rarely suffers loss from being too joyous about one's ruler, whereas a lack of enthusiasm may be costly indeed." Rand nodded—Dorian was right, of course.

The carriages wound their way deeper into the capital until the great boulevard passed through thick walls that marked the borders of the old city. They were now surrounded by the mansions of the noble class. Not long after, the battlements of the citadel itself loomed overhead.

Soldiers in gleaming polished armor lined the passage through the castle wall and stood in ordered ranks in the courtyard within. The royal carriage stopped at the foot of the great stairway to the palace doors. The other carriages swung into rows across the middle of the courtyard. Rand could contain himself no longer; he burst from the Falconer carriage and hauled himself up onto the roof.

He was in time to see the royal carriage open and the looming figure of the Royal Vizier emerge. The man turned and extended his hand, leading Jen out into the light. The crowd in the courtyard was smaller, limited to the members of the noble families, but they and the troops still made an impressive roar at the sight of their new ruler. She was elegant in the gray silk dress and silver circlet that had been given to her by Lord Falconer's Aunt Roberta. She turned and smiled as she raised a hand to acknowledge the cheering people. For just a moment, Rand thought her eyes met his, but in the midst of the tumult she was too far away for him to be sure.

The massive palace doors opened, and trumpets sounded a fanfare. The officials of the court strode out and down the steps to greet Jen with bows and curtseys. Then they turned and joined the Vizier in escorting Jen up the stairs and inside. The doors closed. Officers shouted commands and began marching their soldiers from the courtyard. Carriage drivers began to jockey for position to leave the citadel. As loud and colorful as the procession had been, it was over, and once again Rand felt the emptiness of ending a day without Jen.

Like most prominent noble families, the Falconers maintained a house in the old quarter of Solaria. There Rand settled into his appointed room to await the investiture of Queen Jen. At the table that evening, Lord Falconer once again thanked Rand for serving faithfully in the Gauntlet, and even offered a measure of respect for his having finished so close to victory.

"I think you may find in the end that you will have a better life for not having won the throne. It may seem that a king is the most powerful man in the world, but from what I have observed, the hours of their lives are never their own to spend as they wish. Duties press in on them everywhere they turn, and the power to decide becomes an endless burden."

Throughout the meal and long after, Falconer and Minister Dorian spoke to Rand about the holdings and retinue that would increasingly fall under his administration as the heir of their house. He did his best to attend studiously, but his thoughts were ever on the friend hidden behind the palace walls.

Chapter 50

Love and faithfulness keep a ruler safe;
through love their throne is made secure.

The investiture of Jen as queen was set for noon the following day. Rand sat with Falconer and Dorian in the front row along the right side of the throne room, chafing and sweating in the heavy finery required by the occasion. All of that faded from his thoughts when trumpets sounded and Jen appeared at the entrance to the hall. She was truly regal in golden silks and taffeta, embroidered with silver thread and strings of pearls, and yet there was a delicacy, a fragility to her as she paced forward in time to the slow beat of kettle drums, a slight figure alone at the center of all eyes. She reached the dais and stood, silent and still, before the lord high chamberlain, who turned to one side and lifted the gold and jeweled crown from the large velvet pillow where it had rested.

"Lady Jen," he spoke with voice raised to be heard throughout the throne room, "you have earned this day by right of victory in our Royal Gauntlet, the test devised by our people of old to bring forth the bravest, the strongest, the most cunning among us to lead us. Now you stand at the beginning of a test still greater—to rule our land with justice; to defend our borders with vigilance against every foe; to care for our people with compassion; and to fulfill your office with honor that is above reproach. Do you accept this charge?"

"I do."

Slowly and carefully, he placed the crown on her head. Then he motioned for her to turn and face the assembly. The master at arms pounded his ceremonial staff on the flagstone floor with such force that Rand could feel the reverberation through his feet. At this the chamberlain called out again.

"I present to you her majesty, Queen Jen. Long live the queen!"

All of those in attendance rose to their feet, shouting "Long live the queen!" Rand joined them gladly, shouting so loud that his throat was sore. Jen smiled and raised her hand to acknowledge them, much as she had done on the steps outside the day before. The shouting died down and the crowd returned to their seats. The reigning lord of each noble house came forward, lining up in order of prominence to kneel before her, kiss her hand, and declare their allegiance.

Lord Falconer was near the front of the line and—having offered his fealty—returned to sit beside Rand as the formalities continued. As Rand watched, he thought of Jen's adoptive nobleman, Lord Wilhelm, for the first time in weeks. It didn't seem that any of the dignitaries that were in line to greet Jen were likely to be him. Rand wondered if the man was even aware of what was happening here today.

The repeated oaths of loyalty soon lost Rand's interest. He busied himself by looking over the various officers of the court, wondering what their titles and duties might be. The most striking and imposing figure, standing just at the other side of the dais and a bit behind the others, was the man who had given a speech at the start of the Gauntlet and greeted them afterwards on the dock in Willowberg—the Vizier.

Uncanny and mysterious with his shaven head and curling lines of facial tattoos, he surveyed the nobles, his dark eyes noting and weighing each detail. At one point his gaze shifted and Rand found himself caught in that keen scrutiny. He quickly turned to look at Lord Falconer as if to ask a question, and when he dared to look back, the Vizier's attention was elsewhere.

In due course the formalities of the investiture were concluded. Queen Jen thanked her subjects and excused herself, being led from the throne room by the court officers through a side door. The noblemen and their retainers rose from their seats and began filing out the main doors, pausing to greet friends as they went. So that was it—the Gauntlet was won and Jen was queen. What now? Rand wondered. Would they succeed in the goal that had propelled them to this strange turn? And if so, what then? Jen could hardly free Zekiel from his cell, thank everyone for their assistance, and toss the crown to the floor as she skipped out the palace gates to return to the family fishing boat.

Over dinner that night, Lord Falconer and Dorian talked about the journey back to Serenvale and the keep that would be Rand's new home. They mentioned stopping in Serenhorn on the way and spending a few days in the manor house there, and discussed the merits of Rand continuing his studies at the Academy as opposed to learning the management of the house of Falconer first-hand. Rand picked at his food and nodded or murmured a reply when they happened to address him. His thoughts, hopes, and dreams were elsewhere.

He was snapped from the shadows of his thoughts by a heavy rapping at the door. A footman went to answer it, and returned presently with an envelope on a silver tray. Lord Falconer and Dorian both leaned toward him, expecting it to be a message for one or the other of them. They were all surprised, none more than Rand, when the man instead turned to him.

"Message for you, milord—from the palace."

Rand stared at the envelope, part fascinated, part wary as if it had been a coiled viper. He took it from the tray before the awkward pause could get any worse. The paper was fine and smooth, embossed with the royal crest. The flap was sealed with wax and pressed with what must be a royal signet ring. There was a faint whiff of perfume, and on the other side in Jen's simple but flowing script, "Prince Rand, House Falconer." He opened it and pulled out the folded note inside.

"Come quickly if you can," it read, "we need to see a friend. Jen."

"Milord, the messenger who brought this is waiting with a carriage outside to take you to the citadel," said the footman deferentially. Rand looked at Falconer and Dorian.

"Jen wants to see me," he explained, rising from the table and fumbling for his cloak at the nearby coatrack.

"Very well, young man—you mustn't keep a lady waiting, especially when she is your queen," said Lord Falconer with a trace of a smile. Rand nodded and hastened to the door. There he found a gilded carriage alight with glowing lanterns, harnessed to a pair of immaculately groomed white horses. The driver stood holding the door until Rand had climbed inside, then hopped into his seat and snapped the reins to set off.

Within minutes they were pulling into the courtyard of the citadel. The driver stopped the carriage at an unremarkable entrance that was around the corner and toward the back of the central keep, several dozen yards away from the wide marble stairs of the main doors. There he knocked on the door and handed Rand over to a footman. The man led him through plain, narrow stone corridors until they reached a large, busy kitchen. He pointed to a chambermaid, who was waiting there for them. She waved for Rand to follow, leading him beyond the kitchen and along wider and better-lit stone hallways until they reached a polished wooden door. She knocked, and the door was opened by a well-dressed lady in waiting, who silently led Rand along carpeted and paneled halls and up a spiral staircase until she stopped at a very ornate door indeed.

"Your majesty," she called softly as she tapped twice, "your guest has arrived." She opened the door and waved Rand inside, then closed it behind him without following. He glanced this way and that, to the vast canopied bed, the dressing table with silver mirror, and the massive fireplace where a well-laid fire crackled and popped. A figure rose from a high-backed chair and was momentarily a black silhouette against the flames.

"Jen!" he cried, surprised at how eager and plaintive his own voice sounded. She smiled that wry and impish smile that he knew so well, but her eyes shone with genuine pleasure at the sight of her friend. She walked forward and he saw that she wore a gown of rich velvet, finely tailored but much simpler and more practical than the royal garments of the investiture.

"Rand! I've wanted to see you so much." She came up to him and took his hands. Then, to his delight, she flung her arms around his neck and embraced him. He wrapped his around the soft velvet of her back and gave her a squeeze. His thoughts went back to that day long ago when he had surprised her with repairs and decent furniture in her wreck of a house in Serenhorn, and to a lonely camp in the wastelands of the Gauntlet. She sighed and softly kissed his cheek. He drew back enough to see her face, nuzzled her nose, then gave in to the longing of his heart and kissed her with deep tenderness. She gave a little gasp, then caressed his face and kissed him back with unexpected enthusiasm. Then she cleared her throat and stepped back.

"Well," she quipped, her eyes dancing with a charming mix of amusement and excitement, "more of that would certainly be welcome, but we have a serious matter to attend to. Come sit!" She took his hand and drew him to the fireside, where they sat in the chairs that flanked the hearth.

"It's been a whirlwind since we parted in Willowberg—people trying to teach me and lead me and impress me and flatter me and all manner of things beside! And everywhere that Vizier, staring at me, talking down to me, sizing me up like a cutlet at a butcher's shop."

"The Vizier? He certainly looks fearsome, but he seemed gentlemanly enough when he greeted us at the end of the Gauntlet."

"Don't be fooled, Rand—I trust my instincts, and they tell me he is dangerous. Remember it was most likely him that put Zekiel in prison."

"Zekiel! Have you found him? Is he alive?"

"That is what I hope to find out tonight. I made discreet inquiries among the few attendants who seemed most trustworthy, as to the best way to find and visit a prisoner in the palace dungeon without attracting undue attention. They suggested a guard captain who works the night shift, and is known to be honorable. Let's go and see if he can help us."

Chapter 51

The Spirit of the Speaker is on me, because he has anointed me to declare good news to the poor. He has sent me to proclaim freedom for the prisoners and recovery of sight for the blind, to set the oppressed free.

Jen lifted an oil lamp from a side table and led the way, back out the side door by which Rand had entered and then by many turnings through the back hallways and stairs of the palace until they reached the lower levels where the dungeon was hidden. They came to a guard station where a soldier sat at a plain wooden table.

"Who goes there? Declare your—oh, your majesty! What—what are you doing here?"

"May we speak with Captain Eglund?"

"Of course, your majesty! If you'd just wait here a moment, I will go and get him at once!" The guard rose hastily to his feet and ran to a door farther down the corridor. His chair overbalanced and clattered to the stone floor. Before long he returned with the captain.

"Your majesty, what may I do for you?"

"I have heard that there is a prisoner here by the name of Zekiel—is that so?" The captain turned to the guard, who nodded.

"That's right, sir—cell fourteen."

"I wish to see him, immediately."

"Well, I—that is… forgive me, your majesty, but things aren't normally done this way. Some officer of the court would come on your behalf, during daylight hours."

"The man in question is a friend of mine—an academy professor who could not possibly be a threat to the kingdom or anyone in it. His imprisonment was a mistake made by the previous government and I intend to correct it, now. Show me to his cell, please."

The captain stood for a moment, digesting this information. "Tomson! Is there any risk to her majesty from this prisoner?"

"I wouldn't think so, sir. He was treated harshly by them as questioned him. Hasn't been on his feet for days now." Jen clutched Rand's arm when she heard this, but was careful to give no sign of her distress.

"Very well, then—take us to him, please," said the captain.

Tomson took the lamp from the table and led them down the dank stone corridor. He stopped at the seventh door on the right and took his keyring from his belt to open the door. Captain Eglund took the lamp and entered first. When he was satisfied that Jen would be safe, he waved her in.

Rand followed and could hardly believe that the creature they saw was his teacher and friend. He seemed to be little more than a pile of tattered, dirty robes and matted hair. The old man stirred and moaned, eyes closed and face damp with perspiration. Before anyone could move to stop her, Jen knelt beside his rough prison cot and put her hand on his forehead.

"He's burning with fever—is this the way the prison treats its charges?" That quick anger Rand had become acquainted with blazed in her eyes as she turned toward the captain.

"These stone cells are cold and damp, your majesty—at his age, and if, as Tomson says, he was ill-used, it would not be surprising for him to catch a chill."

"He was imprisoned without just cause and now his health is in serious danger—he must be taken from here at once!"

"Yes, your majesty. I—I am not certain of my authority in such matters. Perhaps you could make up a written order, sign and seal it—that sort of thing?"

"Do you have pen and paper?"

"Yes, at my station."

"Then we will finish it. Tomson!"

"Yes, your majesty?"

"Go and find a stretcher or cart or something to carry him on— we must get him to a warm, dry bed with proper care."

"Yes, your majesty!"

The guard left on his errand and the rest of them went to the captain's office. He produced paper, quill, and inkpot, and even managed to find a pot of sealing wax that he set to work heating while Jen sat and wrote her release order for Zekiel.

Tomson returned with a stretcher, and once Jen had signed the order and sealed it with her signet ring, they returned to Zekiel's cell. They carefully transferred the stricken old scholar to the stretcher, then with Tomson leading and Rand carrying the other end, moved out into the prison corridor.

Rand looked at Jen. "All right—where to now?"

"I suppose we could take him back to my private suite—we could see to it that he got the best of care there."

Captain Eglund cleared his throat. "Actually, your majesty, there may be some... awkwardness if the prisoner remains within the citadel."

"How so?"

"I was going over the duty roster when you came here tonight. There is a public execution scheduled for tomorrow. Your friend there was on the list. I realize you have granted him a royal pardon, but with you having just taken the throne and—begging your pardon—being so young, there may be those among the established officers of the court who would oppose your decision. It might weaken your authority at a critical time of your new reign."

"Let's take him to the Falconer house," said Rand. "Maybe we can get him out of the city before anyone comes looking for him."

Jen considered this for a moment, then nodded. "Captain, is there a nearby door where we could pull up a carriage and transfer Zekiel to it without attracting attention?"

"Yes, your majesty—the gate where we bring in food for the prisoners is not far. Tomson, help carry the prisoner there. I'll see about a wagon with a tarp. I think the plainer things look, the better."

Thus it was not long before Zekiel was concealed in the back of a plain wagon, and a driver who knew the way to the Falconers' city house was taking him and Rand there through the empty nighttime streets. Jen thought it unwise to accompany them, but dashed off a note to Lord Falconer, thanking him for taking care of the old man's needs and requesting that he be conveyed to safety as a favor to the crown.

They arrived without attracting notice, and Rand handed Falconer the note from Jen. He read it and conferred briefly with Dorian before he commanded his servants to bring Zekiel into the house and make him as comfortable as they could in a spare bedroom. Rand thanked the driver and sent him back to the citadel, then joined Dorian and Falconer in the dining room.

"So my adopted son and his friend the queen have presented me with a challenge," said Falconer. "Only one day on the throne and already she spins intrigues and draws me into them!"

"We're sorry to burden you, father, but saving Master Zekiel from prison and possible execution is the reason Jen and I hoped to win the Gauntlet in the first place. It was terribly unlikely, but once we succeeded, and discovered the state he was in, we had to act quickly. All the more so when we learned that he was about to be put to death."

"Oh, I understand, boy. I just want you to understand—this is no small matter. Dorian?"

"Yes, milord?"

"Under the circumstances, it seems best to leave the city at first light as we had planned. If the queen's pardon of Zekiel sets off a storm, I have no desire to be a lightning rod. I'd prefer he have time and rest to strengthen him for the journey, but Jen has asked us to get him out of Solaria and I think that's wise. Could we arrange for an extra carriage, one large enough for him to recline in, with a skilled nurse to attend him as we go?"

Dorian lowered his head in thought, tapping his chin. Then he clapped his hands and laughed. "Yes—it's almost too perfect!"

"Please, enlighten me," said Falconer.

"Of course, milord. Carriages that are long enough to carry a person in repose are not common, and if we go to too much trouble to obtain one, we're sure to attract attention. Unless, of course, we get one that is designed for the purpose, commonplace, and that people prefer not to pay close attention to—a hearse!"

Falconer laughed in spite of himself. "You're right, Dorian, it's perfect! The black velvet curtains drawn and no one eager to peer inside. The somber driver not given to conversation. This should work!"

Dorian began making arrangements immediately. After excusing himself, Rand went to bed, stopping on the way to look in on Zekiel. If anything, the old scholar looked even thinner and more frail lying in the large bed, but he had been given clean garments and his hair and beard were trimmed and brushed. A servant was holding his hand and wiping his brow with a damp cloth. She looked up as Rand stood there in the door.

"It's touch an' go, milord, touch an' go. But he has a good chance, I think, now he's bein' properly looked after. We've been able to get a few spoonfuls of broth into him, though he hasn't yet come to himself." Rand smiled and nodded his thanks, then went to bed.

Chapter 52

The desire of those who do right ends only in good,
but the hope of the evil only in wrath.

In the morning, the funeral wagon appeared as promised, complete with driver dressed all in black, and a tall hat trailing a black crepe ribbon. The hearse itself was also draped with black bunting, velvet curtains drawn tightly. Zekiel was gently loaded into the back, then a nurse with a bundle of healing supplies climbed in with him. All this was done with the hearse backed up to the house in such a way that no curious onlooker would be able to see inside.

Lord Falconer's carriage was ready as well, and just as dawn began to break over the city, they departed. Falconer's guard went before and behind. They all moved as briskly as they could without seeming to be in a rush. They passed out of the main city gate and started up the road to Serenhorn, slipping out of Solaria before the streets began to fill with the bustling business of the day.

Later that morning, Queen Jen sat in chambers with the ministers of the court. They reviewed the list of prisoners who were due to be executed that day, along with their crimes and histories. Jen found the proceedings unpleasant, but could understand why these people had been sentenced as they had. There was a stir, however, when the lord chamberlain brought up the matter of Zekiel's pardon. Several of the court officials were not pleased with the queen's intervention. Jen raised her scepter and the discontented murmurings ceased.

"This man is known to me personally, having been one of my teachers as I prepared for the Gauntlet—a Gauntlet, need I remind you, which I won, and with it the right to rule. I vouch for his character and his innocence, and that is the end of the matter. What is the next order of business?"

The Vizier was livid, but carefully concealed his anger, watching Jen through narrowed lids. He said little, excusing himself as soon as he could to go and prepare to preside over the executions.

Jen observed from her royal box as the grim business was carried out, as was her duty. It was horrible, but in time it was over. The rest of her day was consumed with a seemingly endless procession of affairs of state. After dinner, she changed into less formal garb and allowed herself the small luxury of a solitary walk along a pillared colonnade that overlooked the river. She thought of Rand, wishing for the warmth of his companionship even as she knew that he must get Zekiel to health and safety.

From the shadows behind a pillar, the Vizier watched her. She looked so small and young among the stone columns, alone and forlorn. Very well, little queen, he thought—we will soon see what you're made of.

About the Author

Stephen Kroh has been an avid reader and writer since he was in elementary school. His experiences have ranged from mortuary attendant to editor of college textbooks, from grassroots political canvasser to computer administrator. His perspective has been informed by living in the Pacific Northwest, the South, and the Midwest, along with a two-year sojourn in Europe. He has been pleased to weave several threads of narrative ideas together with his faith to create stories of adventure, discovery, hope, and belief. It is his hope that they will inspire and delight others on their spiritual journeys.

Follow Stephen at www.SteveKroh.com